Suzanne Merchant was born and raised in South Africa. She and her husband lived and worked in Cape Town, London, Kuwait, Baghdad, Sydney and Dubai before settling in the Sussex countryside. They enjoy visits from their three grown-up children and are kept busy attempting to keep two spaniels, a dachshund, a parrot and a large, unruly garden under control.

Michele Renae is the pseudonym of award-winning author Michele Hauf. She has published over ninety novels in historical, paranormal and contemporary romance and fantasy, as well as writing action/adventure as Alex Archer. Instead of writing 'what she knows' she prefers to write 'what she would love to know and do'. And, yes, that includes being a jewel thief and/or a brain surgeon! You can email Michele at toastfaery@gmail.com, and find her on Instagram: @MicheleHauf and Pinterest: @toastfaery.

Also by Suzanne Merchant

Their Wildest Safari Dream
Off-Limits Fling with the Billionaire
Ballerina and the Greek Billionaire

Also by Michele Renae

Cinderella's Second Chance in Paris
The CEO and the Single Dad
Parisian Escape with the Billionaire

Discover more at millsandboon.co.uk.

HEIRESS'S ESCAPE TO SOUTH AFRICA

SUZANNE MERCHANT

CONSEQUENCE OF THEIR PARISIAN NIGHT

MICHELE RENAE

MILLS & BOON

First published in Great Britain 2024
by Mills & Boon, an imprint of HarperCollins*Publishers* Ltd,
1 London Bridge Street, London, SE1 9GF

www.harpercollins.co.uk

HarperCollins*Publishers*, Macken House, 39/40 Mayor Street Upper,
Dublin 1, D01 C9W8, Ireland

ISBN: 978-0-263-32125-8

02/24

This book contains FSC™ certified paper
and other controlled sources to ensure responsible forest management.
For more information visit www.harpercollins.co.uk/green.

Printed and Bound in the UK using 100% Renewable Electricity
at CPI Group (UK) Ltd, Croydon, CR0 4YY

HEIRESS'S ESCAPE TO SOUTH AFRICA

SUZANNE MERCHANT

MILLS & BOON

For THM—who makes the best tea.

CHAPTER ONE

'No!'

Her shout should have been bold and loud, but it came out as a squeak. Scarlett's lungs burned, after fighting the overgrown driveway and her undignified scramble up the crumbling steps. The dash from Cape Town Airport, following a satnav which issued unlikely instructions, had been the easy part. She swiped a grazed palm over her forehead, pushing damp curls out of her eyes. Her face, she knew without the need for a mirror, would be an unattractive shade of puce, clashing furiously with her hair.

None of that mattered. She watched, mesmerised, as the auctioneer, on a stage improvised from a table—*her table*—raised his gavel. The tempo of the world had changed down. Even a clock, hidden somewhere amongst the clutter of the room, launched into its midday chimes at a painfully ponderous pace.

'Going once…' the man's voice boomed with confidence.

Scarlett inhaled a deep, shaky breath. This was her last—her *only*—chance. If she stopped this man from slamming down his gavel, her life could literally change at a stroke. She would no longer be homeless and unemployed, even if healing her broken heart would take a little longer. A lot longer.

'No!' This time she dug up every ounce of conviction, put it all into her voice, and her protest rang out across the room. 'No,' she repeated, and raised a hand, waving above the heads of would-be buyers to attract the attention of the auctioneer and make sure he both heard and saw her. 'You can't sell it.'

He lowered the gavel with what looked like exaggerated patience. He removed his glasses, folded them and placed them on the small ladies' writing desk which balanced on the table in front of him, lending him dubious authority. He scanned the gathering and Scarlett saw his eyes rove past her and then return to her face. Heads turned as people tried to identify the source of this last-minute cliff-hanger of an interruption.

'Excuse me?' The man shook his head. 'Did I hear correctly? Did you say *no*?'

Scarlett nodded vigorously. 'Yes. That is, yes, I did say no. You can't sell the house.'

He folded his arms and rested them on the desktop, shoulders hunched. A flicker of annoyance pulled at his mouth as a murmur of impatience ran through the crowd. 'Would you care then, to explain why?' The sarcasm in his tone was unmistakable. He leaned forward, surveying the upturned faces, and the backs of heads, in front of him. The show he made of looking at his wristwatch would have caused a mime artist to weep with envy and a few people chuckled.

A rush of relief made Scarlett's legs go weak. She pulled in a breath and pushed her shoulders back, bracing her knees and standing tall. 'Absolutely,' she said, making sure no wobbliness escaped into her voice. 'This house belongs to me. It is not for sale.'

A hubbub erupted. The people standing directly in front of her moved away, leaving her in a small, isolated circle. One of the women bystanders frowned, her eyes travelling from Scarlett's face to her feet and back again, and she was suddenly acutely aware of how unlikely her statement must have sounded.

She couldn't remember when she'd last slept soundly for more than a few snatched hours in a bed that wasn't a hammock in the Amazon jungle, with her knees pulled up to her chin, or a friend's lumpy sofa or an economy seat in the back row of the overnight flight from Heathrow to Cape Town. Her jeans and sweatshirt were rumpled and her hair, wild at the best of times, and now scrunched into a messy bundle at the back of her head, felt as if one of the exotic bright parrots, which swooped overhead through the rainforest, had built a nest in it. The palm of her right hand was scratched and bleeding, which meant she had probably smeared blood across her forehead.

Her teeth fastened over her bottom lip as she kept her eyes fixed on the man at the table. He appeared to be lost for words and the small kick of satisfaction she experienced was gratifying.

It was during the charged silence which followed that Scarlett noticed the man standing front and centre of the room, right beside the auctioneer's makeshift podium.

He'd turned, and his eyes, a startling shade of blue even from this distance, scanned the room with an efficient ruthlessness, finding her in a split second and pinning her down with a cobalt gaze which could put lasers out of business. A shirt of fine cotton skimmed shoulders of astonishing width, the pale blue fabric providing an emphatic foil for the deeper blue of his eyes, the sweep of male muscle undisguised by any amount of bespoke tailoring.

Scarlett swallowed; her throat was suddenly dry. She wondered how it had taken all of two long minutes to register his presence. Beside him, the rest of the room faded into a pale imitation of the lively crowd which had surrounded her until a few seconds ago. She chewed on her lip but could not drag her eyes away from his. It felt important that she try, but he seemed to have engaged her in some sort of competition which she couldn't win. She needed him to take her seriously, not treat her like someone who'd wandered in to disrupt proceedings with a baseless claim. Fatigue and anxiety threatened to overtake her, and keeping those two enemies at bay was costing her a hefty dose of mental energy and sheer determination.

As she watched, he ran a strong-looking, long-fingered hand across the back of his neck, the spare gesture displaying a leashed frustration and annoyance. His day had been disrupted, it seemed to say, but only momentarily. He'd sweep this irritating obstruction out of his way but not without resenting the waste of his time. His hand dropped and slid into the pocket of his trousers as he rocked back on his heels. Then he threw a quiet word in the direction of the auctioneer and started towards her. The crowd parted in front of him. She could see he expected nothing less.

Scarlett's gaze was still held in the beam of his, as she watched him approach. He was taller than she'd first thought, and he towered over her own five feet ten inches. She took a step backwards, but he followed. Had he no idea about personal space? But then she recognised the move as a deliberate intimidation tactic and stood her ground. Close up, she could see that his tan was the sort acquired by long hours spent outdoors in the Cape sunshine. His dark hair, brushed back from his forehead, carried a few fine threads of silver at the sides.

To her surprise, he pulled his right hand from his pocket and extended it towards her. *Taking the enemy by surprise*, she thought, trying to kick-start her sluggish brain into action. On autopilot, she allowed him to fold her hand in his. His grip was firm and dry, and she was sure he noted her damp palm, because a fleeting look of satisfaction crossed the hard planes of his face. He raised his chin slightly and finally, *finally*, snapped the link between their eyes and swept his gaze over her. She stiffened, imagining how lacking in every respect he must find her, compared with his sleek elegance and the innate sense of power he wore like a second skin.

'Will Duvinage.' The pressure of his fingers increased slightly. 'And you are…?'

Scarlett scoured her memory but came up with nothing more than a vague stirring of recognition of the surname. Had she read it somewhere? Had Marguerite mentioned it? It was so long since she'd had a coherent conversation with her godmother that she doubted it. Marguerite's mind, clouded by advancing dementia, had, long before her death, ceased to function in any way Scarlett recognised.

'Scarlett Riley,' she said, after a pause which was slightly too long. If he thought she was reluctant to tell him her name, he was right. Something made her want to withhold her identity from him, as if by revealing it she'd be handing over a part of herself that she'd never be able to get back. Instinctively trying to compensate for this imagined loss, she withdrew her hand from his.

He shook his head. 'I'm sorry…' he glanced down at her left hand '… Miss Riley. Your name means nothing to me. It doesn't explain why you might claim to be the owner of Rozendal Manor.'

Scarlett wondered if he'd noticed the band of pale skin on the third finger of her left hand, where until recently she'd worn an engagement ring. Then she decided that nothing would escape his piercing scrutiny. She clasped her hands together, her thumb rubbing over the place where the diamond had been. She'd been surprised by Alan's choice of stone, given how passionately she felt about low-paid workers putting their lives at daily risk in mines deep underground, but he'd assured her in an offhand manner that the gem had ethical credentials. He'd looked so pained when she'd suggested he show her the certification that she'd dropped the subject. With the unimpaired clarity of hindsight, she'd wondered how honest he'd been, given the spectacular dishonesty he'd subsequently displayed.

How, she wondered, had she been so easily taken in by his smooth charm and assiduous attention? His assertion that his way was the right way, his opinion the only one worth considering. Her belief in herself crushed, she'd come out of the relationship certain of only one thing: nothing like that would ever happen to her again.

Scarlett ran the tip of her tongue over her lips. She didn't like the effect this man—Will—had on her. He made her doubt herself even more—question her reason for being here at all. He seemed ready to sweep her aside with a few words, as if she was of no consequence. She didn't know who he was, but she hoped their acquaintance would be brief. If not, his attitude would have to change.

'There is no reason at all why you should know my name, Mr Duvinage.' She articulated his name carefully, giving it the full accented benefit of her fluent French, since she assumed it was French in origin. She remembered Marguerite telling her that many of the vineyards in South Africa had been established in the seventeenth century by French Huguenots fleeing religious persecution in their home country. This man could probably trace his ancestry back to that time, as Marguerite could. She saw his flicker of acknowledgement as he narrowed his eyes, perhaps adjusting his opinion of her.

'Well, then,' he said, his voice dropping to a deeper, more intimate level, as if he wished to talk to her alone, excluding the crowd of curious onlookers around them, 'perhaps you can explain your reasoning?'

Scarlett felt as if she'd been transported back to a university tutorial, with an exacting tutor training the full force of his intelligence on her.

I think this plant is an unrecognised sub-species, because under the microscope...

The past faded away, evaporating in the heat of his focused attention.

'Marguerite du Valois, the owner of Rozendal...' She stopped. Marguerite was no longer the owner of Rozendal. *She* was. *She*, Scarlett Riley, was now the owner—the *chatelaine*, as Marguerite would have said—of this charmed and charming old homestead. She raised her eyes from their study of Will Duvinage's highly polished leather shoes and started again. 'Marguerite du Valois, the—*former*—owner of Rozendal, was my godmother. She died recently and bequeathed ownership of the Manor to me, in her will.'

He blinked once, and the fine broadcloth of his shirt tightened across his chest and shoulders as he inhaled a deep breath. He nodded slowly.

'I see. And the terms of the will…'

'Stated that I must claim ownership, in person, by midday today.'

His eyes were hooded, but she saw the flash of a spark of triumph.

'Some, Miss Riley, might argue that you missed the deadline. The auctioneer had already accepted the winning bid. It was twelve o'clock. Another few seconds…'

'I did not miss the deadline, Mr Duvinage. The deadline would have expired at the last chime of the clock. I had at least…nine seconds…to spare.'

'Mmm.'

In that sound she heard that he'd accepted her argument. She might have won the battle, but he was obviously confident that he would win whatever war he was choosing to wage against her. He inclined his head, one corner of his straight mouth twitching with the ghost of a smile.

'Do you make a habit of living your life on the edge? Sailing so close to the wind? It must be exhausting.'

'No, I don't.' Immediately, Scarlett regretted rising to his bait. She shouldn't feel this pressing need to justify herself to this stranger. She was a scientist. A botanist, accustomed to the rigorous questioning of data, triple-checking results, leaving nothing to chance. She found her position as uncomfortable as he evidently found it amusing. 'The past few days,' she continued, deciding he did not need her to share the forensic details, 'have been unusually challenging. But I'm here, and I can provide the contact details of the lawyers in London and Cape Town, if necessary.'

'I'd be pleased to have those.' A single straight line creased the skin between his eyebrows. 'If I'd had them a couple of years ago, we might not be in this mess now.'

From his words Scarlett understood two things. Firstly, that the bid the auctioneer had accepted had come from him. She had thwarted his plans to own Rozendal. And secondly, he was not pleased about it.

'I don't know what you mean about a mess. It all seems perfectly simple to me.' She kept her voice cool. 'I'll ask the lawyers to contact you.'

'Thank you.' If ice-cold was a grade, his tone aced it. 'Scarlett,' he added, almost as an afterthought. His eyes, unhurried, roved across her face before coming to rest on her hair. She resisted the temptation to raise a hand to check on its state. It could only be worse than she imagined.

She gave him a long look. 'My parents thought it would be amusing to have a red-haired daughter called Scarlett.'

Those eyes, lit with twin blue flames, captured hers again. 'Do they still find it amusing, now that you're grown up?'

Scarlett stared at him. 'I have no idea.'

'Ah.' One of his black brows rose. 'And how do you feel about it?'

She dug her fingernails into her palms, determined not to give him the satisfaction of a snappy reply. She'd tired of that particular joke almost before she could talk. She lifted a shoulder.

'It stopped being amusing a long time ago.'

'You could change it.'

'I could also dye my hair.'

She folded her arms and tucked her hands out of sight, in case he saw their slight tremor. She was exhausted but now she was angry too. Exactly who did he think he was?

His faint smile faded. 'Would you?'

'You have a lot of questions, Mr Duvinage. Do you always get so up close and personal with people you've only just met?'

He slid his hands back into his pockets. 'No. But considering we'll probably be seeing each other quite frequently, it's good to get the preliminary introductions out of the way early, don't you think?'

'Are we?' Scarlett frowned. 'Why?' His supreme self-assurance set all her alarm bells clanging. She was done with men like him, who persuaded you they knew what was best, and manipulated you into doing it. Next thing you knew, you were up the Amazon looking for orchids with a diamond on your finger and a man complaining that his coffee wasn't hot enough. In the *jungle*.

He nodded. 'I think it's inevitable, Miss Riley, since we're neighbours. Welcome to the valley.'

CHAPTER TWO

THE WALK FROM Rozendal Manor back to Bellevale took Will along a well-trodden track. Although the Manor had stood empty for several years, after the latest in a series of unsatisfactory tenants had moved on, he walked this way at least once a week.

Until this afternoon, he'd used the walk as an opportunity for thinking and for planning. As the track mounted the hill behind Bellevale, curving around the shoulder of the hill which divided the two properties, he could look back at the neat, orderly rows of productive vines which covered the acres of his property.

He knew every row because he walked along them as often as possible, looking for signs of disease or stress in the ancient gnarled wood, or for how well newly planted stock was faring. The map of these fields was imprinted on his soul because nurturing Bellevale was something he'd done for most of his life. It was all he'd ever wanted to do.

But a few years ago he'd begun to wonder about Rozendal Manor. The contrast between it and his own vineyards was stark. At Rozendal, nature had taken over and imposed its own chaotic order on what had previously been acreage that produced award-winning wines.

Dimly, he remembered the time during his childhood when the gardens surrounding the old Manor had been famous too. Befitting its name, the rose garden had been world-renowned. Looking down from his vantage point on the hill, it was still possible to make out the shape of it, with rusted metal arbours at the corners and a stone fountain, now buried under ivy and long-since dry, at the centre. Roses rambled over the house too, poking out through gaps in the thatch in places. He suspected pigeons and grey squirrels had taken up residence in the roof space.

In front of the house, the gravel turning circle sprouted a jungle of weeds and the driveway between the avenue of ancient oaks, leading to the original entrance gates, had almost vanished.

It was that way, he mused, that the woman—Scarlett—must have come. How she'd found her way to the disused drive was a mystery, but her scratched hand and the smear of blood on her temple were evidence that she had fought her way through the thickets of brambles. She must have climbed over the ancient iron gates too. Last time he'd looked, they'd been fastened with a hefty chain and a padlock solid with rust.

Had she been dropped off by a taxi? Left a hire car in the overgrown lane?

Nowadays, anyone who wanted to reach Rozendal, and few people did, used the farm entrance at the side, closer to Bellevale. As he watched, the last of the cars which had been parked in the space where the kitchen garden had been, nosed their way down the track towards the main road.

Whatever route Scarlett had taken, she was *there*. He'd left her making complicated explanations to the long-suffering auctioneer, who'd had the not inconsiderable commission for the sale snatched from beneath his nose at the last second. Will could imagine his annoyance and frustration at the turn events had taken. The small crowd who'd turned up to witness the sale, delighted, no doubt, to get a look inside the fabled Manor at last, had had more excitement than they'd ever expected. He, Will, had let it be known that if he secured ownership of the Manor he'd be selling off some of the contents this afternoon. There must have been punters in the crowd who'd had their eyes on the antique pieces of furniture, silver and porcelain. It was rumoured that the French armoire in the dining room was worth the price of an apartment on the Cape Town Waterfront in the right sale.

He hoped the auctioneer had an endless supply of both time and patience. Scarlett Riley had given an impression of strength and determination and he could tell she was not to be messed with. But beneath it, thinly disguised, he'd detected extreme exhaustion and a degree of desperation. Her pale complexion should have been creamy, he mused, but it was dulled by a greyish tinge, with dark shadows beneath her green eyes. The dusting of freckles across her nose stood out in startling contrast to her pallor.

But whatever irritation plagued the auctioneer, it could be nothing compared with his own. The initial flare of fury which had engulfed him when he realised he'd lost the opportunity to own the Manor had settled into a slow-burning annoyance. He wanted Rozendal, and usually he got what he wanted.

He'd had to fight for almost everything he'd wanted in life, and he was used to winning those fights. If someone had asked him what losing felt like, he'd have said he didn't know.

For once, it had seemed as if he was going to get the thing he wanted without a battle. It was obvious that the Manor should be a part of his estate. Who else would be prepared to spend the money needed to bring it back to productive order? Nobody was as fit for the task as he was. The house was almost uninhabitable; the vineyards were unworkable as they stood. Restoring it all would be a massive undertaking and commitment, but to him it would be worth every penny and every sweaty hour spent on it.

And he'd be restoring the boundaries to their correct configuration. Originally, Bellevale and Rozendal had been one estate.

But it seemed he was going to have to fight for it, after all. If Scarlett's claim was legitimate, she owned the property, but he had no idea what she planned to do with it. When she'd had time to have a proper look at her inheritance, she might be willing to negotiate with him on a sale. She must have a life in England to which she'd be anxious to return. Winter was approaching in the Cape, with the oak trees already showing a tinge of colour, and although it was a short season it could be brutally cold and wet here, in the shadow of the jagged mountains which stood sentinel around the valley. A few days of shivering in the damp, draughty old house with the pigeons and squirrels for company would surely make Scarlett see the wisdom of selling to him.

Will shoved his hands into his pockets and remembered that he'd left his suit jacket slung over the back of one of the antique dining chairs. He'd been anxious to get away, to begin planning his counterattack in private, and to escape the noise of the speculative voices in the saleroom.

He dipped his head and then shook back the lock of hair which flopped over his forehead. The day had begun with brilliant sunshine but a bank of cloud had rolled in from the ocean, invisible to the south but a huge influence on the climate of this southern tip of Africa. The light had dampened. He kicked moodily at a pebble and listened as it bounced down the hillside, out of earshot. He looked up to study the sky.

If it rained on her first day at Rozendal, would that hasten Scarlett Riley's departure? And why, he wondered, did the idea of her huddling in the cold and damp bother him? Perhaps he should return to find out what her plans were. He couldn't believe she would be staying the night under that failing roof. He could advise her on accommodation in several nearby towns.

Why did he even care?

Will let out a long breath of frustration and launched himself at the final incline, up the track. From the top, he could look down over his own vineyards. The sight always brought him a sense of peace and immense satisfaction. In time, he'd be able to survey Rozendal Manor and farm in the same way and experience the same deep sense of achievement.

It was just going to take a little longer than he'd thought.

As he descended the hill towards his home he reflected that Bellevale, from any angle, was the perfect example of the Cape Dutch style of architecture. His ancestors had arrived at the Cape from France in the sixteen-hundreds and quickly discovered that the geological composition of the rugged mountains in the area provided exceptional soil conditions for the cultivation of vines.

There had been a Duvinage farming these acres ever since. Their wines were famous, award-winning and deeply respected and that was not going to change under his stewardship. Sure, he'd moved with the times, now producing a percentage of organic wines, as the market demanded. He'd diversified, opening a restaurant which attracted diners from around the world, and establishing a vegetable garden to supply the kitchens. But the principles of the business were unchanged. Attention to detail, a willingness to be flexible and, above all, a deep love of the very soil in which the vines grew remained his mantra. And his obsessive belief that second best was never good enough.

The estate of Bellevale had been his first love. To date, nothing else had come close to challenging it.

He stopped for a moment, surveying the view which gave him such pleasure. The gables of the house were satisfyingly symmetrical, their sharp angles and sweeping curves pristine. The kitchen garden was at its peak, providing an abundance of fresh fruit and vegetables for the restaurant. Several cars were parked in the shade of the oaks alongside the wine-tasting facility, showing it was doing brisk business. Further away from the house, he'd had the original workers' houses converted into holiday cottages, each one decorated and furnished in understated, tasteful luxury, with its own vine-shaded terrace.

Guests from across the globe came to experience the magic of a few days spent luxuriating in the tranquillity and order of Bellevale, but he knew how hard the staff worked to achieve that ambience of effortless ease. He appreciated every single one of them, knew them all by their first names, the names of their children and their grandchildren. He'd grown up alongside some of them and never forgot that his privilege in owning the estate rather than labouring on it was simply a matter of fortune: a toss of the dice.

Now, as he approached the curved steps which led onto the wide thatched veranda, one of those colleagues was waiting to greet him. Grace's mother had worked for his parents, and they'd ensured that her only daughter received a good education. She'd known Will and his brother since they were born. She'd spooned food into their mouths as babies and later dusted them down and patted them better when they fell out of trees or off bikes. It had usually been his brother who'd needed consoling. He had always been the smaller, weaker and less determined of the two of them.

Will felt his jaw tighten, as it always did when he thought about his brother. And his brother's wife.

Grace had made the most of every opportunity which came her way, becoming a talented and well-known chef, and Will had been pleased to offer her the position of restaurant manager at Bellevale. That role had grown to include managing the holiday cottage business. Grace could anticipate problems before they arose. There was nothing she didn't know about Bellevale and sometimes Will thought there was very little she didn't know about him either.

For instance, he'd expected her to be waiting, with a chilled bottle of something fizzy, to celebrate his purchase of Rozendal, but instead she stood at the top of the steps with her arms folded and her features composed into an expression of commiseration.

'News,' she said, 'travels fast. Faster than you, it seems.' She shook her head. 'I'm sorry.'

Will frowned. 'Yeah. Thanks.'

'I put the champagne back on ice. There'll be another reason to drink it before long.'

'What did you hear?' Will reached the top of the steps and began to roll up the sleeves of his shirt.

'That some girl came running in at the last minute and claimed to be the owner who is not selling to the highest bidder. Which was you.'

Will nodded. 'It was. And it was so very nearly mine. I still can't quite believe what happened.' He shook his head.

'Is she legit? Or deluded?' Grace turned towards the double oak doors and pushed one half of them open. 'I heard she had blood on her face and twigs in her hair. Her *red* hair.'

Will paused on the threshold. The idea of this description of Scarlett Riley already circulating in the neighbourhood disturbed him. It had probably reached Cape Town already and the next thing that would happen would be reporters turning up trying to get pictures of her and a story from him.

'You heard right, but she is not deluded. Or deranged, in case anyone makes that suggestion. She is tired, but my instincts tell me that when she recovers I'll find she is fiercely intelligent.'

His words surprised him. What had made him say that? A sense of fairness, he supposed. Of being unwilling to make a judgement without a proper foundation of reason. After all, he should know how that rolled. He had a fleeting memory of the way her expression had closed down, her lids briefly shielding those green eyes, when he'd asked the question about her parents. And then there was that pale circle on her ring finger.

Grace narrowed her eyes. 'Ah. An adversary. Is there going to be a battle for Rozendal?'

He nodded and stepped into the cool, dim interior of the hall. Wide yellowwood floorboards, gleaming with the patina of centuries of polish and wear, stretched across the room, a perfect foil for the glowing colours of the Persian rugs. Copper pans shone on the walls, alongside some of his favourite old oil paintings. He breathed in the scent of beeswax and lavender from the flower arrangement on the circular table in the centre of the space and felt his energy level rise and his irritation and anger subside.

'Yes,' he said, 'there is. It'll be worth the fight.'

Grace studied him. ‘Cup of tea? Coffee?’

He shook his head. ‘No, thanks. But I’d kill for a cold beer. It’ll help me plan my strategy.’

‘Where’s your jacket, Will? You were wearing it earlier.’

He shrugged. ‘I left it at Rozendal. I was in a hurry to leave, but it’ll be an excuse to go back to see how the new owner is getting on. Knowing the enemy is half the battle.’

He opened the fridge and pulled out a beer, cracking open the ring pull and swallowing down a mouthful before wiping the back of his hand across his mouth and pouring the rest of the amber contents of the can into the tall glass Grace held out to him.

She tipped her head towards the folder which lay on the worktop. ‘There’re a couple of things I need to run past you, before you start forming up your battle lines.’ She flipped the file open and ran a finger down a list of items. ‘The couple in Oakdean are film-makers. Apparently, they plan to scope out possible locations. How do you feel about that?’

He frowned. ‘Get more details from them. It’d depend on a lot of things. Mostly on how disruptive it would be.’

Grace nodded and made a note. ‘And we’ve had another query about a wedding…’

Will put the glass down, rested his hands on the worktop and dropped his head.

‘You don’t need to ask me that. You know how I feel about fancy weddings…’

She closed the file. ‘Not all weddings have to be fancy.’

He shook his head. ‘Anyone who wants to get married here wants a fancy wedding.’ Raising his eyes and meeting her gaze, he felt the familiar flare of anger. He hated that she, and others, felt the need to treat him with compassion.

Grace sighed. ‘Yeah, I know. Just thought I’d mention it in case you’ve changed your mind.’

‘When,’ he asked slowly, straightening up, ‘have you ever known me to change my mind?’

CHAPTER THREE

THE WALL OF exhaustion Scarlett had hit felt as solid as if it had been built of bricks and mortar. She felt ready to drop where she stood and curl up on the floor right there and go to sleep. The idea was scarily tempting.

The auctioneer had been the last to leave. She'd done her best to explain the bizarre circumstances which had brought her to Rozendal and given him the name and contact details of the lawyers. She'd apologised profusely more than once, for the disruption she'd caused. She wasn't sure he'd accepted.

Now, alone at last, she walked out through the wide front door, her footsteps echoing in the empty hall. Two elderly armchairs stood on the shady veranda. Their fabric, once a pretty floral, was faded and stained. Some small creature, presumably a mouse, had chewed a hole in one of the cushions and helped itself to some of the horsehair stuffing.

She chose the one that looked marginally less uncomfortable and flopped onto it, toed her shoes off and tucked her feet underneath her.

The view was infinite. In front of the house the gravel drive was thick with weeds, but beyond it she could make out the beginning of the oak-lined avenue she'd fought her way up to get here. She presumed her hire car was still at the gates. It looked as if no other vehicle had used the track for months so she hoped her suitcase and backpack would be safe in it overnight. She had barely enough energy to think, let alone find her way back to the car. And if she did, she'd have to climb those gates again, and she'd never be able to haul her luggage over them.

She'd deal with it tomorrow. What difference would one more night in the clothes she was wearing make?

Beyond the tangle of the overgrown garden, the valley rolled away into the distance. Layer upon layer of rounded hills shimmered in the afternoon sun, the regimented stripes of vines marching over them. She liked the feeling of orderly permanence they gave to the landscape. Compared with the chaos of her recent past, this slice of life, with its atmosphere of timeless peace, felt like a corner of heaven.

The vine-clad hills reached up to the slopes of the mountains which enclosed the valley on three sides. Saw-toothed ridges, like the humped back of a dragon, pierced the blue sky on one side and on another sheer cliffs of rock fell hundreds of feet, to disappear into the scrubby bush at their feet.

Scarlett felt safe—cocooned in her chair, on her own veranda, on her own land. It was a luxury she would like to dwell on and savour, if only she could stay awake.

When she woke several hours later, it was because she was chilled and damp. Darkness was creeping up the valley towards her, although the tops of the mountains were still bathed in a golden evening light. The blue sky had faded to a deep mauve and the first stars glimmered through the dusk. A bank of cloud had built up in the south. Down the valley a curl of woodsmoke rose into the evening air and a dog barked in the distance.

Scarlett pulled herself out of the chair, which seemed to have sprouted lumps while she'd been asleep, and made her way indoors. Little light now penetrated the dust-coated sash windows and the interior of the house was dim. The spacious hall, where the ill-fated auction had been held, looked forlorn, with the small desk perched on a table at the end and a few chairs scattered across the floor. Slung over the back of one of them was a dark suit jacket. She ran her fingers over the fine wool of the wide shoulders and remembered Will Duvinage standing in front of her, his hands thrust into the pockets of his trousers, his shoulders thrown back. She decided the jacket belonged to him.

She wondered if he'd return to collect it or if he'd send someone else. The prospect of seeing him again made her feel uneasy and a little twist of tension tightened around her insides. She shook her head, irritated at her response. She'd talked to him for all of two minutes and in that time had decided he was demanding and over-confident. He seemed like a man perfectly happy to demand the impossible and happy to take it as his due when the impossible was delivered. But, after Alan, she doubted there was a man anywhere whose bad behaviour could surprise her.

Will Duvinage had said they were neighbours, and she wondered exactly what that meant. Here, at the foot of Africa, neighbours could mean driving thirty miles to borrow a cup of sugar. Picking her way across the dusty floor, she rubbed at the grime on one of the windowpanes and peered out into the deepening dusk. There were no friendly nearby lights.

The silence was absolute.

She felt a stab of anxiety. She was used to isolation. Her plant-hunting expeditions had taken her to some of the most remote places on earth, but she'd never been alone. She'd always had the company of other like-minded scientists and the trips had operated to a planned schedule, with every detail thought out beforehand. Things did not go wrong.

Things did not go wrong, until they did. And on the last trip they had gone wrong in a most spectacular way.

The darkness in the room had thickened. With faint hope, she flicked a brass switch near the door and a bulb in one of the old brass wall sconces glowed into life, the light feeble behind a dirty frosted glass shade. Relief loosened the band of panic which had begun to tighten around her lungs, and she breathed more easily.

The antiquated kitchen was at the back of the house and the route to it took her through high-ceilinged rooms with ceiling fans festooned with cobwebs. Stern portraits glared at her through the gloom, and furniture crouched beneath the shrouds of dustsheets. Tomorrow, she thought. She'd deal with all of this tomorrow, when she'd slept, washed and eaten a decent meal.

A loud groan emitted from the ancient brass taps over the stone kitchen sink when she twisted one of them, using both hands to break the seal of rust which held them fast. The pipes gurgled ominously but then a trickle of dirty water splashed from the spout. Light and water, she thought. What more could I want?

A pang of hunger made her realise that what she wanted was food and she would probably not get anything to eat until the morning, when she'd have to retrieve her luggage, make herself presentable and find the nearest town or village. On her mad dash from Cape Town Airport, determined to beat the auction deadline, she hadn't given a thought to stopping for food. There was a bottle of water in her handbag and the little packet of biscuits and plastic-looking cheese from the airline dinner the night before. She'd have to make do with those. In the unlikely event that there was any food in this time capsule of a kitchen, she'd be willing to bet it would not be edible.

The exhaustion that had stalked her all day, and which had been only partly alleviated by her nap in the lumpy chair, hit her again. She returned to the hall, from where a grand staircase curved upwards to the first floor, and began to climb it in search of a bed.

She paused on the landing as light flickered across the night sky beyond the tall window. A few seconds later a distant rumble of thunder rolled over the mountains. What luxury, she thought, to be in a proper house, under a real roof, in a thunderstorm. The rainforest canopy had provided scant protection for her hammock in the jungle, and she'd frequently been soaked to the skin.

Pushing open a door, Scarlett found a bathroom with a huge pink bath and plumbing which looked as if it could drive a steam train. The next door revealed a bedroom with a brass bedstead, bare mattress and pillows and a thin rug folded at its foot.

No bed had ever looked more inviting. Scarlett crawled onto it and pulled the rug up around her shoulders. Lightning illuminated the room and thunder echoed around the valley. As her eyes grew heavy, she heard the muted sound of the first fat raindrops hitting the thatch.

When she jerked awake it was because something had disturbed her. The storm was growing in intensity, but she knew it wasn't that. Storms had never bothered her. It was something much more sinister. She heard a thump, somewhere in the room, and reached for her phone. Then she remembered her bag, containing the airline snack and her phone, was downstairs. As she fumbled along the wall, looking for the light switch, a draught of air lifted her hair and something furry brushed across her face.

She found the door before she found the light switch and dragged it open, flinging herself into the dark passage outside, panic gripping her. Whatever it was seemed to be following her, because she felt it brush against her again and she put her arms across her face, stumbling to where she thought she'd find the stairs.

As she reached the landing, she remembered seeing a light switch next to the window. Her trembling fingers located it and faint light from a weak bulb high up on the ceiling lit the stairwell. A dark shape swooped in the shadows above her.

Her only thought was to escape the furry brush of wings and the unpredictable, jerky loops of the shadow. But as her feet hit the hall floor there was a blinding flash of lightning and an ear-shattering crack of thunder and the faint light high above the stairs flickered and went out. A loud banging came from the direction of the kitchen as a cold draught, carrying with it the scent of rain and damp earth, gusted into the darkness.

A door or window must have been blown open in the storm and she'd have to find it and secure it. Otherwise, who knew what manner of creatures would find their way in to terrify her?

Scarlett groped her way to the kitchen. There was no welcoming flicker from the lamps when she flipped the light switch. Amidst the confusing clamour of the storm, the noise seemed to come from behind a door which she saw, for the first time, illuminated by a flash of lightning. She twisted the stiff doorknob, but it refused to budge. She gripped it with both hands, just as another flash and a roar of thunder ripped through the house. In the inky darkness she heard a sound behind her. She half turned, panic spiralling out of control.

A pair of arms, corded and hard with muscle, closed around her, trapping her arms at her sides and sweeping her feet from the floor.

She screamed, even though the small, logical part of her brain which was still functioning told her it was useless. Because nobody, apart from the assailant who held her in this iron-hard grip, would hear her.

CHAPTER FOUR

WILL SWORE.

Who knew Scarlett's bare heels, hammering against his shins, would be such effective weapons? He allowed himself a moment to be grateful that he had her arms pinned firmly to her sides, or her fists would be raining blows on him too.

A few seconds of silence followed her first scream while she struggled, but he felt her lungs expand as she drew in another breath and then a second scream, even more piercing than the first, split his eardrums.

'Let me go! Let me *go*...'

'Scarlett. Stop it. Stop fighting. It's me. Will,' he shouted, hoping she'd hear his voice through her panic. He'd acted instinctively when the flash of lightning had shown her, poised to push open the door to the cellar steps. He'd stopped her from tumbling into the void, but he might have almost scared her to death.

She didn't scream again, but she continued to struggle. He shuffled backwards in the darkness, relaxing his grip a little but with no intention of letting her go just yet.

'Put me *down*.' It sounded as if she was speaking through gritted teeth. *'Now.'*

'Not now. I need to make sure you're safe.'

'Safe? *Safe?*' He felt her twist her head against him, and a few silky strands of her hair brushed across his cheek. Her scent, floral with a hint of warm spice, wafted over him. He'd noticed it earlier and it reminded him of shady meadows on hot summer evenings. 'I won't feel safe until you've let me go and I've put some distance between us. Maybe several miles. Or at least a locked door...' She kicked again.

Will sucked in a breath, cursing inwardly. There would be bruises to show for this encounter, even though he was wearing jeans.

'Scarlett.' He tried to modulate his voice although his breathing had become erratic and, alarmingly, he was aware that it wasn't only the wild kicks to his shins causing adrenalin to surge through his body and his lungs to feel starved of oxygen. Because, irrationally, he liked the feel of Scarlett's body against his. She felt delicate but strong, and the baggy clothes she wore had disguised the surprising soft curves of the hips which he held, pressed against his own. If he dropped his head slightly, he'd probably find the smooth curve where her neck joined her shoulder and he could take a breath, inhale that scent more deeply...

What the *hell* was he thinking? He snapped his attention back to the present and the immediate problem which he held, literally, in his arms. Carefully, he relaxed his hold and allowed Scarlett to slide down his body until her feet made contact with the floor. He kept his hands closed around her upper arms to steady her and felt a tremor ripple through the muscles under his fingers.

The lights chose that moment to flicker into uncertain life.

Will took a step back. Scarlett stood with her head bent, the pale nape of her neck exposed. He wanted, very much, to place his hand there on her skin, to see if it was as petal-soft as it looked, but he dropped his arms slowly to his sides instead, watching to make sure she didn't fall over.

She raised her head, pushing the mass of her hair over her shoulder, removing the temptation of her nape.

'Are you okay?'

As she turned to face him, he caught the green flash of fire from her eyes.

'Forgive me for pointing out the obvious, but that is a silly question. A furry, flying creature was crashing into the walls of my room. It followed me in the dark. The lights went out and an intruder grabbed me from behind and…' She shook her head. 'Seriously, under the circumstances, would *you* be okay?'

Will felt the corner of his mouth twitch and he pressed his lips together to suppress a smile.

'Put like that…'

'It's not funny.'

'No. Not at all.'

'Then don't laugh at me.'

'I'm not. I'm thinking about the bruises I'm going to have on my shins. I'll have to wear jeans for a week and not go swimming. Or else I'll have to pretend I was kicked by a horse if I'm to have any hope of maintaining my credibility.'

Her eyes dropped and her gaze slid down his body to his feet and back up again.

'Oh… I'm sorry. Are you comparing me with a horse?'

'No!' He shook his head, raking his fingers through his hair. 'I'm sorry I frightened you. I…'

'You didn't frighten me. You terrified me, almost to death.'

'I didn't stop to think. It was instinctive…'

'I think your instincts need work. *Suppressing* work.'

Her breathing was less erratic, but he could still see the hollow at her throat moving in and out, pushing the ends of her collarbones against her sweatshirt. And he had to agree with her, because what his instincts were telling him to do right now was simply unacceptable.

'It wasn't…like *that*. I was trying to protect you.'

'Well, it *felt* like…*that*.' She raised a hand, which shook a little, and pushed her hair away from her forehead. 'Most people would have at least knocked first. So what,' she asked, 'were you protecting me from?'

Will huffed out a breath and pulled a hand across his jaw. 'I'd come over because I thought you might be afraid.'

'It was after you got here that I became afraid. Except of the furry flying thing. Which I presume was a bat.'

He nodded. 'Most likely.'

'I'm used to bats flying around. Just not indoors. They're not scary in the jungle. Also, I'm tired. More like exhausted, and logical thought has become an alien concept.'

'I thought you might be afraid of the storm. The power is unreliable when there's lightning around. I didn't know if you'd have a torch…'

'I'd left my phone downstairs. There was something banging behind that door.' She tipped her head in the direction of the cellar door. 'I wanted to stop it. But you jumped me.'

'That wasn't how it was meant to feel. I'm sorry.'

'I don't know in which alternative universe it could have felt different. Why did you do it?'

'I was at the back door.' He glanced over his shoulder. 'That's what was banging in the wind. In the flash of lightning, I saw you trying to open the cellar door and I had to stop you.' He stepped around her, taking care not to touch her, and twisted the handle, pulling the door forcefully towards him. 'This is why.'

A void, dark as pitch, yawned beyond the opening. Once, a staircase had wound down to the extensive cellars below the Manor, but now the top three steps had crumbled away to nothing, and the remaining treads were rotten and unstable. Will nodded, satisfied that he'd done the right thing. Scarlett would have stepped through the door and into a black space. How long would it have been before anyone found her on the stone flags of the cellar floor?

He glanced back at her. He thought her face, already pale with exhaustion, had lost a little more colour. She raised the back of one hand to her mouth as she peered past him.

The storm was receding and a moment of quiet settled over

them. Scarlett's eyes, wide green pools of shock, met his. He wasn't sure, in the unreliable light, if their shimmer was enhanced by tears or not. Then she turned away, swiping her fingers across her cheeks.

'Thank you.' Her voice was strained with fatigue. 'I'm sorry I kicked you. I would have fallen…'

Will nodded. 'Yes, I think you would have. But you're safe now. Just don't go wandering about in the dark…'

Her narrow shoulders lifted in a slight shrug. 'No, I won't. Anyway, I'm much too tired to wander anywhere else.'

For a reason which Will didn't examine, he hated the trace of defeat he heard in her voice. From what he'd seen of her so far, defeat was probably not a concept to which she gave much consideration. He moved to her side and touched her arm.

'Would you like me to take you back up to bed?' It was too late to take the words back, even as he heard how they sounded. 'That's not what I meant to say. I meant…'

The hint of a smile lifted the corners of her full mouth, showing the slight dent of a dimple in the middle of her left cheek. 'That's good, because I'm in no state to indulge in any bed-related activity, apart from sleep. But perhaps you need to work on your seduction technique, alongside taming your instincts…'

Will's hand shot out to steady her as she swayed on her feet. Then he slipped his arm around her shoulders.

'You're shaking. When did you last eat?'

'That's because of your inappropriate suggestion. And my last meal was an airline one.'

'You haven't eaten? *All day?*'

'Mmm.' She nodded. 'Intermittent fasting is supposed to be good for you.'

'Well, in your case it's going to cause you to pass out, and that will definitely not be good for you.' Will came to a snap decision. 'I'm taking you home to Bellevale. You can sleep in a clean bed and have some proper food while you decide what to do about Rozendal Manor. You'll need to be sharp to talk to the lawyers about planning and timing for the sale.' He bent and put his free arm under her knees. But then he paused. 'Scarlett, I'm going to pick you up and carry you to my four-by-four. It's parked around the back of the house. Is that okay?' Another struggle was the last thing he wanted.

'Um… I suppose so. Yes.' A yawn blurred her speech and he felt her body sag against his. As he scooped her up her head dropped to his shoulder and her hand rested on his chest. Then she raised her head slightly. 'I already know what I'm going to do about Rozendal Manor.'

'Good.' He hoped the relief didn't show too obviously in his voice. If she'd made up her mind it would all happen more quickly than he'd dared to hope earlier in the day. She had determination, he could tell, and was unlikely to change her mind. She must have seen the impossibility of doing anything with the Manor apart from selling it. And he was prepared to make her a generous offer, which she would be foolish to refuse.

'Yes,' she said, her voice soft. 'It's so beautiful here. It's as if the house and garden have been asleep, waiting for someone to wake them up.'

'Tomorrow, I'll take you in to the lawyers' offices in Cape Town, if you're ready.'

Her head dropped back onto his shoulder and he settled her into his arms.

'That's very kind of you,' she murmured, 'but not necessary. I'm not selling. I'm staying at Rozendal. I'm going to rewild the estate.'

CHAPTER FIVE

AS BOMBSHELLS WENT, Scarlett's announcement was up there with the one his brother had made five years ago. After that, he'd vowed he would never be caught out by anyone, ever again.

Since that day he'd been ready for every eventuality, every possibility. Every disaster. He never wanted another surprise. He never wanted to feel that sense of confusion again, as if the person standing in front of him was speaking in a language he knew he should understand but which sounded utterly foreign.

It had felt like a nightmare from which he'd never wake up, and then it had been made worse by the real, proper nightmares that had plagued him for months. He'd woken from those, only to be hit again, each time, by the dawning of reality, the sense of humiliation and embarrassment, and the realisation that you could not trust anyone—not even the people you'd believed were closest to you.

He stumbled, and crashed into the old oak table which stood in the centre of the room. His arms tightened around Scarlett reflexively, protecting her. She didn't react and as he stood, attempting to regain his equilibrium in more ways than one, he realised, from her steady breathing, that she was asleep.

The shock he'd had this morning when she'd appeared, a dishevelled vision with twigs in her incredible hair, to snatch the ownership of Rozendal from him, had been intense. He'd been on the brink of achieving his goal but he'd kept a lid on his temper, knowing only the muscle tightening in his jaw would give it away, and he was almost sure nobody in the crowd had seen that. The rapt attention in the saleroom, which had been focused on him, had switched in an instant to Scarlett. He felt grudging gratitude for that. Some smooth lawyer in a fancy suit, sent to make the claim on her behalf, would not have generated one tenth of the interest she had.

He drew in a calming breath, telling himself that his plans for Rozendal were on hold, not cancelled. Scarlett's appearance and claim were simply a little difficulty he had to navigate, and he was used to managing difficulties. Sometimes he felt as if his whole life, until he'd locked a copy of the deeds of ownership of Bellevale in his safe, had consisted of overcoming one difficulty after another.

Except for that unpleasant business with his brother, which had come a little later.

This was just another one, sent to prove that he would always—*always*—succeed in getting what he wanted.

He carried Scarlett through the open back door and kicked it shut behind him. If there was a key, he didn't care. It had been open when he'd arrived. The stone steps down into the yard were treacherous, the rain having left them slick and slippery. When he reached the bottom, he realised he'd been holding his breath. Falling down the flight with Scarlett in his arms would have been a disastrous end to what had been a difficult day.

Scarlett stirred as he slid her onto the back seat of the Range Rover. She cupped a hand under her cheek before settling into sleep again. Will climbed into the driver's seat and took out his phone, pulling up Grace's number. She never left the restaurant until the last of the diners had taken their leave and the staff had finished clearing up, leaving the tables and kitchens pristine and gleaming, ready for the following day. She'd still be there.

'There's an unexpected late guest,' he said when she answered on the third ring. 'Is there a cottage free?' He refused to face the possibility that there might not be. Of course, he had guest bedrooms in the homestead, but he guarded his space and privacy fiercely, and sharing them with Scarlett would be an absolute last resort. In the background he could hear the sound of the kitchen being cleaned, then a door closed and the noise faded.

Grace could be counted on not to ask unnecessary questions.

'Sure,' she said calmly. 'The couple who particularly requested quiet and seclusion cancelled. One of them is ill. Which means Vineyard Cottage is free, as long as your guest doesn't mind solitude.'

'She's practically comatose at the moment, so she is not going to mind anything.'

There was the briefest of pauses before Grace replied. 'I see. Okay, I'm just finishing up here, so I'll drop by the cottage on my way home to unlock it. Do you,' she asked, and Will could hear the tact in her voice, 'need any help?'

'It's the girl from Rozendal, Scarlett Riley,' he said, deciding to short-circuit any speculation on Grace's part. 'She's exhausted, travel-stained and asleep. Definitely not a subject for you to start weaving a romance around.'

'I wouldn't dream of it.'

'Yeah. That's what you always say. I'll be there in ten minutes.'

When Scarlett eased her eyes open, the first thing she became aware of was the light. It wasn't the greenish, watery light, filtered through the jungle canopy, accompanied by the calls of unfamiliar birds and the squawks of parrots. Neither was it the soft, pale light of an English dawn in spring. It was bright and hard-edged, falling in sharp bars through the wooden shutters onto the pale timber floor. It was completely alien.

Her confusion grew as she studied the room through half-closed eyelids. Nothing about it was familiar.

The walls were painted in a chalky white and green-painted timber framed the window and doorframe. She lifted her head a little and caught a glimpse of the inside of a luxuriously appointed bathroom. With a jolt of surprise, she realised that the jeans and sweatshirt she'd been wearing—for how many days?—lay neatly folded on a low chair. Soft linen, of what felt like a zillion thread count, caressed her legs and the bed was not a hammock or a lumpy sofa, or even an airline seat. It was wide and comfortable and she wanted to stay right here, in it, for ever.

She shot upright. Where was she? And how had she got here? And, for that matter, who had removed her clothes and tucked her into this dreamy bed, leaving her in her underwear and tee shirt?

She pushed back the light-as-air duvet and swung her legs to the floor. It was when she noticed her dusty feet that the scattered pieces of the jigsaw which made up the past few days began to fall into place.

She'd taken off her trainers before climbing into that other bed: the one with the hard pillows and threadbare blanket. And she hadn't put them on again when she'd fumbled her way downstairs, a dark shadow looping above her head, there'd been a storm and the lights had gone out and…

Will. Will had scared her, but he'd stopped her from tumbling down that gaping hole, into the cellar. He'd picked her up. And after that she couldn't remember anything at all.

Had Will brought her here? Had it been Will who had removed her jeans and tucked her into bed? She lifted the hem of her tee shirt and looked at her worn old underwear and groaned in embarrassment, but she suppressed it immediately.

She didn't care if Will had seen her panties. She didn't care who saw them. She was so over worrying about stuff like that.

Standing up, testing her legs because they didn't feel as if they truly belonged to her, she walked to the window and eased back the shutters. The bright African sunlight struck her face, making her blink. From the position of the sun, she thought it must be late morning. It was a long time since she'd slept for so many uninterrupted hours. Her body felt light and energised, her brain clear. The heartache and regret which ambushed her within seconds of waking nowadays had retreated to the edge of her consciousness and she hoped she could keep them there.

Behind the full-length shutters was a pair of French windows which opened onto a deep terrace, shaded by a gnarled vine whose leaves were edged with the first golden tinge of autumn. Rows of cultivated vines divided the slopes which fell away into the valley, while beyond them the mountains etched a jagged outline against the deep blue of the sky.

The scene of orderly tranquillity settled around Scarlett like a comfort blanket as she remembered that she was a part of it now. Okay, Rozendal was neither orderly nor tranquil yet, but she would transform it. The estate would become a haven for wildlife and rare plants, an organic oasis of productivity and creativity. Her imagination raced ahead into the future.

This timeless valley was her home, and Rozendal the only place she'd ever been able to call her own. She felt as if she belonged, even though she'd only been here for a day. She savoured the thought, scarcely daring to believe it. She, Scarlett Riley, was no longer the abandoned, homeless, botanist. She was the owner of Rozendal Manor and its glorious gardens and acres of land.

'Thank you, Marguerite,' she breathed. Her eccentric godmother had rescued her from the ignominy of having to spend the holidays at her boarding school when her hapless parents had failed to make alternative arrangements for her. She'd taken her on adventurous trips, hunting for rare plants, and on chaotic visits to the seaside and up Scottish mountains. She'd been there for all the milestones that her parents had missed. And she'd waved Scarlett off on that last fateful trip to the

Amazon, in a sudden moment of clarity, as if the clouds had momentarily cleared from her foggy mind.

'Be sure that you're sure of him,' she'd said, glancing at Alan's retreating back as he'd marched out of the door of the care home, without waiting for her to follow.

And then, on a rare occasion when she'd been able to connect to the internet at some jungle outpost, she'd learned that Marguerite had died.

Alan had had little patience with her grief, uttering a few empty platitudes before tucking into his breakfast, and Marguerite's words had come back to her.

Was she sure of him? She'd realised she didn't know. And the middle of a jungle expedition was probably not the time or place to start having doubts. She'd deal with them later, when she was back on familiar territory, and when her safety didn't depend on him.

Marguerite had rescued her again, and this time it was for keeps.

Scarlett breathed in a lungful of the warm, scented air. It reminded her of golden honey trickling from a silver spoon, of the lavender cushions Marguerite had tucked under her pillow—'*French* lavender, darling, naturally. *Never* English'—and of the jasmine which had scrambled through the old apple tree in her small London garden.

'Thank you,' she said again, only this time she spoke the words out loud.

Then she noticed two things. Firstly, to her shock, Scarlett recognised her hire car, parked under the towering oak trees which shaded the cottage. And secondly, she saw her battered suitcase standing on the veranda beyond the French windows, her handbag balanced on top of it.

Fumbling with the latch, she managed to open the windows. The tiled surface was warm beneath her feet as she stepped outside to retrieve her luggage.

Then she saw something else. It was Will, and he was striding with purpose towards her. She wondered if she had time to dart back inside and close the shutters again, pretend to be asleep.

But he'd seen her, and he quickened his pace. He looked as fresh as she felt rumpled and undressed. His faded denims encased powerful thighs and she had a sudden, disturbing memory of the rock solidness of them, pressed against her, as he'd held her tightly in his arms the previous night. She pushed the memory away as Will stopped at the foot of the three steps which led up to the cottage, only to focus on the width of his shoulders and the tanned, powerful forearms which his rolled-up sleeves revealed instead.

Scarlett swallowed hard, gripped the hem of the tee shirt, pulling it down so it reached the top of her thighs, and lifted her chin. Men like him should come with a warning.

'Good morning.' His voice was dark and rich. It reminded her of strong coffee and how much she needed a cup of it right now. He glanced at the watch on his wrist, and then back up at her. 'It is still morning. Just. Which means you must have slept well?'

'I…yes. Thank you, I did. I've only just woken.'

'Good. You were practically unconscious last night. I was coming to unlock the door.' He nodded towards the front door behind her and a little to the right of where she stood. 'We locked you in last night, but I knew you could find your way out through the French windows if necessary.'

Scarlett scoured her memory but nothing—not a single detail—floated to the surface.

'We? You and…who else?' She felt a new rush of anxiety and embarrassment at the thought of some other, unknown person taking off her jeans, putting her to bed.

Will smiled, his eyes crinkling at the corners and the lines bracketing his mouth deepening. 'You needn't be embarrassed. You were very tired. Grace, who manages the restaurant and the B and B business, met us here. It was Grace who put you to bed.'

Scarlett frowned. An image of someone willowy and elegant swam across her mind's eye. Someone who worked alongside Will and who he felt comfortable about contacting late at night when he had a problem. A problem in the form of an unexpected visitor who had fallen asleep in his arms. The idea of such a person undressing her and putting her to bed did not make her feel less awkward.

Then she remembered that she was supposed not to care who saw her underwear. She released the hem of her tee shirt and stood a little taller.

'Thank you. Please thank Grace too. I'm sorry to have caused you trouble.'

Will's shoulders lifted. He shook his head. 'No trouble. I'm glad I went to check on you. You were…'

'Yes,' she interrupted. 'I remember. Thank you for stopping me from falling down those stairs too.'

The smile disappeared from Will's face. 'You can thank Grace yourself. You'll see her later.'

'Oh, no, I won't be here long. I need to get back to Rozendal. There's so much to do.'

Will mounted the steps slowly. He stood looking down at her, his hands in his pockets.

'Well, you say you don't mind the bats, so I'm sure you won't care about the squirrels and pigeons living in the attics either. And once you've worked out which boards are safe to tread on, you won't go through the floors. The rusty water—' he shrugged '—it's not drinkable, but you could wash in it, I suppose.' His eyes left her face and moved to her hair.

She chipped in before he could state the obvious. 'So the rest of me will become the same colour as my hair. That'll be interesting. And if you're trying to put me off, you're wasting your time.'

'I'm not trying to put you off. I'm hoping you'll see sense, that's all. The place is unsafe and uninhabitable. The booking for this cottage was cancelled yesterday so it's free for the next fortnight. I can't make you stay here, but you'd be crazy not to.'

His offer surprised Scarlett. After all, she'd thwarted his very nearly successful bid to buy Rozendal from under her nose. Was that only yesterday? Time seemed to have taken on a new dimension and the reality of her last-minute flight and dash from Cape Town felt as if they'd happened in another universe.

If she'd had time to consider it, she would have assumed he'd try to get her to leave as quickly as possible. He wouldn't have succeeded, of course. She'd made up her mind and she wasn't going anywhere, but he wasn't to know that.

His expression was serious as his eyes came back to her face. She looked away quickly, not wanting him to catch her studying him, and found her gaze level with the undone top button of his pastel blue shirt. The exposed vee of skin was smooth and tanned. Was he tanned like that all over? Well, not *all* over, obviously…but then, had he mentioned swimming last night?

Warmth rose in her cheeks, but if he noticed her blush he ignored it.

'I need to get dressed. Then I'll drive over to Rozendal and make a start. If you could direct me to the nearest place where I can buy bed linen, and food…' She stopped. Will's voice had made her think of coffee, but it couldn't have conjured up that tantalising aroma, could it? And layered beneath it was the scent of freshly baked pastries. Hunger, which she'd managed not to acknowledge until now, slammed into her. She resisted the urge to clutch at her stomach. 'Is that…?'

'Here's breakfast. A little late, but I'm sure you're hungry enough to forgive that.'

Beyond Will, an ebony-haired woman had appeared. She climbed the steps and placed the tray she carried on the small, round table in a shady corner under the vine. When she straightened up, she extended a hand towards Scarlett.

'Hi. We met last night, but I doubt you remember. I'm Grace. You must be starving. Enjoy your breakfast.'

Scarlett liked the warm, firm grip of her hand, and the way her smile reached her dark eyes. She was friendly and carried an air of capability.

'Thank you. And for…last night too.'

'You're welcome.' She glanced across at Will. 'I'm practised at putting people to bed. It started with Will and his brother when they were babies. Not forgetting a couple of times when they were teenagers…'

'Okay, Grace, no embarrassing childhood stories. I see there're two mugs on the tray. Is one of them for me, or are you planning on sharing Scarlett's breakfast?'

Grace shook her head. 'Much as I'd like to get to know you, Scarlett, I've got too much to do this morning to spend time drinking coffee. When I saw you chatting, I added another mug to the tray. I'll see you later.'

She left, leaping down the shallow steps and striding away, hips swaying as she pulled out her phone and made a call.

The idea that Grace had helped her to bed made Scarlett feel less uncomfortable. She longed to tuck into the coffee and pastries, but knew she had to put on something more than a tee shirt first.

'I'll get dressed…' She bent to pick up her suitcase, but Will was there before her.

He swung the suitcase up and walked into the bedroom, putting it on a luggage rack at the foot of the bed. 'You'll find a robe behind the bathroom door. Put that on and come out to eat.'

With that, he strode out of the door, his tall frame briefly blocking the light. The room dimmed as he pulled the shutters closed behind him. Seconds later, Scarlett heard him unlocking the front door. She slipped into the bathroom, splashed cold water onto her face and looked in the mirror.

Worse. Much worse than she'd imagined.

Her hair looked as if it had partied all night. She located the scrunchy she knew she'd used to tie it back. Had that been in London? Then she pulled it into an untidy knot on the top of her head. She stripped off the long-sleeved tee shirt and pulled a towelling robe from the back of the door, sliding her arms into its luxurious softness and tying the belt firmly at her waist.

As she walked back into the bedroom, she realised she'd done exactly as Will had told her.

CHAPTER SIX

THE ROBE REACHED to an inch above her knees, but as Scarlett walked towards him across the tiles he caught a glimpse of a smooth thigh as it flipped open. Her slim legs were long, her feet delicate and covered in a layer of grime. She'd pulled her hair onto the top of her head but some of it had already escaped, framing her face in russet-coloured tendrils. As she approached, she tucked them behind her ears and he noticed that her hands were delicate too, with long fingers and short nails.

The movement as she turned her head to look at the tray on the table was measured and graceful and he wondered how she could be so controlled. If he hadn't eaten for that many hours he'd have reverted to a neanderthal, with any manners forgotten.

He pulled out one of the wicker chairs for her and she sat down, her actions deliberate. But when she raised a hand towards the coffee pot it was shaking.

'Let me.' He reached out to grip the pot, his fingers brushing against hers. 'You're trembling, presumably with hunger.'

She nodded. 'Yes, I'm a bit light-headed. Now that food is within reach, I feel almost too weak to eat it.' She slumped back against the deep cushions of the chair and closed her eyes.

Will lifted the linen cloth from the basket of pastries, tore a piece off one of them and reached across the table.

'Eat this, Scarlett. But nibble it. Don't swallow it all in one go or you'll feel ill.'

She opened her mouth and he touched the flaky morsel to her lips. Then she took it from his fingers and ate a piece, swallowing slowly before taking another bite.

'Mmm.' Her eyes fluttered open. 'Delicious.'

Will smiled. 'Good. They're made in the restaurant kitchen every morning. Coffee?'

'Yes, please. I might die if I don't have coffee soon. But, on the other hand, the smell of it makes me think I've died and gone to heaven, anyway. Win-win.'

'It's good that you're feeling better.' He lifted the pot and poured steaming black coffee into the two china mugs. 'Milk? And I think you should have some sugar.' He dropped two lumps of golden-brown sugar into one of the cups.

'I don't take sugar.'

'It'll be good for your energy levels. Just this once.'

'Has anyone ever told you you're bossy?'

He shrugged. 'All the time. I'd worry if they didn't. I'd think I was losing it.'

Scarlett sighed. 'I'll listen. Just this once, then. But no more sugar after that. However, after another couple of those pastries I'll feel fine. And I don't mean a couple of bites. I mean *whole* ones.'

He pushed the basket towards her, trying to stop his brain from wondering what she was wearing under the robe. What was *wrong* with him? He remembered, with annoyance, his slip of the previous evening, when he'd been holding her in the dark, tantalised by her scent and wondering how the skin of her shoulder would feel beneath his mouth…

A leaf from the tangled vine drifted down, one of the first casualties of the approaching change of season. It settled on her hair. Will leaned forward to brush it away but she tilted her head.

'What are you doing?' A wariness in her tone made him stop.

'There's a leaf. It's exactly the colour of your hair.'

'Red.'

'Not red. Russet.'

She patted her head and lifted the leaf between thumb and index finger, holding it up to the light. The sleeve of the robe fell back to her elbow.

'Mmm.' She released it and watched it float downwards to land on the tiles.

Then she helped herself to another pastry and his eyes fixed on her forearm. A series of deep scratches ran from her elbow almost to her wrist. They were healing but still looked angry around the edges.

Too late, he felt her eyes on him. There was no point in pretending he hadn't seen the injury. He could tell she was waiting for the question.

'What happened to your arm?'

'Oh, that.' She pushed up the other sleeve of the robe to reveal similar marks. 'I was looking for orchids.'

'Orchids?'

'Yes.' She gripped the handle of her coffee mug and raised it to her lips, taking a sip and grimacing. 'I'm sure the sugar is good for me. Just this once.'

'Presumably these elusive orchids were not in an English country garden.'

'No. No, they weren't. And, technically, I'd already found them but I'd lost them again.'

He waited for her to continue. She examined the pastry in her hand and took a bite from it.

Will was intrigued. Not just by the lack of information, but by her attitude. By *her*, he admitted with a degree of reluctance. He couldn't remember when he had last found a woman intriguing. Desirable, yes, usually for a very short time, and never by the following morning, which was why he never spent a night in a woman's bed, and never, ever invited one into his.

But intriguing? That was something different. That meant wanting to know more about her. Possibly *everything* about her. And that meant spending time getting to know her, and then she'd want to know all about him, and that was where the story would end. His life was his. Nobody else needed access to it. He had all he'd ever wanted. He had Bellevale.

But, he told himself, perhaps he needed to know something about Scarlett if he was going to persuade her to sell Rozendal to him. Which he was going to do. There was no doubt about that. If he could understand how her mind worked, which buttons to press, the whole process might be quicker. That had to be a good thing. So he asked the next question.

'Where were you hunting for orchids? Where have you been, to get injured like that?'

Scarlett swallowed another mouthful of coffee and put the mug back onto the table. She wiped crumbs from her lips and licked sugar from her fingers—an action which Will found seriously distracting—and pleated the linen napkin on her knee, pressing it down with the heel of her hand.

'The Amazon,' she said, her tone matter-of-fact, as if she'd mentioned popping down to the local flower market.

'The *Amazon*?'

'Yup.' She nodded. 'It's a rich hunting ground. Amazing flora, obviously, for a botanist.' She paused. 'But the jungle is...' she glanced down at her arms '...scratchy.'

Will thought he could come up with several other ways of describing the jungle. Dense, dangerous, scary... Scratchy was not a word he would have chosen. Rose bushes were scratchy. Or thorn trees in the bush. The Amazon rainforest demanded a whole different level of description.

He tried to reassess his opinion of Scarlett. That opinion, after all, was based only on his very brief encounter with her yesterday. She'd appeared from nowhere, seemed chaotic and lost, and her vulnerability had played on his mind enough for him to return to Rozendal last night, in the middle of the storm, to check on her.

But perhaps she wasn't vulnerable at all. She must be strong and intrepid if she'd been plant-hunting in the Amazon. She was a botanist who had the crazy idea of rewilding Rozendal. Perhaps this was going to be more difficult than he'd thought. He glanced down at her hands, but she'd folded them in her lap, on top of the napkin, her right hand over her left. Had he imagined that pale circle on her ring finger? He was sure he hadn't, but he felt wrong-footed, his judgement flawed, so perhaps he had.

'I thought,' he ventured, trying a different approach, 'that you're meant to "take nothing away, leave nothing behind".'

Scarlett rolled her shoulders and her eyes met his. He saw defensiveness flicker in their emerald depths.

'Oh, we… I wasn't taking the orchids away. I was mapping them. All I took away was a photograph. And I left nothing behind.'

He noted that little correction and mentally filed it away for another time. If he always asked the question she expected, she might think he was predictable. He needed to keep her guessing about what he was going to do.

He leaned back in his chair and stretched out his legs, crossing his ankles, trying to look relaxed and not as if he was analysing her every word and action.

'How,' he asked, 'did you get from the Amazon to here? Those scratches look quite recent.'

She went quiet as she appeared to be working something out, her brows pulled together.

'Let me see… I had two nights in London, before flying to Cape Town.' She ticked them off on her fingers. 'Then I spent about six days trying to find my way back to the camp, although it might have been longer. I lost track of time a bit. So they're just about a week old.' She eased the sleeves back down to her wrists. 'And now if I have any more pastry or sweet coffee I think I'll go into a sugar coma, so I'm going to have a shower and change and drive over to Rozendal.' She pushed her chair back. 'Thank you for breakfast.'

Will leapt to his feet. 'I don't think you should drive. Not yet.'

'Why not? I feel fine.'

He crossed his arms, keeping his hands to himself. He wanted to touch her arm, to make sure she listened to him, but he didn't think she'd like that.

'Yes, but you've been very tired. You probably haven't recovered properly yet. And anyway, I should come with you to make sure you don't fall down any steps or through any floorboards.' He tried to sound teasing, but he was aware that he was being overbearing and she might tell him to leave her alone.

The truth was he had an overwhelming need not to let her out of his sight for long. He told himself it was because he needed to keep track of her movements and ideas if he was going to gain possession of Rozendal. He refused to even begin to acknowledge the thought that it was because he wanted to be near her. He hadn't wanted to spend time—proper time—with a woman for years.

Will shoved his hands deep into his pockets and strolled to the edge of the veranda as Scarlett walked away. He was determined not to watch her, but his determination failed. He turned his head just as she turned hers, and their eyes connected. Her stride faltered.

'I'll wait for you,' he said, mentally rescheduling all the things he was meant to do today. The pursuit of ownership of Rozendal was more important. 'Then I'll drive you over to Rozendal.'

Her reply was a toss of her head which dislodged some of the heavy mass of her hair so that it tumbled down her back, a vivid autumnal cascade against the snowy white fabric of the bathrobe. He didn't know if that was an acceptance or a rejection of his offer, but he was prepared to wait for as long as it took to find out.

Scarlett let the robe slip from her shoulders, shed her underwear and turned the shower onto the highest setting. The spray stung like needles on her skin. She tipped her head back, letting the water stream over her face before tugging the scrunchie from her hair.

Will might be waiting for her but she was not going to hurry. She was unlikely to be able to have another shower like this for a while. She'd seen the plumbing arrangements at Rozendal and her expectations were zero.

Bathing in an iron tub in front of a fire might become the height of luxury, at least for a few weeks.

That would not stop her. On numerous expeditions to some of the most remote places on earth she'd showered under buckets suspended from trees, leapt from scalding saunas into icy lakes, or rolled in snow, or swum beneath waterfalls. None of those options had featured four walls or a roof.

Finally, clean and polished from head to toe, courtesy of the array of expensive products lined up on a shelf in the shower, she stepped onto the marble floor of the bathroom and enveloped herself in one of the oversized thick towels which hung from a heated rail.

Studying the contents of her small suitcase, she wondered where her head had been when her hands were packing it. She couldn't remember. She pulled out a fresh pair of jeans and a cotton shirt, applied some sunscreen and lip balm and wove her damp hair into a chunky French plait. Concealer was not much use against the purple smudges of fatigue which lingered beneath her eyes, but tucked into the battered canvas espadrilles at the bottom of the case she found her perfume. Spritzing some onto her wrists and neck instantly made her feel better.

Yes, she was tired, and she had to keep her eyes averted from the bed in case its allure became too great to resist, but she felt purpose and determination rising through her again. Will hadn't mentioned his disappointment at failing to buy Rozendal, but she was sure he hadn't given up his plan. When he made a move, she'd be ready for him.

It seemed Will hadn't waited. He'd gone away and come

back again. At the foot of the steps, behind her small hire car, stood a dark green Range Rover, and leaning against the passenger side door, his arms folded across that broad chest and his eyes hidden behind shades, was Will, looking as if he was prepared to wait all day.

He straightened up as she ran down the steps, turning to open the door for her. As he slid into the driver's seat, he glanced across at her.

'Better?'

Scarlett nodded. She knew she looked better, but his acknowledgment of it brought a flush of warmth to her cheeks.

She noticed how his hands looked light but sure on the wheel and she thought, suddenly, that they would bring the same gentle, confident touch to anything else—an animal…a piece of beloved old furniture…a woman's body.

Not like Alan at all. His touch had been far from gentle. Never unrushed. He had made her feel tense and anxious and then suggested that she was cold and unresponsive.

She shook her head to break her train of thought. She was determined not to need to feel a man's touch again, because she never planned to be in a relationship again. Relationships were the quickest route to heartbreak and disappointment, and she'd had her fill of those. Plants and animals were much more reliable and rewarding than humans. They generally behaved as you expected them to and repaid any care and attention you gave them with devotion and beauty.

Will swung the big vehicle into a bend and Scarlett reached up and held the handle above the door. As they crested a hill, clouds of dust billowing behind them, she saw Rozendal from above for the first time.

It looked more magical than she remembered: a Sleeping Beauty of a house and grounds, waiting for her to bring them back to lush and productive life. Excitement and anticipation unfurled in her stomach and she leaned forward in her seat, watching the property grow nearer as they descended the hill.

Will didn't pull up at the back steps as she'd expected him to. He continued around the side of the Manor and finally stopped on the barely visible gravel turning circle at the foot of the sweeping front steps. Scarlett had a vague recollection of scrambling up those very steps the day before, racing against time. In her haste, she hadn't taken a single second to study the building and later it had been the view that mesmerised her. And by the time she'd walked through the shuttered rooms, amongst the shrouded furniture, she'd been too tired to notice much.

She pushed open the car door and slid out, her feet hitting the tangle of weeds which pushed up through the gravel. Her eyes travelled up the crumbling steps to the wraparound veranda propped up on leaning posts, over the walls covered in cracked plaster and the shutters hanging at drunken angles off their hinges. She saw the moss growing on the thatch and the tree growing out through a hole in it. Perhaps disturbed by their arrival, a flock of pigeons erupted from a different part of the roof, but the large crow, perched on one of the crooked chimneys, one beady eye bent on her, remained at its post, cawing its disapproval.

Scarlett put a hand to her mouth. 'Oh…'

CHAPTER SEVEN

SCARLETT GLANCED OVER her shoulder at Will, who was walking around the front of the car, towards her. She dropped her hand.

'Oh!' she exclaimed again, this time trying to sound delighted rather than deeply dismayed. 'It's so…so…it's so *beautiful*.'

If he thought she was shocked or having second thoughts about her plans for the estate, he would most likely try to take advantage of her—push forward his own ideas and reasons for wanting to buy Rozendal. He was bossy—he'd admitted to that—and he could probably be very, very persuasive. He'd already shown he could get her to do the things he asked, even though most of them had been for her own good. Sleep at Bellevale, take sugar in her coffee, accept his offer of a ride to Rozendal. She'd resisted all those suggestions, but she'd given in. She wouldn't be doing that again.

He was obviously a man who expected to get what he wanted. She wondered if anyone had ever said no to him and stuck to it. If not, she planned to be the first.

So she conjured up her most enthusiastic expression and switched on her widest smile.

'Isn't it just the most perfect house you've ever seen?' She began to pick her way towards the foot of the steps.

'I'm afraid I can't agree with you, Scarlett. Architecturally, I think Bellevale is the better house, and it's structurally sound…'

'You're entitled to your opinion, naturally. And of course

Bellevale is structurally sound. It hasn't been neglected like this.' She swept her arm in a wide arc, encompassing the house and surrounding wilderness that had once been a garden. 'But when Rozendal has been renovated and the grounds restored, it will be unbeatable.'

She hoped she sounded convincing, because the closer she got to the top of the steps, the more devastation she saw and the lower her heart sank. This wasn't something that a lick of paint and a carpenter with a hammer and nails could mend. It was going to take a team of specialists and many months to make it habitable.

The romantic vision of bathing in a hipbath before a roaring fire fizzled and died. If she could get that rusty tap above the stone water trough at the side of the house fixed, perhaps she could wash there.

Will had followed her up the steps and stood behind her, no doubt waiting for her to throw up her hands in defeat. Then he would dive in with an offer to take the place off her, free her of the liability.

There was no way in the world she would be walking away from this. Marguerite had wanted her to have it and it was her home. Her *only* home. That feeling of belonging flooded back through her body, filling her heart to overflowing. It was as if she was already putting down roots, like the trees and plants she intended to introduce to the gardens would do.

She turned to look at Will. He'd removed his sunglasses and his gaze was searching as her eyes met his.

'Scarlett…'

'What?' She twisted round and pushed against the door. It creaked open, just as it had done yesterday, when it had revealed the hall full of people, the auctioneer with his raised gavel.

'You don't have to do this.' He shook his head, his eyes dark. 'It's an impossible task.'

She walked into the house. Shafts of sunlight angled through the tall windows, their multi-paned squares creating geometric patterns on the dusty floor. She could see her footprints on the stairs. The set going up were of her trainers. The one coming down was of her bare feet. Those prints felt like the stamp of ownership. *Her* ownership.

This house had been given to her to care for and she would not neglect her duty. She knew how that felt. How promises could be broken. How love which you took for granted could prove as fickle as a butterfly, flitting from one flower to the next and never fully committing to any of them.

She would never be guilty of that. She loved this house, the garden, the whole valley, and her love would be for ever.

'And yet…' she said to Will, who stood in the doorway, his wide shoulders blocking the light, a ray of sun glinting off his dark hair, his expression grim. 'And yet you were prepared to do it. Just yesterday. If I hadn't turned up and stopped the auction at nine seconds before midday, you'd now be the owner of Rozendal. If it's such a disaster, why did you want it so badly, if at all?'

Without waiting for an answer, she threaded her way through the collection of chairs which had been randomly placed for the punters who'd attended the auction and hooked Will's jacket off the back of one of them, holding it out to him.

'Your jacket. You left it here yesterday.'

Will took it and immediately put it down on a different chair. 'Shall we go through to the kitchen? I think it's slightly more civilised in there.'

'I'll follow you. You said you could show me which floorboards are safe to walk on.'

He didn't reply but led the way through the dark house and in the kitchen pulled out two chairs at the weathered oak table. They sat facing one another.

'Please explain to me why you want to do this, Scarlett, so that I can talk you out of it.'

Scarlett pulled her feet up onto the chair and hugged her knees. She bit her lip. How much should she explain? He'd saved her from tumbling into the cellar last night and given her a comfortable bed and a life-saving breakfast.

Did that mean she had to tell him everything? No, she didn't think so. Not everything. But she could tell him enough to try to make him understand.

'I feel as if this is my home,' she said. 'As if I belong here.'

Will folded his arms and rested them on the table. She felt the force of his intense focus as his eyes drilled into hers, demanding an answer.

'But you must have a home in London. Or at least in England.'

'What makes you say that?'

'You've obviously grown up there. It's logical to assume you'd have a home. A job. Family?'

A couple of weeks ago Scarlett would have said she had most of those things. The speed with which it had all crumbled still shocked her. But Will didn't need to know about that.

'I've never been part of a proper family. My parents,' she said, 'didn't intend to have children. They were as careless about that as they turned out to be about most things, and I was a surprise. Not a pleasant one. Their plans for seeing the world together had to be put on hold and they did not include a plus one. They muddled through childcare for a few years but when I was eight and they felt they'd done their bit in raising me, they sent me to boarding school.'

Will shifted on his chair and ran a hand over his jaw. 'I also went to boarding school,' he said. 'I loved it.'

Scarlett nodded. 'Okay. But I didn't. I was used to solitude. I missed having my own room, with my books and toys, where I spent a lot of time, but my Mum and Dad said school wouldn't be for long. They wanted to travel, but they'd be back to take me home for the holidays.' She picked at a knot in the denim stretched over her knees. 'Only they didn't come back. They sent a message to say they were stuck in Kathmandu, held up by floods, and I had to stay at school, with a couple of resentful teachers looking after me.'

'That's unfortunate. But it was just for one holiday, right?'

'Actually, no. I think they realised how easy it was, just to leave me there. Luckily, it wasn't possible to stay at school through the summer holidays, so my guardian and godmother, Marguerite du Valois, was contacted and asked to take me away. I hardly knew her. She was the original eccentric older spinster godmother. She was shocked to discover what had happened, and she set about changing things.' Scarlett nibbled at her bottom lip. 'Days spent with Marguerite were unpredictable but never, ever boring.'

'Good. But I don't see how that is relevant to you wanting to take on the restoration of this falling-down house.'

'I discovered my parents had sold their house to fund their travels and my school fees. The bedroom I imagined returning to was no longer mine. My toys had been given to charity, along with my books.'

Scarlett felt the pain and anger of that revelation as if it had happened yesterday. She'd kept it a secret from the friends she'd made at school. The romantic narrative she'd woven around her parents' absence had become shallow and false. How could she say they were on an important scientific research expedition in the Himalayas, tracking snow leopards, when she suspected they were sipping cocktails on a beach in Thailand?

'But you must still see them? Unless they're…'

'Oh, they're still alive, and no, I don't see them. They showed no interest in me from the day they drove away through the school gates. They never wanted children, and they'd found the perfect solution for dealing with the child they'd had by accident.'

'They never once came back to see you? That's hard to believe.'

Scarlett felt heat explode in her cheeks, but it was the heat of shame, not embarrassment. All these years later, and the memory could still do this to her.

'My father came back. But I was thirteen by then, and I told him never to come again.'

Will's blue eyes widened and his eyebrows rose. 'Why?'

She puffed out a breath and linked her fingers around her knees again, gazing past him, out to the overgrown garden and the mountains beyond. Just looking at their solid, massive shapes gave her a sense of permanence she'd never experienced before.

'He decided school sports day was a good time to show up with his new girlfriend. She looked closer in age to me than to him. It turned out that instead of finding each other on their travels, my parents had each found someone else. He tried to show his new love interest how young and athletic he was by running in the fathers' race, but he twisted his ankle.' She exhaled slowly, trying to tame her heartbeat. 'I wanted to dig a hole for myself and hide away in it for ever. That's when I told him never to come back.'

'And he never did?'

'No, but his parting shot as he was carted off in an ambulance was that my mother had a new partner too. She'd moved in with her guru in India and was learning to meditate and play the sitar.'

Will's chair scraped across the tiled floor as he pushed it back. Scarlett watched him pace across to one of the windows. He stood with his back to her, his hands in his pockets. It should have been a relaxed stance, but she could see the tense muscles of his shoulders under the taut fabric of his shirt. He turned, dipped his head and ran a hand across the back of his neck.

She had a vivid flashback of him making the same gesture almost exactly twenty-four hours ago, as the ownership of Rozendal slipped from his grasp. Was it an expression of frustration? Anger?

'I'm sorry,' he said.

'Neither of their new relationships lasted and they eventually got back together again.' Scarlett lifted her shoulders.

'You're in touch with them?' He sounded surprised.

She hesitated. 'No...but they can find me through Marguerite's solicitor.'

'That is a very sad story.'

'Don't be sad on my behalf. I was lucky to have Marguerite. She was a great mentor and she helped me to make good choices.' She dropped her eyes, unable to hold his gaze any longer. 'Mostly.'

The pause before he spoke again was slightly too long.

'Did you have any idea about this house? That she was leaving it to you?'

'None at all.' She shook her head and pushed her plait over one shoulder. 'She'd told me stories about the house. They always began with: "There is an old house called Rozendal in a hidden valley at the furthest tip of Africa..." but I always thought it something very much from the past. I didn't know she owned it.'

She glanced around the kitchen, taking a moment to see it properly for the first time. It could be a wonderful room, she thought: the hub of the home. There was a large antiquated range in the fireplace, rows of cupboards along the walls and the huge sink where she'd tested the water supply last night. She could imagine how the ochre floor tiles would gleam once they'd been cleaned and polished, and how the copper pans and brass taps would shine.

Will's gaze followed hers. 'She can't have known it had fallen into such a state of disrepair. Otherwise, surely she'd have left you her house in England instead...'

'That had to be sold to fund her care. Over the past few years I think she'd forgotten all about Rozendal. She had dementia.'

'I see. I'm sorry.' He nodded. 'So you weren't expecting this legacy. I can't believe she would have knowingly burdened you with it.' He crossed back to the table and stood looking down at her.

'It's not a burden, but it was a surprise. A shock. Especially coming so soon after…' She looked away, not wanting him to read her expression, but she wasn't quick enough.

'So soon after what? What happened? Was it something in the Amazon?'

He was worryingly astute, and she bent her head, dismayed by the emotion she felt welling up inside her like a dark tide of hurt and despair, and something else she'd tried so hard to push away: loneliness. She'd lost two people she'd loved and the thought of loving anyone again felt terrifying, and that made her feel not just lonely but *alone*. How comforting it would be to know that someone had her back, to be able to lean into someone for a hug, to feel the warmth of someone's care, just for a moment.

She had to control these feelings because giving in to them was much too dangerous. If Will detected weakness in her he'd think he could persuade her to sell, and she didn't feel strong enough yet to argue with him.

'It's nothing,' she said, aware that her voice was muffled, and knowing he would read all sorts of things into that. 'Nothing that concerns you, anyway.'

'Hey.' His voice had dropped and the word was soft. 'As I see it, you're very much my concern. I am your only neighbour, and you can't do this on your own, if at all.'

Scarlett felt the light touch of his hand on her shoulder. She flinched and pushed her feet to the floor, refusing to admit that his concern was exactly what she craved. Standing up, keeping her back to him, she scrabbled in her pocket for the scrunched-up tissue she was sure she'd find there.

With gentle pressure, Will turned her to face him. There was no hiding the tears that brimmed in her eyes now, or her tremulous bottom lip. The pad of his thumb brushed her cheek.

In the dim kitchen, his eyes were navy blue, the planes of his face shadowed. There was a small scar on his right cheekbone.

'Scarlett,' he said. 'Let me help you.'

CHAPTER EIGHT

WILL WISHED HE could retract those words, or at least reframe them. What if Scarlett thought he meant he could help her to renovate Rozendal? What if she said yes, and asked him for funding to get the project started?

What he wanted her to understand was that he could help her get rid of it.

But he couldn't find the words to express his intention. He was too close to her. Touching her, even just her cheek, had been a big mistake. Her skin was as soft as he'd imagined it would be, and he'd been imagining it way too much since yesterday. It was like stroking a rose petal, not that he'd ever actually done that.

Her eyes glistened and she blinked, but the tears collected, sparkling like tiny diamonds on her lashes.

Her thin shoulder shook and he slipped his hand across her back, splaying it against her shoulder blades, his eyes fixed on her full lower lip.

'Will…'

'Mmm? It's okay.'

Desire rolled over him, hot and urgent, sweeping aside his better judgement, drowning the voice of reason in his head which told him this was a bad—a *very* bad—idea. He *needed* to feel her body against his, to taste her mouth and to inhale that intoxicating scent so deeply he'd never forget it.

It was cool in the old kitchen, on the shady south side of the house, which made the heat spiralling through him even more shocking. Outside, the midday sun blazed from the high African sky, shimmering off the leaves of the trees and bouncing off the mountain crags. The grape harvest was over. The last of the harvest festivities had finished at least a month ago. It was a quiet time in the vineyards, but the rest of the estate was still busy.

He should have been out there, keeping his fingers on all the buttons, all the balls in the air, but none of it mattered. Time had compressed and his awareness shrunk to this place, this moment, and he wanted to freeze it right here. He didn't want it to end.

He stepped closer to Scarlett, pressing his hand against her back, and slid his thumb over her mouth and down to the place above her collarbone where he felt her pulse jumping under his touch.

Her shoulder blades tensed under his hand as she raised her head and placed her hand flat against his chest, but instead of pushing him away she slipped the hand upwards, over his shoulder, to the back of his neck and twisted her fingers into his hair.

For a few seconds his mouth hovered a fraction above hers as he tried to make sense of the longing he saw in the deep pools of her eyes. Then he lowered his head.

She tasted of coffee and almonds and powdered sugar. He tried to hold back, to be gentle and tentative, but he slanted his mouth across hers, knowing the battle was all but lost already. Cupping her head in the palm of his hand, he felt her lips part beneath his and the kiss deepened as she responded to him. Need, all-consuming, throbbed through him, leaving his brain wiped clean of anything but the feel of her body in his arms and the taste of her in his mouth.

Her fingers in his hair tugged him down harder and the small sound of her own need he heard in her throat took him even closer to his limit. He felt the edge of the table behind him and leaned into it, pulling her between his thighs, clamping a hand in the small of her back to hold her steady.

Still he kissed her, exploring the warm sweetness of her mouth, feeling his limbs weakening with desire, his lungs beginning to burn, but refusing to raise his head and break this incredible connection. It was everything he never allowed himself to have, everything he wouldn't let himself feel, and he wanted it to go on for ever. This was all he wanted—all he'd ever need.

But suddenly her hands were on his shoulders, and this time she was pushing him away. For a few dazed seconds he tried to resist, tightening his arms around her, keeping their lips sealed together, but then she tore her mouth from under his and he let her go.

She stepped back, hands on her cheeks, shaking her head. 'No. No, Will.'

He sucked in a long, shaky breath, bewildered, trying to reconnect with his surroundings, which felt dangerously unstable. He'd been transported to somewhere he didn't recognise but where he'd felt infinitely safe, and he didn't want to come back to this world which was tipping on its axis. He'd never experienced the feeling that nothing—*nothing*—outside the moment mattered. Control of his life, of his surroundings, above all, of his emotions, was what he valued above all else. The thought that he could lose it in a few seconds in the arms of a woman he barely knew was unbelievable.

It was deeply disturbing.

'Scarlett, I'm…sorry. That shouldn't…'

Then he realised she was looking beyond him, towards the door to the back steps. He'd kicked it closed last night, he remembered, as he'd cradled Scarlett, asleep in his arms, and carried her to his car. He spun round. The door was open.

'Is anyone here?' Grace's melodious voice called as she appeared, an elegant silhouette against the backdrop of bright sunshine. She stopped on the threshold, her hand raised, about to tug on the frayed length of old rope which hung beneath the brass bell beside the wooden door. 'Will?'

He heard Scarlett's soft gasp and then she stepped round him and ran towards the door like a trapped bird escaping from a dark cage and fleeing towards the light. She bumped into Grace and then disappeared, down the steps.

'Grace?' Will swiped a hand over his jaw. 'What are you doing here?' Stupid question, he realised, and she could ask the same of him. She was probably kindly checking up on Scarlett, whereas *he*...what the hell *was* he doing here?

This sensation of confusion was totally alien to him. He shook his head, trying to find his mental balance. Finding his physical balance was going to be a lot more difficult. He tried to drag his mind back to the present, away from his clamouring body, but he found he was looking to where Scarlett had vanished, wanting to go after her, to finish what they'd started...

Grace walked into the room and stopped, folding her arms. 'What was *that* all about?'

Will pulled shaking fingers over his face, wondering how much his unguarded expression had given away.

'I... I...offered...*suggested*...that she might let me help her with this...situation.' He shoved his hands into his pockets.

'And what was her response to that?'

'She...got a little...emotional.'

'A *little* emotional? Then how come you look like you've been on the receiving end of bad news and she looked like she'd been kissed? Very thoroughly kissed.'

'I was trying to comfort her. It got out of hand. Hell, Grace, that shouldn't have happened. Especially not with her.'

Grace turned and rested her hips against the table. 'What do you mean?'

'She's...vulnerable. A lot has happened in her life. Most of it not good. And that's not counting something I think happened in the Amazon, which she's not talking about.'

'The *Amazon*? Will, are you sure you're okay? You're not making much sense.'

'It's a long story, and she hasn't even told me the Amazon part of it. I just know…'

'Will,' Grace said slowly, 'can you look me in the eye and tell me your aim is to pursue the ownership of this estate? Not the *owner*? Because from the look on your face, and from what I think I interrupted…'

He stared at her, allowing her words to sink in. He could understand why she'd asked the question. The scene she'd come upon must have looked compromising, even if she hadn't witnessed that kiss. Just thinking about it tightened the muscles of his stomach and made him want to do it again.

'For God's sake, get a grip,' he muttered under his breath.

'What?'

His jaw clenched. 'Nothing. But I need to find her. I must apologise.'

'Apologise for what, Will? Didn't she kiss you back? Did she have to fight you off?'

He thought about how she'd pulled his head down towards her, and the urgency of her mouth under his, her soft sound of desire and the look of bewildered longing in her eyes, and shook his head.

'She kissed me back, but then she…as soon as she wanted to stop, I let her go. But I need to apologise for taking advantage of her. She's tired, in a foreign country, surrounded by strangers. I need to find her *now*.'

Scarlett ran headlong down the uneven steps, praying she would not trip and fall but not slowing her pace. She leapt down the last three and kept on running.

The range of dilapidated buildings behind the house looked like a coach house and stables so she supposed this was the stable yard. *Her* stable yard. The buildings were in an even worse state than the house, but she refused to confront that fact now. This was already all too overwhelming.

And what had just happened with Will had pushed her fragile emotions from teetering on the edge of uncontrollable over into the dark regions of completely unmanageable. She could not deal with those feelings, alongside everything else, right now.

Why, *why*, had she let that happen? She'd promised herself—sworn—that no man would take advantage of her ever again. She'd met Alan when she'd been vulnerable and lost. Marguerite had been vanishing before her eyes, into the frightening, fractured world of dementia. The house had been sold to provide for her care and she, Scarlett, had taken a research job based in London so she could visit her. She'd moved into a basement room in a flat-share in Hackney.

Alan had been one of the leading botanists at the facility, responsible for organising expeditions to remote and lost places, mapping the positions of rare and endangered plants, and he'd quickly taken her under his determined wing.

Some of her colleagues had joked that her brain was the attraction, which, they'd suggested, was superior to Alan's own, but she hadn't believed them. At a time when she'd lost her home and the person who'd been mother, friend and partner in hair-raising escapades all over the country to her, she'd felt warmed and validated by his attention.

He'd made her feel needed and safe. He'd offered security when, for the second time in her life, she'd lost hers. When he'd suggested she move into his South Kensington flat with him, she'd been flattered. Looking back, with the acuity of hindsight, she wondered how she'd so easily let go of the independence Marguerite had fostered in her. Alan had presented solutions to her problems and she'd accepted all of them without question. It had felt so simple. Only after it all fell apart had she realised she'd exchanged her free spirit for a level of control she'd found suffocating.

Love, she'd decided, was never straightforward or unconditional. Accepting or giving it came with the possibility of rejection and the need to compromise. She'd learned at the age of eight that trust meant different things to different people. How could she have forgotten?

The news that she'd inherited Rozendal had come when she was at her lowest ebb. It had galvanised her into frantic action, filled her with a renewed purpose. From now on she'd be independent, relying only on herself. She'd make bold, brave decisions and stick to them. She would not be swayed or undermined.

Instead of that, she felt overwhelmed by the scale of the task Marguerite had bequeathed her and she'd allowed a man, who she knew for a fact wanted to wrest the ownership of Rozendal from her, to reduce her to a trembling mess of desire and need and longing with one single kiss: a kiss which she'd wanted desperately, because she'd believed it would make her forget, for a few brief moments.

She was angry with herself, and very ashamed.

And she was furious with Will for being able to crush her defences so easily. If nothing else, that fury would help her to rebuild them, twice as strong, and keep her firmly on the path she'd chosen.

Rubbing a hand across her eyes to scrub away the tears which threatened to blind her, she kept running. This was a monumental undertaking, but she would not give up on it, or give it away to someone else. The vision which had sprung into her imagination, fully formed, of a restored house and rewilded estate, was hers alone. No one else, least of all Will, with his no doubt scientific farming methods, immaculate rows of vines and fancy restaurant and holiday cottages, would be able to bring it to fruition. She *must* do it herself. It would give her purpose, restore the self-belief she'd lost.

Beneath the determination to see her dream become reality lurked another reason. She had to keep up the momentum which had sent her racing to catch that flight to Cape Town to claim Rozendal. If she stopped to consider her position for a moment she might waver, and that would plunge her back into the state of fear which had swamped her when she'd been lost in the jungle. She couldn't afford the time or energy to dwell on that.

Sheer willpower and refusal to give in to panic had got her through that ordeal. It would get her through this too, if she kept that corrosive fear locked out.

Finally, her lungs burning, she stumbled to a stop, bent forwards with her hands braced on her knees and tried to catch her breath.

The valley drowsed in the afternoon warmth, unfamiliar birdsong and a faint rustling in the undergrowth the only sounds.

When she straightened up she realised her flight had taken her into the old rose garden. The formal gravel paths were almost invisible under the rampant weeds, but the shape of some of the beds was almost discernible. Roses which hadn't been pruned for decades sent long stems arching against the sky, above the tangled undergrowth. Fighting her way through the thorny branches, she eventually came to a stone fountain at the centre of the symmetrical space. The octagonal basin was dry and choked with dead leaves, but a bronze cherub which stood on a plinth at the centre, holding a conch shell from which water had once poured, was intact.

This, thought Scarlett fiercely, was where she would begin. And she'd begin now.

She pushed up the sleeves of her shirt and began to scoop out armfuls of dead vegetation, the accumulation of years of neglect, dumping it on the path beside her. She needed a wheelbarrow, she thought feverishly, so that she could cart it all away and put it… She'd have to establish a compost heap. Eventually, the goodness from all these leaves would be put back into the soil in the form of organic mulch. The garden would bloom again. Wildlife would flourish.

That was where Will found her.

'Scarlett.'

She'd been so engrossed in tackling her task head-on that she hadn't heard him approach. She hesitated for a second before continuing to scoop out the crisp dead leaves, ignoring him.

'Scarlett?' He was closer. From the corner of her eye she could see the hems of his narrow jeans, his leather boots, scuffed with wear. She considered offloading an armful of leaves onto them. She wished he'd go away and leave her alone.

'You don't have to look at me, Scarlett, if you don't want to. But I'm not going anywhere until you've listened to what I want to say.'

She shook her head and her plait dropped over her shoulder. 'I don't want to hear anything you want to say,' she said through gritted teeth. 'Please go away.'

His feet moved out of sight, and she released a breath of relief.

'No,' he said, his voice quiet. 'I'm not going away.'

She realised he'd sat down on the edge of the stone basin. She straightened up and dusted her hands together, then looked at him.

Immediately, she wished she hadn't. His gaze was steady. It made her think of the ocean on a calm summer's day, and she wanted her thoughts to be stormy and dark, to fuel the anger she felt towards him.

'I don't think you have anything to say to me, Will. Or me to you. What happened—' she glanced in what she thought was the direction of the house '—back there was a mistake which I won't repeat. If you thought you might somehow persuade me to change my mind by…'

'No,' he interrupted. 'That wasn't… I don't know how it happened, but I'm sorry.'

Scarlett had not expected an apology. If anything, she'd thought he might have followed her to continue his campaign to convince her she couldn't do this. To help her by offering to buy her out. She wiped her hands down the backs of her thighs and raised her eyes to take in the ageless beauty of the valley and the mountains. She belonged here. The thought steadied her.

'You must have noticed,' she said, risking another glance at his face, 'that it wasn't one-sided.' His mouth was set in a firm, straight line and a frown creased the space between those arresting eyes. She wondered how that mouth, so sombre now, could have elicited that explosion of pleasure and desire in her body. How could a simple kiss do that?

She dragged her eyes from his face but they landed on his hands, loosely clasped together between his knees. Those hands had worked their own magic. She still felt the imprint of his fingers in her lower back, and on the place near her collarbone where her wild pulse had betrayed her.

He nodded. 'Yes. I noticed. But that doesn't excuse what I did and I'm sorry.'

'Are you? Or were your actions deliberate? I was already upset, so did you think you might erode my defences even further and begin to persuade me that I can't do this?' She gestured towards the fountain. 'Because if you did, you're wrong. I've already begun.'

She bent to resume clearing the leaves.

'Scarlett, please listen to me. Just for a moment.'

She stood again and shoved her hands into her pockets, biting her bottom lip. 'Will you promise to leave me alone when you've finished?' His hesitation was slight, but she saw it. *'Promise?'*

'Okay. If you want me to.'

'I'm listening.'

He sucked in a deep breath, leaning back, bracing his arms.

His shoulders widened and he looked up at her, the sun glinting on his rumpled hair.

'At that moment, Scarlett, there was nothing on my mind beyond the hope that you would not stop kissing me. You were upset. I offered to help you, and I'm prepared to repeat that offer. All I can say in my defence is that I wanted to comfort you. After that, things became a bit hazy.'

'If Grace hadn't come…' She remembered the grip of his thighs on hers as he'd pulled her close, the heat of his body. 'What did you tell her? Or didn't she ask?' She kicked at a clump of daisies with the toe of her shoe.

'She asked. I told her what I've told you. I wanted to comfort you and I don't regret that, although I'm sorry it got out of hand.'

She nodded. Was that what he thought had happened? It'd got out of hand. Such an ordinary phrase to describe the emotions and sensations which had taken hold of her. The feel of the slide of his tongue against hers, the liquefying of her limbs until she thought she'd fall if he released her, the overpowering single thought that had occupied her brain: she needed more of him.

'How,' she asked, 'were you offering to help?' She wondered if he thought she'd ask him for money. 'Because I'm intrigued to know.'

Will stood up and took a few paces away from her. He bent to pick up a handful of the dead leaves she'd removed from the fountain and crushed them in his fist, letting the shredded flakes sift through his fingers to the ground.

'Look around you, Scarlett. Not just at the rose garden, but at the rest of the estate. At the barns and stables, and the cart lodge.'

Cart lodge, she thought. *Not coach house.*

'And look at the house. I mean *really* look at it. See it for what it is, not for what you wish it was. Restoring all this is an insurmountable task for one woman on her own. It'd take teams of builders and landscape designers, contractors, gardeners and labourers to wrest this place back from nature and make it habitable again. I can make you an offer for twice what I was going to pay for it at the auction yesterday. You can return to your life and work in London, buy yourself a house, live a comfortable life instead of…' He looked around. 'Instead of taking on this impossible project. Please consider it.'

Scarlett studied him. His frown had deepened, and he looked a little pale under his tan. He sounded utterly sincere. Was this really because he feared for her well-being and sanity, or was there some other, more fundamental reason why he wanted Rozendal so badly? Was it just that he'd decided it should be his, and he wouldn't give up until he had what he wanted? According to Marguerite, the other estate in the valley had been in the hands of the same family for longer than Rozendal had belonged to hers.

Will had lived with the certainty of his place in the world all his life. He was rooted in this soil as deeply as the ancient oaks and gnarled vines in the vineyards. He'd never had to wonder where he belonged. He'd always known.

The anger she was nurturing expanded in her chest. She breathed in and out several times, counting backwards in her head.

'If you'll just think…' he said again. 'Try to understand…'

Scarlett gave up the fight. 'I am thinking,' she said. 'And what I'm thinking…' Her voice rose. 'What I'm thinking is that it's you, Will Duvinage, who needs to try to understand something. Because you don't understand at all, do you?'

'Understand what?' He looked shocked, either by her raised voice or by her suggestion. She didn't know which and she didn't care.

'Understand what it's like not belonging. Not *belonging* anywhere. You've lived here all your life. *All your life!* Do you know what that sounds like to me? It sounds like paradise. You've never had to question your right to be here. Probably the furthest away you've ever lived was at boarding school. And I'm willing to bet your parents came to every speech day, every sports day, every match, and turned up on the last day of term to bring you home for the holidays. *Home!*'

'Scarlett…'

She shook her head, taking a ragged breath. 'You've never had to doubt whether this is the life you wanted or deserved. It's been your entitlement since you were born, and the entitlement of all your ancestors, going back centuries.'

She was shouting now, her heart racing, her breath coming in gasps. 'And because of that…*entitlement*…because everything has always been exactly as you wanted it, you believe you can force me into selling Rozendal to you, because you want it. How neat it would have been for you to have bought it yesterday, only I came along and spoilt things. You already have so much. Why must you have Rozendal too…?'

'Scarlett, stop. Please.' He held up a hand, but she was on a roll.

'If you think you're going to take this from me, you're wrong. Marguerite wanted me to have Rozendal and I can see why. It's beautiful and special. Magical. And I've decided I want that magic in my life. This is home for me now. The only home that's ever been truly mine, and I'm not giving it up. If I have to live in one room, cook on an open fire, wash outside in a drinking trough, I'm not giving it up.'

She stopped, horrified by the sting of tears gathering in her eyes. She would never give Will the satisfaction of seeing her cry again.

A long charged silence followed her outburst. When he finally spoke she could tell that he was angry too. His voice shook and colour streaked across his sharp cheekbones.

'You don't know what you're talking about, Scarlett. You're wrong.'

'Which bit of what I said was wrong, Will?'

Her voice was a husky whisper. As the adrenalin took hold she began to shake.

He started to speak then shook his head, appearing to change his mind about what he was going to say.

Finally, he drew in a deep breath and exhaled again. Scarlett wondered how she could note the rise and fall of his broad chest and remember how it felt to be held in his arms, against that wall of muscle, when all she wanted was to forget.

'I'm just asking you to think very carefully,' he said, sounding as if he was maintaining a reasonable tone by sheer effort. 'I'm giving you an easy way out of this. If you insist on continuing with your plan, it's going to cost you a fortune.'

Despite the tears that hovered and the sob that threatened to choke her, she smiled. Perhaps he hoped to lend her money and then call in the debt when she could least afford to honour it. He'd have her trapped then, and she'd be forced to sell to him.

Once, she would have taken such an offer at face value. She wouldn't have suspected an ulterior motive. Once, she'd been naïve enough to trust people.

It was sad, acknowledging that her ability to trust had been shaken, rather like admitting there was no such thing as unconditional love. But she'd learnt to be realistic and pragmatic. Not having to accept financial help was a powerful feeling.

'Luckily, I don't need a fortune, Will,' she said softly. 'Because Marguerite left me hers.'

CHAPTER NINE

SCARLETT WATCHED HIM stride away from her, shoving his way through the overgrown garden. She heard him swear. Perhaps he was venting his anger at her. Perhaps he'd been scratched by one of the ancient thorny rose stems. She glanced down at her own scratched forearms.

Drained, she sat on the edge of the fountain, near where Will had been, and rested her elbows on her knees, closing her eyes. Fatigue, her constant shadow for the past ten days, threatened to overwhelm her and for the first time she allowed herself to wonder what she was doing.

But even as doubt stalked her she knew she wouldn't give in. She had to make a success of this. Rozendal was going to become a shining example of the benefits of rewilding, to the landscape, to wildlife and to ecological systems.

She had absolute faith in her dream. She just didn't know how she was going to achieve it. Will was right when he'd said she'd need an army of helpers. How did she go about finding one?

Her tummy rumbled and her mouth was dry. Admitting that she couldn't concentrate while she was hungry and thirsty, she turned her back on the dry fountain, on which she'd hardly made an impression, and began to find her way back to the house.

The Range Rover was gone. That didn't surprise her. She'd have to walk back to Bellevale to collect her car and her luggage and then ask for directions to the nearest food store. Communications with Will would probably be through his lawyer from now on. *One step at a time*, she told herself. *Don't think beyond that.*

She circled the house, stopping to try the corroded tap at the water butt. It was impossibly stiff and made an alarming grating sound. The pipe vibrated violently before a trickle of rusty water splashed into the stone trough.

Back in the kitchen, she folded herself onto one of the wooden chairs and wondered how she could summon up the energy to return on foot to Bellevale. She wasn't at all sure she would be able to find the way. Should she risk a sip of the rusty water at the sink?

But as she pulled herself upright she heard the sound of tyres on gravel. Through the window she saw Will's Range Rover pull up at the foot of the steps. Its own cloud of dust caught up with it, swirling across the stable yard. The rain of the previous night had been torrential, but it had vanished into the parched earth, leaving it as dry as before.

He was the very last person she wanted to see. Wasn't he? Actually, Alan was top of that particular chart, but Will came a close second. Both were entitled men who'd aimed to manipulate her for their own ends.

The uncomfortable heat of an adrenalin rush pumped through her veins as the rhythm of her heartbeat picked up. Fight or flight? She could retreat upstairs, but he'd find her if he came looking. She could…

It was already too late.

Will had pulled a canvas carrier bag from the back and was pounding up the steps as if he was working out on a treadmill.

He stopped in the doorway, his eyes sweeping across the room and landing on her. He nodded, crossed the floor in two long strides and dumped the bag on the table.

'I've brought food. I decided you were hangry.'

'Hangry?'

'Yeah. Hungry and angry. It's a recognised medical condition. Well documented.'

Scarlett eyed the bag. She was hungry. Very hungry. And her anger, which had been off the scale, still simmered beneath her weariness and the doubt which had begun to niggle at her.

'What made you think that?'

Will began to unpack the bag, glancing across at her. 'You're looking at the bag, so I know you're hungry.' She couldn't decide if the spark in his eyes was one of teasing or triumph. 'Besides, you had coffee and pastries hours ago, and you've expended some energy since then.' His eyes flicked from her face to the watch on his wrist and back again. 'Sugar high followed by an energy crash. Dangerous.' He pulled a bottle of water from the bag. 'And it's past lunchtime.' He put a loaf of bread, ham and cheese and a bar of chocolate on the table. Her eyes went to his strong fingers as they flexed and twisted the cap from the water bottle. He offered it to her. 'As for your anger, I've thought about what you said and I can understand why you might have formed your opinions. But that's a discussion I don't intend to have.'

Scarlett accepted the bottle, his fingers brushing against hers, and the memory of his hand cupping the back of her head ambushed her. Those fingertips exerting gentle pressure on her skin had felt…amazing. Exciting. And his mouth… What would it be like to feel those hands, those long, capable fingers and those deft lips, exploring the rest of her body? She closed her eyes. A headache began an insidious throb behind her eyes and she longed for a cup of tea. There was no chance of making one in this kitchen.

Will opened a couple of drawers, humming under his breath, until he found a breadknife, plates and cutlery.

'Give these a wipe, Scarlett.' He dug in the bag for a cloth. 'I think they're only dusty, but it would be sensible to check before using them.' She took the cloth, taking care to avoid his touch this time.

'You're very organised.'

He shook his head as he gripped the loaf and the knife. Scarlett tightened her hold on the plate in her hand, watching the action of the muscles and tendons of his tanned forearms as the blade sliced into the bread.

'I asked Grace to sort out some food from the restaurant kitchen. It's unlikely I would have thought of putting in a cloth.' He peered into the bag. 'Or wine, for that matter.'

He made sandwiches, peeled the wrapper from the chocolate and snapped it into squares. Then he pushed a plate across the table towards her. 'Sit and eat.' He pulled out a chair. 'You'll feel better. Then we can talk.'

'Thank you. You must think I'm hopeless. But normally I'm very good at taking care of myself.'

'It seems you've had a stressful, possibly traumatic time lately.' She saw the searching look in his narrow gaze and dropped her head to bite into a sandwich. 'This—' he gestured around the room '—is a huge change for you. It's not surprising if you're feeling disorientated.'

Scarlett decided to swerve that conversation. 'Is this bread local? It's delicious.'

'It would have been baked in the restaurant kitchen this morning. Grace tells me she's perfected the art of the sourdough loaf.'

'I think I agree.'

'I'll tell her. The food we serve is all local. There're very few food miles on this table. It's a source of pride at Bellevale, although it can be a challenge too.'

Scarlett felt a stirring of surprise and she tried to adjust her perception of Will. She'd imagined Bellevale to be a state-of-the-art estate, and if asparagus needed to be flown in from Mexico or cheese from France she wouldn't expect him to bother about the air miles.

'I'm surprised you care about things like that.' She swallowed a few mouthfuls of water from her bottle.

'I care about Bellevale. That is my bottom line. And I know that what is good for the planet is going to be good for the estate. That's a no-brainer. The methods we use for farming and winemaking are cutting-edge and world-class. And that goes for every part of the operation. There is always a waiting list for the restaurant and the cottages. The food, service and accommodation are all five-star.' He pushed the chocolate across the table towards Scarlett then leaned back in his chair. 'But we try to ensure, at every stage, that nothing we do is harmful to the environment.'

'And the wine? Obviously, you export. You can't avoid those food miles.'

He nodded. 'You're right. We can't. But our marketing and sales teams spread the message that the estate is ethically run. Visitors, and we have many, are welcome to talk to any member of staff. They will always tell the same story: people love working here because the conditions are excellent. Our organic wines are growing in popularity.'

'It sounds as though you set high standards.' She took a square of chocolate.

'My standards are super-high, but I lead by example and the results speak for themselves.'

'Is that another way of saying you always expect to get your own way?' The chocolate melted on her tongue, smooth and bittersweet with a whisper of flaky salt.

He shook his head. 'I'm reputed to be single-minded and aloof, and I don't dispute that, although I think *determined* is a better word. And if I get my own way, it's because most of the time it's the right way.' His smile was self-deprecating, robbing his words of the arrogance she might have heard in them. 'But,' he continued, 'enough about me. How about you?'

'What about me?'

He chose a chair opposite her, balancing an ankle on a knee and folding his arms across his chest.

'Scarlett.' His tone was softer. 'You're exhausted and stressed. You need to be sensible.'

'I won't change my mind. You'll be wasting your time if you try to make me.'

'I recognise your determination, and I admire that. What *would* be a waste of time would be having to check up on you twice a day to make sure you're okay.'

'Why would you do that?' Surprise made her look up, her eyes locking with his.

'Because we're your only neighbours, and you're on your own. It's how we operate around here. We look out for each other.'

'What do you want me to do? Check into a hotel? Is there one?'

'Yes, there is. It's called Bellevale, although, strictly speaking, it's not a hotel.'

Scarlett shook her head. 'I can't do that.'

'Tell me why not.'

'It would be an imposition. And you and I…we're not on good terms. We'd argue…'

'If it bothers you, you can pay for Vineyard Cottage. It's available for two weeks. And I can help you to get your project up and running.'

'Why would you have any interest in doing that? You don't agree with what I want to do.'

'I'm not sure I fully understand what you intend to do, apart from making this house habitable. If we can sit down and talk about it some time it would be helpful for both of us. Meanwhile, you need to recover. You've suffered a bereavement, had a long flight, a traumatic experience last night. All of that would take its toll on anyone.' His eyes went to her arms, but she'd rolled down the sleeves of her shirt, covering the damaged skin. 'And before that…'

She shook her head, making it clear that subject was not open for discussion.

'Your forehead…'

He rubbed his fingers across his left temple. 'It's just a scratch. Those rose thorns are fierce.'

He was quiet for a minute. Then he stood up and walked over to the ancient fridge in the corner and pulled the door open.

'Mmm. When the power is on this will probably work, after a fashion. The cooker… I'm not sure about that. It looks dangerous. The water is not drinkable and if you wash in it you'll turn a rusty shade of orange all over.'

'Like my hair.'

He turned his head, his eyes resting on her hair. 'Not at all like your hair.' He slammed the fridge shut but it sprang open again. 'Nothing really works. But some of it could be made to work, and I and the team at Bellevale are the people who can make it happen.'

He returned to stand in front of Scarlett, hands in his pockets, rolling his shoulders. 'Give yourself time, Scarlett. There's been a lot going on in your life. You may be strong and independent, but right now you're vulnerable and that's nothing to be defensive about. You're alone, and I feel responsible for you. Your life has changed and that has been a shock, but you showing up unexpectedly like that yesterday was a shock to everyone in the valley too. We all need to adjust. Yes, you have turned my plans upside down, but I'll make new ones.' He paused, shaking his head. 'That's what I've always done.' His voice dropped. 'And some of the changes I've had to make have been huge.'

Scarlett dropped her head into her hands. 'You make it sound as if I have no choice.'

'You do have a choice, but if you choose to stay here it will be difficult for everyone, mostly for you. You'll spend so much time and energy simply surviving that you won't achieve anything else. There's no internet, no phone signal. How are you going to organise anything? Winter is approaching and it'll be cold and wet. Colder and much, much wetter than you probably imagine. We have almost all our annual rainfall in three months and it's not gentle English rain.' He pulled his hands from his pockets and turned his palms upwards. 'Please, Scarlett, be sensible.'

Being sensible, Marguerite had always said, usually meant being boring. She tried to imagine what her godmother would have done in this situation. It wasn't easy. Would she have raised two fingers at Will's offer and toughed it out on her own? If she tried to do that and failed, she'd have to come to Will for help anyway, admitting defeat. The idea rankled.

If she accepted the accommodation at Bellevale, and help from Will now, it wouldn't be for long. If she stayed there just long enough for the roof at Rozendal to be repaired, the power and water supplies to be secured and until she'd been able to hire some help for the garden…

'Scarlett.' His voice sounded strained, as if he was doing his best to hold something back. 'Come home with me. Please.'

Scarlett sighed, pushing her fingertips into her hair and massaging her temples.

'Are you okay?' There was a thread of concern in his voice.

'Yeah. Just…memories.' She didn't have to explain that some of them were old, but some were as recent as this morning. She scraped her chair away from the table and stood up. 'Okay.' She breathed out a long sigh. 'But whatever the state of the house, when I move out of Vineyard Cottage in two weeks I'll move in here. That's not negotiable.'

Relief softened Will's expression. The lines of anxiety faded, and he smiled. 'That's the right decision.'

'And just to be clear, this is not you getting your own way. It's me deciding how to do it.'

His smile vanished, but the amusement in his eyes lingered. 'Of course.'

'You mentioned wine? And the chocolate is *really* good.'

'It's made by a small bean to bar operation in Cape Town.

They source their ingredients from sustainable cocoa plantations in West Africa. When they were looking for investors to start up, I provided a major stake. The company continues to grow.'

Scarlett peered into the bag Will had repacked.

'The wine is in there?'

'It is, but I think it's grown a little warm. Let's head back to Bellevale and pop it into the fridge at Vineyard Cottage. You can have it later.'

'You'll know where I am at Bellevale, so you can avoid me if you want to.'

He hoisted the bag from the table. 'Sure,' he said easily. 'But I won't want to do that.'

'You'll want to know what I'm up to, so you can continue to plot how to get hold of Rozendal.'

'Absolutely.' One corner of his straight mouth lifted, and the trace of a dimple ghosted across his cheek. 'Except I don't plot,' he said, holding her gaze. 'I plan.'

'There's a difference?'

'I think you'll find there is. And I also prefer to meet problems head-on.'

'And I'm a problem for you?'

'More of a challenge.'

CHAPTER TEN

RELIEF MADE WILL breathe more easily as he left the cool kitchen and stepped onto the *stoep* outside the door. He checked to make sure Scarlett was following him. What would he have done if she'd stubbornly refused to take his advice? He knew he could pick her up and carry her, but forcing her would not be acceptable, under any circumstances. But he couldn't have left her here either.

Now he had to let her draw the conclusion that this was the correct decision. He had to try to make things a little easier for her—show his willingness to listen to her plans and to offer any help he could. If he could establish a good working relationship with her, encourage her to trust him, he'd have a much better chance of achieving what he wanted later.

He had already changed his plan.

He had to concentrate on that. His goal was to unite Bellevale and Rozendal. With his sharp business sense and experience, his persuasive tactics, he should be able to do it. She'd agree with him in the end, he was convinced.

What had happened between them this morning had complicated things more than a little.

Her taste, the urgency of her response, had played havoc with his mind all day and his level of achievement had dropped below what he expected of himself. Way below.

He'd lost count of the number of times his concentration had lapsed, or he'd lost the thread of a conversation, as he tried to identify her scent. Perhaps he could find a way to ask her, without it sounding too personal, although when was asking a woman about her perfume not personal? And why did he think if he knew the answer he'd somehow be able to let go of it?

'There's no key to the door,' he said over his shoulder, 'but close it firmly. You don't want the resident troop of baboons moving in.' He scanned the mountain crags. 'They're probably watching us right now, just waiting for an opportunity.'

'If they're so keen to get in, surely they'd have found a way before now?'

'The house has been abandoned for a long time, but they'll have noticed the human activity here, yesterday and today. Humans mean food to baboons. They'll be down to investigate opportunities for stealing anything they can find.'

He started down the flight of steps, hearing the door close behind him. He slung the bag into the back of the big four-by-four and held the passenger door open for Scarlett.

When she was strapped in and the door was shut he'd relax.

He took the drive slowly, skirting potholes and bumps on the track and pointing out landmarks on the way.

'When you drive over on your own, look out for that old oak barrel.' He pointed. 'That is where you turn down towards Rozendal. Years ago, it had the name and an arrow painted on the side, but it's illegible now.' He negotiated the turning. 'The sun fades things.'

The road leading to Bellevale was well maintained and Will pressed the accelerator and the vehicle picked up speed. He noticed Scarlett looking around, taking an interest in the landscape, and when he swung the wheel and they turned in between the solid old white gateposts of his home he heard her quiet intake of breath. He glanced across at her.

'Yes, it's beautiful.'

The sight of the avenue of ancient oaks, flanked by acres of immaculate vineyards, never ceased to give him the kick of pleasure he'd been experiencing ever since he could remember. Best of all was the view of the matchless house, the parabolas of its sweeping white gables perfectly symmetrical, the honey-coloured thatch gleaming in the sunshine. It was framed perfectly in the distance. A fountain played in a pool in the middle of the gravel turning circle in front of the homestead, serene white water lilies floating on its surface.

Will took a turning to the left and followed a narrow track between the vineyards, waving to a distant group of workers. They all raised their arms in a salute.

'They're checking the vines for signs of stress or disease.' He hauled the wheel round to the right and pulled up behind Scarlett's hire car, under the giant oak trees. 'We use organic methods of pest control, but we have to be vigilant.' He cut the engine and looked across at Scarlett. 'Vineyard Cottage. Your home for a fortnight.'

Scarlett had slid from her seat before he reached the passenger side of the vehicle. He followed her up the shallow set of steps, reaching around her to open the front door, catching that scent again.

'What…?' he began, but stopped himself. He had to keep this relationship on a business footing. Questions about perfume would never be appropriate. But then his gaze fell on the nape of her neck as she walked through the door ahead of him. The creamy smooth skin was soft, inviting a caress. He knew, because he could still feel the sensation of it at his fingertips. How would it feel, and taste, under his mouth?

Trying to get a grip on the need which stalked through him and making a super-human effort not to haul her into his arms and see what happened next, he carried the grocery bag through to the built-in kitchen in the corner of the open-plan living area.

A packet of tea and a sealed bag of coffee sat next to the kettle. He opened a cupboard to reveal a glass jar of fruited and nutty muesli, alongside pots of local jam and marmalade. The small fridge contained juice, milk, eggs and butter, to which he added the leftovers of Scarlett's late lunch.

In the middle of the small round table an earthenware bowl contained a collection of peaches, plums and apples. Their colours glowed in a shaft of afternoon sunlight. He knew if he opened the brightly coloured tins on the marble worktop he would find them filled with crisp, buttery shortbread and possibly a crumbly fruit cake.

Will straightened up from slotting the bottle of wine into the fridge and closed the door.

'Where did this food come from?'

He lifted his shoulders. 'We always stock the kitchen with basics for our guests.'

'But the guests cancelled. And I'm sure none of this was here this morning. There must have been some mistake.'

Will gave up. 'Okay, I asked Grace to arrange for the cottage to be stocked, as usual. It's no big deal.'

'Maybe not for you. But I can't keep accepting your hospitality. I thought I'd been clear about that.'

'Why? This is just to tide you over. You need to eat, and you probably don't feel like going out, or eating in the restaurant tonight.'

'No, I don't. But every time I accept something from you it puts me in your debt, and that's not a place I want to be.'

'That's not how I see it. This is just our usual way of welcoming guests.'

'Maybe, but I'm not one of your usual guests, am I? And you obviously didn't doubt that I'd agree to come. That is an even bigger problem for me.'

Will strolled over to the window, buying time.

'Why,' he asked eventually, 'is it a problem?' He turned back to face her. She stood in the middle of the room, her hands on her hips, a frown creasing her smooth forehead.

'You seriously can't see why?' She huffed out a breath. 'It's because it means you were confident you'd be able to make me do what you wanted. That you could manipulate me.'

'No.' The shake of his head and his tone were decisive. 'Manipulate is an unpleasant word. It smacks of control and coercion, and that's not how I work. I—*hoped*—I'd be able to persuade you to see that living here for two weeks was the sensible option. And I succeeded.'

He watched, fascinated, as an expression of frustration crossed her features and a spark of emerald flashed in her eyes. Her teeth indented her full lower lip and then the tip of her tongue smoothed over the mark. Her heavy russet plait hung over one shoulder, the blunt end of it, tied in a green ribbon, resting on the curve of her breast.

He found it hard to breathe.

She pushed the braid away, the movement one of contained irritation, and he could see the dip at her throat, where her ivory skin stretched over the tips of her collarbones, moving in and out as she tried to slow her breathing.

If he placed his fingers there, where they'd been earlier today, just above that delicate bone, he knew he'd feel the quick flutter of her pulse. It had been driven by desire, and some other, hidden need. He was sure of that. Now, she was the victim of a different sort of emotion.

She turned on her heel and walked through the door into the bedroom, her plait swinging between her shoulder blades, her hips, curving out from her narrow waist, swaying.

Of course, he knew what she was saying. But if she felt indebted to him, surely that was a good thing? If it made her feel at a disadvantage, so much the better…

His thoughts stalled. He did not want to think about Scarlett at a disadvantage, or in any situation in which she felt indebted or trapped. Her strength and determination were admirable and not something he wanted to be responsible for crushing. He had to be subtle about this. If she no longer wanted to keep

Rozendal, Scarlett had to come to the decision on her own. Or she had to believe she had…

He'd help her with her project, but he'd help her see his point of view too.

Her slender figure was silhouetted against the light pouring through the tall window, the slanting rays of the sun illuminating her bright hair. She'd removed her shoes and came, soft-footed, towards him, tugging at the ribbon which fastened the end of her plait. She raised her arms, the cotton fabric of her shirt tugging tight against her breasts, and threaded her fingers through the strands of hair, letting them part and shaking the coppery mass over her shoulders and down her back.

With her full, rosy mouth and the slight flush on the alabaster skin of her cheekbones she looked as if she'd stepped out of a Pre-Raphaelite painting.

Will clenched his fists, his breathing losing its rhythm, wanting it to be *his* fingers easing into her glorious hair.

He had this under control, he told himself. It was a long time since he'd spent more than a few hours with a woman. He always left them safely at their homes or hotels. None of them ever came here, into his personal space.

That didn't mean he couldn't handle this. His self-control was legendary, his determination unshakeable. His mental strength was the reason he was here at all. Contrary to what Scarlett believed, he'd had to fight for Bellevale, the undisputed love of his life, and the fight had been bitter. Taking possession of it had only been the beginning because bringing the estate back to useful productivity had taken several seasons of curtailed sleep and nail-biting uncertainty.

Last year the rains had failed. Farming in Africa, he reflected, was governed by flood or drought, feast or famine. If the rains this winter weren't sufficient, the harvest would suffer, and so many families depended on their positions here. But now he had a plan.

God, she was beautiful.

He clenched his jaw, gritting his teeth.

If he had this under control, why did he feel he was in so much trouble?

Darkness had fallen, with its African swiftness, beyond Will's study window. He exited the program on his laptop and flipped the lid closed. A strip of light shone beneath the door, and outside a slice of the moon hung above the mountains, tracing their outlines in silver. If he looked the other way, down the valley, he'd see the Southern Cross in the velvety sky.

But his gaze was turned inwards. He tapped his knuckles on the lid of the computer and raked his fingers through his hair, turning over in his mind what he'd read.

What would we do without Google? people often asked. Far more secrets could be kept, he mused. In this case, he wasn't sure that would have been a good thing.

His day had been disrupted and unsatisfactory and he'd come to his study to catch up on some paperwork. But the cause of his disturbed day had continued to get between him and anything else he'd tried to do. His concentration was shot, he'd admitted to himself, unless he was thinking about Scarlett. He had no problem focusing on her at all.

Hell, the thought of her was driving him insane. Kissing her had been one of the sweetest, most erotic experiences of his life, and also one of the most stupid things he'd ever done. The memory of those few intense minutes continued to play havoc with his emotions and his self-control.

As he'd discovered last night, she intrigued him, teased his senses and drove him to unfathomable feelings of protectiveness.

He was a rational, practical man and he didn't understand this irrational and totally unreasonable reaction. He needed to understand her, a little, if he was going to get any peace.

He'd put aside his paperwork, opened his laptop and typed her name into the search engine.

It didn't take long to find her.

She was a botanist. He knew that already. She was highly regarded in her field of research, for her ability to spot minute differences between plants, and had discovered several new species. She'd travelled to some of the most remote, hostile areas of the world. There was a picture of her in the jungle in Borneo, observing wild orangutans.

But the information about her most recent trip to the Amazon was disjointed. The press reports were speculative, in the absence of any verified facts.

Reading between the lines, some of which were from shouty, sensation-seeking tabloids, she'd been lost in the jungle, feared dead, for six days. A cloud of suspicion hung over the expedition leader, unsubstantiated reports accusing him of abandoning her.

The latest report said she'd returned to England and promptly vanished. She was known to have been staying with a friend in London who now refused to speak to the press, saying only that Scarlett was safe and needed to be left alone.

Will pushed away from his desk and stood up. He needed to think, and he did that best outside. Pulling on a sweater, he left the house, the chill of the autumn evening sharpening his senses and clearing his mind. He took his usual route, around the grounds, to the edge of the vineyards.

The night was still. Bright stars were scattered across the sky and the moon had almost set behind the mountains. High up, among the crags, a jackal barked, the harsh sound echoing through the ravines, and from somewhere close came the double hoot of a Cape Eagle Owl, on the hunt for small mammals.

What was Scarlett running from? Or who had frightened her into disappearing?

Will intended to find out. If he could unravel the mystery surrounding her sudden appearance at Rozendal, he hoped the hold she had taken on his mind and body would loosen.

His walk brought him to the collection of cottages he'd had

converted from labourers' quarters to luxury holiday accommodation. He'd built a new, modern complex of houses for his staff, closer to the main road, from where the children could more easily access the bus service to school.

On a normal night he would have turned back towards the Bellevale homestead at that point, but tonight he was drawn onwards, past the cottages, towards the one which stood, secluded and separate from the others.

Vineyard Cottage, so-called because it bordered the vineyards.

The shade of the oaks was deep. He stopped on the edge of it and took a sharp breath.

Scarlett sat on the terrace, under the vine. A candle flickered in a blown-glass shade on the table, throwing dancing shadows across her face. The bottle of wine, frosted with condensation, which he'd put into the fridge earlier, stood open, alongside a half-filled glass. Her hair flowed in a dark, molten mass over her shoulders, and she'd wrapped herself in one of the woollen throws off the sofa, to ward off the cool night air.

He moved forwards, out of the oak shadow, wanting to talk to her but afraid of startling her. Autumn leaves rustled beneath his feet and she turned her head slowly, searching the darkness.

'Scarlett?'

'Will.'

'May I join you?'

CHAPTER ELEVEN

SHE SHOULD HAVE apologised to Will, or at least thanked him.

When she'd watched him walk away from her, vanishing among the thorny bushes, she didn't expect to see him again. But he'd brought lunch to her at Rozendal, and insisted she return to Bellevale with him. Stocking the kitchen had been thoughtful, and she was grateful for the meal she'd put together from the collection of groceries she'd found in the fridge and cupboards.

She'd barely thanked him for either act of kindness. She'd been too busy insisting she could look after herself, that she didn't need his help.

She'd been rude to him and she didn't trust him. He was single-minded, and absolutely focused on what he wanted. All his actions, even if they appeared to be kind and thoughtful, would be geared towards adding Rozendal to the property he already owned.

It would be far too easy to slip into a mindset of believing him, relying on him—*trusting* him.

All these thoughts churned around in her head as she took a long shower, washing away the dust of her battle with the choked fountain. She looked at the wide bed, made up with sumptuous embroidered linen, and knew she was not ready for sleep.

The bottle of wine she'd opened with her meal stood in the

fridge, her glass next to the sink, and she gathered them up and opened the door to the terrace.

The night air was cool, almost cold, after the warm day, and she hesitated, but she put the bottle and glass on the table, returned to the living area and pulled the soft woollen throw from the back of the sofa, wrapping herself in its folds. The cream alpaca fabric was as soft and as light as down, enclosing her in a cocoon of warmth and luxurious comfort. She snuggled into the deep cushions of one of the rattan chairs and sipped from her glass.

How unusual to find crystal as fine as this in a holiday cottage. Like everything else, from the throw to the one thousand count linen and the Persian rugs on the oak floors, it lent another layer of opulence to her surroundings.

The wine was exquisite. Crisp and zesty, its fresh notes seemed to help to clear her head. It was one of the Bellevale whites, of course.

The air was still, and the sounds of the African night were unfamiliar to her. Unfamiliar, and completely different from the sounds which had surrounded her in the Amazon.

But the rustle of leaves nearby did not fit. The disturbance was too loud to be a mouse, or even a snake. The pattern of the noise was unnatural.

It took a second for her to process this. She tensed, annoyed that she'd put herself out here, in a vulnerable position, where she was unlikely to be heard if she called for help.

She eased her head around to face the sound, hoping not to draw attention to herself. The candle on the table gave off very little light so perhaps she'd be invisible to someone prowling in the shadows of the trees.

A shape detached itself from the deep darkness and Will's voice, low and steady, said her name.

She watched him climb the steps. He stopped at the top.

'I'm sorry if I startled you. I was trying not to.'

Scarlett smiled. 'Any dark shape emerging from the trees in

the night is going to be at least a little scary, don't you think?' She tipped her head towards the green glass bottle. 'Wine?'

He hesitated for a moment, then nodded. 'Thank you. I'll grab a glass.'

Scarlett pulled the throw more tightly around her shoulders as she waited for him to return.

He poured himself a glass of wine and raised it to her. 'Have you eaten?'

She nodded. 'Yes, thank you, I have.' She took a sip from her glass. 'This wine is excellent. One of yours, obviously.'

Will swallowed a mouthful. 'Mmm. I'm glad you like it.' He put his glass down and leaned back in his chair, linking his hands behind his head.

'The glasses are pretty special too.'

'Yeah. When we equipped the cottages, I sent buyers round all the antique markets in Cape Town, looking for crystal. Fine wine should be drunk from fine crystal. Sometimes the glasses are mismatched, but personally I think that adds something to the overall feel.'

'The rest of the cottage is beautiful too. Last night…well, last night I hardly woke up enough to know where I was. And this morning I didn't really take much notice. But I've had time now, and every detail is perfect.'

'Perfection is what we aim for.'

'Do you ever miss the target?'

A corner of his mouth lifted. 'More often than you might think, but we usually manage a cover-up.'

'I find that hard to believe. You have your fingers on all the buttons all the time, by the look of it.'

He was quiet for a moment, then he unlinked his hands and leaned forward, his forearms on the table. 'It's how I live. I'm not comfortable any other way.'

His gaze, deep blue in the dim light, fastened on her, steady and intense. The black wool sweater he wore framed his powerful shoulders and with his arms in that position the sleeves were pulled back a little, revealing his tanned forearms, sprinkled with fine, dark hair.

An intense awareness of him shivered through her.

'Do you ever take a break?'

'Not unless I'm forced to. Tell me,' he said, taking her by surprise, 'about the Amazon.'

Scarlett played for time, slipping out a hand from under the comfort of the throw and picking up her glass. Her teeth nibbled at her bottom lip and she saw his eyes drop to her mouth, his gaze heated and explicit.

'No,' she said softly.

He nodded. 'No,' he agreed. 'Not now.'

'Not ever.'

How much did he already know? Had he looked her up? Most likely, she thought. He'd have done his research. She watched as his fingers gripped the delicate stem of his glass and raised it to his mouth, his eyes returning to hers.

'What do you want to know?' she said after a pause.

'Everything. Except that the jungle is scratchy. I know that already.'

'You haven't been there? Maybe on a cruise up the river?'

He laughed. 'A cruise? I wouldn't last a day before throwing myself to the piranhas. Or worse, throwing someone else to them.'

Scarlett shrugged. The throw slipped, exposing her left shoulder. She glanced down, hoping he wouldn't notice, but she should have remembered he noticed everything. He reached across the small table and lifted the fabric, tucking it around her neck again.

'Thank you,' she said stiffly.

'Soft,' he murmured, 'like your skin.'

She felt heat bloom in her cheeks and her eyelids dropped, as she almost fell victim to the quiet seductiveness of his velvety voice.

Then she straightened her spine, tipping her head back so

her hair fell down her back. 'Just one of the touches of luxury with which you indulge your guests,' she retorted. 'Do you like jungles?'

His smile narrowed his eyes, and they crinkled at the corners. She saw that fleeting ghost of a dimple revisit his cheek.

'No. I prefer wide open plains. The savannah. Give me a desert before a jungle, any day.' He looked out into the darkness. 'Although right here is where I always want to be, wherever else I go.'

'I like deserts too.'

'Do you?' He swirled the wine in his glass. Those fingers, she thought, could snap that delicate stem in an instant. 'For someone of your profession, I would have thought a desert is rather lacking.'

'You'd be surprised what can be found growing in a desert, if you know where to look. The Empty Quarter in Arabia…'

'Scarlett—' he interrupted her '—you've changed the subject. Now, please tell me something else about the Amazon.'

'Okay.' She pulled her feet up and tucked them under the blanket. 'It's dense, hot, steamy. And incredibly noisy. There're squawks, hoots, grunts and rustlings. The sounds, especially at night, are completely alien—totally different from the ones you can hear now, if you listen. The colours are intense. There're blue, red and rare hyacinth macaws in the canopy. You'd never believe there could be that many different shades of green. And the plants…' She stopped and shook her head. 'A few square metres of the forest floor could keep me entranced for hours. There is so much…*so much*…to see and discover.'

That, she thought, was my mistake, although Alan must have been watching and waiting for me to make it. I left the path, and I was too absorbed in the search. She'd been over and over those minutes in her mind, endlessly. Had it been minutes? Or longer? She'd probably never know…

'Go on.'

Will's low voice broke into her thoughts. For a few seconds

she was confused, but then his serious face, his eyes intent on hers, came into focus again and she dragged herself back to the present.

'That's what it's like. Why I like…*liked*…being there.'

'And in your search of the forest floor, did you find what you were looking for?'

'It wasn't anything…' But that wasn't true. She—the expedition—had been looking for something very specific. 'We were looking for orchids. Especially one orchid, which was thought to be extinct.'

'Did you find it?'

She shrugged. 'A needle in a haystack would be no challenge at all compared with searching for one small flower in the Amazon rainforest.'

'So that's a no. Will you go back and try again?'

She was quiet for a long time. Then she uncurled her legs from beneath her and put her bare feet on the tiles. She gripped the edges of the throw across her chest.

'I doubt it. This is where I plan to stay now. At Rozendal.'

'Why, Scarlett? Your enthusiasm glows when you talk about plant-hunting. I don't know if Rozendal will ever be worthy of that degree of passion.'

'Oh, it will be. It's my home. Like Bellevale is yours. Would you ever give up your home?'

'Never. But it's been my home for a long time. This is all new to you. It takes years to build up a relationship with a place.' He drained his glass. 'But then it's a relationship that's solid. Trustworthy.'

Scarlett remembered what she'd said—shouted—earlier. 'Yes, I suppose so. I've never had the opportunity to find out until now. But I'm sorry for shouting at you. I think I was just beginning to realise what a huge undertaking the restoration will be. I felt overwhelmed and a little panicky.'

Will rubbed his fingers across his forehead. 'I sensed that, and I'm sorry too. I shouldn't have pushed you like I did.'

'You saw an opportunity to get past my defences and you took it.'

'Yeah. It's how the hard-edged world operates. You have to take your chances and watch your back. It's not what you're familiar with, I'm sure.'

If only you knew, she thought. Those rules applied to everything in life. You had to be on your guard, ready for things to go wrong, so when they did you were prepared. She'd believed her parents when they'd said they'd be back for her in time for the holidays. She hadn't been prepared for that. She'd believed Alan loved her completely, not just for the use he could make of her mind and her research.

She'd believed she'd loved him back.

The only thing left to believe in was herself.

'And the scratches on your arms? Are you going to tell me about that?'

Scarlett clutched at the blanket and stood up. The edge of the soft fabric brushed against her calves. She took a step back from the table, lifting her chin a fraction. 'No,' she replied. 'I'm not.'

Will rose from his chair in a controlled movement. She had a wild and irrational desire to lay her cheek against his chest, to see if his sweater was as soft as it looked. It would be comforting. For a moment she'd feel secure, but it wouldn't last.

'What happened, Scarlett?'

Her throat and mouth were dry, but she couldn't risk reaching for her glass to take a mouthful of wine.

'Nothing that matters.'

'I don't think that's true. I think you're hiding something. Or from someone.' He moved towards her. 'And I think it does matter. Maybe quite a lot.'

He raised a hand and brushed the back of his fingers across her cheek. She turned her head away.

'I'd like you to go now.'

'Wouldn't you like a nightcap? There'll be liqueurs in the minibar. It might help you to sleep.'

'No, thank you. I need to have a clear head in the morning, if I'm going to make a start on Rozendal.'

'Come to my office at ten. Up the steps at the front of the homestead and down the passage on the right. We'll drive over and decide where to begin.'

'I can do that on my own.'

'Yes, you can. But it will be quicker and a lot easier if you let me help you.'

He reached past her and opened the door, stepping back as she walked inside.

He waited until he heard her turn the key in the lock and slide the bolt, before turning away. She was safe, although not from whatever demons were bothering her.

At least she was safe from him.

CHAPTER TWELVE

HE'D SAID SHE should come at ten o'clock, but he'd been pacing the floor since nine-thirty. He'd tried to spend the time usefully, answering emails, but his concentration was fragmented. Lack of sleep normally didn't bother him at all. He could power through on just a couple of hours a night, but perhaps it was catching up with him at last.

Not that he felt like sleeping. He felt like punching something or tackling a triathlon. Anything to release this pent-up frustration and energy which bubbled inside him, making him move restlessly around his office like a caged animal, wearing a track in the carpet. It tugged at his gut and captured his muscles in an unfamiliar grip of tension, and he didn't know how to escape it.

He picked up his phone and scrolled through his contacts. Maybe he should get in touch with that blonde he'd met last month. Dinner and then sex back at her apartment. That would surely afford him at least a few minutes of oblivion.

He dropped the phone onto the desk, swearing under his breath. Nothing felt less appealing. He did not want to wipe the thought of Scarlett from his mind. He wanted to keep her image there. He wanted her in his arms. He was notorious for getting what he wanted. But no matter how much he wanted this, he could not have it. Could not have *her*.

A glance at the antique carriage clock on the mantelpiece told him it was still five minutes to ten. Perhaps the clock wasn't working properly. It tick-tocked steadily, as it had done for more than a hundred years. Why should it slow down now?

His phone vibrated on his desk and he snatched it up, but his frustration ratcheted up another notch as he saw his brother's name light up on the screen. What the hell did he want, and why *now*? He considered rejecting the call, but he knew if he did it would ring again. And again, until he gave in.

'Yeah?'

This conversation was one he'd had many times and would no doubt have to have many times more. He marvelled at how his brother could keep asking. It must be because his wife was standing next to him, telling him what to say. He knew she was because he could hear her voice.

His answer was never going to change. Richard had been quick to accept the deal he'd offered him. Happy to shed his responsibilities. Not that he'd had much choice. It was that or bankruptcy.

He ended the call, tucked the phone into the back pocket of his jeans and ducked his head to scan the grounds through the window. There was still no sign of Scarlett.

'Will?' He swung round, startled even though he was expecting her. That was how frayed his nerves were. 'Is everything okay? If you're busy I could…'

She stood at the door, in snug-fitting jeans and a loose cotton jumper the same green as her eyes. Her braided hair hung over one shoulder and there was a cool box at her feet.

Finally, he understood the meaning of *breathtaking*. The frustration of the past few hours, as he'd waited to see her again, the irritation with his brother, all drained away and he felt something unravel inside him, releasing the knot in his gut. Relief at the sight of her almost made him light-headed.

'Scarlett. No, I'm not busy. Just a…business call. Come in.'

He wondered how much of his conversation she'd heard. It didn't matter. She'd only have heard his string of refusals.

And the expletive with which he'd punctuated the end of the call, as he stabbed at the button.

She didn't move. Her eyes ranged around the room, taking in the pictures on the walls, the antique furniture, the rugs. Her gaze swept over the surface of his desk, with its desktop and laptop computers, beyond to the bookshelves, packed with wine auction catalogues and books on the history of wine-making in the Cape. A slight frown drew her brows together.

He glanced around and saw the room as she might see it. The pale green walls provided a perfect foil for the dark mahogany furniture. The brass which bound the large chest positioned against one wall gleamed with polish, and the richly coloured rugs glowed on the pale wooden floor. A collection of Delft blue and white china filled a glass-fronted cabinet.

It was a beautiful, satisfying room but it was utterly impersonal. That was how he liked it.

The photos on the walls were all of awards given to Bellevale wines, or of staff members celebrating a significant moment of the harvest. One showed a smiling Grace beside a world-famous chef, outside the estate restaurant. The man had given the food a five-star rapturous review and then tried, and failed, to woo Grace away, to work for him.

There were no family photos in silver frames on his desk. No travel souvenirs or childhood mementos.

He wondered if Scarlett would comment.

'You said ten o'clock, I think.' She glanced at the clock as its silvery chime began marking the hour.

Will skirted his desk, exhaling, dropping his shoulders. 'I did. I'm ready to go.'

He'd been ready for hours. He flipped the laptop closed and picked up his car keys.

'I've made a picnic lunch, from the food at the cottage, so you can just drop me off at Rozendal. I'll be fine…'

'I've cleared my schedule for a few hours. Is there enough for two? If not, I can ask Grace…'

'But you're so busy. I'm sure you don't want to waste any more time.'

'My time is my own, Scarlett. The only person I answer to is me. And you haven't answered my question.'

'That depends on how hungry you are.'

Ravenous, he thought. But no picnic, however lavish, was going to satisfy this particular hunger.

Three hours later, Scarlett sank into one of the ancient lumpy chairs on the veranda of Rozendal and closed her eyes.

Plans, facts and mostly figures filled her brain so that her head buzzed with information, although she felt physically exhausted. The temperature had climbed and at noon, when they'd been at a point furthest from the house, inspecting the old walled garden with its broken glasshouses and storage sheds, it had felt hot. The ancient walls had reflected the heat of the sun, generating warmth which would linger long after the sun had begun its descent towards the west. It would be a perfect place to establish a nursery garden for growing rare plants from seed, if the seed was available. Scarlett made a note to find out.

She'd compiled lists under endless headings on her phone, cataloguing the basic repairs which needed to be carried out and equipment which had to be replaced.

Most importantly, she'd listed all the plants she could name in the gardens and taken dozens of photographs. Will had promised to lend her a book on the historic flora and fauna of the region. She was looking forward to sitting down later, with a glass of wine at her elbow, when she could begin identifying some of the plants and trees, both native and invasive species, and begin to plan her rewilding strategy.

Will lifted the cool box, put it on the rickety table between the two chairs and sat opposite her.

'Tired?'

'Physically, yes. But my brain is in overdrive. So much to think about.'

'So much to plan.'

They'd dodged around each other all morning. Making sure he didn't touch her had taken a degree of concentration he usually reserved for tasting a new wine or playing a game of poker.

The simple brush of his fingers against hers might cause him to lose it. He couldn't risk that. Another kiss and she'd retreat, refuse to engage with him, and this would all end up taking much longer than necessary.

Time, or the lack of it, was the issue. He had to move the project along as quickly as possible and that meant being with her, helping her. And ultimately persuading her to help him.

He'd discovered she was clever, thoughtful, astute. And she was gorgeous.

His body buzzed with awareness of her: her long, denim-clad legs as she walked in front of him along a narrow path; a glimpse of creamy cleavage as she bent to examine a plant and exclaim over its beauty or unfamiliarity; the fabric of her cotton shirt pulled tight against her perfectly rounded breasts as she stretched up to take a leaf between finger and thumb.

How long could he do this for? A week? Two? Watching her push her fingers into her hair and stretch out her legs made both those estimates seem far-fetched. Right now, his limit was so close he didn't dare to calculate it.

If he reached the end of the day without pulling her into his arms and kissing her until neither of them knew which way was up, he'd consider himself superhuman.

She caught him watching her and he felt another layer of awareness thread through his body. How much had she guessed about the desire that gripped him, dictating his every careful movement?

How much of it did she share?

'What are you thinking about?' The words were out of his mouth before he could stop to consider them.

Scarlett blinked, dark lashes feathering over her cheeks. Across her cheekbones her pale skin was stained with pink.

'That I should have worn a hat?'

'I should have suggested it. The sun…'

'Actually, that wasn't what I was thinking.' She dropped her head against the back of the chair, exposing her smooth throat and neck.

Will swallowed. 'No?'

'No. What was on my mind was something you said yesterday.'

'What was that?' A knot of warning tightened deep inside him. He needed to keep the conversation light and he needed to control it.

'You said I have turned your plans upside down. I think those were your words. What did you mean?'

Will put his glass down. 'Why do you ask? I was simply explaining that your arrival has meant I've had to change my plans. I've done it before. It's possible.'

'Yes, I get that.' Scarlett pushed a tendril of hair off her forehead with the back of a hand. 'I'm just curious to know what huge changes you've ever had to make. From my perspective, you've had an easy life. Your family have owned Bellevale for generations.'

'That's right.' He nodded. 'Centuries. Since they arrived from France, fleeing religious persecution. The date on the main gable of the Bellevale homestead is 1687.'

'And its succession from one generation to the next has always been smooth, without any major upheavals? A good marriage always made, a son born to inherit?'

'Mostly.'

'Mostly? You see, I can't imagine what that must feel like. Growing up with that certainty, that security, of knowing where you belong, all your life, feels mind-blowing to me. I lost my security when I was sent away to school. I was eight.'

'But then you found your godmother, Marguerite. You got it back.'

Scarlett smiled, and it made his heart turn over. 'School holidays with Marguerite were interesting. Often fun. But I was never secure. I never knew what scheme she would come up with next, or what corner of the country we were going to be dashing off to, on some crazy whim. Some days she forgot about food altogether, so I took to hiding biscuits and pieces of cheese under the mattress. And sometimes she'd disappear, and I wouldn't know when, or even if, she was planning to return.'

She pulled her knees up and wrapped her hands around her shins. 'Sometimes I really did not want another of her adventures. I craved normality and all I wanted to do was lose myself in her overgrown garden. I treasured the time I spent there. I felt safe. It's where my obsession with plants began.' She leaned forwards, resting her chin on her knees. 'When I arrived for my school holidays, I'd rush straight to the garden to check on the plants. Knowing they'd be there, following the seasons, flowering and setting seed and reappearing in the spring, gave me a sense of continuity and security I couldn't find anywhere else.' She sipped from the glass of lemonade Will had poured for her. 'I'm wondering what blip in your never-ending line of certainty could be called huge?'

Will listened, trying to imagine a childhood where no two days had been the same, when the only certainty had been the changing seasons.

He'd believed Bellevale was home. He knew and loved every inch of the house and the estate, but that wasn't all of it. Like Scarlett, he loved the seasons which came and went with such dependability, year in and year out, whatever was happening around him. He loved the sheltering mountains that enfolded the valley. He loved the animals that roamed the wild places beyond the boundaries, and the birds of prey which soared on the thermals, high above in the endless blue, their haunting calls echoing off the crags.

It was all an intrinsic part of him.

But from a very early age he'd known that, like Scarlett, he hadn't been wanted and that Bellevale would never be his.

That knowledge, which had felt like a shard of glass embedded in his heart, had forced him to become tough and relentless. Some called his business practices ruthless, but he disputed that. Toughness and determination were what had got him where he was today. Ruthlessness would mean he cared only for himself and that wasn't true. He cared for his staff, deeply, and would do anything to make their lives easier. They returned his care with loyalty and trust, qualities which he valued above all else.

He could not say the same for his family, but that was something he did not discuss, with anyone.

He watched Scarlett as she waited for him to reply and decided to turn the conversation around.

'I can't imagine what your life was like,' he said. 'You lost your ability to trust when your parents deserted you, and your godmother was unreliable, even if she had the best intentions.'

'I suppose you could analyse it like that.'

'And then you found security again, and someone you could trust, but…'

Her green eyes flew wide. 'What do you mean? I haven't said anything about…'

'You haven't needed to.'

Will dropped his eyes to her hands, where they were loosely linked around her legs. A few days of working in the garden, in the autumn sunshine, and that pale band of skin around her finger would fade, erasing all evidence that she'd worn a ring there.

She looked as if every muscle in her body had tensed, primed to flee. He shifted forward in his chair, ready to catch her if she tried to run. That need to keep her safe engulfed him again.

The thumb of her right hand shifted, to rub at the base of her ring finger. 'I…it's nothing. I'm fine with it.'

'Was that what happened in the Amazon, Scarlett? Did he say he'd changed his mind? Ask for the ring back?'

The thought of anyone hurting her made him burn with anger. He'd like to get hold of whoever he was and…

'No,' she replied suddenly, her voice stronger. 'It wasn't like that. Not at all.'

'Then how was it?'

'I gave the ring back. Well, actually, I posted it to him.'

'You broke up with him by *letter*? Not even email or, God forbid, a text? That's so old-fashioned…'

'No letter. Just the ring in an envelope, but I couldn't find one of those padded ones so I wrapped it in a tissue. He didn't need an explanation. He knew what he'd done.'

'What? What had he done, Scarlett?' The need to know felt urgent. 'Had he cheated?'

'No. Not in the way you'd imagine.'

'I don't understand.'

She shrugged her narrow shoulders and twisted round, peering into the picnic box.

'You don't need to. It really doesn't matter now. Would you like a sandwich? Ham or cheese?'

Scarlett walked over to the veranda railing and dusted the crumbs from her hands. A sparrow immediately swooped from the overgrown shrubbery and pecked at them on the gravel below.

She'd avoided Will's questioning, simply by refusing to answer. She'd learned enough about him in the brief time she'd known him to suspect he wouldn't be satisfied with that for long.

'The birdsong this morning was beautiful. I must get a book so I can identify them.'

'I'll lend you one, along with the one about the flora of the

Cape I mentioned.' He stood up and packed the remains of the picnic into the box. 'Shall we have a look at the house now?'

She turned as he straightened up, the muscles of his back flexing under the pale blue linen of his shirt. She remembered the smoothness of those muscles beneath her hands, as he'd cupped her head and stroked her collarbone. Had that happened only twenty-four hours ago? The memory felt as if it had always been a part of her: how his back had expanded under her touch as he inhaled, filling his lungs, but then stayed broad as he'd kissed her, not breaking the contact, not even to breathe out.

His long thighs had supported her, steadied her as she'd leaned into him, lost to everything but the exquisite immediate moment.

How could she have forgotten so quickly that those feelings were never meant to last? They were as fragile as spun glass, made to be shattered by the whim of another, just like the trust of a child could be.

The promise she'd made to herself, to banish such feelings from her life, had been swept away the moment Will's mouth had brushed hers and now that memory was bound to her soul. She knew she wouldn't ever be able to shift it.

Will's kiss had felt like nothing that had gone before. The combination of place, circumstances—*him*—had created the perfect storm and she'd been sucked into its peaceful eye where, for a few brief moments, she'd soared, weightless and cherished, while the trauma and chaos of her life had tumbled away.

Luckily, she'd crashed to earth before things had got out of control.

'Yes,' she agreed. 'Let's look at the house. Its condition can't be worse than the gardens and outbuildings.'

But examination of the house proved to be less daunting than she'd anticipated. The roof needed to be rethatched but once the building was watertight and the pigeons and squirrels had been evicted from the loft, redecoration would quickly make a huge difference.

Scarlett followed Will's lead, avoiding floorboards that he decreed unsafe. They peered down the lethal staircase which led to the cellar and closed the door on it.

Scarlett glanced at his grim expression. 'Thank you for saving me from that,' she murmured. 'Even if you gave me a terrible shock in the process.'

'I'm sorry I frightened you. I had to make the decision in a split second.'

Outside, they found a low door beneath the kitchen stoep which gave safer access to the dark semi-underground space.

Huge oak barrels ranged along the walls, a legacy of the time, long gone, when Rozendal had produced wine. Massive beams, festooned with generations of cobwebs, meant Will frequently had to duck his head. It was dry and smelled of ancient wood and dust. Scarlett was relieved to step back into the warm sunshine of the stable yard.

She turned her face to the sun and shivered. 'I don't like it in there. That's not somewhere I'm going to spend much time.'

Will ducked through the door and pulled it closed behind him. He brushed cobwebs from his head.

'You won't need to. It's about the only part of the house that needs no work done on it.'

They returned to the interior, noting holes in skirting boards which mice had probably used on a nightly basis when there'd been food to forage in the kitchen, broken tiles in bathrooms and a broken window under the eaves.

'That's where the haunting bat will have got in.'

'Is the haunting bat related to the ghost bat and the terror bat?'

'Closely,' he said with a smile. 'They all come out at night to prove people wrong who say they're not afraid of them.'

'Hey, I'm not afraid of them. I was tired and confused and I didn't know the thing thumping around my room was a bat.

It sounded huge. I've been up close and personal with a *vampire* bat before now.'

'Not too close and personal, I hope.' He lifted the end of her plait and peered at her neck.

Scarlett went very still. Her eyelids dropped and her breathing grew shallow, waiting for the feel of his mouth on her skin. She didn't know what she'd do, but she'd have to stop it, somehow. Her pulse accelerated and she knew he'd see it beating at her throat.

He dropped her plait. 'Can't see anything.' A note like a stretched wire ran through his voice.

'No,' she murmured. 'I didn't let them get *that* close.' She pulled her head away.

Their eyes met, understanding arcing between them. Scarlett dragged hers away first, turning blindly towards a door and pushing it open.

It was the bedroom where she'd tried to sleep that first night. The daylight through the grimy window showed it up in glaring reality. The bare mattress and ancient pillows were lumpy, and the thin rug was threadbare and moth-eaten.

'This is where I tried to sleep. It's where the haunting bat found me.'

Will stood just inside the door, hands on his hips. 'God, Scarlett, I should never have allowed you to stay here.'

'I was determined.'

'Has anyone ever told you that you're stubborn?'

Scarlett lifted her chin and pushed her hands into the pockets of her jeans.

'I'm not stubborn. I'm strong-minded.'

'There's a difference?'

'Definitely. The first has connotations of unreasonably obstinate behaviour, whereas a strong-minded person is recognised as having a vigorous mind. It's how emancipated women were once described.'

'Presumably by those who disapproved of them, for wanting

to separate themselves from a life of drudgery at the kitchen sink?'

Scarlett laughed, and the tension between them faded.

'Probably. Anyway, I don't like being told what to do.'

'I've noticed.' He spoke with feeling, but she saw his mouth lifting at the corners.

They returned to the car in silence but instead of climbing behind the wheel, Will folded his arms and rested them on the top edge of the door, looking up at the old house. Its lines were graceful and pure. Even though chunks of plaster had fallen from the walls and the thatch was green with moss, the classic bones of the structure were undeniable. The date on the tall central gable was no longer legible but it could be discovered and reinstated. He was sure it was only a few years younger than Bellevale.

He wondered what had made his ancestors choose the land they had, rather than this neighbouring piece. He knew it had all originally been one estate and Rozendal had been sold off, either to raise money or reduce the size of Bellevale to make it more manageable.

That made sense, except Rozendal had the water supply which never failed, even during the severest drought. It hadn't been possible to divide that.

By uniting Bellevale and Rozendal he'd simply be reinstating the original boundaries.

He turned to look at Scarlett. She was standing at the edge of the pond which formed the centre of the gravel turning circle. A couple of inches of green, slimy water covered the bottom and long-dead waterlilies drooped from baskets.

'It will be so pretty,' she said, 'when I've fixed it. And I'm going to reinstate the original drive.' She pointed to the place where the two lines of ancient oak trees marched away from them.

He would have described the undergrowth beneath them as

impenetrable, but he knew Scarlett had forced her way through it, to burst in on the scene of the auction. No wonder she'd had twigs in her hair and looked wild, but she'd probably thought it easy compared with the Amazon rainforest.

Stubborn, he thought, *associated with unreasonable behaviour.*

'If you do that, you'll have to have the lane leading to the gates cleared and resurfaced too. I don't know how you got that hire car down there. It'd be a challenge for a tank.'

Actually, he did know, because he had gone to look for it yesterday morning. He'd found it parked at a rakish angle and, unbelievably, the keys had still been in the ignition and her cabin baggage in the boot. He'd eyed the tall, rusty gates and wondered how the *hell* she'd managed to climb them, and then he'd taken half an hour to turn the car and bump his way, very slowly, back up the track to the road.

It was well known that in situations of extreme stress the human body, pumped full of adrenalin, could accomplish feats of strength that would normally have been impossible. Scarlett had known the clock was against her, that the auction was happening, and nothing was going to stop her. She'd been desperate not to lose Rozendal.

It was not in the least surprising that she'd crashed so spectacularly afterwards, as soon as she'd known she was safe.

He thought she would have crashed wherever she'd happened to be, but he was glad she'd been in his arms.

They climbed into the car and Will turned to face her.

'I know a builder who'd be perfect for this job.' He nodded towards the house. The sun was lower and the white gables were taking on a softer, buttery glow. 'He owes me a favour.'

Scarlett sighed. 'But that would mean I'd owe you a favour too, Will, and you know I don't want that.'

'Tell me then, how you're going to find someone to do the work.'

'I'll ask around. Grace will…'

'Anyone you ask will tell you to ask me, and I'll recommend this guy. If you use that vigorous mind of yours, you'll see at once that my way will be quicker and better.'

Scarlett leaned back in her seat and folded her arms. 'I don't want…' She turned her head towards him. 'I don't want favours, Will.'

'Now I think you're being stubborn.'

'Will...'

'This man, Peter Langer, is semi-retired and will have the time. I'm not suggesting he does it for a preferential rate. It will be expensive. This kind of specialist restoration work needs to be done with care and sensitivity by someone knowledgeable, like him. He'll also be able to find someone to take on the rethatching. That isn't easy. Shall I call him?'

'Give me his number and I'll call him.'

'Okay. But the first thing he'll do is call me to get the low-down on you, and the job. It'll take longer, and the result will be the same, but the choice is yours.'

'I did tell you that you're bossy, didn't I?'

'Yup, you did. But tell me something new about myself. I already knew that.'

He watched her bite her bottom lip and he thought she was trying not to laugh.

'Hey, you'll hurt your mouth and…'

And then I'll be compelled to kiss you better, carefully but very thoroughly. And all the defences I've spent today building will crumble. Immediately.

'You're bossy, but you're kind too.'

'Kind? Me? If you go around spreading that sort of talk I'll lose my hard man image. I'm ordering you to keep it to yourself.'

'Bossy. *Again.*'

'Difficult to break the habit of a lifetime, even if I wanted to.'

He pressed the ignition switch and eased the big vehicle into gear. He steered around the pond and then stopped at what had been the entrance to the oak-lined driveway.

'How did you do it, Scarlett?'

'How did I do what?'

'How did you fight your way through that jungle, after first climbing the gates? And why did you approach by that route?'

'It's the way the satnav took me. I wasn't in a position to argue with it. Not that time. And I can't remember much about it. Remember I'd been lo… I'd been in the Amazon. My jungle skills were finely honed.' He intercepted her sideways glance.

'And,' she said, 'I'm strong-minded.'

Just how strong-minded she was, Will was beginning to appreciate. He drove her back to Vineyard Cottage and pulled up at the foot of the steps.

'Useful day?'

'Useful, but daunting. How about you? Have you figured out a way to part me from Rozendal yet?'

'Harsh words, Scarlett. I want you to reach your own conclusions about Rozendal. I'm ready to listen when you want to talk.'

He had a sudden, vivid vision of her leaving, broken and defeated, and he hated it. He hadn't expected to enjoy the day but he had, even though he'd spent a lot of time dancing around her, being ultra-cautious. He liked her company and loved it when her guard dropped, letting her sense of humour escape. At least, he thought, he might enjoy the time she was going to spend here. Afterwards, it was unlikely their paths would ever cross again.

For a reason he was unwilling to examine, the idea of never seeing her again felt impossible.

He opened the door, but she raised a hand.

'There's something I'd like to ask you.'

He snapped back to reality, wariness instantly in place. He hadn't answered her earlier question. Was she about to ask it again?

'What?'

'I'll need to see the lawyers in Cape Town, to arrange access to funds. I'll have to make an appointment. Is it an easy city to navigate? I can find my way through uncharted jungle but I'm not so good with the urban kind. Driving in heavy traffic makes me nervous.'

Will drummed his fingers on the steering wheel, setting up a quick rhythm. Scarlett getting to see the lawyers was not going to be difficult. They'd most likely clear their diaries and roll out the red carpet, definitely crack open the sherry, when they knew she was coming to call. Last night he'd looked up Marguerite du Valois. It was startling what you could discover on the internet. Most startling was the information regarding her estimated net worth. He wondered if Scarlett knew just how much of an heiress she was.

'Give them a call in the morning and see how they're fixed,' he said. 'Have you got your phone working?'

Scarlett nodded. 'And my laptop. I found the Wi-Fi instructions.'

'Good. I need to go into Cape Town one day this week, to see our exporters. I could take you.' He needn't mention his intended visit to the company who made hydro-electric components.

'I could drive myself…'

'Yeah, you could.' His fingers resumed their beat on the steering wheel. 'But the freeways are busy, and the driving is nothing like in England. Lane discipline as you know it doesn't exist. And, depending on where you're going, parking can be tricky, if all the pavement space is already taken up.'

'You can park on the *pavement*?'

'You can park anywhere you like. The difficult bit is avoiding the traffic wardens. They take no prisoners.'

'Oh…'

'But I know what a strong-minded and independent woman you are, so…'

'Stop it, Will.'

His fingers stilled. 'Okay. Let me know what they say. I could show you a bit of Cape Town at the same time. I'm a great guide and good company.'

'Really? Who says?'

'Really. And you don't want to know who says.'

He walked round the car to open the door for her and she slid to the ground. Then he followed her up the steps of Vineyard Cottage, stepping back as she unlocked the front door.

'Thanks for today, Will. It was kind of you to be so generous with your time, although I know you also want an excuse to keep an eye on what I'm planning to do.'

'You noticed? I'll have to learn to be more subtle.' But he dropped his head, wanting to hide his expression. It might give away just how much he'd enjoyed being with her and how very hard it was to let her disappear into the cottage and return on his own to the large, empty homestead.

But he'd negotiated the day and he hadn't slipped up. At times the desire to slide his arms around her and feel her pliant body against his, her satiny skin beneath his fingers, her lips under his mouth, had been more powerful than he believed he could resist.

That moment when he'd lifted her hair and studied her neck had been reckless. He'd heard—*seen*—her breathing change, her pulse rate pick up, her pupils dilate. She'd wanted more, just as he had.

But he'd resisted even that.

Move over, Superman. He'd just proved himself to be superhuman.

CHAPTER THIRTEEN

'THEY SAID ANY time is fine.'

Will ran down the steps and turned at the bottom, jogging on the spot. 'I'll collect you at two.'

She watched him disappear along the track, into the trees, plugging his earbuds into his ears, the movement of his arms and legs smooth and coordinated.

She returned to her bedroom and looked at the meagre collection of clothes she'd brought with her. There were jeans, shirts and jumpers. A jacket which, if Will's information about the Cape winter was accurate, was not going to keep her either warm or dry in the months ahead.

The skinny jeans she'd pulled on earlier would do. She swapped yesterday's emerald jumper for a pink one which almost clashed with her hair and slipped her feet into a pair of flat bronze pumps, the only shoes she had packed which were neither walking boots or trainers.

When Will had interrupted her breakfast to ask if she'd spoken to the lawyers she hadn't expected things to move this fast.

'I hope they're reputable.' Now, Scarlett glanced across at him. He hadn't spoken since they'd driven through the gates of Bellevale and he'd lowered his window to call a greeting to a staff member.

There was no hint of the stubble which had roughened his jaw yesterday, so she wouldn't have to try to block the fantasies about how its scrape would feel against her skin. As he'd leaned into the car, pulling the seatbelt out to hand the buckle to her, she'd caught the citrus and sandalwood scent of his cologne, sharp but with underlying notes of smoky sensuality. His hair was damp, towel-dried after a shower, brushed back but curling slightly at the ends, and he'd swapped running shorts and a tee for khaki chinos and a cream linen shirt, top button undone, cuffs rolled back from his wrists.

His straight mouth was set firm. She wondered if he'd even heard her.

Then he flexed his fingers around the wheel and looked sideways at her. 'What makes you say that?'

'The fact that they said I could come and see them any time.'

'So?' Was it her imagination, or did he sound amused? She turned to study his profile again.

'So my point is, they can't be very busy.'

'If it makes you feel better, they are the most prestigious firm of lawyers in the country. They have offices all over the world.'

'Well, I wonder why…'

'Scarlett.' The way he said her name like that—just her name—his voice dropping on the second syllable, did something strange to her insides. It caught her attention and held it. 'Scarlett,' he repeated, 'you're an heiress. They're going to fit you in.'

'I don't like that word. What does it even mean? Anyone who inherits anything is an heir or heiress, even if it's your grandmother's favourite earrings. You were an heir. You inherited Bellevale. It doesn't make you special.'

She saw his jaw tighten and he took one hand off the wheel, pulling his fingers across the back of his head.

'Maybe not,' he said, his eyes fixed on the road as they approached a tight bend. 'But money changes people sometimes, and it also changes how others perceive you.'

'Well, if you perceive that I'm becoming unreasonably demanding, and obsessing over which tree in Italy my olive oil came from, will you tell me? Nip the diva in the bud?'

Will pushed back in the seat, bracing his arms against the wheel. 'Sure.' He sounded amused. 'It'll absolutely be my pleasure.'

Scarlett felt the blush spreading up her neck, over her cheeks. A glance in the wing mirror confirmed that she now had the appearance of a sun blush tomato. She'd walked right into that. She sneaked a look up at him from under her lashes.

The faint comma lines at his mouth had deepened and his eyes sparked.

She went back to studying her hands in her lap. 'I didn't mean…'

'You're blushing. Did I say something to embarrass you?'

'No. I think *I* did.' She raised her head. 'Oh!'

'I wondered when you'd notice. By the end of today you'll have seen it from different angles. I think it's beautiful from all of them.'

In the distance, Table Mountain seemed to rise from the waters of Table Bay, its top hidden under the famous white 'tablecloth' of cloud. It poured like a thick, continuous curtain of candyfloss, disappearing magically at a precise distance from the summit. To the right and left, wrapped in their own ribbons of cloud, stood two lower mountains.

'It's…breathtaking.'

The mountains loomed steadily larger as they sped along the freeway towards the city and soon Scarlett could make out the shimmering steel and glass of towering buildings on the foreshore, green spaces and colourful old houses climbing up the steep streets in cheerful rows.

'Cape Town is in its own mountain amphitheatre, right by the sea. It must be one of the most beautiful cities on earth.'

Will shifted, adjusting his grip on the wheel. The traffic was heavier now, and he braked sharply as a small van cut in front of them.

'Glad you didn't drive yourself?'

'Very. But mainly because I wouldn't have been able to admire the mountains if I'd been concentrating on the traffic.'

'Mmm.' Will glanced at the satnav screen on the dashboard and indicated left, pulling onto a looping off ramp and entering a maze of busy streets. 'I'll drop you at the door. Send me a message when you're ready to be picked up again.'

CHAPTER FOURTEEN

WILL'S PHONE BUZZED two hours later. When he pulled up at the kerb he saw two men in suits shaking Scarlett's hand. One of them opened the passenger door, nodded to Will and closed it again as she fastened her seatbelt.

'You must have made their day.'

He saw a gap and pulled into the traffic. 'They were very helpful. I had no idea about the money. When I said Marguerite had left me her fortune, I didn't realise it was *a* fortune.'

'How does it feel? Powerful? Exciting?'

'Overwhelming. It'll take time to get used to the idea. But the lawyers have arranged everything. My new bank card arrived by special courier, while I waited. They've suggested making some investments, only they called it "wealth management". I'll have to come back in a couple of days, to sign some papers.'

'Tea? I know a place you'll like.'

'Yes, please. You sound very sure.'

'I am.'

He drove out of the city, the road hugging the curving foot of the mountain.

'Look. Table Bay is behind us and False Bay ahead of us. The flat plain connecting the two was once the seabed, when this peninsula was an island.'

'And on this side the climate is obviously different. It's much greener and there're forests.' Breathless excitement bubbled over in her voice.

'This southern side of the mountain gets almost twice as much rain annually as the city.'

He left the freeway, swooping onto a tree-lined avenue.

Scarlett's response to her first views of the peninsula were joyful and enthusiastic, and he could identify with her feelings. They mirrored his own. Every time he made the journey to Cape Town he marvelled at the spectacular setting, the majestic mountains, the vibrancy of the culture.

They had tea at the Kirstenbosch Botanical Gardens, tucked onto the slopes of Devil's Peak, where the array of indigenous plants and trees fascinated her.

'Did you know there're more than twenty-one thousand plant species in South Africa?' she asked him, looking up from an information board, her eyes lit with passion. 'And many of them are under threat of extinction. They're creating their own seedbank but at the moment seeds are stored at the Millennium Seed Bank run by Kew Gardens, in England.'

'Would you like to see another endangered indigenous species?' Will glanced at the sky. 'There's time for that, and a visit to Cape Point, if we go now.'

They drove towards the wide curve of False Bay, the road climbing and dipping, revealing a new view around every corner. When he pulled into a car park he saw Scarlett's expression of delight as she read the sign.

'Penguins! Is this the famous colony of African penguins?'

He nodded. 'It is. More than two thousand of them. Come on.'

Low slopes covered in coastal bush sheltered the coves below them, where the sea swirled around enormous granite boulders. The waves of False Bay curled onto the sandy beach, each one bringing a group of sleek penguins bodysurfing to the shore.

From the boardwalk which snaked through the bush, they could see the birds and their nests, amongst the roots of the scrub. He watched Scarlett crouch down, intense concentration on her face, as she studied the penguins at close range.

'This is wonderful, Will. Thank you for bringing me here.'

She glowed with enthusiasm and Will wanted to capture her face between his palms and claim her mouth, see her eyes darken with desire. He pushed his hands into his pockets and looked away, wondering why he was submitting himself to the exquisite torture of being close to her when he knew he could not give into his impulse to hold her. He should have collected her from the lawyers' offices and driven her straight back to Bellevale.

Half an hour after leaving the penguin colony at Boulders Beach, Will turned into the Cape Point car park. It was a half mile walk up to the Old Lighthouse at the most south-westerly tip of the African continent, and it was steep, but when they reached the top Scarlett stopped so suddenly that Will cannoned into her. She felt his hands close around her upper arms as he steadied her and she fought the impulse to lean back against the hard expanse of his chest and let him hold her. All afternoon she'd waited for him to touch her hand or sling an arm across her shoulders, but he'd kept his distance and now he dropped his hands as she turned.

'This is amazing!' The steady gale snatched at her words, and he bent his head towards hers. 'Amazing!' she repeated, and he nodded. She stepped towards the stone wall surrounding the base of the lighthouse and leaned into the teeth of the wind.

A fierce gust seized her hair and whipped a strand of it across her face and she lifted a hand to push it away, leaning further out. Far below at the foot of the cliffs the sea churned and boomed, flinging up curtains of spray. She laughed, exuberant, loving the power of the wind and the taste of salt on the air. Suddenly, it felt as if the trauma of her recent past had been swept away, leaving her filled with freedom and excitement.

Anything was possible, with the legacy Marguerite had left her. All her plans and dreams for Rozendal could become reality. She would never have to depend on anyone else again. She let go of her hair and flung her arms out, feeling almost strong and light enough to fly.

'Scarlett!' Will's arms clamped around her waist, pulling her back against his chest.

She turned her head to look up at him, surprised at the anxiety etched on his features. She dropped her hands over his.

'I'm okay, Will.'

She didn't know if he could hear her above the roaring wind and the crashing sea, but he nodded and rested his chin on her head. Then he steered her away from the edge, into the shelter of the lighthouse.

'What were you doing?' he asked when it was possible to speak. 'I thought…' He shook his head. 'I thought you were going to be blown away.'

'I think part of me did blow away.' She turned to face him but he kept his arms around her. 'I'm free, Will. It's starting to sink in, and I feel so strong and powerful, as if I can do anything I want. Because I can, with Marguerite's legacy.' Dizzy with emotion, she rose onto her toes and kissed him quickly before stepping out of the safe circle of his arms. 'You don't need to feel responsible for me any longer.' She reached out a hand and touched his shoulder. 'Hey, I thought you'd be happy about that. I can hire a driver to bring me to Cape Town next time. And I can find someone to advise me about the work at Rozendal.' She smiled up at him. 'Think of all the time and trouble I'm saving you.'

As they set off down the steps, she slipped her hand into his. She glanced up at his austere profile, his wind-whipped hair and straight mouth. Now that she knew her independence was assured and that she'd never have to sell Rozendal, she felt safe with him instead of threatened.

His blue eyes locked with hers and her joyful heart turned

over. Doubt nudged at her. Did she really want to find someone else to drive her, or to advise her? Nobody else would be fun to be with, or make her feel safe, like Will did. Enjoying his company, feeling that connection between them didn't mean she was breaking her vow. It wasn't as if she was letting him get close to her or falling in love with him.

She let go of his hand, to prove to herself that she could.

Will negotiated the early evening traffic in silence, reluctant to interrupt Scarlett's thoughts. He supposed she was making a dozen plans which did not involve him and he tried not to let that bother him.

The idea of her being free made him anxious. He told himself it was because it threw his plans to acquire Rozendal into jeopardy, but he knew the truth was that he wanted her to need him. And with that came the dangerous thought that he was beginning to need her in return.

Was it possible to spend time with her and yet maintain his emotional distance? Allowing himself to admit to an emotional need was unthinkable, and yet with her he felt some of his iron-hard rules softening.

'You're very quiet, Will.'

Her voice startled him. He glanced across at her, noting her expression of concern.

'You're not exactly chatty.' He accelerated past a truck. 'Making plans?'

'Plotting?'

He allowed himself a smile. 'Yeah, plotting how I can convince you that you don't need to hire a driver.'

'How are you getting on with that? Because…'

'I need to be back in Cape Town in a couple of days. If you let me know when your papers are ready to sign, I'll co-ordinate my meeting with yours.'

'Oh…' He thought he detected relief in her voice. 'Because I was going to say I don't really want another driver, if you'll bring me. I…enjoy being with you. I haven't had fun for a long time, but I had fun today, and I hope you enjoyed it too.'

Will felt himself relaxing. He tipped his head back against the seat headrest for a few seconds.

'I love showing newcomers the sights of Cape Town.' He braked before a bend. 'And I… I like being with you.'

'You were right.'

'Aren't I always?'

'No. But this time you were. You're a good guide and great company.'

'We didn't finish the tour today.'

'Perhaps that's a good thing. Any more stunning views and surprising wildlife and I might have started taking it all for granted.'

'I'll make sure that you don't.'

CHAPTER FIFTEEN

'THE TABLECLOTH HAS VANISHED.'

It was two days later, and Scarlett studied the mountain as they sped along the freeway. The wind had dropped and it was a golden autumn day.

Will nodded, feeling relieved. He'd wanted to show her the mountain without its mantle of cloud. He hoped the day would hold its warmth later on.

He'd collected her from the lawyers' offices and drove them around the base of the mountain, past the university and Kirstenbosch, and Groot Constantia, one of the oldest wine estates in the Cape.

The winding route took them over a dip in the mountain range, which stretched all the way from the city, along the spine of the peninsula to Cape Point, and by late afternoon they were cruising along the spectacular Chapman's Peak Drive, the twisting route carved from the sandstone of the mountainside, swooping down to the stretch of glittering white sand which fringed the beach at Camps Bay.

He pulled into a parking space and they climbed out, leaning against the front of the car. A brisk sea breeze tugged at the loose bun of Scarlett's hair, whipping curls around her face. She laughed.

'Shall we swim?'

'This is the Atlantic. The water is freezing. And I didn't bring swimming things.' He leaned back, resting on the warm metal of the bonnet. 'Did you?'

'Wimp. And no, I didn't.'

'If you want to swim, I can take you to a place in the mountains behind Rozendal. Autumn isn't the best time—it might be chilly—but it's remote, the views are stunning, and we won't have to share it with anyone else.' He scanned the crowded beach. 'None of these people know about it, or they'd be there instead of here.'

'And you wouldn't let them in. You'd stand on the track and repel them all. Single-handed.'

'Bare-handed.'

'Bare-chested.'

'Perhaps we should stop there?'

'Okay.' She swiped the hair from her forehead. 'It's a date, though. A swimming date.'

'A date? I don't date.'

Dating implied thought and possibly planning another meeting. Candlelight and flowers. Those weren't the things on his mind when he scanned the contacts list on his phone.

'An appointment, then. I'm sure you do those.'

From the terrace of the graceful old Mount Nelson Hotel, where they sat sipping cocktails, Scarlett tilted her head to look up at Table Mountain.

'This is perfect.'

Will watched her stir her drink with a striped straw. He'd scarcely been able to keep his eyes off her all afternoon. She was beautiful, with her lustrous green eyes and hair the colour of autumn leaves, threaded through with strands of gold. But her beauty seemed to come from within, a glowing warmth and enthusiasm which he envied.

He remembered the energy with which Scarlett had erupted into Rozendal, robbing him of his victory at the last second, and the determination which had driven her to get there, against all odds. He remembered how the room had buzzed with renewed life, everyone turning to focus on the source of it.

It had been frustrating to have his plans thwarted, but now he wouldn't change it. He wouldn't have missed these times spent with her, watching her relax in his company, her delight in nature and enjoyment of life. He'd get what he wanted, eventually. Having Scarlett as a sparring partner along the way was making the ride far, far more interesting.

Partner. His mind snagged on the word. She'd had a partner. He glanced at her ring finger again. What had happened between them? How could any man have allowed a jewel like Scarlett to slip away? He must have been an idiot. And careless with her. Anger simmered in him at the idea that she'd been hurt.

He stopped, remembering that not everyone, himself included, needed a partner in life. Perhaps the man had realised his mistake and called it off before it became too messy.

Better a broken engagement than a train smash of a marriage.

'Will? *Will?*'

He dragged his mind back to the present.

'Scarlett.' She stilled, and her teeth scraped over her bottom lip. 'I'm sorry. I was thinking.'

'I could see that. Anything interesting?'

'No.'

'I don't believe you.'

'Sensible. Are you hungry?'

'I will be by the time we get back. Should we leave? It's so perfect here…'

'We could come back another day, if you like.' His mind leapt ahead, racing along a forbidden path. A single call to the concierge would secure one of the grand bedrooms…

But her face clouded and she shook her head. 'I'm going to be much too busy. I shouldn't take any time off. But today has been wonderful.'

'It's not over yet. Today, I mean.'

'I don't know if I can absorb any more beautiful views.'

'That's a pity. I had one more planned.'

'Well, if it really is only one, and it's truly beautiful…'

'You can be the judge.'

He clasped her hand to pull her out of her chair and he didn't let go of it until they reached the car.

They retraced their route, up the steep hill towards Kloof Nek, where the road would tip over the brow of the hill and plunge in a series of bends through the pines, down towards the sea again.

But just before the top Will swung the car to the left.

'Where are we going?'

'To dinner. On the mountain.'

Scarlett leaned forward and looked up. 'In the cable car? Oh, Will…'

'Well, it's a bit late in the day to start walking up, and in those shoes…' He shook his head at her ballet flats.

A stream of vehicles was coming towards them, leaving the lower cable station.

'I think we're too late. Everyone else is leaving. What time does the cable car stop for the night?'

'I have no idea.'

'Oh. We should have skipped the cocktails, or I could have drunk mine more quickly. But it's okay. The view from here is pretty special.'

Will pulled up, leaving the engine running, and took Scarlett's hand to help her from the car. A uniformed man stepped forward.

'Good evening, Mr Duvinage. Enjoy your trip.'

Will nodded. 'Thank you. I'll message you when we're on our way down.'

Scarlett looked up at him, confused, as the stranger drove away in the Range Rover.

'But Will, we don't even know if we're in time…' She turned her head and watched the car disappearing around a bend in the road.

'We don't need the last one, Scarlett. I've booked our own private cable car.'

'You can *do* that?'

'Stop asking questions and I'll show you.'

She took his outstretched hand again.

The ride was spectacular. The floor of the car revolved, giving them a three-sixty view as they ascended, the mountainside quickly dropping away beneath them. Scarlett's knees weakened as they climbed, and she found she was still clutching Will's hand.

She kept her gaze level. At the halfway mark the descending car passed them, packed with noisy trippers on their way down.

'In a few moments, Scarlett…' Will turned his head '… you'll be able to see down to Camps Bay.'

The car swung upwards, seeming to barely clear a jagged ridge of rock, and then the mountain plunged away beneath them, sheer cliffs falling towards the sea.

Scarlett gasped and squeezed her eyes shut.

Will's fingers tightened around her hand.

'Are you okay?'

'Not that good with heights…'

'God, Scarlett, why didn't you say? We didn't have to do this.'

She opened her eyes and found his blue ones, filled with concern, looking down at her.

'I didn't know we were going to do this. And anyway, I wouldn't have missed it…even though it's scary.'

She swayed and Will pulled her against him.

'It's okay. Just a minute to go.'

He put his arm around her shoulders and held her tightly against him. She felt wrapped in safety and put a hand flat against his chest, keeping her eyes fixed on his. The steady beat of his heart thumped beneath her palm and that elusive feeling of belonging—of *fitting*—made her want to stay there in his strong arms, inhaling his scent and feeling the brush of his fingers across her back. Darts of sensation arrowed through her body, meeting at a point in her abdomen, and she pressed herself against him, not caring about letting her feelings show. His hand covered hers and he lifted it, brushing his lips across the tips of her fingers.

The car slowed, inching towards the docking station, swaying slightly. The doors slid open and they stood there for a moment, then Will, keeping an arm around her shoulders, guided her out of the bubble, before slipping several folded notes to the operator.

'Thank you, sir.' The man raised a hand. 'See you later. Whenever you're ready.'

Dusk, thought Scarlett. The perfect word to describe the softly fading light. She looked up into the deep sky and turned in a circle. It was quiet, high above the sounds of the city. Far below, lights had begun to flicker on, spreading a jewelled net over the darkening streets and buildings.

On the western side, the sun was poised above the ocean, its rim seeming to test the water before committing to a swim. The sky flushed orange, pink and then lilac as it sank, spreading the last of its rays over the dark blue and silver of the sea.

'Are you ready for dinner?'

'I think we're too late. The café is closed.'

He smiled. 'Come this way.'

A gazebo, housing a table and two chairs, had been set up, facing the view. Candlelight glowed in glass lanterns and a picnic hamper stood open on the ground. Each chair had a woollen rug folded over the backrest.

Scarlett stopped, a hand going to her heart.

'How did you do this, Will?'

He shrugged. 'I made some calls.'

Will placed a hand on the small of her back and urged her towards the table, pulling out a chair for her. Then he released the ties on three sides of the structure, letting the canvas roll down to protect them from the cool breeze, but leaving the side facing the view open.

He pulled a bottle of local sparkling wine from a cooler

and eased the cork from the neck with sure fingers. Honey-gold bubbles fizzed into delicate flutes and he raised his towards her.

'To the heiress.'

'If this is the life an heiress leads, perhaps I could get used to it.' Scarlett sipped. 'Do you live like this all the time?'

'Not *all* the time, no.'

'When you inherited Bellevale did you celebrate like this?'

Will thought back to the day when Bellevale had finally become his. There'd been no champagne opened, no toasts drunk, just a sense of having finally achieved what he'd been striving for since he'd been a boy. It had been a bitter process.

In the confines of this tent, enveloped in Scarlett's burgeoning acceptance of her new status, he felt uneasy. He hated talking about his past, but he didn't like that she had a skewed perception of him. If he tried to explain how he'd come to be the man he was today, would she begin to understand what drove him? Why, when he'd set his mind on something, he couldn't rest until he'd achieved it?

'Will? I'm sorry. Obviously, you didn't celebrate, because your father must have died when you took over Bellevale.'

'Scarlett.' She stopped, her eyes fastening onto his. 'Scarlett, my parents are still alive. I didn't inherit Bellevale. I bought it.'

Her mouth opened and all he could think was that he wanted to kiss her.

'You…*bought*… Bellevale? But you're a Duvinage. Your family have owned the estate since…'

'1687.'

'Yes. I'm sure you can see why I'm confused.'

'Of course. Why wouldn't you be? Your logic is faultless.'

Will gripped his hands together and looked out into the darkness, wondering why he'd thought starting this conversation was a good idea. He'd made it known to his friends and associates that this was something he would not discuss, under any circumstances. His family didn't count. He discussed nothing with them, anyway.

Nothing about the past could be changed. The subject stirred up feelings of bitter resentment, animosity and, he had to admit, although he wasn't proud of it, an empty sort of triumph.

It was best kept under the carpet, where he'd insisted on sweeping it. Only now he'd lifted a corner…

'Will? I'm sorry. I can see this is difficult for you. If you'd rather not talk about it, I understand.'

It was her empathy which made him want to carry on. She wasn't pushing him for details. He knew he could let the subject drop, if he wanted, and she *would* understand. It felt safe.

'Like you, Scarlett, I was a surprise: the unwelcome and unwanted baby.'

Shock showed in her wide eyes and the small frown between her brows.

'But your parents must have wanted an heir…'

He nodded. 'Oh, yes, they wanted an heir to take over Bellevale. But only one. They weren't—*aren't*—invested in family. "One and done" was their plan, and they had my brother.'

'But if they already had a son, why…?'

'Why did they have me? They never intended to, but I came along anyway.'

'So it was your brother…'

'Richard.'

'It was your older brother, Richard, who took over Bellevale.'

Scarlett reached out a hand towards him. He'd held it many times that day, but now he let her hand, with the pale stripe around the ring finger, lie unclaimed on the linen tablecloth.

'You got that in one.'

'Don't, Will. Don't do that.'

'What?'

'It's not a joke.'

'People joked that I had the passion for Bellevale but it wouldn't be mine, while Richard… All it achieved was to make me determined that I would, ultimately, own it.'

Scarlett withdrew her hand. 'Do you want to tell me what happened?'

Will pulled a hand across his face and took in a long breath.

'Long story short. Richard was raised to run the estate. He was told from day one where his future lay.'

'And you?'

'I was told my future lay anywhere but at Bellevale. There was room for one owner and that wasn't ever going to be me. I can see that the way our parents handled it resulted in an outcome precisely opposite from the one they intended.' He shook his head. 'Richard was never given a choice and he rebelled against the restriction. Everything my parents did was directed towards his future ownership. It was understood that I would leave and stay out of the way.'

'Did you rebel against that?'

'I suppose I did, in a different way. Richard became a sulky teenager, resentful of being expected to learn about viticulture and oenology, while I was hell-bent on learning as much as I could. I also had to make enough money to buy him out one day.'

'And you did.'

'I did a maths degree and joined a software company in the States. Then I saw a gap in the market for a piece of software. It was such an obvious thing, which is probably why everyone else had dismissed it as irrelevant. I raced to develop it, and it was so successful I was able to start my own company. And then, as happens, I was taken over by one of the giants. Suddenly I had billions and there was only one thing I wanted to spend them on.'

'You're a tech billionaire. Did you make him a hugely inflated offer?'

'Considering the condition the estate was in by then, my offer was generous. Our father had retired and Richard had let everything slide. He simply didn't possess the interest or drive to keep up the momentum which running something like a vineyard requires. It's not easy. Farming is precarious, dependent on so many variables. Droughts are more common than they used to be and there is so much more pressure on water supplies, with the increase in numbers of people living in the Western Cape.'

Scarlett nodded, her lips and cheekbones highlighted in the glow of the candles, her eyes forest green. 'It's a beautiful environment.'

'The rainfall is unreliable, and the one thing everyone needs is water.'

'And your brother wanted out.'

Will chewed his lip. 'I…suggested to him that he might be happier living a different life. Bellevale is isolated. He spent a lot of time driving to and from Cape Town, socialising. Being on his own doesn't suit him.'

'Perhaps if he'd had a partner, it might have been different.'

'Maybe, but he didn't. He, with our parents encouraging him, asked for more money. I upped the offer several times, but they knew what I was worth, and how much I wanted the estate. They'd always known I loved it, so they kept pushing. Eventually I paid him an obscene amount, but I made the conditions very clear. There would be no more money and they—all of them—were to stay away from me and from Bellevale.'

'You don't ever see them? Talk to them?'

'Oh, I do. He still asks for more, quite regularly. He grew up believing the world, or rather Bellevale, owed him a living. He has never understood the concept of earning it.'

'I'm sorry, Will. I've wished I had a family: parents who cared; a sibling who understood. It's lonely without someone to share everyday life with. I think that's why I…' She shook her head, reaching towards him again, and this time he closed his fingers around hers.

'Why you did what, Scarlett?'

'It doesn't matter. This isn't about me.'

'This is about you. I wouldn't have arranged it for myself.' *Or anyone else.* He looked at his watch, angling his wrist to read the time by the light of the candle. 'I think we'd better call for our glass coach and get back down the mountain.'

'It'd be tricky if it turned into a pumpkin.'

'And you ran away…'

'And lost a shoe…'

'Like I said, *those shoes.*'

He stood, picking up the rug from his chair and shaking it out before tucking it around Scarlett's shoulders.

'Surely we should leave the rugs with the picnic things?'

He allowed his hands to rest on her shoulders. 'I'll make sure this one is returned to the restaurant tomorrow. You need it now. The temperature has dropped.'

She turned to face him, holding both his hands. 'Could we stay a little longer? It's not midnight yet…'

He bent his head and rested his forehead against hers. 'It's not, and I'd love to stay longer, but the cable car operator will need to get home, as well as the car park attendant.' He kissed her temple and she shivered. 'And you're cold.'

'That wasn't a cold shiver. It was a…'

He pressed a finger to her lips. 'Shh, sweetheart.'

He pulled out his phone and sent a message, then used the phone flashlight to light their way over the rough ground. Their arms bumped together as they walked side by side to the cable station.

'Going down will be less scary because you won't be able to see how far away the ground is.'

Scarlett laughed. 'My imagination will make it far worse than it is.'

Will took her hand as they stepped into the dimly lit car. 'Imagine you're Cinderella and the worst thing that can happen is that your glass coach turns into a pumpkin.'

'That *is* the worst that could happen. It'd be catastrophic.

Suspended from a cable at three and a half thousand feet? In a pumpkin.'

He laughed. 'As you said, it's not midnight yet so I think we'll be okay. But I'll call for the Range Rover, just so we're prepared.'

The driver had the car waiting for them, engine running, when they stepped out of the lower cable station.

'Still think the view is special from here?' Will spun the wheel and pulled onto the road.

'Mmm.' Scarlett snuggled into the folds of the blanket, her head turned towards him. 'Yes. And the view of Cape Town is stunning too.'

'Scarlett. Are you flirting with me?'

'Possibly.'

'I thought so.'

He kept his eyes on the road, the headlights slicing through the dark. *Home.* Her use of the word made him feel good, until he remembered he wanted to part her from her home, or a piece of it. He exhaled deliberately, trying to focus his thoughts on the day they'd spent together, and not on a future in which they'd clash.

She was so still that he thought she'd gone to sleep. He glanced across at her, lifted a hand off the steering wheel and tucked the blanket around her more securely.

'Will?'

'Sorry. Did I wake you?'

'No. Do you regret telling me about your family?'

'I try not to regret things. It's a waste of energy.'

'But what if you really, really wish something hadn't happened? And it's hard to stop the wishing?'

He thought for a while. Did she wish she'd never been engaged, or had a relationship with the idiot who'd broken her heart? Or did she wish she was still with him, her heart intact?

He needed to know the answer.

'Perhaps if you learn from the thing that happened you won't let something like that happen again.'

'If only I could believe I'd learned. And Will?'

'Mmm?'

'That blip which disturbed the line of inheritance of Bellevale was significant.'

'Yeah. It was notable.'

'I'm sorry about the things I said that day in the rose garden.'

'That's okay. You made the obvious assumption.'

He hadn't told her everything. What he'd kept hidden made him feel ashamed and betrayed. It had upended his life and the scandal had played out in the glare of publicity.

But he'd learned never to make *that* mistake again.

Thinking about it made him want to punch something. *Someone.*

The throb of the engine died into perfect silence. Vineyard Cottage was shrouded in darkness, although he knew a motion detector light would come on at the front door.

He listened to the quiet for a minute, unwilling to end it—to break the spell.

Scarlett slept in the passenger seat, her cheek cupped in one hand. Will opened her door and carefully stretched across her to release the seatbelt buckle.

He shook her shoulder gently. 'Scarlett. We're home.' He smoothed a lock of hair back from her forehead. 'You need to wake up so you can go back to sleep in your own bed.'

The urge to kiss her was almost more than he could resist. He lifted his hands and gripped the edge of the roof of the car. Her lids fluttered and he saw the confusion in her eyes, and then clarity dawning as she focused on him.

'Thank you, Will, for such a fun day.' She pushed herself upright. 'But I'll need to edit my TripAdvisor review.'

He tried to release his clenched jaw so he could reply.

'What do you mean?' A whisper was all he could manage.

'You're a great guide and *very* good company.'

'I am?'

'Mmm.'

She reached out her hand and touched his cheek, but he circled her wrist with a finger and thumb and moved her hand away.

'Come on. Bed.'

'With you?'

She slid to the ground and he put a hand on her back, guiding her towards the steps. The light came on and she blinked.

'You're flirting again, Scarlett.'

'Just asking a question.'

As she stepped onto the bottom step, he brushed his mouth over her temple.

'Goodnight, Scarlett.'

He left the car on the drive and took the steps two at a time. The familiar smell of leather and beeswax polish hit him as he pushed open the dining room door and crossed the floor to the drinks cabinet. As the amber whisky swirled into the heavy tumbler gripped in his hand he sniffed deeply, hoping the peaty smell would drive Scarlett's scent from his memory.

He eyed the bottle. How much more of its contents would he need to drink before sweet oblivion overcame him?

Scarlett pushed the door closed behind her and leaned against it, pressing her palms against the cool wood. She breathed slowly, trying to regulate her heartbeat. If she'd repeated her question, would he have followed her in?

She didn't know. What she knew was that she'd wanted him to. Her heart broke for him. She wanted to hold him, comfort him, tell him how amazing he was. And she wanted to experience that sense of safety and belonging again. She thought it could become necessary to her, as fundamental as air and water.

Perhaps she should be grateful that he'd shown more willpower than she had.

CHAPTER SIXTEEN

SHE HADN'T SEEN Will for over a week.

He'd vanished from her life, but he'd put several things in motion towards the renovation of Rozendal, without asking her.

The morning after their magical dinner on Table Mountain, Peter, the builder, had knocked on her door, at his shoulder a man who could rethatch the house and outbuildings.

She'd asked for contracts to sign but they'd shrugged their shoulders. They'd worked for Will for years, they said. His word was good enough.

'You're working for me,' she'd replied acidly, and they'd laughed and left.

After that, everything moved quickly.

Scaffolding went up around Rozendal. A huge tarpaulin shrouded the roof.

'Just in case the winter rains come early,' Jonas, the thatcher, said, looking skywards.

Peter had a man for everything. A plumber restored the water supply so the water ran clear and smooth, the noisy hiccoughs cleared from the pipes. An electrician frowned and sucked his teeth over the fuse box and muttered about rewiring the entire house, but made it work, anyway.

Scarlett needed it to be weather-proof for the coming winter, with a functioning kitchen and bathroom and a bedroom where she could sleep in a warm, comfortable bed. And she had to be out of Vineyard Cottage in a week.

Everything else could wait for the spring.

* * *

Then, early one morning, she looked up from polishing the bronze kitchen taps and Will was standing in the doorway, leaning a shoulder into the frame.

It was eight days since she'd seen him, not that she was counting.

He pushed away from the door and stepped over the threshold.

Scarlett dropped the polishing cloth into the sink and wiped her hands down her jeans.

'Will.'

'I've been away. Board meetings in Johannesburg and Cape Town.' He leaned across her and twisted one of the taps. A stream of clear water ran smoothly into the sink. 'No more rusty water.'

A mix of emotions chased through Scarlett. She felt a little flare of pleasure, knowing he'd been away, not simply avoiding her. She took a steadying breath, filling her lungs and exhaling slowly. This was Will, and they'd had a beautiful afternoon and then, two days later, an enchanting evening in Cape Town. He'd gone away without telling her. Big deal. Huge. She told herself to get a grip. He did not have to tell her anything.

So why was her heartbeat ignoring her stern inner voice and beating to an entirely inappropriate rhythm? She remembered, uncomfortably, how she'd brushed her fingers across his cheek and he'd gently removed her hand, the gesture speaking louder than any words could have done. And she'd nonetheless half suggested that he come to bed with her. She felt heat flare across her cheeks.

His navy-blue eyes skimmed her face and settled on her mouth for longer than they should have. Her pulse leapt again as she swiped the tip of her tongue across her lower lip.

One corner of his mouth lifted a fraction and his gaze shifted to lock with hers.

'How's the rewilding project coming on?'

Scarlett looked out over the neglected gardens and fields, to the towering mountains beyond.

'I've been in touch with the Seed Collections Officer at Kirstenbosch and he's keen to help. Everyone has been enthusiastic.' She pushed herself upright. 'Except you.'

'Mmm.'

'Have you come to check on progress?'

'No. I've come to make an appointment with you.' He turned and leaned his hips against the worktop, pushing his hands into his pockets. 'A swimming appointment.'

'Oh… I thought you'd forgotten…'

'Scarlett.' She wrapped her arms across her waist, allowing his soft pronunciation of her name to settle over her. 'Why would I forget?'

It felt as if a chasm had opened up between them: between the relaxed easiness of the days they'd spent together and now. Had Will used the time away to withdraw from her? Had her half-joking invitation made him cautious? That was how it seemed. And Scarlett felt tongue-tied and awkward, as if they were strangers striking up a conversation on a station platform.

'No, of course you wouldn't forget. But if you've changed your mind you don't have to…'

'I'm not known for changing my mind, Scarlett. But if you've changed yours…'

'No! No, I haven't.' She stumbled over her words. 'I'd love to go swimming, only you said autumn wasn't the best time and…'

Then she remembered how she'd stepped out of Vineyard Cottage that morning and been shocked by the temperature. A hot, unsettling breeze had whipped her hair across her face, and the air smelled of dust.

'A day like today is perfect for swimming. There's a berg wind blowing. It's the hot, dry wind which comes down from the high escarpment in the interior. By tomorrow it could be twenty degrees cooler, with mist and rain.'

Scarlett looked out at the sky, its blueness dulled by the dusty air. It was hard to believe it might rain soon and grow cold.

She knew Will's eyes were on her while he waited for her answer. It would be difficult to come up with a reason why she didn't want to go swimming. And anyway, she did. She just wasn't sure she *should*.

'Scarlett?'

'Yes. I mean, *yes*?' She pressed a palm to her forehead.

'Hey.' His voice gentled. 'Even if you don't want to swim, I'd like to show you the place.'

The track twisted up the slope behind Rozendal, through outcrops of grey boulders and clumps of pine trees. The air was thick and warm in her throat and lungs.

'After the cooler temperatures of the past week this feels unnatural.'

'Yeah.' Will settled into a steady pace, just ahead of her. 'It only ever lasts a day.'

The pool lay in a basin of rock. Shelves of sandstone surrounded the clear water and smooth pebbles lined the bottom. Water tumbled down the mountainside beyond and over a lip of rock, creating a gentle splash, and near to where Scarlett stood beside Will it overflowed over a much higher cliff, plunging onto rocks far below before gathering itself to flow in an even stream through the valley.

Scarlett spread her arms wide. 'This is the most perfect place.' She pushed her fingers through her hair, fanning it out over her shoulders. 'Better than any beach.'

'The Rozendal boundary lies just above the waterfall.' Will extended an arm to show her. 'This is your pool. And that's the river which flows along the edge of your estate.'

'It's beautiful.' Scarlett sent a silent message to Marguerite, as she did every day, thanking her for rescuing her when she'd most needed it, and for delivering her to this place. 'I feel so…lucky.'

Will bent to untie his boots. 'Time to cool off.'

'And no crowds at all.'

'I said I'd fight them off.'

'Bare-handed.'

'Bare-chested, I think you said.'

'You said we should stop there…'

Will began to undo the buttons of his shirt. His teasing gaze held Scarlett's anxious one.

'Wimp?'

'Not fair. I was referring to the cold water. Not…'

'Not what, Scarlett?'

If her cheeks hadn't already been flushed from the exertion of the hike, she knew they'd be burning now. She clamped her arms across her chest.

'Not being afraid of seeing you strip your clothes off. And I'm not.'

Will peeled off his shirt and she felt her stomach lurch. His shoulders gleamed, smooth and golden in the sun, while his sculpted chest and abs tapered to slim hips. A dusting of dark hair narrowed to a line which disappeared, tantalisingly, beneath the waistband of his jeans.

As if her gaze had some sort of power, his fingers popped the button and he pushed the jeans over his hips.

'God, Will…' She turned away.

'It's okay, Scarlett.' There was laughter in his voice. 'I'm wearing shorts underneath.'

Scarlett risked a glance over her shoulder, in time to see him stretch his arms skywards and dive in a clean arc from the rock platform, slicing into the crystalline water.

He surfaced near the edge, tossing his hair from his eyes and scattering a bright shower of droplets over her. The spatter of water was deliciously cool on her skin.

'Are you coming in?'

'I…don't know.'

'You said you were going to change into swimming things.'

'I did.' The blinding truth, that it would have been way safer to swim with Will at a crowded beach than alone in a wild pool high in the mountains, hit Scarlett. 'But I'm not sure…'

He swam to the edge and rested his folded arms on the rock, looking up at her.

'What aren't you sure about? It's perfectly safe. No sharks. No piranhas.'

Just you, she thought desperately. 'It's not that…'

Too late, she saw his arm stretch out and felt his fingers circle her ankle.

'Come on, Scarlett. It might be your only chance. You can't say you went to South Africa and didn't go swimming.' His touch was light, but she felt the stroke of his thumb on her inner anklebone. Who knew the anklebone was such a sensitive spot? A hot current of sensation zipped up her leg.

Piranhas. His words cut through the confusion which clouded her brain, jolting her back to reality. He was so sure of himself, she thought. So determined that he'd get Rozendal, and she knew he wouldn't care what happened to her, once he'd got what he wanted. She'd been stupid to allow the romanticism of a candlelit picnic skew her judgement.

Were all men the same, or had she been unlucky to meet two similar ones in quick succession?

She wasn't going anywhere, except maybe into this water. A hot gust of wind ruffled the surface and scorched her skin. She really, really wanted to swim. His body made her want to run her hands over him and drive him wild and his eyes were daring her to do exactly that. None of that was going to happen. His reaction to her touch, late that night, had been decisive. Was he testing her, to see if he could provoke her to do it again? Playing with her emotions?

'If you'll let go of my ankle, Will, I'll come in.'

He released her and pushed himself away from the side, floating on his back, kicking out into the middle of the pool.

Scarlett turned and pulled off her boots, jeans and shirt, fumbling with the buttons in her haste. For a second, she wished she'd worn a black one-piece swimsuit and not a purple bikini, but she pushed the thought away, refusing to allow herself to be intimidated.

Over her shoulder she could see that Will was still floating on his back, his eyes closed. She stepped to the edge and slid into the silky water.

The icy temperature was so unexpected that she gasped.

Will rolled over onto his stomach and dived beneath the surface. She watched him swim towards her, underwater.

He surfaced close to where Scarlett was suspended in the water, one hand gripping the ledge of rock. Goosebumps roughened her skin and she shuddered.

'You didn't say it was cold.'

'It's water off the mountain, Scarlett. It's always cold.' He sluiced water from his hair. 'Swim a bit. You'll warm up if you move.'

Scarlett released her grip on the rock and he watched her swim with long, steady strokes across the pool. He caught up with her as she reached the waterfall. Ducking beneath the curtain of water, he emerged in the space behind it.

'Will?'

'Come in here. It's…'

She appeared next to him in a shower of bubbles and droplets. Her hair, darkened to the colour of polished mahogany by the water, floated behind her. The emerald of her eyes was intensified by the greenish light reflected off the shadowed water. Close up, he could see a new, faint sprinkling of freckles across the bridge of her nose.

'This is beautiful.' She looked up. Moss and ferns grew on

the underside of the lip of rock. Another shade of green, he thought. 'Have you always swum here?'

Will nodded. 'We came here all the time as kids. Whoever was living at Rozendal never seemed to mind.'

He wondered what the hell he'd been thinking, encouraging her into the water with him, and then, even worse, bringing her into this secret place behind the waterfall. It was closed off from the outside world—cool and quiet and…*intimate*. The word beat repeatedly in his brain. This was all kinds of crazy, but when he was around her he felt as if his compass swung out of control. Scarlett became his true north.

He'd stayed away longer than necessary. She'd become almost irresistible, that afternoon in Cape Town, and it had taken all his willpower not to follow her into Vineyard Cottage that night. The pull she exercised over him was unfamiliar and therefore not to be trusted. It was outside the parameters of his experience, and he dared not explore it.

A week should have been long enough, but he could see now that no measure of time away from her would be sufficient to snap this thread that pulled them together. With her, he behaved in a way he didn't recognise. He should have been cool and distant this morning. If he gave into this temptation—this *need*—which had invaded his mind and body, leaving space for nothing but thoughts of how she'd feel in his arms, under him, the barriers he'd built to keep himself safe would crumble.

He couldn't face that. He'd be vulnerable again, in a way he'd only ever been once in his life. The thought was terrifying.

'Will?' Her voice was puzzled. 'Are you okay?'

He shook his head to clear his thoughts, trying to focus on something other than her toned limbs moving in the water, the purple bikini covering, but not concealing much, her body taut with the cold, her rounded breasts peaked beneath the silky fabric.

'Yeah.' His voice felt as if he'd swallowed sandpaper. He wished he hadn't mentioned piranhas. It had made her drop that shutter he'd seen before, when he'd tried to talk to her about the expedition to the Amazon, and he hated that he'd triggered a bad memory for her. 'Just thinking that you're cold. Maybe we should get some sun to warm us up.'

And get us out of here.

She shuddered as a spasm of shivering shook her, turning herself in the water. 'Okay.'

As she moved, her fingers trailed across his chest. He felt the light rake of her nails and his mind blanked. She kicked away but her legs tangled with his as he did the same and suddenly they were face to face, skin to skin, behind the waterfall.

Will felt himself going into freefall and there was nothing he could do to stop it—nothing he *wanted* to do. He slid an arm around her waist to steady her and ran his other hand over her hair, pressing it away from her forehead, his palm coming to rest on the side of her neck. His thumb stroked along her collarbone as his fingers curled over her smooth shoulder.

Her hands rested on his chest and he waited for her to push him away. When she didn't, he pulled her towards him, holding her gently enough so that she could resist if she wanted to. But her hands moved from his chest, round to his back, and he felt her palms pressing against his shoulder blades.

'Scarlett.' It was almost a groan, as if all the forbidden emotion he'd kept tightly coiled inside him for ever was being released at once.

'Mmm?'

He thought he might drown, not in the water but in the depths of her eyes, and in the wave of desire, pure and focused, which crashed over him.

Her breath feathered across his cheek, and he found her mouth. Despite the cold, her lips were warm and soft, and he held back, tasting her, licking the drops of water from her skin before returning to the kiss.

They'd kissed before and he had a vivid memory of how he'd wanted it to go on for ever. This was on another level. There was no space for wondering if it would end. Time ceased to have any meaning at all.

He'd wanted this, dreamed about it, knowing that having it would leave him on the edge of self-destruction, but now that it was happening all his instincts for self-preservation had evaporated. He clung to his self-control, desperate to have more of her but afraid of taking too much, too soon. He brushed her bottom lip with the tip of his tongue, nipped at it with his teeth and he felt her shudder and her mouth open.

Still he resisted, knowing that once he'd crossed that line all other lines would blur. Her back arched and her aroused body scraped against his chest. One of his hands drifted around her waist and came to rest on her ribs, beneath the swell of her breast, his thumb perilously close to its peak.

Then she went rigid in his arms and suddenly there was cold space between them, her hands on his shoulders, her mouth dragged away from his.

'Will, no!'

This time, he didn't know how he'd be able to stop. Scarlett was pulling away from him, shaking her head. He'd promised himself he'd let her go if she resisted him, but instinctively he felt himself trying to hold onto her. His body clamoured for more. His drugged brain was being slow to catch up.

'Scarlett. Please...'

Her fingers gripped his biceps and then went to where his hands spanned her ribcage. She unpeeled his fingers but wrapped his hands in hers.

'I'm sorry, Will...'

'No.' He finally managed a coherent thought, dragging words up from somewhere. 'I didn't mean this to happen.' He pulled in a breath, trying to find oxygen. 'Please don't apologise.'

'I'm sorry,' she said again, her teeth beginning to chatter. 'I just...can't.'

He swam alongside her to the edge. When he put his hands

on her waist to help her out of the water she didn't protest. He stayed submerged for a few more minutes, trying to get his thoughts into some sort of order, and his ragged breathing under control. He felt as if he'd tried to run a marathon and not made it to the end. He'd fought a battle with himself and lost.

His mind, so trained to control his environment, had failed to control his body.

Scarlett sat with her back against a rock, in a place sheltered from the wind. She wore an expression of fierce concentration as she squeezed water from her hair. She did not look up as he sat down a safe distance from her, leaning back on his hands and stretching out his legs.

There was no way he could pretend it hadn't happened. They both needed to acknowledge this thing which burned between them.

Every cell in his body wanted her—wanted to hold her, kiss her, make love to her. But what if he found that wasn't enough? He couldn't risk that.

She wanted him, of that he was sure, but something stopped her.

Perhaps he should be grateful for whatever it was.

She looked up at last, and their eyes collided. She chewed her bottom lip and bent her legs up, hugging her knees to her chest. Was she trying to ensure there was less of her to see, or was it an unconscious gesture of self-protection?

'Scarlett…'

'Will.' She held up a hand, palm flattened towards him. 'You don't need to say anything.'

'You want me.' Those weren't the words he'd planned to say, but they were the ones hammering in his head. Her eyes flew wide and she opened her mouth to speak, but he interrupted her. 'Don't deny it. If you choose not to act on it, that's fine, but just don't…*deny* it.' He rubbed his forehead, fighting to keep his voice steady. 'Because that would be a lie.'

He thought she'd be angry, perhaps walk away, but she dipped her head and linked her fingers around her shins.

'Yes,' she said, her voice quiet. 'I want you. So much it's almost…too much to manage. But like I said—' she glanced across the pool towards the waterfall '—I just…can't.'

'Can't, or don't choose to?' He shook his head. 'You suggested I might come to bed with you.'

'I wanted you to, but you were right to refuse. I'm not in a good place.'

The droplets of water on her skin were drying quickly but a trickle still dripped from the ends of her hair across her shoulders. His eyes were drawn to the slight movement as her hands tightened their interlaced grip, just below her knees.

The band of paler skin around her finger had almost disappeared and a piece of the puzzle that was Scarlett clicked into place in his brain.

'What happened, Scarlett?' He kept his voice even and low. 'What did he do to you?'

CHAPTER SEVENTEEN

SCARLETT SQUEEZED HER eyes shut and shook her head. 'You don't need to know.'

'Maybe not. But I'd like you to tell me.' Will bent his legs and propped his forearms on his knees. 'Sometimes talking can help.'

There was bitterness in her quiet laugh. 'Says the man who doesn't talk to his family. Have you ever thought it might help you?'

'I drove what happened between my brother, my parents and me. There is nothing to discuss. But it sounds as if whatever happened to you in the Amazon was out of your control.'

She didn't answer. He was right and she was sure he knew it. She tried to suppress the rising sense of panic she felt, if she allowed her mind to travel back to that place.

'Have you talked to anyone?'

She breathed in, counting, and then out again. Not panicking had kept her alive. She could deal with this.

'No. I haven't. There wasn't anyone…' Her voice wobbled.

'Scarlett.'

It was the way he had of saying her name. It soothed her like a balm, made her relax, and relaxing her guard was the worst thing…

Too late, she felt tears clogging her throat, stinging her eyes. She squeezed her lids together but the scalding tears spilled onto her cheeks.

She scrubbed at them angrily with the heels of her hands, biting her lip to stop it from quivering.

'This is so stupid. I don't cry…'

She didn't hear him move but she felt him beside her. His arm was gentle around her shoulders as he pulled her against him, cradling her head onto his chest. She tried to curl into a ball, but he kept her there, wrapping his legs around her, trapping her between his thighs.

'Scarlett, sweetheart, talk to me. Tell me what happened.'

'I'm sorry…'

'If you apologise again, I may get impatient.'

'I'm saying sorry for crying.'

'Not for kissing me?' He spiked his fingers into her hair, pressing her cheek into his chest. 'Well, if you're not sorry, perhaps we can…'

She gulped in another breath, but her shoulders stopped heaving. She shook her head.

'No, Will. Stop it.' She lifted her head and looked up at him. His eyes were serious, his mouth, which had almost driven her over the edge, was a straight, composed line.

Scarlett shifted until she could lean her back against his chest. He wrapped his arms across her waist and his thighs pressed lightly against hers. She felt safe and protected. She rested the back of her head on his shoulder and felt the brush of his jaw across her temple. She knew that she wanted to tell him.

'We were engaged.'

Will lifted her left hand and ran his thumb over the faint mark on her finger.

'I know.'

'He recruited me to join his research team, so I was already flattered. Then when he paid me attention that was more than professional, I was more flattered still.' She wriggled to get more comfortable. 'I was so, so naïve.'

'Don't beat yourself up, Scarlett. It wasn't your fault.'

'If I hadn't been so desperate to find some sort of security—*stability*—I might have been more clear-sighted. *Strong-willed.*' She huffed out a sigh. 'Marguerite's house had been sold to pay for her care, and I was losing her too, a little more each time I visited. I clung to the first straw that floated past and unfortunately it was Alan. I know now that he'd identified me as someone who could be useful to him in the research field. I'd built up a bit of a reputation…'

'For being good at what you did?'

She nodded. 'He was putting together a team for the Amazon expedition, looking for the orchid I told you about, and he took me with him. I didn't want to go—there were others who deserved the trip more—but he insisted. Then he proposed. Now I think he did it so I wouldn't back out.'

'What made you end it?'

Scarlett chewed her lip, struggling to frame the sentence she'd never spoken out loud.

'He abandoned me in the jungle.'

'So the reports on the internet were true.'

His arms tightened around her, but his chin lifted from the crown of her head. 'Tell me what happened.'

'He left me behind. The team had divided into two and he and I had been trekking for three days. It was tough. Hot, obviously, but so much more than that. He was bad-tempered and critical. Everything either stung or bit. Although, if you could ignore all that, it was very beautiful and so full of energy, teeming with life.'

She could feel his heartbeat against her back and the rise and fall of his breathing, but Will had assumed an absolute stillness.

'Go on.' She felt the words rumble in his chest.

'I found the orchid. I thought he'd be pleased but he seemed angry. He took photos of it, and we mapped its position and then he said we should head back towards the main camp. "Mission Impossible accomplished". Those were his words.'

'Sounds like a pompous bastard.'

She felt his anger in the way his arms tightened around her.

'The rainforest is dense, and so full of noise, it's possible to get disorientated very quickly. I moved on a bit, looking for more flowers, thinking he'd wait for me, and then I couldn't find him, or the orchid. I think he dug it up. He didn't get the memo about taking nothing away and leaving…nothing behind.'

Her body tensed, remembered panic tugging at her. Will lifted a hand and grazed his knuckles across her cheek.

'It's okay.' His voice was rough. 'I've got you. You're safe.'

She swallowed.

'The jungle covers tracks very, very quickly, and the canopy is dense. It's hard to fix on a direction without reference points or the sun. I was lost within minutes.'

'For how long?'

'Six nights.

'I had some biscuits in my backpack and there's an endless supply of water. Because of my botanical knowledge I knew I could eat some of the fruit and plants.'

Will swore.

'I did panic, in the first few hours, but I managed to do one sensible thing, which was to follow a stream flowing downhill. I came to a small settlement where the people were kind and took me to a larger one. From there someone took me upriver, back to the camp. The others weren't surprised to see me. Alan had returned to England, saying I'd chosen to stay in the jungle with some local people for a few days.'

'He'd gone back to England? Presumably to claim the discovery of the plant as his own?'

She shrugged. 'That's what he did. But if he stole it, he can't let anyone else see it. If he did, his reputation in the scientific community would be destroyed.'

'But you haven't let him get away with it? You've reported him?'

'It's his word against mine, and it happened a long way

from English law. He knew I had no family, and it would be a while before my friends began to wonder where I was. And if the question arose, I *had* been with local people. That suited him perfectly. Communication is difficult and sketchy in those conditions. Things get lost in translation. I was never going to be able to prove what he'd done.'

'He hoped he'd never see you again.'

'His wish has been granted. He need never see me again now. But he knows what he did.'

'It sounds as though that won't bother him for a moment. I'd like to…'

'Please don't tell me what you'd like to do to him. I might have nightmares.'

She felt spent, a lethargy creeping over her which she knew came partly from the relief of telling the story. She didn't want to accept that the other part came from the security she found, wrapped in Will's arms, feeling the regular thump of his heart beating with hers. This was a false security. It could never last.

'*Do* you have nightmares?'

'Sometimes I have to sleep with the light on. But now I only have myself to believe in, and I'm determined that I will. I thought he loved me. How could I have got it so wrong?'

Will dropped his cheek onto her hair. When he eventually spoke, his voice was muffled.

'Do you still love him?'

She knew the answer she should give. It was the only logical one, and she felt in the hitch of his breath, as she hesitated, that it was the one he wanted to hear.

'I…don't know if I ever really did. I hate him for what he did. I despise him. Love shouldn't be something you can simply switch off. It has to fade until it turns into something weak that no longer has the power to control or hurt. I thought I loved him, but now I can't even remember how that felt. I think for me he was a convenient safety net and he manipulated me into believing him. I think my judgement is flawed—skewed by my childhood experience of love, or the lack of it. If I can't trust myself, how can I ever learn to trust someone else? And I believe trust has to be a fundamental part of love.'

Will abandoned his desk. He'd given up trying to concentrate on anything constructive, his thoughts filled with the man who had been happy to leave Scarlett in the jungle, perhaps hoping she'd never find her way out. Prepared to destroy her life, her ability to love, her willingness to trust, for the sake of being a footnote in the world of botany.

He found her acceptance of such a shattering betrayal incredible. He'd have wanted to go after the man—Alan—and throw every book at him, legal or otherwise. He'd have wanted to see him brought down.

But, he wondered, how would that have been for Scarlett? It would have dragged her name into the public eye, a sordid case of betrayal for the media to pick over and then discard. Better that she'd left Alan with his small triumph and the corrosive knowledge of what he'd done.

Rozendal had come to her when she'd needed it most. But the visit to the pool high in the mountains had not only been to show it to Scarlett. After his discussions with the engineering company in Cape Town which specialised in hydraulic machinery, he knew the pool and waterfall would serve his purpose perfectly.

If he explained his intentions to Scarlett, would she see his point of view? Harnessing the river would go against all her principles of rewilding and returning the land to its natural state. But the future of Bellevale might stand or fall on the supply of water from Rozendal. The river had never been known to dry up, even in times of drought.

But if he acted on his feelings for her, would he simply be manipulating her into giving him what he wanted? He couldn't do that to her, or to himself.

It was late and very dark when he left the house. The scorching wind had turned chilly, carrying with it the scent of rain.

His nightly walk took him around the edge of the vineyards, past the cellars, the restaurant and the cottages. He narrowed his eyes, looking through the trees towards Vineyard Cottage. A glimmer of light flickered through the restless branches. Was Scarlett sleeping with the light on tonight?

A single thought beat in his brain: was she all right?

The security light came on as he leapt up the steps and knocked on the door.

'Scarlett?'

It could only have been thirty seconds before the door opened, but it felt like for ever.

'Will? What…?'

'It's late and your light was on.'

She stepped back. 'Come in.'

'Are you okay?' His eyes took in her cotton shorts and camisole, pink gingham with a satin bow. His mouth dried. This was a bad idea. Of course she was all right. She'd think he was crazy. And he was, he admitted silently. Crazy for her.

'Not really.'

She'd caught the sun and her cheeks and nose were tinged with pink but beneath that her skin was white. She looked exhausted.

'You look tired. You should be in bed.'

'I might have to remind you that you're bossy, and telling a woman she looks tired is not normally regarded as a compliment.'

'Yeah, you might, but it won't make a damn bit of difference. You look as if you need a good night's sleep.'

Scarlett lifted her arms and bunched her hair in her hands. He tried to keep his eyes from straying down to the narrow band of skin which appeared as the camisole rode upwards.

'I tried sleep. It didn't work out.'

'Any reason why?'

'You noticed the light was on so you know why, Will.' Without warning, she put her hands to her face. 'Will…'

In two strides he had his arms around her. She didn't resist him, falling against him, her arms banding across his back.

'It's okay. I've got you.' He smoothed a hand through the silky length of her hair, resting his cheek on her head, breathing in her scent of flowers and rain.

'It's not okay. I'm afraid to fall asleep. Talking has brought it all back, in HD and Surround Sound. I have my own private IMAX theatre in my head. Every sound I hear takes me back there.' Her voice rose. 'If I put out the light, I hear the jungle closing in on me. I should never have told you about it. I should have kept it locked up, where I didn't have to admit it was true.'

'Scarlett.' He felt the almost imperceptible release of tension in her body. 'I'm so sorry, but I'm glad I saw your light was on.'

'I wanted to call you.'

'Why didn't you?'

'Because I have to manage this on my own.'

'No, you don't. I want to kill him for what he did to you.'

'Thank you, but I don't think that would help.'

'What *would* help?'

She was quiet, then she took a deep breath and spoke. 'You help. You've made me see I can still have fun.'

His fingers followed the line of her spine up her back, exploring. He discovered that her breath stuttered when he found a particular place under her left shoulder blade. His other hand rested on her hip, his thumb tracing a circle over the bone beneath the cotton of her shorts. Her breath had become quick and shallow, feathering over his skin at the vee of his sweater.

The wildness of their earlier kiss had to be contained. He didn't want to frighten her by losing control. And, he told himself, he didn't want to scare himself either.

'Will?'

'Mmm? Tell me how I can help…'

'Kiss me.'

'Scarlett…'

'Please. It'll help…'

She moved a hand from his back and lifted his palm from her hip, drawing it up close to his chest. Her thumb moved over the inside of his wrist.

He felt his restraint dissolving, his willpower falling away, and all that was left was the need to kiss her, absorb her scent, close any gaps that remained between them.

'God, Scarlett,' he breathed. 'Are you sure?'

'Yes.' The word was scarcely more than an exhale. 'When we kiss I forget everything else.'

When their lips met, tentatively, he buried his hands in her hair, holding her head steady. Her eyes were dark with desire, a deep sea-green. Her lips, pink and so soft, parted as his mouth hovered over hers, inviting him in.

It was deep, immediately, as if the previous times had been preliminaries which they could skip now. His tongue probed the astonishing sweetness of her mouth, intimate and explicit. Soft sounds of pleasure and need came from her throat, making him band her to his hard body more tightly.

It wasn't enough. This would never be enough. He slid a hand down her back, slipping his fingers into the waistband of her shorts, and she arched into him.

All thought vanished from his brain except the knowledge that this was what he wanted and the joy that she wanted it too. Her warm skin and silky hair drove him wild. He wanted to bury his face in the russet mass and lose himself in her completely.

Holding her steady, he kissed her still, while one hand roamed her body, eliciting gasps of response and shivers of ecstasy. She felt like molten fire in his arms, hot and dangerous but irresistible.

His hand came to rest on her ribcage and then his palm brushed over her straining breast.

At last, he stopped the kiss. He needed to feel her skin against his, see her perfect body, wanting him. He lifted her arms, gripped the edge of the camisole and pulled it over her head, dropping it on the floor.

For a moment he drank in the sight of her. Her ivory skin glowing in the soft light, the curve of her waist and dip of her navel. Her perfect breasts, rosy tipped. Her lips, red and swollen from his mouth and her eyes, hazy with desire.

'You're the most beautiful thing I've ever seen. Scarlett...'

Then he put an arm behind her knees and lifted her against him. She pulled his head down towards her, fusing her mouth with his, as he carried her to the bedroom.

CHAPTER EIGHTEEN

SCARLET LIFTED HEAVY LIDS. Grey light filtered through the shutters and she heard the muted thrum of rain on the thatch.

It had been raining for three days and nights, ever since she and Will…

She turned her head on the pillow, not surprised to see the space next to her was empty. He left her as dawn broke. He liked to start work early, he said, before the endless interruptions began. She could still feel the weight of his arm across her body.

But he hadn't left, she realised, as she heard a tap running in the bathroom, the clink as he hung up a towel on the metal ring.

A minute later he crossed the dim room and sat on the edge of the bed next to her.

'Hey.'

He bent and kissed her, slowly and thoroughly. She slipped a hand round the back of his neck, her fingers into his hair, raking her nails lightly across his scalp.

He groaned and moved her hand away. 'Enough. I need to go. But I'll see you later. I've booked a table for us in the restaurant tonight.'

Her eyes widened. 'Are you sure? Are we celebrating something?'

'No.' He ran a finger down her cheek, his thumb across her bottom lip. 'But there's something I'd like to talk about.'

'We can make it a celebration of my move.'

'Your move? You're going somewhere?'

'The two weeks are up, Will. I'm moving into Rozendal today.'

'But the thatching isn't finished yet. The rain…' He glanced towards the window. 'Listen to it.'

'It's a beautiful sound, and the house is waterproof under that tarpaulin. Not a drop of rain has found its way in. I've painted my bedroom, the bed has arrived, with my gorgeous new linen, the bathroom and kitchen work, mostly. It's all worked out.'

His jaw tightened and she put a hand against his cheek.

'Stay a bit longer.'

'Two weeks was the deal, Will. I don't want any more favours, remember. Anyway, Vineyard Cottage is probably booked from today.'

He shook his head. 'I booked it for a month, in my name. You can stay.'

Scarlett shuffled up the bed and leaned against the headboard. She tucked the duvet around her as his eyes darkened, fixing on the shadowed dip between her breasts. Desire tightened her abdomen.

'Being able to stay here has been a lifesaver for me, Will, but I want to move. And it is a cause for celebration. It's the first home of my own I've ever had.'

'Yes, I know.' He pulled a hand over the back of his head. 'It's just that…'

'This is convenient for us, I know.' Each night he'd come to her after his late walk, when the rest of the estate was asleep, and he left early. She didn't think anyone else knew they were sleeping together.

To be with her at Rozendal he'd have to drive over, and back. Perhaps he'd no longer want to spend the night in her bed.

She'd told herself that was fine, but now, faced with the reality of it, she felt less certain. The thought of him not being there, warm and responsive, when she woke in the night, made her feel hollow. She loved waking and turning into his arms, finding his mouth, feeling his body respond to her. She loved the way he tucked her against him, his chin resting on her head, as they drifted off to sleep.

How would she cope if it ended? She couldn't begin to imagine. They were so perfect together. Without him, she was afraid she'd never feel complete again.

How had she allowed this to happen?

'Convenient, yes.' He nodded.

'Not romantic.'

'I don't do romantic, Scarlett.'

'I know.'

'That's okay, then.' He smiled, his dimple creasing his freshly shaven cheek. He reached out to run a finger along her skin above the duvet, pausing at the dip in her cleavage. 'Go back to sleep, Scarlett. It's early.' He kissed her forehead. 'I'll collect you at seven-thirty for dinner.'

'From Rozendal.'

Scarlett had spent the day moving into her home.

The house still looked like a building site, but it was dry, and she thought her bedroom was beautiful. She'd painted it a shade of soft white and had a cream carpet laid. Her new bed, dressed in a cream silk valance, had a curved headboard covered in buttoned, pale grey velvet. She'd made it up with the fine cotton sheets and duvet she'd chosen, edged with delicate embroidery. A luxurious velvet throw lay folded across the foot.

Nightstands, lamps and a dressing table were on order, but she was happy to wait for them. Nothing could blunt the excitement of spending her first night at Rozendal.

She'd showered in the ancient bathroom. The water was hot and clean, although the pressure wavered between force eight and a trickle.

On a visit to Franschhoek, choosing paint colours for the drawing room, she'd fallen in love with a green watered silk dress, and now she was glad she'd bought it. Since she would be dining with the owner, she supposed she could wear whatever she liked to The Stable Yard Restaurant, but the occasion felt special enough for her to dress up.

She was waiting on the veranda when the Range Rover pulled up. She watched Will climb the steps towards her and her heart turned over in her chest.

It was hard to believe that this man had shared her bed for the past three nights. She knew the long, sleek planes of his body almost as well as her own. She knew how his shoulders felt beneath her hands, how he liked the feeling of her fingers raking across his back and chest. She could make him gasp with pleasure by kissing him along the collarbone, or groan with need by trailing her fingers across the small of his back.

Their lovemaking was gentle and slow or quick and sometimes a little rough, but he was considerate, always asking if she was all right, calming her with tender kisses when she called his name, and holding her as she fell asleep.

The nightmares had faded; the memories of Alan had shrunk into insignificance. Nothing that had gone before could compare with how she felt in Will's arms.

He reached the top step and wrapped her in a hug, kissing her hair and tipping her face up to move his lips to her mouth.

'Scarlett. You look…breathtaking,' he murmured, between kisses. 'Did you buy that dress to match your eyes, or was that an accident?'

She laughed. 'Did you wear that shirt to match yours?' She slid two fingers between the buttons and scraped his skin, feeling goosebumps roughen the smoothness. 'Oh, your eyes are darker now. Not such a good match.'

'Any more of that and I won't need a shirt at all, because we won't be going to dinner. We'll be going to bed.'

'Mmm. But I'm hungry.'

'So am I, but there're different sorts of hunger.'

'Perhaps we can satisfy them all?' She withdrew her fingers.

'If we're going to have time for that we'd better get started.'

* * *

Grace met them at the entrance to the restaurant.

'I've put you at your usual table, Will.'

She led them past the bar, busy with guests enjoying pre-dinner drinks, to a table in a corner next to a tall window, with a view of the room and of the garden. The vineyards beyond had already faded into the evening light, and the spectacular mountain backdrop was dark against the azure sky.

Scarlett knew the restaurant was famous for its relaxed atmosphere and superb food. The kitchen was visible at one end over a modern granite worktop, but the rest of the interior had a timeless charm, with a terracotta tiled floor, white walls and reminders of the building's original purpose.

'I'm surprised you don't prefer one of those tables.' She looked towards the back wall, where several of the stalls had been converted into private, intimate dining spaces.

Will shook his head, holding her chair for her. 'I like to see who else is here. And this table is quite secluded.'

He closed the menu and handed it back to their server. 'I'll order for both of us.'

'Bossy?'

'No. It's all good.' His eyes met hers, navy blue and filled with intent. 'And…' his voice dropped, warm and smoky '… I know what you like.'

'I might prefer the tasting menu.'

'You can have that later.'

Scarlett had to admit that he was right. The food was delicious, and he'd chosen the perfect pairing of wines.

Will lifted a bottle from the bucket at his elbow and topped up her glass. He raised his own, his eyes intent on her face.

'Here's to my new home,' she said, touching her glass to his. 'Is that what you want to talk about?'

He replaced his glass but kept his fingers on the stem. Scarlett swallowed as she watched them caress the delicate crystal, then she pulled her eyes away, trying to compose her expression.

'In a way, yes.'

Something in his eyes released a curl of unease in her. His gaze was intent on her, but it was because he was watching for her reaction to whatever he was going to say, not because he was remembering how it felt to kiss her or hold her. Some part of him had withdrawn.

She folded her hands in her lap and straightened her spine, leaning away from him.

'What is it, Will? And why do I think I'm not going to like it?'

He lifted his chin, a shadow of surprise flickering in his eyes.

'I'd like,' he said, 'to buy a part of Rozendal.'

The disquiet faded a little. This wasn't news. She'd known it since she'd stepped into the middle of that auction. Was he going to make her an offer he thought she wouldn't refuse? Did he even *know* the size of the fortune Marguerite had left her? Had he not even begun to understand the reasons why she'd never give up Rozendal?

Then the disquiet returned. Did he think sleeping with her for three nights would have made her easier to persuade? She crushed that thought. He was private, difficult to get to know, and complicated, but she didn't think he was manipulative, and she didn't think he could have faked what they'd shared…but then she remembered how she'd asked him to kiss her—made it plain that she wanted him to take her to bed.

I haven't had fun for a long time... she'd said.

For him, had it just been fun?

It had become so much more than fun, for her.

Smoothing the white linen napkin over her knees, she met his steady gaze with her own.

'Only a part of it? I thought you wanted all of it, and me out of the way.' She tried to smile. 'And I thought you never changed your mind?'

* * *

Will felt cornered. That was what happened when you set such categorical boundaries for yourself, he thought, but it was the only way he knew how to live his life. He'd declared he would own Rozendal, but he now had to admit that in Scarlett he'd met his match. She was not going to take the money and run.

She had every reason to stay at Rozendal indefinitely and to put her New Age ideas into practice, when he could be using the land to increase the size of his estate, turn the house into a high-end boutique hotel and restore the boundaries to their original configuration, before one of his feckless ancestors had sold out to one of the du Valois family.

Moreover, the past three nights had seen him break his own unwritten rule, for the first time ever. He'd spent three nights in her bed, and if his brain had told him he was being reckless, compromising his safety for the sake of waking up and finding her in his arms, his body would have told his rational mind to go to hell, because every second had been exquisite, every touch mind-blowing.

She was not in the market for permanence and that suited him just fine. After her experience with her previous partner—her *fiancé*—she'd admitted she'd never trust anyone again; in future she'd only ever depend on herself.

Faced with her absolute determination to carry out her plans, he'd changed tack. *His* plans for Rozendal could be shelved, for a while at least, but he needed the rights to the pool and river.

He had all the facts and figures at his fingertips, and he expressed them fluently and clearly. But he could see stubborn refusal gaining strength in her eyes. What was that she'd said about being strong-minded? Here was the proof.

She listened, but she interrupted him.

'I plan to use the water from the river, and to encourage the natural development of the riverbank, once the invasive plants have been eradicated, Will.' She began to shred a bread roll onto her side plate. 'Your plan doesn't allow for that.'

He had an answer. 'If your estate is truly to be returned to its natural state, you shouldn't use the river for irrigating or watering. You should rely on the seasonal rainfall.'

'The rose garden was famous once, and I intend to make it famous again. I'm not rewilding that; I'm restoring it, like the house. I need the water for the garden. The river has never dried up, ever, and that means I can rely on it.'

'How do you know it's never dried up?'

'One of the elderly men helping me in the garden told me. It's well known amongst the local community that there is always water at Rozendal, even in the most severe drought. I don't intend to change that. The river is not for sale.'

Will felt frustration rising, tightening in a band around his chest, making his jaw ache. He gripped his hands together on the tabletop, hanging onto his temper.

'I don't understand,' he said at last, 'why you want to turn the clock back, impose the past on the present and the future. It's counter-productive…'

'Will.' Her voice was quiet, but he recognised the thread of steel running through it which he'd only heard when she was expressing her passion for the land. 'I'm rescuing species that have thrived here for millennia, but which will disappear in a generation if they're not given the space and conditions they need to grow.' She drew a deep breath. 'Rewilding restores relationships between animals, plants and the environment. I'm not turning my back on science or imposing the past. I'm applying a different science and securing the future.'

'Scarlett.' Her eyes softened a fraction but her body still looked taut as a bowstring. 'You and I…'

He thought he saw a faint tremor in her bottom lip, but her teeth closed over it briefly and her mouth firmed.

'When you asked me to come here for dinner, Will, I thought perhaps it was you and me you wanted to talk about.'

He tried to interrupt her, but she raised a hand. 'No. Let me finish. Please.' She dropped her hand to the tablecloth and his eyes went to the almost invisible evidence of her past trauma. Hot, acid guilt made him look away. 'I thought you might want to discuss how we might…manage…once I'd moved into Rozendal. I'm aware you want to keep our…*us*…a secret. That's fine. It'll be less messy when we decide to end it, if nobody else is aware of it.'

'*End* it? Scarlett, it's not…'

'I don't know what it is, Will. I don't know what's between us. Perhaps we're just two people who need each other at this moment, for different reasons. Neither of us wants a permanent relationship.' She hoped he didn't notice the tremor in her voice. 'But I hope… *I hope…*you haven't thought having sex with me would make me easier to persuade. I enjoy your company. The sex is off the scale, but if it's had any other purpose for you besides enjoying it, your behaviour is little better than Alan's.'

Will pushed a hand through his hair, adrenalin burning through him, trying to find the words to convince her that she was wrong, but his brain had gone into a tailspin and if he didn't find a way to pull it back soon, like in the next few seconds, he was going to crash and burn.

'That's not true,' he grated at last. 'He left you in the jungle. You might have died and never been found.' He tried to take her hand, but she moved it away. 'I would never, ever do anything to hurt you. Being with you is like nothing I've ever experienced before, and I don't only mean being in bed with you.' He wiped a hand over his face, searching for the right words. 'You make me smile. You challenge me. You make me want to…'

'What, Will?'

'You make me want to break all the rules, but I daren't…'

He raised his head, scanning the busy restaurant, hoping nobody would notice the drama playing out in the corner.

Grace caught his eye across the room. She looked anxious and she shook her head, her gaze sliding away from his, to a noisy crowd around the bar.

She set off towards them, weaving quickly between the tables before arriving at theirs.

'I'm sorry, Will. They came in with a group. Their names weren't on the list…'

'Who?' He was aware of Scarlett turning her head to look at him, but he followed Grace's gaze.

His body stilled; every muscle tensed.

'Will? Are you okay? You've gone very white.' Scarlett's voice seemed to come from far away, but he knew she was right there, where he wished he knew she'd stay. But that was unrealistic. Women didn't stay. They grabbed the next, better opportunity and left ruins in their wake.

He'd let her get too close. Dropped his guard and let her in.

'Will?'

He turned to look at her, to tell her they had to leave, and saw her expression change, her look of concern replaced by one of incredulity, and he understood it perfectly. Because coming towards them, his eyes fixed on Scarlett, was his identical twin brother, and behind him was the wife who should have been his.

CHAPTER NINETEEN

UTTER CONFUSION SWAMPED SCARLETT. She felt like an audience of one, watching a play unfold and she didn't understand the plot or even the language.

She saw the moment Will used his iron will to crush his emotions. He stood, every movement spare and controlled, and watched his brother approach.

She rose to stand beside him.

'Will!'

Up close, subtle differences emerged between the two men. Richard was fractionally shorter than Will, and of a lighter, softer physique. There was no evidence of the hard, toned muscle which she knew lay beneath Will's linen shirt. Richard's dark hair was longer, slightly unkempt. But it was his eyes that marked him out as different from his brother. There was no warmth in his ice-blue appraisal.

'Richard.' Will extended his hand for the briefest of greetings. His eyes flicked to the small, curvy woman at Richard's side. 'Melanie.'

'Good to see you, bro. And with a stunning companion…?'

'This is Scarlett.'

Scarlett nodded to them both.

Melanie laughed. 'Scarlett? Well-named.'

'Scarlett and I were just leaving.'

As he moved around the table she entwined her fingers with his.

He turned to look at her. His eyes rested on her face, faintly surprised, and she squeezed his hand tightly. The surprise faded, to be replaced with something that shook her to the core. He held her gaze for seconds and then he turned away, but Scarlett had recognised what she'd seen in his eyes because the connection which had arced between them in that moment was as strong as titanium but gentle as dew.

'Oh…' Richard stepped back. 'I was hoping we could have a chat, Will. Scarlett and Melanie could get to know each other…'

'We have nothing to say to one another, Richard, and Scarlett and Melanie don't need to get to know each other. I doubt they would have anything in common.'

Scarlett felt him urging her close to his side. He untangled his fingers from hers and clamped his arm around her waist, walking her towards the door.

It had all taken less than two minutes. Was that enough time for her whole world to have changed?

Grim-faced, his knuckles white on the steering wheel, Will brought the Range Rover to a jerky stop in front of Rozendal. The rain had begun to fall again, sifting down in drenching sheets.

'Would you like to come in?'

Will shook his head.

She jumped from the car and raced up the steps, out of the rain. He hadn't uttered a word since leaving the restaurant and she didn't expect him to follow her. He needed time to gather himself, she thought. He needed space.

She didn't understand the extreme animosity between him and his brother. She longed to hold him, to try to soothe him, but she would hold back—let him come to her when he was ready.

'Scarlett.' The strain in his voice tore at her heart. She turned, ready to take him in her arms.

His expression stopped her in her tracks, stealing her breath. Her heart began to hammer at her ribs.

'Will? What's wrong?'

He shook his head, then pushed his damp hair off his forehead. 'I'm sorry.'

'Sorry? It wasn't your fault. You didn't know...'

'No, I'm sorry for this. For us.'

Her disquiet swelled into something much more dangerous. Fear lapped at her, like a malevolent tide. She'd vowed no man—no other person—would ever again wield power over her emotions. What didn't kill you made you stronger, and she was alive. She was the independent woman Marguerite had exhorted her to be. Wasn't she?

But what she'd seen in Will's eyes had destroyed all that. It had been the briefest flash, but she'd seen it and she'd known she was lost.

'What about us?' Her voice came out as a whisper.

'I haven't been honest with you, Scarlett.' He pushed his hands into his pockets and moved back a step. 'I might have let you think there was something between us, and I'm sorry if I've misled you.'

'*Misled* me? How?'

'I thought I might be able to convince you to sell to me—first the whole estate, but then the pool and water rights.' He shrugged, the movement of his wide shoulders brief, and she wondered how he could be so cool, when her heart was being ripped to shreds.

'That's all you wanted?' Her hands hurt as she twisted them together.

His eyes were devoid of emotion, his mouth set. That mouth...

'Yes.'

Her head snapped back, as if he'd hit her. She wouldn't think about his mouth ever again. Or his hands, or...

Her silk dress was spattered with raindrops, and she shivered with cold. She bit her bottom lip, hard, the hurt helping her to focus on something other than his crushing words. She stared at him.

'You said I'd be lying if I denied there was anything between us, Will, and I don't know why you're denying it now. You weren't quick enough to hide your true feelings. I saw, and I don't believe you. It's you who's being untruthful, to me and to yourself.'

Will drained his glass. He'd lost count of how many shots of whisky he'd drunk, and he didn't care.

His head throbbed with fatigue, but the alcohol had neither numbed his pain, stilled his fear or knocked him out.

It would be a waste of a good hangover.

He was waiting for the light to begin to silver the dark sky behind the mountains. Then he'd take a shower, cold if he could bear it, drink black coffee, as hot as possible, and, as soon as the time was civilised, he'd go to Rozendal.

He'd tried to blank her agonised expression from his mind, without success. He'd chosen each word to crush her, and he thought he'd succeeded. But then she'd accused him of lying.

How could she see into his soul with such clarity when his own perception of things was so muddled? He cursed Richard and Melanie for showing up at the one restaurant in the Cape where they were explicitly unwelcome. But he despised himself for not handling the encounter with more dignity. He should be able to dismiss them with the lack of regard and attention they deserved.

He hated the thought that Scarlett had seen his reaction, and he intended to attempt to explain it to her. If she was going to judge him, she needed, at least, to have all the facts.

At eight-thirty he pulled up outside Rozendal, parking amidst the builders' trucks and decorators' vans. Rain dripped at a steady rate off the giant tarpaulin covering the house and the steps looked slippery. He should warn Scarlett…

Scarlett, he thought, would dismiss his warning with contempt.

She stood outside the broad front door. The brass handles she'd polished with such enthusiasm shone. She wore jeans and a jacket and her hair was in a neat French braid. A set of car keys jingled in one hand, and she held the handle of her small cabin bag in the other.

Shock punched him in the gut. He tried to breathe in, but oxygen seemed to be in short supply.

'What are you doing here, Will?'

'Why? I… You're going away. Where to?'

'I don't know why it concerns you. I'm sure you'll be pleased not to have me around.' She took a step forward. 'I'm going to England.'

'*England?* Why?'

'For some reason I was having trouble sleeping and I checked my emails early this morning. My father is ill.'

'You're going to see your parents? But I thought you had no contact with them…'

'I've always made sure they could contact me if necessary, and now they have.'

'That's outrageous. All these years…everything you've been through, and they've never supported you. Yet you get one email and you're going…'

'They're my parents, Will, and they have nobody else. I'm going to see if I can help them. I'm grateful that I can.'

Will propped himself against the balustrade. 'I think you're crazy.'

'What you think doesn't matter. I'm doing what's right for me. Possibly you should try reaching out to your family, instead of perpetuating an argument you've already won.'

Anger, hot and damaging, coursed through his veins. He folded his arms to stop himself from punching the wall.

'Scarlett, you have no idea what you're talking about.'

'Well, try explaining it to me then, Will.' She glanced at her watch. 'You have approximately five minutes.'

Will swallowed, at a loss as to how to do this. The words to articulate exactly what had happened were buried deep inside him. They'd never been used. He had to dig deep. Breathing was suddenly painful, his constricted lungs unwilling to expand.

'She was going to marry me. Melanie. We were engaged.'

The words hung between them, out in the universe for ever. Watching the colour drain from Scarlett's face should have given him a scrap of satisfaction but it made the hurt worse.

'Oh, Will. I'm… That's shocking. I'm so sorry.'

'Don't be,' he snapped. 'I'm grateful not to be married to someone who could do what she did.'

'Yes…yes, I think you should be.' She stepped forward, putting out a hand towards him, but he flinched away, out of her reach. 'What happened?'

'I…' He rubbed his burning eyes, raw from lack of sleep, wishing he could leave now, and not go through with saying this. 'I'd taken ownership of Bellevale. It took two years to get into shape, to be able to start planning to expand, open the restaurant, convert the cottages. Melanie is an events organiser, and she came to look at it with a view to using it as a wedding venue.'

'You don't do weddings.'

'We don't. She fell in love with the idea of the place—its romantic past, the old buildings, even older oaks. She decided the first showcase wedding, which would attract dozens of other would-be couples to tie the knot, would be ours. I was sucked into it. I was working eighteen-hour days, seven days a week, to get the vineyards productive, to become successful. Success has always been my goal. I've always had to win.' He shook his head. 'Sometimes I wish I was less competitive. I didn't notice that Melanie was growing dissatisfied. She'd met Richard in Cape Town and decided life with him would be a lot more fun than with me. He had the money and didn't have to work. I was determined to make Bellevale a huge success and never stopped long enough to see it wasn't the life she'd envisaged, as my wife.'

Scarlett nodded. Her teeth were fastened, hard, on her bottom lip. He wanted to reach out and run his thumb over her mouth, tell her to stop it, but he could no longer claim that privilege.

'She and Richard married at what should have been her wedding to me. She said she refused to let all that organisation go to waste. It was the first and last wedding to be held at Bellevale.'

'Will, I'm sorry. I should have realised there was a good reason behind your estrangement from your family. Your parents…?'

'Couldn't see what the fuss was about. From the time Richard was born, seventeen minutes before me, he'd always come first. That's why I always have to win. Coming second at anything is never good enough. I hope seeing your parents brings you some closure. Just don't judge me for not seeing mine.'

He fixed his eyes on her face, trying to imprint all its details on his memory. Her beautiful amber hair; her eyes that changed from emerald in the sunshine to deepest forest in his arms at night; her full bottom lip which felt like peach blossom under his thumb and tasted like honey on his tongue; the ivory skin of her throat, where that pulse reacted so swiftly to his touch.

Then he stepped back.

'Will?'

'Yes?'

'Do you still love her?' Her voice was unsteady.

He knew the words which would keep him safe. If he said them, he'd drive her away for ever, and that was what he needed to do. But she'd already accused him once of lying and he knew he had to be honest.

'No,' he said. 'I realised last night that I never had.'

CHAPTER TWENTY

SCARLETT LEANED AGAINST the sink. Grey rain lashed the windows and cold seeped up through the tiles under her feet. The mountain had almost disappeared under a thick layer of cloud.

She pressed the heels of her hands into her eye sockets, trying to relieve the ache of fatigue. Getting her parents settled into their assisted living apartment and putting their cottage on the market had been stressful. The journey to London from Yorkshire had been long, and even though the overnight flight had felt interminable she had dreaded arriving.

But now that she was here she needed to contact Will as quickly as possible. She wanted to control the situation, not dread bumping into him by chance. She did not want to see him at all, but she had to tell him how she felt, whatever the outcome. She pulled her phone from her bag and scrolled through it, then she took a deep breath and unblocked his number. She'd bring in her luggage and then she'd call him.

Her phone beeped as she stepped back through the door. His name on the screen confused her. How did he know she was back? She'd told nobody she was coming home. She read the message and her hands began to shake. He'd tried repeatedly to contact her, he said. He was trying this last time before leaving for the airport, on his way to find her in England.

Scarlett looked at the time and picked up the car keys, her heart racing. She'd be too late to stop him if he really was leaving immediately. But she might be able to catch up with him at the airport. Her fatigue forgotten, she ran out onto the veranda and down the slippery steps.

The road to Bellevale was awash. It looked as if the rain hadn't stopped since she'd left, a month ago. She groaned in frustration as she had to slow down to negotiate a flood where the river went under the bridge. Then she accelerated, not caring if she hit a hidden pothole or skidded around a corner. She swung the car between the white gateposts and continued up the drive between the avenue of oaks.

The Range Rover stood in front of the homestead and she exhaled. Then she thought he might have taken a taxi, or Grace might have driven him. The car slewed to a stop on the sodden gravel and she flung herself out of it, up the steps and through the front door.

'Scarlett?' He looked more shocked than she felt. 'What are you doing here?'

'I…got your message.'

'I'm…' He pulled a hand over his face in the gesture she had grown to love in a few short weeks. 'When did you arrive?'

'This morning.' She moved further into the hall. A suitcase stood at the door, a jacket on top of it.

'I've been trying to contact you…'

'If you'd like me to go…'

'You didn't answer your phone or pick up messages.'

'I blocked your number.'

'Grace wouldn't tell me how to find you. Nor would your lawyers. I practically begged.'

'I'm glad to hear they listened to me. Only I didn't ask Grace…'

'She said I should leave you alone and you'd contact me if you wanted to.'

'Good advice. What did you want to say to me?'

'That you were right.'

'I thought that was your prerogative. Aren't you always right?'

'Scarlett, please…just listen to me?'

She felt as though she was held together by a single thread which was in imminent danger of snapping and allowing her to unravel in an untidy and messy heap at Will's feet.

'Okay. I'm sorry. I'm tired and…' She wanted to add that she was sad. That the past month had been the hardest of her life. That her heart had lurched every time she remembered a snatch of conversation they'd had or glimpsed a bottle of Bellevale wine on a supermarket shelf. Who knew there were so many ways in which she could remember him, and every one hurt.

'You were right. I lied, because I was afraid. I thought I was immune, after what happened with Melanie and Richard. I thought no one could ever get past my guard. I was determined never to let anyone close to me, so that I could never be hurt or humiliated again. I'd fought against being second-best all my life, and I'd finally achieved what I wanted. Then Melanie and Richard…'

'It was a double betrayal, Will. I don't know how you deal with something like that.'

'You were betrayed in a much worse way, yet you didn't want revenge. And you owed your parents nothing, yet when they needed you…' He took a step towards her. 'You enchanted me, Scarlett. I wanted to be with you and then I realised I was in too deep. It terrified me. I'd broken all my own rules and I was spinning out of control. I deliberately set out to hurt you, to drive you away, because that was the only way I could see of protecting myself. It was cowardly and unforgivable and if you never want to see me again I'll understand, but I need you to know how sorry I am.'

'Will, I knew you were lying because of what I saw in your eyes that night. My whole world turned upside down because I knew I'd broken my own rules too, by falling in love with you. I never wanted to depend on anyone else ever again, but

I knew at that moment that we were soulmates and without you I'd always feel incomplete. When you told me you only wanted the water rights, my heart broke. I knew it wasn't true and that you were afraid of what had happened between us, but you wouldn't let me help you.'

Somehow, his arms were around her in an embrace so tight she could scarcely breathe. She was content to listen to his heartbeat through the soft sweater against her cheek, but he tipped her chin up. His mouth brushed her forehead and he kissed her temple, spreading his hands across her back.

'Scarlett,' he muttered into her hair, 'look at me.'

Her lids fluttered up. His gaze was dark—the dark blue of the deep ocean—and what she saw in it made her catch her breath.

'Yes,' she said, putting a hand to his cheek. 'That's what I saw, and that's how I feel. I love you, Will. I never thought I'd be able to say those words to anyone again, but saying them to you is so easy.'

His mouth took hers then, in a kiss as deep and passionate as the ones which had haunted her dreams. He cupped her face in his hands to keep her steady, until he broke the contact and cradled her cheek against his chest.

'I've missed you so much. I've missed everything about you. Your smile and the joy of hearing you laugh, the feel of your hair through my fingers, your warmth, your scent. I promised myself if I ever got the chance I'd ask you what it is, so I need never be without a reminder of you.'

Scarlett smiled up at him. 'It's called Je Reviens. And I have come back.'

'If you'll give me your heart, I'll mend it so it's stronger than before and I'll take care of it for ever. Being without you has been unbearable, my love. I thought I'd lost you for ever, but now that you're back I don't ever want you to leave again.'

Scarlett reached up to touch his cheek. 'My heart belongs to you. I didn't know it until that night at the restaurant, but I'd already given it to you.'

* * *

Much later, Scarlett turned in his arms and rested her head on his chest. Will tucked her into his side, sliding his hand under the duvet and resting it on her stomach. Her skin quivered under his touch. He dropped a kiss onto her head.

Scarlett lifted her hand and raked her fingers across his chest, and he groaned.

'Please don't ever stop doing that. And please stay.'

'I intend to. Rozendal is my home.'

'I meant here, at Bellevale. All night. Every night. Always.'

'Isn't that breaking all the rules?'

'I love you.' He kissed her shoulder. 'And with you there are no rules because my love is unconditional. I don't want to be apart from you ever again. Will you marry me, Scarlett?'

Scarlett pushed herself upright and turned to look at him.

'Will…'

He pulled her down onto his chest, hooking a leg across her thigh, spearing his fingers into her hair. 'Please say yes.'

She bent her head. 'Yes,' she whispered into his mouth. 'Yes.'

* * * * *

CONSEQUENCE OF THEIR PARISIAN NIGHT

MICHELE RENAE

MILLS & BOON

CHAPTER ONE

"ABSOLUTELY NOT!"

The woman who'd flatly refused Sebastian's proposal and shoved the engagement ring he had just shown her back in his face, grabbed the car door handle and opened it. She thrust out a designer-shoe-clad foot toward the curb and then turned to look over her shoulder to waggle a finger in his face.

"You, Sebastian Mercier, are a rogue. You don't want to marry me because you love me. You just want to control your family's company. And I will not be bought. Oof! Men!"

With that, she fled the limousine in a rage of silk and silvery sequins, a burst of fluffy white marabou fluttering in her wake.

Sebastian leaned back and closed his eyes. That had been his second failed proposal in a six-month period. And he'd thought finding a wife would be easy!

Apparently, a man with money, a luxe Paris home and social connections to everyone who was anyone wasn't motivation enough to entice a *yes* from a woman.

Well, he wasn't an imbecile. Women required an emotional commitment. A sparkly ring was not sufficient incentive.

He'd had to give it a go. He and Amie had dated for three weeks. Had seen each other every day. Had enjoyed great sex. As a fashion influencer followed by tens of millions, Amie had been a perfect candidate to step into the role of his wife. His family approved of her old money and fashion connections.

But…after a recent media leak, the competition between him and his brother, Philippe, was no longer secret. And such information tended to matter to some, especially if it affected their future. And their heart.

The refusal did not upset him as much as expected. He hadn't been in love. Nor, he suspected, had Amie. Theirs had been an affair of passion. Love must not intrude on such a cold business transaction. Love and the emotional attachment that came along with it must not interfere in his quest to find a bride.

Will you marry me and have my child so I can then take control of the family company?

Besides, what did love even feel like?

He'd try again when the opportunity presented itself. He must. Philippe must not win. He'd regroup and begin the wife search again after—well, after a good, stiff drink. A man did have a right to mourn his loss, didn't he?

Tucking the ring box away in his suit coat pocket, he leaned across the seat to grab the open door when a woman's shout—in English—called for him to hold the door.

A stunning vision sprinted toward the limo. A floaty pale pink dress dazzled with glints and sparkles. And wearing that lovely creation was a beautiful blonde with arms spread in a plea to wait as she neared.

Sebastian leaned back just as the blonde plunged inside the car, changing the very air with her arrival. He felt suddenly lifted, and curious. She shoved a heap of purse—and some sort of clothing—onto his lap, blew out a panting breath, grabbed the door and closed it.

"Drive!" she demanded of his driver with the pound of a dainty fist against the seat. "Please! He's chasing me!" She swiped a dash of wavy hair from her eyes and her panicked look took him in. "I'm so sorry, but could you…just drive me a few blocks from here? There's a man. He's after me."

Gorgeous, pale blue eyes surrounded by the lushest black lashes frantically met his. "Someone is after you? Whom do I have to fight for your honor, my lady?"

"It's the photographer. He took off after me because I kicked him in the—"

Still panting from what must have been a high-speed run, she patted her chest. His protective instincts in high gear, Sebastian glanced out the back window. No sign of the perpetrator. He nodded to the driver to pull away. Why not play along with this interesting insertion of feminine audacity into the evening?

Her huffing breaths settled a bit as she nodded and patted his hand. "Thank you. I'll get out soon. I just need to put some distance between us."

"If you are in trouble…"

"You'd fight for my honor?"

"But of course, mademoiselle. My limo is at your disposal."

"I'll take a rain check on that fight. But don't think I won't forget the offer."

"Anything for a damsel in distress."

Her worried moue crinkled into a smile. Freckles that dotted her entire face got lost in a few of those crinkles. Cute.

"This is your limo? Oh, dash it. I'm really sorry about all this."

"Don't apologize. I've never had the opportunity to rescue a damsel before. This one will look good on my résumé, eh?"

She laughed and shook her head. “Oh, it will.”

“If I may ask, why the kicking of something or other and the resultant dash?”

“Well.” She smoothed out the sparkly skirt. “My girlfriend gave me a princess photo shoot as a treat,” she said. “Because of the breakup, you know. I dated Lloyd for six months. I thought for sure he was going to propose. So that night at the fancy restaurant I asked if he wanted to have kids and he laughed. Hated kids! Can you believe it?”

Sebastian wasn’t sure if she was angling for an answer or some kind of affirming gesture. But he didn’t have time to shrug as she continued her breathless ramble. It seemed her fear was streaming out in words, and he wasn’t about to stop her, especially since she was already fearful of one man.

“And then!” she continued dramatically. “Lloyd confessed he’d slept with my flatmate, who was also my boss at the flower shop. Who—let me tell you—had the audacity to insist I move out of our flat while *they* were away on vacation.” She paused, winced. “Sorry. Too much information? Probably. I’m frazzled. Anyway! I was so excited about the photo shoot. It was a means to forget about that awful breakup. And this dress is so posh…” She spoke as quickly as he suspected she must have been running. “And look at my makeup and hair. I look like a princess, right?”

He nodded, unable to resist a smile. A princess with freckles and looking more like an imp lost in a glamorous world that was perhaps not her natural habitat. But what did he know? If she truly had been in danger, he was just thankful she’d jumped into the back of his car.

Azalea was rambling! It was a bad habit that always swooped upon her when she was nervous. Or afraid, as the case was. Though her fears were reduced knowing they were driving away from the scene of the crime. And the man sitting next to her seemed quite gentlemanly. So handsome. His dark hair was short but looked as though it deserved a good finger tousle. A sharp jawline and the hint of stubble suggested an elegance that matched the fitted black suit. Was that a glint of diamond on his cuff links? His look said corporate raider with a softer touch of international jewel thief. She loved a good heist movie with a charming rogue robber. And his eyes held genuine concern. Offering to rescue the damsel?

Yes, please!

"I can't imagine a life without kids and family, you know? I love children!" Azalea added, because she didn't want the man to think she was totally off her rocker.

Just stop rambling, then!

She nodded to her inner thoughts. Yes, shut up. And perhaps they'd driven far enough by now?

"Children are lovely," he offered with a bemused tone. "You seem to have calmed a bit. I hope the photographer did not do anything untoward?"

"Well." She sighed heavily. "He made terrible, lewd remarks. And he touched me! Not where a girl wants to be touched by a stranger, either. So I panicked."

It had all gone knees up when that sleazy photographer had slipped his mitts up under her skirt, insisting he was making an adjustment—and then he had gone too far.

Azalea had reacted. Her father had taught both her and her sister, Dahlia, if they ever felt unsafe around a man to kick first, ask questions later. And forget questions, actually. Just run. Which she had done.

"My dad taught me self-defense. My kicking skills are excellent. Got him right where it counts. Then I grabbed my stuff. And…"

She leaned back and blew out a breath. She'd made it away safely. Thanks to some quick thinking and maintaining her wits. Yet now the adrenaline rushing through her system made her jittery and she just wanted to go somewhere and cry.

No. She was stronger than that. Find a hotel to stay the night, and text Maddie about never recommending that photographer again, and then head back to Ambleside in the morning. The day had been a bust. No princess day for Azalea Grace, after all.

On the other hand, she had run into a rescuing knight.

"Tell me where they are and I'll take care of them both," Sebastian offered.

She shook her head. "I wish you had been around a few weeks ago when Lloyd broke it off. Oh, and now. I just… want to forget about this day." She grabbed her stuff from his lap. "Sorry. I've been rude. I'll pay you for the ride."

"No apologies necessary. What matters is that you are all right."

"I'm good."

"Can I drop you somewhere?" he asked.

"I…uh…was going to rent a hotel room for the night. My girlfriend and I spent the afternoon together. It was so good to see Maddie again. We grew up together. She headed to Paris the moment we finished our A levels. Anyway, she gave me a coupon for a hotel in the tenth arrondissement, I believe. It's in my purse somewhere." She began to dig inside her bag. "What an awful way to end what should have been a perfect day. I'm just…ooh, I need a drink, actually."

"I was just thinking much the same before you graced me with your presence. I have a proposal for you," he said.

"Yeah? Does it involve alcohol?"

"It could. It may also involve decadent treats and tiny hors d'oeuvres."

The way he said that, with a hint of a tease, made her smile. And nothing about him screamed lecher. The expensive suit—and his elegant manners—also made her want to hear more regarding this proposal. Instinctively, she felt he was someone she could trust.

She shoved her purse aside and leaned an elbow on the armrest "I'm listening."

"I was on my way to a party. Until my date…"

"I saw the woman leaving this car! I thought she was being left off by a cab. She was your date?"

"Yes, but no longer. We had…"

"A bit of a row?"

"Something like that. Heartbreak." He winced. Heartbreak could only mean they must have broken something off. Poor man. He needed a hug as much as she did.

"I suspect you want to forget your troubles?" he asked.

"I do."

"And while I sympathize for what you've just experienced, I wonder if a little dancing and champagne might lift both of our spirits?"

"I do like champagne. And dancing. And you mentioned tiny hors d'oeuvres?"

"I did indeed. I should not be so bold as to press you to join me. I am a stranger."

"That you are."

He offered his hand for her to shake. "Sebastian Mercier."

The warmth of his hand clasping hers sent a delicious shiver across her shoulders. Her rescuing knight even smelled good, like vanilla and cedar. Azalea had always prided herself on being a good judge of animals. Were they wild, persnickety, trusting or fearful? Judging people was a little hit-or-miss for her. And yet, there was nothing about the man that sent up a warning flag for her. They were comrades in broken hearts.

"Azalea Grace," she said.

"After the flower? It suits you."

"Thanks. My friends call me Lea."

"Would you like to spend a few hours with me in an attempt to forget our troubles? You are dressed for the soiree."

She smoothed a palm over her bespangled skirt. "This dress doesn't belong to me. I'll have to return it. Oh, how do I dare? I can't set foot in that studio again."

"I can see to its return. After the party. You've clothes here?"

She sighed and rifled through the tangled clothing on her lap. "Looks like I only grabbed my jeans during my quick getaway."

"No worries. I will make sure you are properly clothed before the dress is returned. But right now, there's the party."

"I thought it was a soiree?"

"Same thing. Basically. Are you in or out?"

As she let her gaze wander over his face, she exhaled, her shoulders relaxing. Sebastian was not of the same ilk as the man she'd just run from. He was a gentleman. He'd even offered to defend her honor. No man had ever done such a thing. And while she was not so stupid as to be won over by a handsome face and charming manners, the man was also heartbroken and probably felt as rough as she did. What terrible woman had been so cruel to break it off with this gallant knight?

A few hours at a fancy soiree? Her heart leaped before her brain could caution her.

"I'm in," she announced with an effervescent lilt to her tone. "Let's party!"

CHAPTER TWO

AZALEA WASN'T SURE what fantasy world she had entered since plunging into the back of the limo, but she was going along for the ride. Literally. And seated beside a sexy Frenchman wearing an impeccable suit, who kept giving her a smile and a nod? The smolder in his eyes was making parts of her shiver. And in a very good way.

The day had started well. She had been moping over the breakup with Lloyd for weeks, so Maddie had decided to grab her by the fetters and toss her back into life. Before the photo shoot, she and Maddie had done lunch, and then strolled the Jardin du Luxembourg, chatting about their jobs, men and life. Tears had fallen as Azalea had rehashed her recent breakup with Lloyd Cooper. She had genuinely expected him to propose that night at the ritzy restaurant. And to prepare, she'd determined that she must know how he felt about having children before she could answer such a question as a marriage proposal. She'd casually mentioned children over the first course. Lloyd's answer had stunned her. What sort of monster thought children wild and unsuitable for a proper lifestyle?

Then, her heart had crashed. Lloyd had shoved aside his plate and said he couldn't wait one moment longer. He had to confess. He'd hooked up with the woman who owned the flower shop where Azalea worked. The very woman who was also her flatmate! Lloyd had had the audacity to insinuate Azalea was unsophisticated. And she would never fit into his lifestyle, implying that she was a simple farm girl unfit for his important London friends. He and his new lover—her boss!—were headed to Greece the next day for a holiday. They'd insisted Azalea vacate the flat while they were away. So she'd packed her things and trundled home to Ambleside to stay with her dad on the family farm until she could figure out her next step. Finding a new job. And reclaiming her tattered heart.

Why did she always make the wrong choices? If it wasn't a haircut with a seventies-style fluff, it was a horrible spur-of-the-moment lipstick purchase. Why had she thought the eggplant would work against her pale complexion? And had she ever dated a man who hadn't wanted to change her in some way? Even Ralph Madding, the chicken farmer down the road, whom she'd dated when she was nineteen, had complained about her independence. Told her that he required a woman to cook, clean, and have babies with him.

She had nothing against cooking and cleaning. It was the *expectation* of such things that rubbed her the wrong way. Why couldn't men simply exist alongside women and allow them their space while also embracing them? Was that too much to ask?

A night in Paris with a sexy Frenchman she had only met moments earlier? Talk about busting out of her unsophisticated norm! She intended to end this miserable day with a bang.

This dress felt like fairy tissue sprinkled with stardust. The pale pink chiffon floated and was topped overall with a layer of silver-star-bedazzled mesh. Her long, wavy blond hair had been swept up and pinned with sparkling clips to match the stars on the gown. Her makeup was subtle and hadn't succeeded in covering her freckles. And the makeup artist had given her the perfect lip color. Hot pink. Who would have guessed!

Despite growing up on a farm and embracing her inner tomboy, she loved a girlie outfit and the chance to play princess.

She cast a sneaky glance at the seemingly very kind man who sat next to her on the back seat. He could turn out to be another sleaze. But no, she suspected he wasn't. How many men offered to fight for a woman's honor after knowing her for only a few minutes? She'd be cautious of his smolder, though. Those sexy bedroom eyes and devilishly coiffed dark hair melted bits of her.

She couldn't make two bad choices in one day. The odds must be in her favor!

The car arrived at a fancy building that featured an actual red carpet stretched from curbside and up a flight of stairs to the front doors, where neon lights flashed and music bounced out.

Funny, she'd always thought soirees were more refined, and possibly included tea.

"What kind of party is this?" Now a little nervous, she gripped the door handle. Paris was not her usual stomping ground. She didn't even speak the language. Hobnobbing with an elite crowd was not her style, but a rave or something wild like that would also set her off-kilter.

"A launch bash for Jean-Claude's latest perfume release. It'll be fun."

She liked perfume. And yet. "It looks fancy. Are there celebrities in there?"

Sebastian shrugged. "Probably." When he leaned closer, she inhaled the exotic vanilla and cedar. It tickled at her nerves and softened them. The man was teasingly edible. "I dare you," he offered.

What was it the French declared when taken by something wonderful? *Mon Dieu! Oh, mon Dieu*, this man's eyes. And his smooth baritone voice.

What had he said? Oh, right. He'd *dared* her to go into the party.

Much as whatever waited beyond the red carpet was probably far out of her league, and as unsophisticated as she might be, Azalea wasn't about to be taken down again today. This choice would not blow up in her face. And she wanted to get her mitts all over the promised champagne. And the food. She was hungry! And if opportunity presented, she wouldn't refuse a dance or three.

"Sebastian, right?"

He nodded. "At your beck and call all night, mademoiselle. It'll be fun. Promise."

A promise from a Frenchman wielding a smile that could lure her between the sheets was the most exciting thing she'd ever experienced. She took his hand. And he led her up the red carpet. At the door, a bouncer in dark sunglasses nodded to Sebastian and ticked something on the list he held. If Lloyd could see his little farm girl now!

The ballroom was vast and set in an old building that was tiled, columned, buttressed and everything else one could imagine from ancient architecture. Probably kings and queens had danced across the elaborate marble-tiled floor. The high, curved ceiling featured stained glass Art Deco designs. Mylar streamers, colorful balloons and shimmery fabric hung everywhere. The crowd was dressed to the nines. Diamonds and jewels dazzled.

And… Azalea noticed a lush perfume hanging like an invisible fog over it all. Must be the perfume being launched at the party. It smelled expensive and sweet, like candy.

Then she noticed the word hung overhead, dashed in bold pink neon. *"Câlin?"* she asked.

"It means a hug or something like a cuddle," Sebastian explained. "An odd choice, really, since we French are not keen on hugs. It is the name of the perfume."

"No hugs, eh?"

She imagined wrapping her arms around Sebastian's wide shoulders, fitting her body against his tall figure, and bowing her head against his shoulder, but a kiss away from his alluring mouth. He deserved a hug for rescuing her. As a balm to his own heartbreak. But she didn't want to scare him away—the French weren't keen on hugs?—so she offered up her pinky finger crooked before him.

His quizzical look made her giggle.

"Pinkie hug," she explained. "In honor of the perfume."

He twined his pinkie with hers. Could he contain that smolder that involved a sexy quirk up on one side of his mouth and a soft gaze, or was it a natural movement? "I fear we will both reek of expensive perfume even after leaving."

"It's very nice."

"Smells like something you could eat, yes?"

She nodded her head to the catchy music. "Yes, they must be pumping it into the air. Whew!"

Time to forget her troubles. Forget Lloyd. And the photographer wouldn't be manhandling anything but his private bits for a while. She was here to party.

"Would you like champagne?" Sebastian asked loudly so she could hear over the noise.

"Not yet. I need to dance!"

When she grabbed his hand, he followed her to the center of the ballroom. They insinuated themselves in a spot where they could get their dance on. Three or four songs passed while Azalea's energy soared. Movement always lifted her spirits. The man whom she had literally dragged onto the dance floor showed no signs of wanting to slow down. Undoing the buttons on his suit coat, he countered her moves with some surprisingly rhythmic moves of his own.

When had a man ever matched her silly dance floor energy? Certainly, Lloyd hadn't been able to deflate his pompous upper lip long enough to actually let loose. And despite Sebastian's fancy suit, the diamonds glinting at his cuffs, and what she guessed must be a ridiculously expensive haircut, he danced as if he didn't care what the world thought of him. He'd been dumped by the woman who had fled the back of the limo? Poor guy. They both needed this night.

Grabbing her hand, he twirled her a few times. They developed a dance language with some hip bumping, slides and spins. Azalea laughed and tilted back her head, lifting her arms to become the music.

When the music slowed, she spun and caught her palms against Sebastian's chest. The lights dimmed as the DJ announced a romantic interlude and they swayed beneath the constellation of glimmering party decorations. His cologne tangled with the sweet, perfumed air. Heady and delicious. She inhaled, drawing him into her pores. A girl could lose herself in a moment like this. And maybe she already had.

Something about the enchanting Frenchman reached inside her and tickled her battered heart. Offered some hope. Even a breathless dare to try again. Might she have a fling with a stranger? It sounded brazen and taboo to her practical heart. But it felt…like something she deserved. A one-night stand? She'd see where the evening led them.

"Are you having a good time?" he asked.

"The best!"

She held up her pinkie and he linked his about hers. "Me as well."

"You're not sorry you're here with someone other than the person you intended to bring here?"

"Not in the least. I've already forgotten her name. You are a spitfire of dance moves and freckles. I could fall in love with you, Azalea Grace."

She laughed, tilting back her head, and he spun her out. Twirling back to hug up against him again, she shook her head and said, "Fall in love all you wish. I would never marry you."

"No worries, my family would never—erm. Why is that?"

His family wouldn't approve of her. That was what he had almost said, but had realized his faux pas. Didn't matter to her. She knew they were not in the same social class. This was just one night. Nothing would spoil it.

She wiggled her shoulders, then shrugged. "Marriage isn't in the cards for me." Because—much as she craved a family of her own—she'd been hurt by expecting it to happen. And really? She, married to this fancy, obviously wealthy, man? A ridiculous dream. She must not be crushed twice. Or ever again. "But you know what my next goal is?"

"Do tell."

"Champagne!"

Hours into the party, Sebastian was on his third glass of champagne, as was Azalea. Lea was what she'd said her friends called her. He'd shortened her name to Zee. He was feeling the alcohol, but not drunk. His senses were sharp and acutely aware of every brush of her skin against his, each sweet smile she cast his way, and her bodacious laugh that seemed to birth from her belly and echo out and spread like the crystal stars suspended over their heads.

This night was multitudes better than he'd expected it to be. And he had expected to be engaged right now.

"Do you know all these people?" she asked as they stood, looking over the dance floor. Somewhere between dances they'd become comfortable with holding hands. It felt as though they'd been holding hands all their lives. "They all seem to recognize you and are so friendly."

"I do know most. It's a tight social circle. My brother was supposed to be here tonight, but I haven't seen him."

Of course, if Philippe had shown he'd have flaunted his latest paramour and inquired why Sebastian was here with an English woman. Not that his family was against the English. It was just that Sebastian tended to date closer to home.

"A Parisian girl will suit you," his mother, Angelique, had a tendency to remind him. *"Not too smart, but beautiful,"* she'd add. *"And don't worry about love, Sebastian. No one marries for love anymore."*

He'd almost blurted that awful statement about his family not approving of her. Uncouth. Yet she hadn't seemed to take it to heart or even notice. *Good save, Sebastian.*

While he hadn't the luxury to waste his time dating a woman of whom his family would never approve, this night wasn't about the competition between himself and Philippe. It was a means to get over tonight's rejection. And apparently, as Zee had spewed out in the limo, she had been rejected recently, too. Her boyfriend hadn't wanted children? And she'd been expecting a proposal?

She was a perfect candidate for Sebastian's win. He could not have placed an order for a more suitable wife. And he even had a ring in his pocket. But…no. He wasn't so heartless that he could bounce from one woman to the next over the course of a few hours. And he would not take advantage of Zee's broken heart and battered ego after he'd promised her a night of fun.

The live band sang pop songs that spanned decades. When they launched into an eighties' hit, Zee bounced giddily and turned her gleeful eyes to him. He didn't even have to ask.

He took her empty goblet and set it on the bar behind them. "Let's dance!"

Sebastian had never found a woman who liked to dance as much as he did. And who had the energy to keep up with him. Or who couldn't stop worrying about her hair or nails, or her expensive dress, long enough to simply let go and move.

He fit his hands to his surprise date's hips, and they joined a makeshift conga line. What a night! He'd never felt freer. And it was an easy kind of freedom that allowed him to be more intimate with her than he might have thought possible. She didn't mind when he clasped her hand and leaned in close to talk against her ear. She smelled like starlight. And that kind of romantic thinking was what tended to get him into trouble.

This was a one-night adventure. No reason not to enjoy.

After a few songs, he tugged her from the dance floor and to the opposite side of the ballroom. "Did you notice the life-size dioramas?" he asked her. "They're for photographs. Let's do some!"

Staged along the wall were makeshift rooms with props and colorful backgrounds for couples or groups to take fun photos to remember the event. Sebastian strolled toward the first, which featured a setting with paper palm trees. A tropical vacation called to him. A week or so to soak in the sun and forget the demands of work and family.

Suddenly he was jerked to the right.

"This one!" Zee called. "I want to hold the balloons!"

The scene featured a massive bouquet of red balloons set against a cerulean sky background. Zee stepped onto a stepstool and grabbed the balloon strings. Sebastian handed his phone to the assistant that manned each diorama. Then he positioned himself to grasp Zee's legs.

Photo taken, the assistant handed him his phone and Zee bounced up beside him to check the image. It looked as though she were floating away and he was trying to keep her grounded.

"I love it!" she announced, then flitted off again. "I want to do the one with the blossoms!"

Handing his phone to another assistant, Sebastian followed the bouncing woman under a massive paper tree festooned with pink paper flower blossoms. They fluttered everywhere and he had to admit the scene was incredibly romantic. Add to that the perfume that filled his nostrils—and likely all his pores—and he surrendered to the dreamy moment. They took a few shots smiling at the photographer.

Then, she stepped back to take in the overhead blossoms. "This is amazing. So creative."

Sebastian signaled to the assistant she might take a few more shots. He then took Zee's hand and spun her beneath the paper tree. "I'm glad you're having a good time."

"This is a bit of all right! Pinkie hug?"

"Pinkie hug." They linked fingers.

She sighed and tilted her head against his shoulder. Tendrils of her hair had tumbled from the upsweep and she looked tousled but more beautiful for the disarray. The warmth of her body and the press of her breast against his arm lured him to kiss the top of her head.

They met gazes. She smiled and her eyes dropped to his mouth. It felt perfectly natural to kiss her. Softly. Just a brush of his mouth over her pink lips. The sweetness of the moment teased at his emerging desires. When had he shared such a simple yet breathless moment with a woman? Whom he barely knew?

With a tilt of her body, she pressed harder into the kiss and threaded her fingers into his hair, teasing his surprise desires to alert. She tasted of champagne and the too tiny hors d'oeuvres she'd laughed over and then had popped into her mouth between dances. The warmth of her body melded against his as he slid a hand down her back. This dance move was subtle, reading her body, tasting her mouth. She electrified the air and his every desire.

This night could end one of two ways. Delivering her safely to a hotel or…taking her home with him. He knew which of the two he preferred. His inner rogue was not entirely tamable. Nor did he wish to tame it.

And yet something about this woman felt…remarkable. And so different from any woman he'd ever dated.

When suddenly she ended the kiss with a giggle, he turned her in another twirl and then she spun out in search of the next diorama.

The assistant handed back Sebastian's phone to him but muttered as she did so, "I switched to video. Seemed… special." With a wink, the woman turned to accept another phone from a partying couple.

Sebastian sought where his impromptu date had gone. He spied her snagging another tiny treat from a passing silver tray. "She *is* special."

Azalea clutched Sebastian's hand as they wandered along the edge of the dance floor. He'd spoken to so many people, in French, which she didn't understand, but he'd remained cognizant of her presence and those conversations had been short. He would often squeeze her hand and tilt down a smile at her. Gray-blue eyes stood out on his angular face beneath the dark brown, almost black, hair. So sexy. Handsome. A gentleman. A remarkable dance partner. And a hot kisser.

That kiss! What a way to get over a bad breakup. Might Sebastian be considered a rebound guy? Only if they went further than a kiss. And…that was not off the table as far as her desire-filled brain was concerned. A fling might make her feel better about men in general. Boost her confidence. At the very least, she'd leave Paris with a night to remember.

Not that this hadn't already turned into a memorable night. Hand in hand they wandered toward the exit, both in favor of some fresh air. Outside, the warm spring air swirled through her hair and restored her wilting energy.

After texting his driver for a pickup, Sebastian tucked away his phone and slid an arm around her shoulder. She leaned against him as if they were old friends.

Or new lovers. Could she?

Of course, she could. She wasn't that unsophisticated girl Lloyd had so rudely dismissed. Azalea Grace was a beautiful woman who could do anything, and have any man she desired.

"I've never had a better time," he said.

"Same. I sort of wish it wouldn't end."

"It doesn't have to." He saw the limo and waved that he'd seen him. Then he swept Azalea into his embrace.

The kiss was quick, passionate, and it said exactly what she had been considering: *we should take this to the next level.*

"I'm not a hookup kind of guy. But just one night…?"

He held out his hand and she glided hers into it. "Yes, just one night. I want that."

And she did.

CHAPTER THREE

AZALEA OPENED HER eyes to stare upward. The pale morning sky caressed pink-tinged, puffy clouds. With a twist of her head, she could just see the elegant Eiffel Tower in the distance. The two-story-high windows that curved over the bed she lay in captured the top of the city skyline and the dreamy sky. The bed sat on a wooden base, luxurious with sheets that boasted a thread count she was pretty sure exceeded the thousands. An ultrasoft comforter hung to the thick, plush rug spread on the herringbone-patterned wood floor.

Everything smelled like sweet flowers and candy. A hug? What had been the name of that perfume? Câlin. The scent certainly had followed them home. Good thing she liked the smell. But it was all so much.

Sebastian was so much. So much of a good thing.

Sebastian... Sebastian... What was his last name? He'd told her it, but she couldn't recall it.

Azalea suddenly remembered that she wasn't in bed alone. Clutching the sheet to her bare chest, she turned her head. Sebastian lay beside her, his eyes closed, pillow partially over his face and an arm wrapped over the end of it. A strolling gaze traveled from his square jaw with the hint of dark stubble to his broad yet smooth chest that displayed the hard muscles she had traced with her fingers last night. And down to his abs, well-honed and tight. And down farther… Oh, baby, what a night!

Never in her life had Azalea hooked up. Not with a complete stranger. She'd only known the man for hours before following him into bed! Yet from the dancing to the champagne, to the delicious sex, she didn't regret one moment of it. This trip to Paris had turned out to be an uplifting treat after all.

But now the walk of shame. Or rather, the day's journey back to her dad's cottage in Ambleside, where she must finally see to putting her life back together and reenter said life with a plan to move forward. Which entailed…

She didn't know what it entailed. But she did know it was time to stop moping over a failed relationship and get on with it.

Yet the thought of leaving Sebastian's side firmly tugged against the nudge to get up and move on. Maybe a few more minutes lying here, taking it all in.

The man was a dream come true. He ticked all the right boxes, including being a dance phenom, and she did recall at some point he'd offered to defend her honor. She'd loved every minute of the fancy soiree. And the dress had allowed her to easily fit in with the elite crowd. Perhaps being away from home and knowing absolutely no one had allowed her to let loose. Her inner wild child had jumped to the surface. What fun to find a man who enjoyed dancing, being a little silly, and embracing life. They'd pinkie-hugged into one another's lives. Their own secret handshake, of sorts.

Of course, she could have no clue what he thought of last night. Perhaps it was his manner? Hookups might be usual for him. In which case, he might expect to wake and find her gone.

Good plan. She'd gotten what she wanted—a night to remember.

It could never be more than one night. They'd both been burned in a relationship. Last night had been rebound sex. Nothing more. Certainly not if this stylish, big-city man ever learned she was but a simple country girl.

Right. She was out of her league here. Time to shuffle back home.

She carefully slid from the bed to seek out the bathroom. The spangled dress lay on the floor. Had Sebastian said something about returning it for her? *Yes, please.* She didn't want to face the photographer again. Though he'd been a creep, she had actually stolen a valuable gown from him. She'd leave a note with the name of the studio and trust the dress, along with the heels, would be returned. But that meant she had only her jeans and no shoes or shirt to wear home.

She wandered into a closet whose interior was the length of the bedroom wall. With the ceiling constructed entirely of glass, she could see the elegant suits, shoes and accessories neatly ordered. Each hung exactly two fingers apart. And all colors were arranged by hue in rainbow order. Someone had a bit of fashion OCD. Excusable. She wasn't going to judge a man who had given her, oh, so many orgasms. Had Lloyd even been capable of finding her *on* button? Not without some direction from her. Idiot.

Toward the back of the closet were folded slacks and a couple of neatly folded T-shirts stacked from neutrals to a soft heather tone. She plucked up a black one and held it against her bare chest.

"It'll work."

Grabbing her pants and purse, she slipped into the bathroom and carefully closed the door so as not to wake the sleeping prince who had rescued her from the lecherous villain.

Deciding against a shower because she didn't want to make noise, she splashed some water on her face and borrowed the comb that lay perfectly arranged in the side drawer.

Slipping on her jeans, she then pulled the T-shirt over her head. The scent of Câlin filled her nostrils. She suspected it might have to be sandblasted off her skin. At the very least, it did smell nice. And it reminded her of laughter, dancing and a kiss under pink paper flower blossoms.

Her phone vibrated, and, thankful it wasn't set to ring out loud, she quietly answered when she saw Maddie's name on the screen.

"How'd the photo shoot go?" her friend inquired cheerfully. "Must have been great, because I know what you did last night."

"You...know?" Meaning, the party? The man? The sex? How could she possibly...? "The photo shoot was a bust, Maddie. I had to run—"

"Run? What?"

"The photographer was handsy and a total sleaze. I took off. With the dress. Which I promise I'll return today."

"Oh, my God, Lea, I'm so sorry. I had no idea. I had heard good things about the photographer."

"It's...in the past. I got away from him. And..." Landed in a much more respectful pair of male hands. Who certainly knew how to push all the right buttons on her anatomy. Whew! Surely, that third orgasm had been worthy of her gasping shouts.

"And..." Maddie prompted expectantly.

"Well, you said you knew what I did last night. What did you mean?"

"Câlin," her friend pronounced as if declaring the name of the mysterious fiend on a late-night show.

"How do you…?"

"It's all over social media, Lea."

"You know I don't do social media. What are you talking about?"

"Seems you went to a fancy party last night. A perfume release by Jean-Claude? He's a Parisian icon, Lea. How *did* you manage that invite?"

"Well." Pausing to listen for sound on the other side of the door, Azalea sat on the toilet seat and explained everything from jumping into the limo, to the invite, getting her boogie on, and then landing in bed with the sexy Sebastian. "I'm in his bathroom now."

"OMG! When you get over an ex-boyfriend you really do it right. The photo of you and Sebastian is stunning. He's got you in his embrace and you are laughing. You look so happy. And he is the definition of sexy. Sebastian Mercier." Maddie sighed. "What a catch. But seriously, Lea, you don't want to get involved with that family drama."

Still stuck on his last name—she'd only heard him say it once last night—Azalea wondered why it sounded so familiar.

"Lea, are you listening to me?"

"I am. I wonder what photo that was?" From one of the diorama shots? Though, she did recall some shots taken in the crowd. Sebastian had slid an arm about her waist and leaned in to pose for a number of people. Had one of them been a reporter? "Why does his last name sound familiar?"

"L'Homme Mercier? Remember, Lea, we rented tuxes from them last year for my wedding?"

"Wow—the most famous menswear designer in Paris?"

"Yes, dearest, *that* Mercier family. They own an elite

atelier in the sixth and another shop in the Place des Vosges. And, apparently, you are not aware of what the poster wrote about that family's current competition."

"Competition? I don't understand any of this, Maddie. And I'm hungry. I need eggs and toast. With beans and tomatoes and a few of those curly onion bits sprinkled—"

"Lea! Focus. Listen to me."

Visions of steaming eggs set aside, Azalea nodded. "Right. Fill me in."

"So apparently your sexy dance partner and his brother are in a competition to win the CEO position of the family company. The first brother to marry and produce an heir wins."

Azalea's jaw dropped. Her sweet, sexy lover who could dance her into dreams both on the dance floor and in between the sheets was…looking for a wife? And an heir? As part of a competition.

Suddenly she wished for a toothbrush because the bad taste in her mouth stunk.

"That doesn't…" Sound like the man who had saved her last night. And had given her a taste of real, delicious passion.

But she knew nothing about him. So, he loved to dance. And make love. And was kind. An actual rescuer of lost, makeshift princesses. But had such amiable heroics been a ruse? The woman who had dashed away from the limo—Had he been trolling for a wife last night?

"Lea? Talk to me."

"I…thanks for telling me that, Maddie." This was a lot to process. "But don't worry about me. It was just a hookup. I'm not in the market for a husband. You know marriage is not on my list."

"Is that so? It was on your list. Your goal of having kids

and raising them wild and feral on a farm isn't going to happen without a man, Lea."

"That goal can be attained. Doesn't mean the participating man has to be my husband." Oh, how she lied to herself!

Maddie sighed. "Sebastian Mercier is worth millions."

"So? I'd never marry a man just because he's got money. You know me better than that."

"I do. And I believe that sweet, quirky Lea landed in the arms of a millionaire by accident and was swept away on a fantasy night of dancing and passion. And you know what? You deserve it. A night on the town. Doing as you please. With whomever you please. But it's a new day. What are you going to do now?"

"I'm heading home. I had my fun." And had made another wrong choice! Just when she'd thought she'd turned a corner on her bad decisions. Argh! "Time to get back to my life."

"Which means…? Are you going to find work in London and rent a new flat?"

"Well." Staying at her parents' farm provided a convenient hideaway from the real world.

"Lea. Don't let Lloyd's rejection bring you down any longer. You're better than that. And you don't have to go back to that flower shop. Find a new shop that's not owned by a backstabbing, boyfriend-stealing witch. You'll find something."

"I know I will." Pausing to listen for sound on the other side of the door, she was reassured by the silence. "I gotta go, Maddie. I want to duck out of here before he wakes."

"Oh, baby, you've had a night. Just don't trip and land in his arms again. That man could prove a real problem."

"No kidding. I'm not that stupid. At least, I'm not going to be that stupid about a man anymore."

"Hallelujah!"

"Talk later, Maddie."

She hung up and stuffed the phone in her purse. Then she faced the woman in the mirror. Hair tousled but still a bit wavy from the updo. She shook her head and exhaled.

"It was a fun night." No way would she deny herself that win. "But you need to dash before you do land in his arms again."

Because Maddie knew she had a weakness for a sexy man with pleading eyes and a heroic heart. What woman would not? But apparently this sexy man needed a wife and child. To consider such a fulfilling prospect—no. This wasn't her world. Azalea Grace loved her small life. It made her happy. Besides, a relationship with Sebastian would lead nowhere. How could it? He had a wife to find. A company to win! Better to walk away with her heart intact while the walking was possible.

With a firm jut of her chin, Azalea pulled on her metaphorical big-girl knickers—because in reality she was sans knickers—and snuck out of the best thing that would never happen to her.

Sebastian pulled up a pair of soft, jogging slacks and called out to Azalea. He assumed she was in the bathroom, though he didn't hear any running water. He raked his fingers through his hair.

The petite bit of freckles and blond hair had rocked his world last night.

They had danced like no one was watching. Laughed until his jaw had ached. Had sex. Really amazing sex. They needed to do all of the above again. Before she left and returned for home.

"Zee?" He wandered over to the bathroom door and

rapped with his knuckle. A twist of the knob, and he slowly opened the door… "Zee?" He scanned the penthouse behind him, not seeing any sign of her.

His gaze landed on the dress folded neatly on the vanity. The shoes were placed next to it, along with a note written on a piece of cardboard torn from a soap box.

Sebastian, it was an amazing night. I'll never forget it! Saw social media this morning. You're in a competition with your brother? Time for me to leave. Only good memories. Promise. You said you'd return the dress for me. Here's the address...

Sebastian cursed under his breath. She'd learned about the competition on social media? He rushed out to the bedroom and grabbed his phone to open the one social media app he used and searched for his name. A photo of him embracing a laughing Azalea popped up.

"So gorgeous," he whispered. "And happy."

And yet, after the night they'd had together she'd decided to sneak out without saying goodbye? Would she have waited and spent some time with him had she not seen the post? He would never know.

Sebastian looked out the window and ran his fingers through his hair. Had the best thing that had ever happened to him just slipped away?

No, it had been a one-night fling. In a few days he'd forget all about Azalea Grace. And her cute freckles. And her bubbly presence. And her delicious and surprisingly commanding kisses. Life would move forward. Back to the wife hunt.

He turned his phone over to peer at the social media post. Her smile was so effusive. Her entire face squinched and her eyes closed, drawing all attention to those remarkable freckles. He could hear her laughter even now and smell…well. *Mon Dieu*, that perfume had followed them home. They'd literally danced it into their systems. Despite its pleasantness, a long shower was in order.

Before tossing his phone to the bed, he recalled they'd taken some shots in interactive stages featured around the ballroom. Flicking through his camera files, he found the photos. In one, Azalea grasped a bouquet of balloons and stood on a concealed stool that made it look as though she were floating upward. Arms wrapped around her waist, he appeared to bring her back down as he looked up adoringly at her.

Sebastian smiled. Tapped the photo until it wobbled with a trash can on the corner of the photo. And then… he shook his head.

"No, I don't want to forget you."

CHAPTER FOUR

WITH THE SUN setting soon, Azalea found her bicycle parked behind the bookstore where she'd left it yesterday morning before catching a train to London to make the trip to Paris. She knew the store owner and had gotten permission years ago to use the rack. Everyone in Ambleside knew everyone else. It was a tourist town renowned for its hiking trails and beautiful scenery. It was one of many small towns in the Lake District that sat upon Lake Windermere.

Her dad, Oliver Grace, had texted her around noon. He and his girlfriend had left to catch their afternoon flight out of London to Australia. Would she be home soon to tend Stella? Yes, not to worry.

The bike ride was a pleasant meander along the paved roads and cobbled Ambleside streets to country lanes lined with mown grass and bright yellow buttercup and pale pink thrift. Inhaling the fresh air, she allowed the remaining sunshine to beam through her pores, reviving her muscles after the tedious hours of travel. Still, the perfume lingered on her. Most likely she'd left a scent trail on all the trains she taken from Paris to home.

One night in Paris? Well spent when she considered her sexual needs had been met. Big-time.

It was that pinkie hug from Paris that she needed to forget. And that smolder. The man was in a competition that required him to find a wife and have a child? Might Azalea Grace ever manage to pick a normal man?

Apparently, she was not meant to find a happily-ever-after sort of guy. At least, not the sort who could meet her expectations of what she wanted in her future. Country cottages and barefoot children, anyone? Yes, please. She'd meant it when she'd told Maddie marriage was off the table.

Maybe.

Dash it, her heart knew that was a lie. Her idea of the perfect life did involve marriage, and not living on her own, children or no children. But she would not marry a man simply because he'd rocked her world and needed her to win a competition.

"Forget about him," she muttered to her pining heart.

Once at the cottage, set in a dip beyond a sharp right turn and but a stone's throw from the lake, she parked her bike against the weather-bleached fence that had once kept wild rabbits from the garden but now tended to merely entice them to try their hand—or rather, paw—at wiggling through the wide gaps between slats.

She wandered into the cozy, brick-and-stone, nineteenth-century farmhouse that had been completely renovated two decades ago. In the kitchen, she filled a water bottle and walked out to the creaky yet comforting porch, where she sat on the steps overlooking a tidy and currently rabbit-less yard. Sunlight glittered on the wildflowers to her right and on the pond surface where a couple of wild ducks floated.

After a day filled with abrupt naps and rude awakenings—she could never sit on a train and not fall asleep within minutes—finally she had a moment to breathe.

She kicked off the cheap trainers she'd purchased at a tourist shop before hopping a train at the Gare du Nord and leaned against the porch railing. The wood was worn and smooth at her back because this was where she had sat all her life.

And soon it would be no more.

Her dad intended to sell the farm and cottage. Grace Farm had taken in and rehabilitated animals for almost three decades. Oliver Grace had started it along with Azalea's mother, Petunia. Now her dad wanted a new adventure. Which he had gotten with his girlfriend, Diane, a woman who defined the term *wanderlust* with a sparkle in her eye and occasional bits of grass in her hair and personal possessions proudly confined to but a rucksack.

Azalea was happy that her dad was moving on after her mother had divorced him three years earlier. Petunia Grace had told Azalea she felt confined. Needed to be free. It had been as amicable an ending as a thirty-year relationship could be. Her mom had moved to Arizona to start a crystal business with a longtime friend. A male friend who had read Petunia's aura and declared them soul mates.

So that was how freedom looked? Apparently.

The divorce had finally forced Azalea to move to London. Yes, she hadn't left home until she was twenty-two, being perfectly content to live on the farm and have no aspirations or ambitions other than to breathe fresh air and befriend any animal the farm took in.

London hadn't been so much a rude awakening as merely a much-needed rousing. Azalea had discovered a world beyond the confines of the country, and she'd enjoyed most of it. She'd stayed a few weeks with her sister, Dahlia, a lawyer. Dahlia had left the farm at sixteen, never to look back, compelled by the beck of the busy city and all its opportunities. She'd helped Azalea find a flat and a lovely job as flower arranger for a tiny shop tucked between a bookstore and a vinyl record shop. It had suited her. She had been happy. Much as Dahlia gently prodded her to aspire for something higher, more fulfilling, Azalea had never felt the need to enter the corporate rat race. She preferred a simple life, with simple things.

And though a tomboy at heart, she did have aspirations to become a princess. That childhood fantasy still held space in her heart. Not real royalty, but rather, well...last night had contributed to the fantasy. Fabulous gown, pretty makeup and shoes, an elite event filled with stardust and champagne. And a handsome knight.

Azalea inhaled the perfume that coated her skin and which had even imbued the T-shirt she wore. *His shirt.* She wished it smelled like him—sultry vanilla and cedar—but no such luck. A lovely parting gift to remember her one night in Paris?

Last night's fling had been amazing. Not a thing to complain about when viewing the larger picture. Sebastian had been perfect. Handsome. Kind. Fun. Even a little silly when they'd been dancing up a storm. An excellent lover. Obviously rich. But apparently in the market for an instant wife so he could gain control of the family company. That pesky detail could not be dismissed.

And he hadn't considered *her* a possible wife? He'd started to say something about his family not approving, but she'd forced herself to ignore it at the time. She had a right to be miffed at that exclusion. Even if it felt as if she'd dodged a bullet. So, like she'd written to him, she would remember the night, cherish it, but it was time to move on. More wrong choices to make, don't ya know?

A sneaky little devil landed on her shoulder and prodded her in the heart.

You liked him. A lot. Don't act like you wouldn't jump if you saw him again.

She sighed, catching her chin against her palm. Her heart did have a tendency to leap before her brain could stop her. Here she sat in a little piece of heaven on earth, undisturbed by the rush of the real world, and still Sebastian Mercier haunted her thoughts.

There was one problem. She hadn't given him her phone number and she'd not gotten his contact info. Though certainly she did know where he worked. L'Homme Mercier was a well-known Parisian brand. Maddie had mentioned the two ateliers. A quick browse online could easily locate them. She could make contact.

Yet, that felt like diving into something she wasn't sure was good for her. If he wanted to see her again, he'd find her.

And if she never saw him again, she'd have to accept that was how it was meant to be. Obviously, the man had a wife to catch. And she was all about not becoming a wife now.

Azalea sighed. Her relationship with Lloyd had broken her in a surprising manner. And one night with a stranger hadn't been able to pry the memory from her brain cells. Because of that breakup she'd developed a healthy fear of commitment. Marriage? Once it had been all she'd desired. Until Lloyd had reduced it to a condition of social status, and Sebastian had further cemented it with his emotionless quest for a wife. And while her parents had shown her that anything could be broken and still survive, she didn't want to touch the idea of an extended attachment with someone she didn't love or a man she might even eventually fall out of love with.

Yet her romantic heart still wanted love and a relationship. She wanted to be cherished, admired, and be a friend and lover. She wanted to be a mother.

Well. Wasn't as if Sebastian had intended to propose to her anyway.

Which left her here. Alone and unsure what her future held.

A moo from the barn clued her it was feeding time. Her dad, a bovine veterinarian, had taken in injured or sick cows for decades. He cared for them, tended their injuries and nursed them back to health before they were either returned to their owner or, if abandoned, lived in happiness on the lush acres of Grace Farm. Stella, a highland cow with a long brown coat and pearly white hooves, had given birth to a calf two months earlier. The little one was so fluffy it looked like a walking plushy. Her dad hadn't named the newborn, insisting he didn't want a reason to get attached when his plans involved selling them both before summer's end. In the few weeks Azalea had been staying here, she and the cow had become best of friends.

Stella wandered toward the wooden fence attached to the side of the barn and Azalea stepped down onto the grass in her bare feet.

"Stella!" she called. "You'll never believe the night I've had."

In a quiet office on the top floor of a 6th arrondissement building the Mercier family had owned for over a century, Sebastian leaned back in his chair. Two stories below, the atelier created bespoke suits for an elite clientele. The shop on the Place des Vosges carried their prêt-à-porter collection. Both shops drew clients worldwide.

L'Homme Mercier had begun in the 1920s as a tailor shop set up by Sebastian's great-great-grandfather and had grown exponentially over the years. It was a Paris icon. Their clients were rich and many. Yet the company prided itself on individual attention and exquisite detail to every piece of clothing it produced. Never mass-scale production. And marketing was tasteful yet sensual.

Philippe's suggestion that they integrate women's wear into their *oeuvre* was unthinkable. But his brother, just down the hall in his office, was moving ahead with plans, designs and clothing sketches. While their father, Roman, had not approved of the idea, neither had he rejected Philippe's ruse. That glint in Roman Mercier's eyes always indicated that he had set the parameters for the future of L'Homme Mercier. And those parameters would be controlled by whichever son first married and produced an heir.

A competition declared just weeks after Roman had suffered a stroke. It had only put him in the hospital overnight. The doctor had said Roman was very lucky in that his girlfriend had recognized the signs—one side of his face had drooped and he'd not been able to get his words out—and had immediately taken him to the emergency room. But that little brush with mortality had set Roman on a quest to secure his legacy.

Sebastian had never viewed the competition as silly or unthoughtful. Or even out of character for his father. It was what he knew. All his life he and Philippe had competed, be it on the lacrosse field, or attracting *Le Monde* for a feature article, or at boat racing at Marseilles. They earned their worth through their father's nod of approval.

And while this new competition would involve another person—and *creating* another person—his child—Sebastian set his heart to it as with all other competitions. And this time he must win. L'Homme Mercier would not be diluted by mass marketing and—by all the gods—a women's clothing division.

Did the battle require he be in love? Not at all. In fact, the idea of love equating to marriage was not a Mercier philosophy. Roman Mercier had four sons. By three different mothers. He'd never married any of the women. And while Sebastian knew there was something not quite right with that family structure, he also knew nothing else. Which did make the marriage stipulation a little strange.

Why did Roman insist on signed legal papers? Shouldn't an heir be enough? And really, was Sebastian supposed to put some woman's name on a piece of official paper that granted her half of everything he owned? That did not sit well with him. So he'd be sure to have a prenup drawn up.

Sebastian was very capable of taking control of the family legacy. He knew the company from bottom to top. He'd started in the sewing department when he was thirteen, learning the trade and taking pride in the occasional nod of approval from the tailors. Later, he'd moved up to promotions and design, and now he was in charge of the finances, shipping and suppliers. As well as sharing marketing duties with Philippe. Just last week he'd worked men's fashion week, which was held annually in Paris. It was always a whirlwind of fashion, celebrities, news media, interviews, parties and pressing flesh with all the right people. Philippe had missed half of it because he'd been in Marseilles schmoozing with an Austrian royal of the female persuasion. So, who was *really* devoted to the company?

Yet, during that exhausting week of fashion shows, Sebastian had struggled with distracting thoughts of *her*. Azalea Grace of the freckles and bubbly laughter. A woman who had leaped into his life, swirled him dizzy on the dance floor, and then dashed out as quickly.

But not without a pinkie hug. He smiled to think about that little gesture they'd developed between them within the short period they'd been together. The woman had dug up his fun side and he'd reveled in it. He hadn't felt so exhilarated and unguarded since he was a child. It was almost as if he'd been swept away into a fairy tale. Silly to think like that. Though she had mentioned something about feeling like a princess. And hadn't he been her rescuing knight?

A tilt of his head confirmed that bemusing thought. And yet. It had ended abruptly. Didn't feel right, either. Like Zee had left behind a hole in him with her sneaky departure. And that hole needed to be—well, he wasn't sure. Was it that he merely lusted after her? Or was there something more? The affection she'd given him so easily had felt genuine and surprisingly new. She hadn't asked for a thing in return, save another dance.

Had he seriously not gotten her contact info? Stupid of him. All he knew was her name and that she lived in England. Some village, or tourist town called Bumblebush. Or Anglewood. Or…he couldn't recall. He must remember the name. Because he wanted to see her again. Even as he'd schmoozed and shaken hands with the press and talked to all sorts at cocktail parties last week, whenever a beautiful woman had caught his eye, he'd looked away. Thought of Zee's springy blond hair. Those bright blue eyes that had reflected joy. And so many freckles.

And that kiss under the paper cherry blossoms. He'd

watched the video of it every evening, remembering the softness of her skin, the warmth of her sigh, the utter indulgence of her body melting against his. She'd gotten under his skin. Even more so than that blasted perfume.

Such nostalgic longing wasn't like him. Sebastian Mercier was a playboy. Just like his father. He loved women. Had found the process of frequent dating in his search for the perfect wife not at all taxing. And yet, for some reason, he hadn't hooked up with a single woman since the night of the perfume debut party. Quite out of character for him.

He toggled the mouse to bring his computer screen awake and decided to search for the name of the English village. If he could figure that part out, it shouldn't be too difficult to then find a woman named Azalea. He did have the photos of them from the party. He wondered if he could search for her that way. Might bring up a social media page?

His phone rang and, just when he thought to ignore it, a text popped up from his brother at the same time. Curious.

Sebastian answered the call, which was also Philippe, "What is it?"

"It's Dad. He's had another stroke."

CHAPTER FIVE

Months later

So MUCH HAD happened as summer swelled. And so much had stayed the same.

Azalea's dad had called during week six of his vacation asking her if she wouldn't mind keeping an eye on things a bit longer. A few more weeks? Of course, that was no problem, she'd reassured him. And it wasn't. She loved the farm. She and Stella were best friends. And the half dozen chickens weren't too much trouble, save for Big Bruce, the cockerel, who had a habit of scampering off to the neighbor's farm and—well, she'd gotten more than a few rude phone calls pleading her to keep her cock locked up.

She'd gotten over the breakup with Lloyd. His loss. And with his lack of empathy, he would have never made a good father to her future children. Because, yes, children were her future.

And yet, the one thing that had altered in Azalea's heart lately was her need for companionship. It was more an inner blooming that pressed her to figure out her life. And to do it quickly.

Would she remain on this farm forever? No. It would go up for sale as soon as her dad returned. But where would she go and what would she do? London had been fine, but it had never felt like her place. Like a forever home. It was too busy. Too crowded. Too…just, too.

Even more, now she sought stability and comfort. Protection, even. In a sort of "man wrapping his arms around her and keeping her close" manner. Had she blown it by walking out of Sebastian Mercier's life?

She shook her head. Even if they had continued to see one another, she could have never been assured he wasn't using her simply for the wife and child stipulation that would have won him the CEO position.

Yet still, she was frustrated.

"Things have gotten complicated." She swore a bit more loudly than usual. Sometimes a well-intoned oath was required.

"Stella…" Azalea swept hay from the barn floor while the cow watched through the open gate at the end of the breezeway. "You and Daisy seem to get along well on your own." She'd named the calf. Difficult to keep calling her *little one*. And the little plushy did enjoy nibbling daisies in the field. "You think I can manage?"

The cow rubbed her cheek against the worn door frame, a favorite place to scratch.

"I am very capable of living on my own," she defended to no one but herself. Taking care of her own, she thought with a proud lift of her chest. "And I will find a job. I enjoy arranging flowers. There's a florist in Ambleside next to the ice cream parlor."

Yet it might never pay enough to ensure even the simple lifestyle she desired. She needed to get serious and figure out a means to an income to support herself.

Having been content on the farm for such a long time, she'd never considered pursuing higher education to enable her to get a nine-to-five job. Dahlia was the go-getter, the woman with a plan and a target. That target being becoming partner in her law firm and a million-pound home in Notting Hill. Dahlia knew her little sister was not so financially ambitious and had never tried to provoke her toward something beyond what she aspired to. Yet, Azalea was well aware she'd become complacent. Set in her ways.

Her parents' divorce had shaken her out of that complacence. Once located in London, she'd realized the only jobs she was qualified for were fast-food slinger—ugh; hotel maid—she did not like touching other people's messes; rubbish collector—seriously?—or simple yet creative jobs that she could easily learn, such as floral arranging. She didn't regret not furthering her education. The world was filled with self-starters, independent minds who made their own way. She just needed to make some life changes. Focus on her strengths. And…sooner, rather than later.

Because she'd taken a pregnancy test twice now. Both times it had confirmed the new life growing inside her. She'd only smiled about it since. Not once had she felt regret.

Honestly? Very well, anxiety had struck. And tended to wake her in the middle of the night. Could she do this? Could she actually be a mother? And do it alone?

What about Sebastian? He was the father, no doubts on that one. Should she include him? Did she want him in her life once the baby was born? Of course, the father should be allowed that option. But what if he insisted she marry him? He did, after all, outweigh her when it came to power, influence, and having access to hard-hitting lawyers. She barely knew the man. Might she risk getting trapped in his competitive plans for marriage? Plans that did not include love.

"Love is important," she muttered.

Stella mooed, as if in agreement.

"Exactly." She hung up the broom and slapped her palms across her khakis to disperse the hay dust. "I don't think I can tell him."

Stella's next moo was more admonishing. Azalea had debated with her nearly every evening when she went to muck out the stable. Should she or shouldn't she tell Sebastian?

Yet another moo and a curt dismissal as Stella turned to find Daisy. The cow left Azalea standing there with her hands on her hips. And her heart begging to be included in the debate.

"But there's no way to tell him," she insisted.

Another lie she told her heart. She'd already marked the GPS location of L'Homme Mercier on her phone. Flying to Paris and showing up at the atelier to announce Sebastian was going to be a father was not an impossibility.

"I don't know. I just…don't know how to do it in a reasonable and nonconfrontational manner. There will be a row. Loud words. Accusations. Questions. So many questions, surely. I've got enough to deal with in figuring out this pregnancy thing."

Put her indecision down to hormones.

Then she reprimanded herself for having normal doubts any new mother must experience. She was thrilled over being pregnant. Having a baby as a single woman hadn't been a choice she'd made in the moment. She and Sebastian had used protection. What was it she'd heard about a condom's failure rate? Something like two percent? She wouldn't even label it wrong. This baby felt right.

With or without Sebastian.

Wandering outside, she nearly slipped in the mud that curled around the barn but caught herself with a swing of her hand just dipping into that muck.

Swiping a palm over her thigh, she lifted one foot, clad in a mud-coated wellie, and the suction released her. Farm life. If she didn't end the day with mud, straw or some unidentifiable substance stuck to her hair, skin or clothing, it just wasn't a day.

"I'm going to shower, then take a walk in the field to collect some cornflowers for a bouquet," she told Stella. "You and Daisy might join me if you care to. Be back in a bit."

She strode to the back of the cottage, where a makeshift, outdoor shower fitted over a stone mat was useful for clearing away the mud. But before she could turn on the spigot, she heard a car. Driving *away* from the cottage? The property was in a neat little private area, sporting a long drive lined with hedgerows. Had someone been up to the front without her knowing? Possible. When in the barn it was difficult to hear beyond the back of the cottage. She wasn't expecting any deliveries.

Swinging around the side of the cottage, Azalea dodged the overgrown vines that she swore she'd tend soon and pushed open the creaky iron gate. A man stood on the fieldstone pathway curling to the front door. A smart black suitcase sat on the ground beside him. He was quite well-dressed. In a stunning suit—

Azalea swore under her breath. In an instant her heartbeat went from calm to freakout. She patted her frazzled hair, which she might or might not have combed this morning.

At the sight of her, he waved. Even at this distance his smile danced into her heart and giddied in her belly. He'd seen her! No chance to duck away and hide. To fix her hair. To—she studied her dirty hands—yikes, did she have mud in her hair, too?

How had he found her? Why was the sexiest man

in Paris standing before her cottage with a smile that shouldn't be there if he could get a good look at her?

"Zee!"

He could call her all he liked, but that didn't make her feet move forward. She was frozen in shock. And not because she must look a fright. Well, yes, there was that. But because—her hand went to her belly.

"Sebastian," she said on a gasp.

She'd gone over this moment many a time with Stella. How to tell him? *Should* she tell him? The answers depended on whether she'd see him again. And now here he was. Standing in her front yard. And she had not practiced for this scenario.

Seeing her frozen there, dumbstruck, Sebastian stepped carefully on the overgrown grass, and beelined around a crop of fieldstones that were supposed to be yard decoration but really her dad had tossed there because he didn't want to haul them to the back of the property.

When he stood before her, Azalea still felt like a statue that could barely breathe. Her insides were rushing, gushing and flip-flopping all at once. And the little tyke growing inside her had many months before it began to move about, so she knew it was nerves.

"I found you," he announced. "And believe me, it wasn't easy. But once I figured out that you lived in Ambleside, all I had to do was go around with your photo and ask—"

"You have my photo?" she dumbly blurted.

"Yes." He tugged out his phone and turned the screen toward her. The screensaver showed them in that silly pose they'd taken at the party with her flying away, balloons in hand, and him grasping to pull her down. "Everyone had a good laugh at the photo. They all knew it was you and where you lived. Though I must admit, finding a place 'just beyond the dip' was an interesting excursion."

"Yes, the dip in the road."

She gestured toward the road, realizing it was stupid to even converse about the condition of the old, winding road when the man of her dreams stood before her. Looking like a god who could conquer all of womankind with his smolder and a tug at his perfectly fitted suit. And she looking like the one who got trampled on by the masses as they rushed him for his favor.

"I'm sorry it took so long to come see you," he said. "I've thought about you every day."

"Same," she whispered more softly than her heart screamed. She must tell him.

Oh, heart, be quiet!

"After you left Paris, I was busy with fashion week. Which takes up a few weeks business-wise. And then my father had a stroke. Another one, actually. It was difficult to get away."

"Oh, dear, Sebastian, your dad? Is he all right?"

"Yes, he's recovering and dealing with some speech issues now. The old man needs to slow down. Take things easy."

And insist one of his sons get married and have a child so they could take control of the company? The thought shoved Azalea like a bully with his hands to her back, but she swallowed down a yelp, or worse, an oath.

"Is it all right that I've come?" he asked.

He took her in, his eyes gliding over her. Gray-blue irises caught the sunlight and toyed with her sense of personal space. Her newly acquired need to protect her growing family at all costs. And yet, all she wanted was to claim a hug from the man who had explained that the French simply didn't do that.

"You don't look pleased to see me."

Azalea exhaled and shook her head. "I am pleased. I think. I mean, well, it is a surprise, isn't it? I hadn't thought to see you again. Though…yes, I am pleased. Well. I feel a bit mussed right now. Been mucking out the barn. Would you like to come inside while I refresh?"

"I'd love to."

Sebastian had risked rejection jetting off to London, then on to the little village of Ambleside without having a means to notify Zee he was on his way. He'd gone from a café to a pub and, photo of Azalea displayed on his phone, had gotten lucky at the second stop. A young man around Azalea's age knew her from school and had directed Sebastian to take the west road for a distance, then turn right after the dip.

Surprisingly, the driver had found the place.

Now he sat at a round table graced with a bouquet of wilting blue flowers. The house was small and epitomized cottage core, with the checked curtains, cozy rugs, low ceilings and tidy cupboards. He heard a cow moo in the distance and the occasional crow of what he guessed could be a cockerel. That night at the party he'd guessed she wasn't of his world, but he'd not expected an actual farm girl. He was not put off but he also wasn't sure what to expect. He'd only ever dated city girls, women who'd given a care for their hair, nails and always the perfect outfit.

What sort of travesty had been those rubber boots covered in mud? And even more mud in her hair and on her face?

And yet, at the sight of Azalea—his Zee—his heart had

bounced. Almost like a dance he'd shared with her at the party. He'd found her. The woman who had jumped into his life and as quickly jumped out of it.

He'd had to make this trip. He wanted to get to know her. To see if this compulsion to find her was something more. But also, since his father's second stroke, the pressure to win the competition and take control of the company had increased. The risk that his father might have another stroke was high. And he might not survive the next one. L'Homme Mercier must be put in order before then, with the long-established traditions firmly in place without threat of change.

And if Zee had been on his mind so much, then, Sebastian had reasoned, perhaps he should entertain the idea of making *her* his wife? They both got along. And she had mentioned something about wanting a family and children. He'd come here to learn if she might be amenable to the idea. But even more so, he wanted to learn if he still felt the same way toward her. If they spent the night squabbling or couldn't find a common interest, then he'd mark the trip off as closing the door on a wonder that had prodded at his heart for months. On to the next potential wife. It was something he had to do for the company.

"Sorry to keep you waiting," she announced as she sailed down a curved stairway hugging a stone wall. "I didn't realize how much mud I had on me. It's Stella's fault."

"Stella being…?"

"Uh…my best friend."

The crinkle of her brow was so cute. Everything about her, from the tips of her now bare toes, up to her freckled knees, and the simple green checked dress to her button nose and more freckles on her checks. Her hair was fluffed and a little wet, and those bright eyes. The woman was simply stunning.

"So you found me." She stood at the base of the stairs, hands fidgeting before her.

Approaching her, unsure if she would allow it, Sebastian watched for a panicked look but only got a stunned blink of her eyes. Damn it, he'd been dreaming about this reunion for weeks. And it always started with a kiss. So he kissed her. And, thankfully, she didn't resist.

It had been too long. He'd thought about her kisses, her bare skin, the warmth of her body gliding against his. Her sweet murmurs as they'd made love that night, over and over. How the moonlight had glowed like pearls over her naked body. The two of them smelling like that crazy perfume and giggling about it. Now she was back in his arms. And a sweet murmur reassured him he was not overstepping any lines.

Something about holding Azalea Grace felt…fragile. Yet also a greedy desire prodded at him. He wanted the thing he wasn't supposed to have. And the little boy in him wouldn't allow any others to take it away from him.

When he pulled away to study her reaction, she nodded and said, "Yep, not a mistake."

"What's a mistake?"

"Nothing's a mistake. I was just remembering our night in Paris. It wasn't a mistake. That kiss reminded me of how real and fun it was."

"It was fun. And real. But too quick." He held up his hand, pinkie finger extended.

She twined hers with his. "Yes, too—well!" She quickly disengaged. "Now that you've found me, you must realize that I am a farm girl. Definitely not the type you're accustomed to dating. I'm not sure why you'd even bother coming to see me."

"Zee, I can't look at another woman without comparing her to you. I had to find you to see if the feeling I get every time I think of you was real. And well, it is real. I'm feeling those same flutters. Hell, it's like an animal pull to hold you, touch you, make love to you all over again. And I don't care if you're a farm girl."

"Yes, you do."

He shrugged, then chuckled. "There are certain odors out here, aren't there?"

She laughed. "But not me, I hope?"

"No, you smell like summer."

"And you…" She sniffed and then crinkled her freckled nose. "Do you smell of Câlin?"

"That perfume seems to have gotten into every fiber of clothing in my closet. I thought I'd aired it out but apparently not."

"That's crazy." She strolled to the sink, flicked on the faucet and grabbed a glass. Distancing herself from him? Not a good start.

"I wish you hadn't left without kissing me goodbye. But I understand. I'm sorry you had to find out about the competition from social media."

"I had to sneak out. I wasn't prepared to do the morning-after awkwardness. And the competition means nothing to me since we're not even a thing."

"We could be a thing."

"Listen, I'm not a fool, Sebastian. I'm so out of your social echelon."

"Oh, we're talking echelons now? Those are fighting words."

She laughed over a sip of water. "Be serious, Sebastian.

You asked that woman to marry you. She fled. You didn't ask me to marry you because I do recall you saying your family would never approve."

He should have never let that slip! "Do you want me to ask you? I recall you saying you'd never marry me."

"You got that right."

He clutched the back of a chair before the table. He hadn't expected this to be easy. "Still don't understand why this visit bothers you."

"It's just that, why waste your time on me? Surely you and your brother are in a race to win the prize. And with your father—oh, I'm sorry. I shouldn't make assumptions regarding his health."

"Assume anything you like. Philippe and I *are* in a race since Father's second stroke. It affected him more this time around. He can no longer go into the office. I've had to take over dealings with his special client list and Philippe has been traveling nonstop. We…" He shoved a hand over his hair and splayed it out before him. "Zee, can this just be what it is? I had to see you again."

"So you've seen me." She crossed her arms.

Not going to give him an inch? What had he done to make her so…disinterested? He'd thought they had parted on common ground, both quite pleased with their time spent together. Although she must've been miffed to learn about the competition. He'd give her that.

"Give me twenty-four hours," he challenged.

"What for?"

"To talk to you, get to know you." Find that crazy, silly happiness they'd shared with one another when they sailed around the dance floor. "I just want to be with you, Zee."

"Have sex with me, is what you mean."

"That would be ideal, but it's not a requirement."

She shook her head, then spread a palm over her stomach. “I don’t know.”

“You don’t want to entertain a visitor for a while? Come on, Zee, give me a chance. Show me around. Take me into town. Introduce me to Stella. Can you tell me you haven’t thought of me once since fleeing my home?”

“I didn’t flee.”

“You exited without saying goodbye, which is the definition of fleeing.”

“Fine, I fled. And…very well. I’m not hating you being here in my home. My dad’s home. I’m just watching the place until he returns from vacation.”

“Tell me about it.”

“Seriously?”

He spread out his arms. “You can’t get rid of me now. I sent the driver away.”

It took a while for her smile to blossom, but when it did her nose wiggled and her eyes brightened even more. She was so adorable. And he had just won the next twenty-four hours with her.

CHAPTER SIX

AZALEA OFFERED TO make a light meal, so a salad it was. Everything was fresh from the garden or field, even the mustard seed dressing. She and Sebastian sat out back on the porch, plates on their laps, wineglasses close to hand. Of course, she only had cherry-flavored sparkling water. In the background, a portable radio played her favorite station at a low volume.

Having combed her hair and gotten over her initial shock that Sebastian had actually come looking for her, she'd decided she would use this time to learn more about him. Her future, and the family she would create, required it of her. Because some day she'd have to tell her child about his or her father. What kind of man was he? Was he here to cajole her into marrying him to win that stupid competition?

Dare she let him into her life, allow him to learn more about her? It would be a cruelty if she ultimately decided against allowing him to participate in her child's life.

But that decision had not yet been made. And it was a big decision. One that needed all the supporting data she could acquire. Because no matter what, they would always be linked through their child. And that was an immense future to consider. Her wanting heart gushed and pleaded for her to invite him in and make him her own, while her logical brain put up a fit and insisted she ignore emotion and strive for practicality.

Stupid brain.

"It's peaceful out here," he commented as he set his plate aside. "Reminds me of summers at my grandparents' house south of Paris."

Pulled from the argument of brain versus heart, Azalea set her plate aside and rested her elbows on her knees, tilting her head to take him in. "Did they have a country place?"

"I suppose you would call it a château, but it was small and on many acres. Grandmother was the barefoot gardening sort who always greeted me with a spin."

"A spin?"

"She loved to dance anywhere, any time. She's the one who gave me a love for dancing."

"I don't think I've ever had more fun dancing than that night with you." Nor had she been more attracted, and downright sexually invigorated by his refreshing demeanor. Not what she'd expected from a man who knew how to wear an expensive suit. "Not many men care to loosen up like that. Especially one in such a fancy suit."

He brushed a trouser leg. He'd abandoned the suit coat, undone a few buttons at his collar and rolled up his white sleeves. Azalea decided it was his idea of comfort. "I'm all about suits, Zee."

"I suppose, since it's the family business. But with a little dancing included now and then?"

"Absolutely. I looked forward to those summers my mom would deposit me at the château to stay for weeks while she gallivanted off with her latest lover. My grandparents had a mangy dog and some chickens. And an insufferable goat."

"Goats are like that."

"They are. I even used to run barefoot in the grass." He eyed her bare feet. "So I'm not a complete slicker."

"You do earn points for that. But when was the last time your feet touched grass? I'm betting it hasn't been since those childhood summers."

"Is that a challenge?" He leaned in, tipping his glass against hers. "Because I'm all about challenges."

Yes, like finding a wife to give birth to his heir? Dare she spend the next day with him *without* telling him she carried his baby?

Oh, brain, just concede to heart!

"What's going on in there?" He tapped her temple and shifted to sit closer to her. "You're too serious for the fun-loving Zee I remember."

"You hardly know me."

"That's why I'm here. To learn more."

"Hmm, well, I do have moments that do not involve dancing wildly and tossing down champagne and tiny snacks."

"Oh, yes?" He paused, tilting his head to listen, and she noticed the sprightly song on the radio. "You know this one?"

At her affirmative nod, he stood and tugged her to stand on the porch. He spun her once under his arm, and they swirled into a few steps.

"Did your grandmother teach you this?" she called between bounces. She didn't know the dance exactly, but Petunia Grace had once been a competitive dancer during Azalea's preteen years.

"Of course! Grandmama loved the American dances."

With that he lifted her and twirled her around. Azalea thrust out her arms, her hair spilling out and a laugh gushing up. And when they whirled to a stop and he carefully set her down, he slid a hand along her cheek and studied her eyes with his beautiful, soulful, gray-blue eyes. From the frenzy of the dance to the sudden overwhelming *connection* of his gaze. She swallowed. Her heart resumed its swell in response. Tilting onto her toes, she kissed him.

A familiar place, this kiss. She didn't feel tentative or wary. Sebastian's heat coaxed her deeper and she reveled in the easy clash of tastes, textures and a hint of cherry sparkling water topping it off. As she leaned against his chest, her hands glided up and along his shoulders. Broad and straight. Her mighty rescuer in tailored armor. Her Parisian hero.

Breaking the kiss, she tilted her head against his shoulder and they swayed to the slower song that whispered behind them. The moment felt perfect, like something she needed to preserve in memory. So years from now she could tell the tale to her child.

"I'm glad you found me," she said without thinking her words through. It had been a confession. A true one. Her heart always spoke before her brain. "I missed you."

"I'm here now."

Yes, now. For less than twenty-four hours that she must wrap her arms around and squeeze out every moment. To remember forever. To tell stories about the man who danced her so silly they immediately followed it up with making a baby. Never would she have planned such a situation. However, this was not one of Azalea Grace's bad choices. And there was not a thing about it she would change.

If only she could blurt it out…*tell him.* But something kept her tongue in place. A worry that she might lose what little hold she yet had on him. Or more so, that he may want her for something she wasn't willing to agree to.

Behind them Stella mooed. The cow didn't need to be fed. And Azalea had no intention of listening to a cow's insistence she tell the man *right now.*

"Do you have a guest room?" he asked on a whisper.

Her dad called her old bedroom the guest room now. A hint that she should be moving along?

"It's my room."

His brow quirked. "I wasn't going to ask to sleep separate from you tonight. And it seems that we are both guests in this home. Shall we?" He hooked an arm and she glanced down at the plates and goblets. "We'll clean that up in the morning. Right now, I need to kiss your skin. Everywhere."

A quiet hush gasped from her very being. "Yes."

Hours later, both of them lying naked on the bed, with the sheets off and the open window beckoning inside a sultry breeze, Azalea turned toward Sebastian. It was dark in the room because there was no moon. One of the things about living in the country? No ambient city lights. She loved it. Though she would like to see his eyes right now.

Stroking her finger along his face, she followed the jut of his jawline back to his head and up to his earlobe.

"What are you doing?" he asked quietly.

"Memorizing you. You've got a sharp jawline. I like it." She trailed her fingers down his neck and along his shoulder to a bicep. "I'm guessing you do more than dance at perfume parties to get these muscles. Gym?"

"There's a weight room in my building. But I do run when I can."

"So, you could chase me across a field?"

"I'll certainly give it a go if the opportunity presents itself." He leaned in and kissed the base of her neck. His soft hair tickled her chin. "It's nice out here. So peaceful. Where will you go when your dad sells this place?"

"Not sure yet. I enjoy wide-open spaces. But I like the connection that London offers and sometimes all this rural charm really does annoy a girl. I mean, it takes some effort to pick up a few snacks."

"Sounds like you're stuck between the convenience of a big city and the peace of a smaller town."

"I suppose I am."

"What about Paris? It's a big city, but there is something less busy about it than London."

"Are you suggesting I move to Paris?"

"I wouldn't mind you living in my city. I'd get to see you more often."

"Sebastian..." She dropped her hand to the sheet. "What are you doing? This thing between us, you know it's only a..."

A fling? What *was* it? Because it felt big. Like something she could welcome into her life. Something she *should* welcome into her life. Into her burgeoning family. And yet... It could only ever be a dream. And wouldn't it be best to simply leave it as a dream?

"I don't want it to be a fling, Zee."

Neither did she. But she also knew what she didn't want. "I don't want to do a long-distance relationship."

"You could move to the French countryside?"

"Sebastian."

"What? I'm tossing out ideas."

"We've known each other for less than forty-eight hours. And yes, what we have when we're together is good. Really good."

"Feels soul-deep," he said. "I mean, I can just be with you, sitting on a porch, and that feels right."

Darn him for picking up on that intense connection. But thinking in such terms would only distract her from her staunch need to not settle for something that could never be real. Her mother had left her dad because she'd felt confined, stifled. How could Azalea possibly feel free under the thumb of a millionaire who wanted her for reasons that had nothing to do with love?

And yet, her fantasies of marriage and family had been recently renewed, treading right alongside the desire for a man who seemed too good to be true.

"Just because we're getting along well doesn't mean it will always be good," she said. "Besides, how will my living closer to you work when you have a wife and child?"

He rolled to his back and sighed. "I don't know."

That he didn't protest such a scenario meant it wasn't something he wanted to budge on. He had to find a wife. And have a child.

"I haven't seriously thought about that competition in weeks," he offered in the darkness. "I've been too focused on my dad's recovery and…you. Despite my busy schedule, I had to get away to find you. And now that I have, I question how to move forward. I want us to be a couple, Zee. But it feels as though you don't want it—"

"I do," she rushed out. A foolish outburst?

Oh, heart!

If she told him the real reason she wanted him, it would be as forced as his needing to find a wife. She wanted to be with Sebastian because she was falling in love with him, not because she felt beholden to him. Or because she was having his child and needed an official paper to give the baby legitimacy.

You want to make a real family. Mother. Baby. And father. You know you do.

He kissed the top of her head and slid a hand down to cup her derriere. “Let’s sleep on it. Tomorrow is a new day. And I get to spend it with you.”

He didn’t say anything else. He didn’t need to. She felt the same. Getting to spend time with him was a treat.

He would leave tomorrow, though. The idea of telling him she was pregnant suddenly felt manipulative. Like a means to keep him in her life. It wasn’t like that. She’d thought about it. Debated the pros and cons with Stella. She was prepared to do the mother thing on her own. With the support of her family. She’d told Dahlia about it and her sister had offered to help her find a place to live and a job and day care. She hadn’t told her dad yet. She would when he returned from vacation.

Now, to tell the man who needed a wife and child in order to secure his future that he’d already succeeded in meeting half that stipulation? Or to just step back and allow him to leave and have his own life in a world that she felt wasn’t quite the right fit for her?

CHAPTER SEVEN

A DREAM-OBLITERATING SOUND woke Sebastian. He bolted upright in bed and muttered, "What the…"

It sounded again, long, obnoxious and…crowing. His entire musculature twinged tightly.

He swore.

The gentle touch of a hand to his back soothed reassuringly. He remembered where he was. On a farm. *Of all places*. But he was with her. And that made the next crow—still annoying.

"It's just Big Bruce," Zee whispered. "He's waking up the flowers. Lay down. It's early."

No kidding, it was early. Waking up the flowers? He didn't understand that. What did a cockerel have to do with—? Another crow crept into his spine and froze there.

The room was dark. He…couldn't exactly form thoughts beyond that. But the hand stroking his back chased away the chill and lured him to snuggle against the delicious warmth of Azalea. His Zee.

No obnoxious, crowing fowl could spoil that wondrousness.

Azalea rolled over in bed to find Sebastian smiling at her in the soft morning light.

"That cockerel is not my favorite part of this visit," he said quietly.

"Big Bruce is a noisy fellow."

"Agreed. Let's stay in bed all day and do what we did last night six more times."

"Six? You're awfully motivated."

"Too much? I'll settle for five."

She leaned in and kissed his nose and snugged her entire body against the length of his. Mmm, he was firm in all the right places. "Five, it is. But."

"But?"

At that moment, Big Bruce crowed.

"That," she said. "If I don't head out to feed the wildlife there will be a revolt."

"The life of a farmer?"

"I prefer rural princess, actually."

"Has a nice ring to it. Can I distract you for five minutes before you rush off to tend the animals?" He nudged the firmest part of him against her thigh.

"Absolutely."

After Zee left the bed, Sebastian showered and dressed. They'd only had time for two orgasms before she'd fled to tend the crowing and mooing menagerie. He'd claim the other three, or four, later.

The room was small but the bed had served as a cozy love nest. The entire place was minuscule compared to what he was accustomed to. But for the lack of maids who left his towels out and organized his fridge ingredients by color, he found he didn't mind the tiny home. Everything was an arm's reach away. He'd not had to walk across a vast closet to find anything.

The cockerel's crow tightened his muscles.

"Big Bruce and I will have words today," he muttered.

As for him and Zee, they had come together as if they'd

never been apart. Sure, she'd been initially awkward, but a dance and some kisses had reminded them both that what they had was magical.

"There you go again," he muttered as he wandered down the hallway, "thinking like a romantic."

He hadn't a romantic bone in his body. Truly. Hell, Sebastian Mercier didn't know a thing about romance and love. He'd not witnessed as much growing up. No heart-fluttering, gushing examples had filled his learning brain. Affection had been so fleeting he felt quite sure he was incapable of loving another person.

And yet, the fact he stood here in this tiny cottage, had been woken at dawn by an annoying bird, and now sought to spend the day with a sweet rural princess must allude to some part of his heart softening to the idea of love and romance.

Or was it that he simply needed a wife? A means to an end. And Zee offered an option.

When he thought of it that way, his skin prickled. It sounded so clinical. And certainly, Zee was not the sort of woman who would ever agree to become a convenient bride. Yet he could never give her the love and romance she deserved if he hadn't a clue how those emotions worked.

He'd thought to come here to see if they still had a connection. If not, he'd have headed home to pursue the next candidate for wife. Yet their reunion had been anything but cold and distant. The passion they shared filled him in ways that surprised him. Could he possibly convince Zee to marry him?

Down in the small room before the back door he studied a neat shelving unit that housed shoes, boots and various caps, hats and gloves. Ah, here was a tidy setup. The rubber boots on the bottom looked about his size. And they fit.

"When in Rome," he muttered. Make that *when on a farm.*

He gave a stomp to each boot. Not much for comfort, but they would serve a purpose. The mud-green color clashed terribly with his gray, checked trousers, but he'd not packed comfort clothing, so this look would have to do.

"They could be more stylish with a buckle and perhaps a leather pull tab," he decided.

L'Homme Mercier did not offer shoes in their line. Something to consider? If they ever went with a rustic line, for sure.

Stepping outside, he wandered across the tidy porch and stepped down onto a neat stone walk. The outdoor shower deserved a nod of approval. A few decorative pots of frothy grass rose almost as high as his head and gave off a lemon scent. The path veered in a curving fashion toward the blue barn. With the sun high in the pale sky he wished he'd worn a T-shirt or something lighter than his white button-up, but a roll of each sleeve provided some relief from the humid heat.

He could do rustic as well as anyone. Who would have thought? Certainly, though, his family would scoff to see him now. If it wasn't luxury, artisan-made, an original, or reeking of old money, it wasn't worth the notice. Cows and cockerels? The indignity!

His family didn't have to know about this trip to Ambleside. Nor did they have to know about Azalea. She was…

What was she, exactly? She had stuck in his brain for so long that he'd had to find her. And now that he had, he wanted to stay and never leave her side. Find a way to keep her in his life. Though he much preferred they be together in a less rural setting, he could manage for the duration of this visit. Which would be too short.

If he got involved with Zee, then what would become of his quest to find a wife? He couldn't have a lover and a fake wife. Or? Well? No. It just wouldn't do. He was not a French king or even the president of the country. Despite the press's tendency to label them careless, pleasure-seeking playboys, even the Merciers had their standards.

Might Zee consider becoming his wife? A name on an official piece of paper, who wasn't required to love him or receive love in return. But certainly, it did demand she give him an heir.

Sebastian scrubbed his fingers across the back of his head. He could never fake it with Zee. And not faking it would only complicate it all and confuse his emotions.

Then again, he was no man to back down from a challenge. Especially one that offered such a delicious prize as the freckle-faced rural princess. And the clock was ticking.

"Play it by ear," he muttered as he wandered toward the open barn door. "It's only been a day."

Yes, and things could change. His heart might simply be in the throes of a new and unique interest and passion. Everything cooled. That was a given. As his father had so often said to his sons, "The glow rubs off quickly. And then you're left with disinterest and the itch for something new."

Easy enough for Roman Mercier to say when he hadn't been presented with a win-it-or-lose-the-company ultimatum. There was nothing Sebastian wanted more than to claim the CEO position of L'Homme Mercier.

Not even Azalea Grace? his inner devil whispered.

Well. Which did he want more? Could he really claim attachment to a woman he knew so little? The CEO position meant more. It did.

"Zee?" he called as he entered the cool shade of the barn.

No reply. He wandered through and spied the blonde combing a rather monstrous cow with a long brown coat that flowed over its eyes and horns.

Sebastian had never been around large farm animals. He was rarely around dogs or cats, though he did favor a mellow, napping cat over the oft-rambunctious dog. Those stays at his grandparents' had only ever introduced him to one old dog who could barely wander from his bed to the feeding bowl. There had been the occasional turtles and snakes. Creatures that had fascinated his younger self. And heaven forbid he ever encounter another goat.

Slowing his pace, he cautiously approached, noting there was a smaller cow at the end of a fenced area, nipping at foliage that grew wild against a fence post.

"Why do you call me Zee?" she asked, keeping her attention on the midsection of the beast that she combed.

"You don't like it?" He winced at the scent of manure that rose from all around him. Yet it was topped with a sweet grassy note. He much preferred a perfume-doused room.

"I don't mind. Most friends call me Lea."

"Well, I'm not a friend." But what was he exactly? "Is this beast what you would call a bull?"

She smirked at him as he stopped a good five feet from the animal. He glanced back to the barn. Sprinting distance, if necessity required.

"Stella is a girl. Not a bull."

"*This* is Stella? I thought she was your best friend?"

"She is."

"I see." And here he'd thought her best friend would be a human. Well, he should have guessed, eh? "But she has horns."

"Girl cows can have horns. Specific breeds, that is."

"I didn't know that. She's…" He bent to find the creature's eyes but the long coat covered them completely. "How can she see?"

"Her coat moves when she walks. She knows where you are. She smells you."

"As I smell her." The beast snorted and bobbed her head. Sebastian took a precautionary step back. "Sorry," he provided. "I'm sure you smell lovely to other cows."

"I see you found my dad's wellies," Zee said.

"Do you think he'll mind?"

"Not at all. It's messy out here. Come closer. Give my girl a pat on the nose. She likes affection."

"Very well." Not about to appear afraid of an animal she was obviously comfortable to stand beside, he carefully approached, stretching out an arm until he was just near enough to gently pat her nose. It was…warm and had a soft leathery texture. The beast nudged against his palm. So he stepped closer and gave her nose a gentle rub. "She likes that."

"Stella is a flirt. She'll have you wrapped around her horns in no time."

"I'm not sure I like the idea of such a scenario."

"I didn't mean it like that. Like having you wrapped around her little finger. You know. Maybe you don't. It might have gotten lost in translation."

"Indeed." And yet, he was perfectly content should Zee wish to keep him wrapped about her pinkie finger.

The smaller cow now wandered over, its nostrils flaring as it scented him. Sebastian stepped closer to Azalea.

"She's only five months old," she said. "I think she's going to take after her mom. Goes for the handsome men, she does."

Patting the little one's nose, he was happy to note that

it stopped the beast from getting closer to him. "Do you have a lot of handsome men visiting your animals?"

She chuckled. "Nope. Well, my dad is handsome. And he babies them like they were his children. I think that's good, Stella. You look gorgeous." Zee wrapped her arms about the cow's head for a hearty hug.

"You don't worry about those horns?"

"I'm careful. So." She tucked the comb in a pocket of her overalls. "I'd offer you breakfast but I haven't had time to do grocery shopping. How about we head into the village for a hearty British brekkie?"

"If that means protein and eggs, I'm in."

"Great. You like to ride a bike?"

Sebastian strode after her as she headed through the barn, hanging up the comb as she did. "Bike? Are you serious?"

"Would you prefer we jog?" She chuckled but didn't reassure him that she was indeed joking with him.

And Sebastian swallowed to think that this trip to find the woman of his dreams might just challenge him in ways he never could have imagined.

They did not bike into the village. Azalea had been teasing. The look of utter horror on Sebastian's face when she'd suggested they might pedal in was probably the exact look she hadn't been able to see when Big Bruce had woken him before the crack of dawn.

Poor guy. Farm life could be tough for the uninitiated. But hadn't he said he was a runner? Probably he required fancy running togs and a dedicated path through a city park for such a venture.

Parking her dad's old car on a side street, she then led Sebastian down the quaint cobbled street to her favorite breakfast café.

* * *

After a huge breakfast of bacon, eggs, beans and toast, and a rosemary-seasoned blend of summer vegetables, she led Sebastian on a walk along the river that was hugged on one side by tight hedgerows. He snapped a few selfies of them standing before the Bridge House, then she tugged him down a pathway. The hiking trail was well worn, so the fact that he wore designer shoes without rubber treads wouldn't be a problem.

"It's beautiful out here," he commented as they paused on a hillock to look over Lake Windermere.

A corvid flew over their heads, frighteningly low.

"They're looking for food scraps," Azalea explained. "From the tourists. They come here for the hiking and scenery. It is a lovely place."

"A place you plan to stay in forever?"

He really wanted to nail down her future plans. He'd asked much the same last night in bed.

She leaned against a wood fence post and studied his profile. If she checked the entry for handsome in the dictionary, she felt sure to find Sebastian's picture there. With an addendum warning all women to proceed with caution.

"I fled London to lick my wounds after I broke up with Lloyd. I have a tendency to make bad life choices when it comes to men."

He flicked a concerned look her way.

She shrugged. "I'm not sure where I'll go after Dad returns from Australia. I don't want to intrude on his new relationship. He and Diane are quite smart together. She makes him smile again. And that's a good thing. Besides, he plans to sell, so I need to pack up and find my own place in this world."

And if they continued on this course of conversation,

she'd have to tell him everything. That information was not something she wanted to reveal with tourists wandering by.

"Tell me about your parents," she said. "Are they the sort who would welcome you to stay after a breakup?"

"Perhaps my mother would if she was staying in Paris at the time. My parents are… My father has never married any of his children's mothers."

"Oh. So you and your brother…?"

"Philippe has a different mother than mine. It's why we are only six months apart in age. And I just got a new set of twin brothers nine months ago. Another girlfriend for my dad. Good ole Dad is still single."

"I think they are called playboys. Or baby daddies."

Sebastian laughed and clasped her hand. "That is most definitely Roman Mercier. The man is set in his ways."

"And those ways involve pitting his sons against one another and forcing them to marry? I can dismiss his roguish ways, but really, Sebastian, a man who has never married is asking his sons to do so? I find that hypocritical."

"I try not to consider it too much. And since the strokes, I've noticed more urgency to his manner. He's tasted mortality. He wants to ensure L'Homme Mercier is in good hands before he leaves this world."

"I don't see why both sons can't work together."

"If you knew about the changes and direction Philippe wants to take the company you would understand. He wants to add a women's division."

"And you don't?"

"What part of L'Homme Mercier says women's clothing?"

"Nothing wrong with expanding, is there? The women's market must be much bigger than the men's."

He shook his head and scoffed. “We are a menswear company. Always have been. And should remain so. I’m not against taking the brand to new levels, keeping up with the trends, but there’s no need to cater to the female clientele. So many other designers do it and do it well.”

“I understand that.” She tilted onto her toes to kiss him. A means to assuage what she guessed was a touchy subject that might have just raised his blood pressure a few digits. “I hope you win.”

“You’re just saying that because you like me.”

“I do like you. You’re smart. You’re handsome. And you like to dance. We have fun together. But.”

The fact that he’d tracked her down meant that he hadn’t advanced his plans to find a wife. Or had he? Oh, bother.

“But?” He clasped her hand and pressed the back of it against his lips. Thinking something through? “Am I one of your bad choices, Zee?”

Damn. She shouldn’t have put that one out there.

“Not completely. But well, what *is* this, Sebastian? You’ve already told me you wouldn’t consider me marriage material.”

“And you’ve told me you’d never marry me.”

“I would not. I don’t want to be a pawn in your family competition.”

“I get that but… Zee, I like you. Very much. And that *like* puts a wrench in the competition.”

“How so?”

“I’d much rather spend time with you than seek a potential wife. A woman I fully intend to marry only on paper. Show my father the male heir. Deed done.”

“Sebastian, how can you say that? Much as I care about you, it offends me that you’d treat a woman like that. And use a child in such a manner.”

"I don't know how else to do this, Zee. Unless the perfect woman falls into my arms, I will be forced to find a facsimile wife to win the company. And I must win because L'Homme Mercier must remain as it is."

He couldn't know how hearing that devastated her. Azalea bowed her head. She could understand his desire to keep the family business as he wished it to remain. That his father had set such a ridiculous requirement was cruel to both his sons and to the woman trapped in a loveless marriage, and the resultant baby.

And that made her even more reluctant to reveal her news to him. He didn't need to know. Well, he did. But he didn't need to be a part of her life. Nor she his. That was optional. A choice she mustn't allow to be wrong.

How could she possibly tell him she was pregnant?

"Let's walk back to town and try out the bowling green I saw in the little green square near a pub," he suggested. "I haven't played the game since I was a kid."

"Sure." She clasped his hand and he led them back to the trail. "You're a bit of a kid yourself," she decided. "You like to have fun. That'll be a good thing when you're a dad."

"You think?" He squeezed her hand. "I do enjoy when I see my little brothers. They're adorable. I will strive to be a much different father to my children than my father is to me and my stepbrothers."

That was hopeful to hear. But the idea of raising a child in the Mercier family of men who did not feel love was necessary to commit did not appeal to Azalea at all.

CHAPTER EIGHT

SEBASTIAN WAS SURPRISED at how the red-feathered hen had settled comfortably against his stomach as he held it. Trusting. Zee had shown him how to carefully pick it up, protecting its wings and cupping its feet. Now he stroked its head softly and whispered in French that she was pretty.

Zee sat beside him with another hen in hand. She winked at him. Her wavy hair spilled across her cheek, and if he had not had his hands full, he would have brushed it aside.

How to convince her that marrying him would make them both happy? Did he believe that they could be happy together? It felt as though happiness were a possibility. And really, if he had to marry, why not to a woman with whom he genuinely enjoyed spending time?

"You're a natural," she said. "Ginger is in love with you."

"Ginger, eh?"

"Yep. And this is Posh." She tousled the elaborate feathers that spouted bodaciously from the top of her chicken's head as if a cheerleader's pom-pom. "That's Scary over there with the missing tail feathers. And… Sporty is over there chasing Daisy. She's the most athletic of the crew."

"Where's Baby?"

Zee sucked in her lower lip and cast him a worried

glance. "Dad and Diane made coq au vin before they left for Australia."

"Oh." At that horrifying statement Sebastian could but hug his content fowl closer. Might he ever enjoy a chicken meal again after bonding with the sweet and snuggly Ginger?

"I know," she said. "But despite her name, Baby was getting long in her years. She wasn't laying anymore. She lived a good life."

"And you think *I'm* callous about this whole marriage thing."

"I would hardly compare eating a pet hen to faking a marriage."

"It's not—"

He wanted her to be wrong but she was closer to the truth than he was. How else *could* he manage such a situation? He wouldn't know love if it smacked him in the face. And that was what it was wont to do if it did occur and he had the audacity to insist on marriage.

"Let's not talk about that right now," he said. "I'm enjoying this moment with you. I like that we can sit together and be quiet."

She laid her head on his shoulder. "And hug chickens."

"It's a nice break from my usual hectic schedule. And the sunset is unreal."

Pink, violet and brilliant streaks of gold painted the sky. He'd not taken a moment to notice the sunsets in Paris. It was a vibrant masterpiece. Just like Zee. And Ginger. The colors made him think of the first time he'd been introduced to embroidery work by one of the tailors. It wasn't utilized in suit-making but had been a hobby. The old man had crooked a finger, urging a young Sebastian to follow him into the back room at L'Homme Mercier. With a gleeful flash of his eyes, he'd then opened a sewing box to reveal a rainbow of embroidery threads and shown him the various needles. Sebastian had run his fingers over the silken threads, in awe. Perhaps that had been what had cemented his true interest in the creation of fine clothing, from the very basic stitches to the elegant fabrics and quality craftsmanship. It beat out machine-made factory clothing by everything.

He hadn't worked hands-on creating a suit in years. But there were days he wished the old tailor with the sparkle in his eyes was still around. Sebastian would like to explore his collection of colored threads and create something.

As CEO of L'Homme Mercier he would take on more responsibility, yet at the same time he might be able to delegate to others some of his current duties that were tedious. It was his life. He honored hard work and talent, but he also appreciated this trip that allowed him to relax and not think about shipping schedules or clients or vendor complications.

"I don't want to go home," he blurted.

"I was wondering when you were going to leave. You said you would stay twenty-four hours. That's right about now."

"Do I have to leave?" he asked himself. Then he looked to Zee. "Do you want me to leave?"

"I want you to stay as long as you like."

"Then I'll stay. Because leaving you doesn't feel right. Don't you agree, Ginger?"

The chicken cooed quietly. Content. As he felt. Sitting beside Zee felt right.

"You don't have work to get back to?"

"I can manage another day," he decided. Maybe two? "I have a meeting on Friday with a supplier that I mustn't miss. He's traveling from Dubai."

“That gives us two more days.”

“My stay won’t be unwanted?”

“Honestly? I wish you could stay all summer.” She kissed him and in the process her chicken squawked and made a fuss so she set it free. “How about I go in and make us something to eat.”

“I’m quite hungry after our adventurous day.”

“Great. I’ll make chicken!” She got up, leaving Posh on the ground by his feet, looking up at him with a worried fowl stare.

“I’ll protect you,” he said to the hen. He scanned his gaze around the yard, sighting the other two birds. Stella wandered near the fence. “Should have done a head count on the poultry earlier.”

On the other hand, if Big Bruce were sacrificed, he would not argue the quiet.

The next afternoon they hiked out across the hillocks and stones of the countryside along the bank of Lake Windermere.

Azalea chose a spot next to a low stone wall and laid out a plaid blanket near a crop of wild poppies, while Sebastian snapped some shots of the glassy blue lake and the lush greenery hugging it. It truly was as gorgeous as the tourist advertisements made it look. And it smelled like the real world, so verdant and full. And as luck would have it, she’d led them onto an unmarked trail that only the residents knew about, so unless some tourists got curious, they’d have this cozy little patch to themselves.

She’d packed a simple lunch of sandwiches, fresh fruit, cheese and bottled water. Diane had made cream cheese cookies before leaving on holiday and had left them in the freezer. Azalea had been judiciously thawing but one a day as a treat. Today, she'd packed four.

Taking the stone path carefully, Sebastian returned to sit on the blanket beside her. "You say people come here to hike the mountains?"

"Yes, it's a big tourist draw. I mean, I don't know if the summits qualify as mountains but they give good exercise."

"Have you hiked them?"

"Yes, all around the area which is the National Forest. I can start out in the morning and not be seen until after sunset. There are sweet surprises all over, like tiny stone bridges, or enchanting tree-covered paths, and the Stagshaw Gardens. There's a waterfall that way in the Stock Ghyll woods. It's a lovely way to while away an afternoon. Oh, and there's the champion trees. It's a pretty walk among hundreds of different types of trees. My favorite is the sequoia."

"You're a real nature girl. I understand now why a big city does not appeal to you."

"And yet, a big-city man does offer appeal." She handed him a bottle of water, and he took her wrist and pulled her closer to kiss her.

Feeling like a heroine from a nineteenth century novel, Azalea decided the flutter in her chest and the warmth enveloping her neck was a genuine swoon. The man could own her with his slow and deep kisses. And that was a dangerous realization.

He bowed his forehead to hers and tapped her lips. "I'm glad your heart is not determined to find a rural lover wielding a pitchfork and wearing wellies."

Recalibrating her malfunctioning common sense, she sat up straight and lifted her chin. "Nothing wrong with that type. They are dependable, hardworking…" And yet… the one she had briefly dated had wanted her barefoot, pregnant and subservient. "Though I feel sure my princess inclinations would not be weathered well by such a hardy rural man. I do like to dress up and do the city life once in a while."

"You balance between the wilds and the urban," Sebastian said. "Princess one day, cow whisperer the next?"

"Works for me. But what about you? I don't fit in with your lifestyle, do I? I mean, Lloyd said it best when he—"

Another kiss made her realize that she had been about to spout nonsense and silliness. Lloyd was her past. The comments he had made about their differences were just his perspective. Common sense wasn't always fun, nor should it ruin a perfectly lovely picnic.

Sebastian said, "We are different, Zee. My grandmother used to read me a story when I was little. Something about a country mouse and a city mouse?"

"I think that story was more about one's ambitions and desires. Each has their own comfort zone. Of course, I believe it was the city mouse who lived in fear of the cat all the time. The country mouse was quite content to return home after a brief adventure in the big city."

"You think my ambitions are too much?"

"If they involve marrying a woman merely on paper to achieve a position?" She busied herself with unwrapping the sandwiches and cookies. It had just come out. It was the truth, to her. Even Sebastian had said as much.

"You think I should concede to Philippe in order to avoid a moral misstep?"

Who was she to tell him what he had the right to do or how to live his life? She couldn't even come to terms with how to proceed with her own life!

She handed him a sandwich and shook her head. "I think you should be true to your heart." And her heart performed a double beat in response to that statement.

Listen to me, it seemed to beg. *Are you being true to your heart?*

He nodded, taking a few bites. "I'm not even sure what my heart's truth is right now."

"My heart has a tendency to think before my brain does. It can sometimes be annoying. And I regret the things I do. But later, it always seems as though it was right."

"Even when it was a bad choice?"

"Even so." He wouldn't let that one drop. Sebastian Mercier was not a bad choice. Well, not as bad as some of her choices had been. "My heart speaks my truth. I just have to learn to listen to it and stop arguing for something different."

"What arguments have you with your heart right now?"

If he only knew. The one where she wanted to wrap him in her arms and never let him go. Tell him she was pregnant as a means to keep him in her life. Win the man she adored.

Stupid heart.

In this particular situation, her brain knew better. Nothing good could come of such a relationship because her heart could never really know if Sebastian's feelings for her were true or just manufactured to obtain the CEO position.

"Wow." He brushed breadcrumbs from his pant leg. "There really is an argument going on in there." He pointed to her chest, there where her heart pounded to be heard, to be acknowledged, to simply be followed. "Is it about me?"

She smirked and leaned back on her palms, stretching out her legs. "You know it is."

"I am honored to have found a position in your heart. Though it saddens me that it causes you internal struggle."

"Sebastian, you are a charmer. But we both know this can't go anywhere. So why not just enjoy what we have right now?"

"Then walk away from one another and proceed as if it didn't even happen?"

"Oh, I'll never forget you."

"Nor I you." He took her hand and pressed it over his heart. "My heart developed this weird little hole the morning I woke up and found you had snuck out, never to be seen again. And since then, it's been wanting to fit you into that hole. Someway, somehow."

Such a confession kicked her own heart, trying to convince it to comply. To be honest with her needs for her future. But her brain held her back. So much to consider now with the way her life had begun to unfold.

Shrugging, she offered him a treat. "How about a cookie to fill that hole?"

With a smirk, he took one and bit into it, turning to look across the lake. And Azalea knew that with or without him in her life, he would always be a part of her world.

She couldn't decide whether that was good, bad or ugly. But mostly, she just wanted her heart to get its act together and win.

They walked back through Ambleside just as a city parade was coming to an end. The streets were packed with tourists and residents and so many children.

Sebastian noted they carried wood frames covered with flowers and long weedy leaves. "What did we miss?"

"It's the annual rush-bearing festival. Celebrates the cleaning out of the rushes from the churches. I guess it's become so commonplace to me I didn't even think to ask if you wanted to watch. Those wood frames are rush bearers. And the leafy things are rushes. They used to place them on the floors in medieval times as rugs and to keep things cleaner. Seems to me they might have been more of a big mess."

"Interesting." He paused at the edge of the crowd, taking in a crew of bustling children dashing about with rushes and flowers in hand. One of them ran up to him and with big, beaming eyes offered him a white flower.

Sebastian bent and took the flower. "Thank you."

The little girl, no more than five or six, winked at him, then performed a twirl and spun back into the procession alongside her friends. He stood and sniffed the blossom.

"You are a lady killer," Zee muttered. "But that was also the most adorable thing I've ever seen."

The look she flashed up at him landed in his heart like a warm beam of sunshine. It felt like admiration, perhaps even pride. And Sebastian had never felt more worthy of a woman's regard in his lifetime. Wow. It wasn't an overwhelming feeling, yet it seemed to flood his system with a knowing warmth, a quiet joy. The noise of the parade faded out and he smiled to himself, sinking deeply into the moment. It needed to be honored, recognized. And enjoyed.

Azalea Grace had a power over his heart that should frighten him, but instead he wanted to sway toward her and allow her open access to it. To him. To anything she desired that would see that look of pride beaming at him again.

"Sebastian?"

Surfacing from the feeling with a tilt of his head that allowed back in all the ambient noise of life, he gripped her hand and gave it a squeeze. Tucking the white flower into Zee's hair, he kissed her forehead.

"Back to the farm," she said, unaware of his incredible journey of emotion. "You've got a train to catch."

After witnessing Zee in her natural environment, Sebastian realized what he wanted was not something he could have. They were two different people. Living in two very different places. With two different focuses. And while millions of couples all around the world obviously made similar situations work, he sensed Zee's reluctant to give it a go. She pulled him to her while at the same time pushed him away. Such inadvertent machinations had the potential to drive him mad.

So he must be done with it.

All the proud, admiring glances in the world would never change their situation.

If she wasn't willing to give this thing they had a try, then he must set back his shoulders, chin up, and walk away from her. Much as he adored her, if she couldn't see a future between them, then he must stop trying to prod the dead horse, so to speak.

Thinking of animals, he thought of Zee, out in the barn tending Stella and Daisy.

He paused in folding the dress shirt he'd packed and peered out the window. He'd called for a car, which would arrive soon. And then he would leave. Never to see her again?

He stuffed his shirt and trousers into the suitcase, not caring if they wrinkled. Perhaps he had one last chance to woo her, to convince her that they could be more than just a brief fling. Should he take it? Would he wound her by further involving her in the mess of a future life he must create to win the prize?

"One more try," he muttered.

CHAPTER NINE

AZALEA PRESSED HER palms against the wood fence behind the barn. With a few deep inhales, the wooziness she'd felt passed. Morning sickness. It had occurred two or three times in the last month. And not necessarily in the morning. A quick online search had told her it could occur at any hour. She hadn't vomited yet. But the nauseous feeling rose so quickly all she could do was focus on her breathing until it subsided.

She could be thankful it hadn't attacked when in Sebastian's presence.

By her calculations she was three months pregnant. When she'd taken the test a month earlier, she'd surprised herself with her reaction. No tears. No regrets. She'd been excited to know a new life was growing inside her. While she'd not come to a decision regarding whether to tell Sebastian—that nasty competition spoiled everything—she did realize she was strong and independent. Women did the single mother thing all the time. She could manage.

"Really?" she scoffed. "How's that going to work without a job or home?"

Sure, she could stay here at Grace Farm. But her dad intended to put up the For Sale sign when he returned from Australia. And she was quite sure she couldn't tag along with him and Diane to their next location. If they even bought a permanent home. The twosome planned to travel for a while before settling down. Azalea would not be a third wheel, even if one of the other wheels was her dad. Especially so.

She needed to find a home and a job within the next few months or she would be left homeless and sporting a baby propped on her hip. Not the way she wanted to begin life as a mother.

She could ask Sebastian for help. But that would mean revealing all to him.

Sebastian had disconcerting views about family and children. The family he created in order to gain control of L'Homme Mercier would be fake. And the idea of even considering them as a couple, possibly married, didn't sink in right. She might never know if he were marrying her because she was the mother of his child or because he wanted to win a competition.

And even if love were involved, she would never force a man to marry her just to make things look right. The world had changed. Single mothers were no longer ostracized or sneered at. And forcing a man to be a father, simply to make a family, could go the wrong way and the child could suffer because of it.

Though she wouldn't mind a little financial assistance from him.

"What to do?" she asked Stella, who currently rocked her head against the fence for a good scratch. "I have to tell him. It's only fair. But I don't want him to feel coerced. Or to take advantage of the situation. How am I going to do this?"

He was leaving soon. An important meeting tomorrow morning required he return to Paris. She couldn't guess how he would react to her news. She didn't want it to turn into an argument or a sob-fest or, worse, an obligation.

She stroked the cow's side, giving her a firm pat. "What do you think, Stella? The next step I take is going to steer my life. I just want to make the right choice this time."

Rain seemed appropriate for his departure. It began fitful and heavy, then settled to drizzle. The air smelled like ozone and flowers. It really was a kick to notice that unadulterated scent.

According to the tracking on his app, the car he'd called for would arrive in about twenty minutes. His suitcase sat near the front door. The wellies he'd borrowed were cleaned and placed neatly in their cubby. And Zee… She'd been strangely aloof since they'd returned home following the rush-bearing festival. When he'd suggested they have sex one last time she'd said she needed to feed the cows.

Really?

He suspected she might be feeling the same way he did. Parting would tear out his heart. As much as he wanted to stay forever, though, it wasn't possible. She'd drawn a line. He must respect that. And remember that for one amazing moment he had earned that look of pride from her. A look he would never forget.

In the kitchen, the white flower blossom gifted him by the little girl sat in a small glass vase on the table. He heard the back door swing shut on its creaky hinges.

"Zee?"

"Right there! Just washing the mud off my legs."

When she wandered into the kitchen, she was barefoot, wearing a simple floral dress that was a little wet from the rain. Her hair hung in loose wet waves over her shoulders. A beautiful mess.

"You're ready to leave? I'm so sorry I lost track of time. When does the car arrive?"

"Soon." He set his coat on the suitcase and took her in his arms. He swayed, sliding a hand up her back. "One last dance?"

Hugging up against him she followed his slow steps, her head against his shoulder. They didn't need music to find their rhythm; they'd been in sync since the moment they'd met. Every move, every glance, every shared smile felt meant to be. Fated? He'd never thought much about fate and destiny but it did feel special.

And yet, he noticed her careful separation from him, the sudden absence of her head from his shoulder, the misstep as she turned the opposite direction he'd intended.

Sebastian blurted, "You've been avoiding me since we returned to the cottage."

"I..." She exhaled and stepped from his embrace, nodding. "Sorry. This is difficult."

"I feel the same. But I thought you had decided this wasn't possible?"

"This?" She blew out a breath and rubbed a hand over her belly.

"Well, us, of course. Have you had a change of heart? Zee, I know this whole marriage thing isn't fair to you. But I need you to understand that you are set aside from that. That's an odd way to put it. You—I care about you, Zee. I think I could fall in love with you."

She tugged in her lower lip and winced.

"Please don't make that face. I'll take it personally." He held up his hand, pinkie extended.

She sighed but didn't return the pinkie hug. Oh, the unbearable weight of rejection.

"I'm sorry. It's just the love thing," she said. "You only think you're in love. Or could fall in love. You can't say, with certainty, you are in love. I know it's complicated.

Oh, Sebastian. There's something I need to tell you. And I've been sitting on it since you arrived, unsure how to reveal it."

At that moment a car rolled up the drive and honked.

Sebastian took out his phone and texted the driver that he'd be five minutes. "What is it, Zee? When I say I think could fall in love, that's it exactly. I'm not sure I've ever been in love before. And God knows it's not a thing I've ever gotten much of in my life. This is a new feeling for me. Allow me some measure to figure that out?"

"You weren't in love with the woman who fled the back of the limo that night we met?"

"No. Amie and I had dated for only three weeks."

"Why did she run off?"

"Because for some reason she was offended by my proposal." He knew the reason. Amie was not stupid. Love was an important ingredient to marriage. Or so he suspected. She'd made the right choice. "She tossed the ring at me and left. I was honest with you about that situation. It's the past. Has no bearing on what's going on with us. Zee, we can make this work. Paris isn't that far away—"

"Sebastian, I'm pregnant."

"And I can— What?" The heartfelt argument sluiced from his brain like a flood. What she'd just said. Had he heard her correctly? "You just said…"

Zee splayed out her hands. "I took a test—two of them—and I'm pregnant. It happened that night in Paris. I haven't been with anyone else, so I know it's yours. Promise. And I know what this means in the competition sense of things to you. But it can't be like that. I won't allow it to be."

He took her by the upper arms. Big blue eyes peered up at him. No freckles caught in the crinkles though, because she wasn't smiling. Was that sadness in her irises? Why was she not bubbling over with joy? Did she not feel the same, sudden intensity of emotion that he did?

"Zee," he breathed. His heartbeats raced. Every muscle in his body wanted to follow that race. What a rush of emotion and— "Do you tell me true?"

She nodded.

"But that's..."

What was that? He was going to be a father? That sealed that part of the competition—but no. He mustn't react that way. It was... Not right. Unfair to Zee. Unfair to his own feelings.

What *were* his feelings about this unexpected announcement? Besides the fact that he felt as if something inside him were actually bubbling. Was it joy? It felt akin to the feeling he'd savored while they'd stood watching the parade.

"Really?" A smile wiggled on his lips and he didn't fight it. This news felt...not wrong. Though he wasn't sure if it was quite right, either. At least, not to judge from her lack of enthusiasm. "Zee, I wish you had told me about this sooner. We could have talked about it."

He'd given up on asking her to marry him after seeing her thriving in her natural habitat, but with this news... might he have asked her after all?

"There's nothing to discuss. I've decided that I don't want to involve myself, and this baby, in the Mercier family drama. I just thought it was only fair to tell you about it. You are the father. You have a right to know. I'll be fine on my own. I'm not going to ask anything of you."

"But you must. Ask me for everything! Zee, this is *my* baby."

The car honked.

Sebastian cursed. He stuck his head out the doorway and gestured for the driver to be patient. “I can’t believe this. I need to process this. We must discuss what this means. Zee?”

“I know. I apologize for saving this for the last minute. I think this is as cruel as I’ve ever been to a person. And I’m not proud of that. But I was scared of your reaction. That you might want to use me and the baby to win the game you’re playing with your brother. Even though I do desire family and…finding someone who cares about me.”

“But—”

She thrust up a palm to stop his desperate plea. “Just accept that I have to do it this way.”

He nodded, though it wasn’t a means to agreement. It was merely a reaction to—such a surprise. Processing it would take some thought. Never would he have expected her to reveal such a thing as… “I’m going to be a father?”

She shrugged. “Well, it’s your sperm. I’ll be doing all the mothering and childcare.”

He didn’t like that she put it that way. It relegated him to the side, to not being a part of the baby’s life. Did he want that? He needed a child. But that was a need created by his desire for career advancement. For the very thing he most wanted in life.

Another honk annoyed him, but he reacted to the rude prompt—and Zee’s seeming indifference to his heart—by grabbing his suitcase. “We have not discussed this properly. You owe me that much. Promise me, when your father returns, you’ll come to Paris so we can talk about this like adults. Zee?”

She nodded. “Of course. It’s only fair.”

She was so resigned. His heart broke. No joyous bubbles. Just utter ache. Was he not worthy of her recognizing him as the father of her child? Did she not want him in her life? And here he'd made plans to attempt to woo her one last time…

"At the very least don't you want to come to Paris to see me again?" It felt like a childish plea, but he was at odds, unsure about anything right now.

"I do, but… This is just so big, Sebastian. I need time—"

"I do, too. But I also need us to handle this. Together." He opened the door. "When will your dad return?"

"A few weeks."

"Then…here." He took out his phone and started a text. "I'm sending you my address…along with all the digital entry codes. As soon as you can, come to Paris. If I'm not home, you walk right in. My place is yours." A tap of his finger sent her the information. With reluctance, he lifted his head and nodded. "I'll see you in a few weeks?"

She nodded and managed a weak smile.

A kiss would be most appropriate, but something held him back from leaning in to claim that delicious connection. Things had changed between them. So suddenly. And he honestly didn't know whether to label it good or terrible.

No pinkie hugs this time. He'd lost that connection. Or rather, she had indicated it wasn't what she wanted.

Turning and taking the cobblestone pathway to the waiting car was the hardest move Sebastian had ever had to make. Raindrops spat at his skin. He put his suitcase in, slid into the back and closed the door, and the car rolled away. Away from a woman who dazzled him. A woman for whom his heart beat. A woman who allowed him to see the world in a new way, or rather, reminded him of a simpler time when he'd been a child and had enjoyed life.

A woman…who carried his child.

"Mon Dieu," he muttered as he rubbed a temple.

Was he doing the right thing? Walking away from her right now? The meeting could—well, it was important. But he could reschedule. The client was flying in from Dubai but he could put him up in a hotel for a day or two…

"No." Zee had asked for time to think about this. As well, he needed to think about it. A few weeks before her father returned?

This was going to be the longest fortnight of his life.

CHAPTER TEN

Oliver Grace and Diane had returned to the farm a week ago. After Diane left for town to pick up groceries, Azalea decided it time to tell her dad she was pregnant. He'd looked surprised but had immediately pulled her into a hug and kissed her forehead. Motherhood, or rather nurturing, had always been her true calling, he'd declared. Then he'd asked if the baby would call him Grandpa or maybe Pops?

That had been much easier than how she'd expected the talk to go. Even the information about Sebastian, and his family competition, had been listened to with a quiet nod from her dad.

"You've got to do what feels right in your heart," he said now as they sat out on the porch steps. "I'm here for you, Lea, you know that. And I agree that London isn't the place for you. But..." He sighed. "You can't hide here forever."

"You posting the For Sale sign out front yesterday was a very obvious clue."

"It's not even that, Lea. If you wanted to stay here and we could work out a means for rent, I'd be behind that."

Yet she knew he needed the sale of the land and house to finance his future. A future of new dreams and adventure that Diane had been detailing since they'd returned. Next stop? The United States, starting with New York City!

Diane had already booked a room and purchased Broadway tickets for October in hopes the property sold quickly.

"But speaking as a man," he said as he clasped her hand, "Sebastian does deserve more than the quick five minutes you gave him before he had to leave."

The manner in which she'd told Sebastian, as the driver waited to whisk him away, had been cruel. She'd panicked, prolonging the reveal for far too long. He would have stayed if she'd asked it of him. But the moment had felt like ripping off a plaster. She'd just wanted to toss it aside and not look at it, so seeing him off had been all she could manage at the time.

"Go to him, Lea. Talk to him."

"I will. I just…"

"No more excuses. Stella will survive without you. In fact, I spoke to Burke the other day." The owner of the farm on the opposite side of the lake from Grace Farm. "They lost two of their calves to sickness last winter. He's interested in buying ours. As pets," he reassured when she almost protested that the neighbors tended to butcher their cows for the table.

"I know a trip to Paris is necessary. I do want to see Maddie again."

The air felt heavy with things she should say, truths she wanted to confess about how she felt about her baby's father, emotions that rose when remembering how they simply seemed to belong with one another.

Her dad smoothed a palm over the back of her hand. "Is he so terrible, then?"

"Sebastian? No. He's possibly the most wonderful man I've ever known." She knew what her dad alluded to: then why avoid him? "He didn't ask me to marry him. And I didn't expect him to. Nor did I want him to, knowing what it might mean. And after how things went with Lloyd… And Mom deciding to leave…”

“Oh, Lea, you mustn’t believe the divorce was anything but meant to be. We talked about this. It was a mutual parting.”

“I know, but Mom said she felt confined. And you know how I love my freedom. But also…” Now she was just grasping for excuses. Her heart would never give up the dream of having family.

“Marriage is different for everyone. Your mother and I shared thirty wonderful years. People change. They grow apart. That doesn’t mean you should never give a person a go on the off chance the same might happen. Life is meant to be lived. Live it without looking into the crystal ball and asking about your future. Take a chance!”

She sighed. “Maybe my heart was waiting for that proposal from Sebastian after hearing about the baby. Just so I know it was something he would have considered.”

“He’s being smart. Maybe even cautious of your heart. If he had asked you right away, I would have been suspicious. Like he was only trying to do the right thing.”

“Maybe.” What was so wrong with that? Well, everything. At least, as far as she’d decided. “Oh, Dad, this is difficult. I should be focusing on finding a job and a place to live. In less than half a year I’m going to be a family!”

“I can’t wait to welcome my grandbaby! Heaven knows, Dahlia will never make me a pops. I think we’re going with Pops, yeah?”

“Sounds perfect, Pops. I’m glad you’re excited about this. It makes everything feel a little easier in the grander scheme of things.”

“Raising children is never easy. It’s messy, emotionally

trying and downright frustrating at times. But it is also wondrous, joyful, and so worth it."

She tilted her head against his shoulder. "I love you, Dad."

"I promise to love the heck out of my grandbaby. I might even save some space in my heart for the tyke's father, too."

"Sebastian takes up a lot of space," she started to say, but swallowed and couldn't bring herself to finish the last part—*in my heart.*

Her dad pulled her into a hug. "It'll all go as it should, Lea. I promise you that."

Days later

Azalea had asked the taxi driver to drive to the L'Homme Mercier atelier and home office in the 6th arrondissement. She'd considered being dropped off out front, but then she'd decided that walking in with suitcases in hand, looking like the last woman the posh Sebastian Mercier would ever involve himself with, would be bad form. She couldn't do that to him, so she redirected the driver.

A small corner hotel offered an available room. It was literally just a room, like in someone's house, with a basin and a bed and a window that looked toward Notre Dame. She plunked her suitcase on the lumpy bed and went to freshen up in the closet-sized bathroom. The lavender soap made her dizzy, so she tucked it away in a drawer.

She hadn't texted Sebastian to let him know she'd be coming to Paris. He'd texted her over the weeks since he'd left the farm. He hadn't asked after the baby, just sending notes to let her know he was thinking about her.

You are in my thoughts.

I miss your bright eyes.

We dance well together.

She appreciated his careful distance. But it also put dread in her heart.

A very rich and powerful man now held a claim to her unborn child. If she didn't go along with whatever he wished, would he take it away from her? It was a dramatic scenario, but she'd played it over many times. Sebastian had been brought up by a father who had many children, all by mothers he'd never married. Could this baby be the first in a collection that Sebastian would grow just as he'd witnessed his father do? After all, he'd known nothing else.

A terrible thought. But something she needed to have answered while here in Paris.

To look on the plus side, she felt great. The morning sickness had passed, though her aversion to smells had grown. Her appetite had also increased. As had her gut. Though she'd yet to pop out with an apparent baby bulge. So far, her middle had thickened, overwhelming what had once been a slender waist. Not the most appealing shape. She'd begun to wear looser clothing—today a spaghetti-strap sundress—to accommodate the weight gain.

Checking her phone, she vacillated between going for a walk and calling him. Sebastian had given her his home address, which was in the 6th arrondissement. The entry codes, for gosh sakes! But it didn't feel right walking in and making herself at home. Much as part of her felt a certain right to do so. Carrying the man's child, anyone?

That did grant her some clout. But no. She wasn't the sort to expect anything of him.

Yet why not? And really, *shouldn't* she expect something? And if not from Sebastian, then certainly she must figure in her own expectations for this strange but curious affair of having the rebound man's baby.

"Such dramatics," she muttered. A chuckle was necessary. She was a rural princess, not some wayward romance heroine desperate to claim her baby's father.

"Maybe a little," she then whispered.

And her heart remained hopeful in response to that realization.

Since it was early, she decided to ring up Maddie. Her girlfriend was hopping a flight tomorrow for Berlin, so they arranged to meet at a café in half an hour. Starting this trip with some friend time was what Azalea required to bolster her courage.

Finding the café with ease, Azalea crossed the street. Maddie, seated at an outside table, waved, gold bracelets clinking. She stood to kiss Azalea on both cheeks as she arrived. "I can't believe you're back in Paris. I wish I'd known sooner. We could have spent more time together. So, what's up?"

Azalea sat and took a sip of the water already at the table. "A lot, Maddie. Are you ready for this?"

Her friend wiggled on her chair and excitedly said, "Always!"

CHAPTER ELEVEN

JUST AS HE was leaving the office for the evening, Sebastian received a text from Zee. She was in Paris. An utter explosion of relief loosened muscles that he hadn't realized he'd been holding tight for…possibly weeks. He texted her back that he was on his way to pick her up.

He'd given much thought to the idea of becoming a father. While it hadn't been something he'd planned, it was also something that he'd sought. Weirdly enough. He'd thought of his baby every day since learning she was pregnant. Most of the time he smiled. A few times he shook his head. Was he even ready to become a father? How to be a good parent when all he knew was…well, it was what he knew.

And now he'd been gifted with the very thing that could catapult him to the win.

But a softer, more caring side of him admonished that he couldn't very well take the baby and run, while seeking another woman to marry him. Azalea did not deserve such cruelty. Yet if she wouldn't marry him, what was he to do? If he made the wrong choice, he could very well lose not only the CEO position, but as well, the only women he desired.

How to have both?

He hadn't come to any sane means to obtain Zee's hand in marriage without offending her morals. Kidnapping, threatening and coercion had only been temporary, ridiculous thoughts. He wasn't that man.

Gently wooing her might work. Could it?

For the first time in his life, he struggled with his feelings for a woman. And that was remarkable to realize. Was this, in fact, for the first time in his life…love?

He'd told Zee he thought he was falling in love with her. But at the time he hadn't known for sure. And he wasn't even sure now. The idea of love excited him. And it worried him.

Love might spoil any plans of gaining control over L'Homme Mercier.

Half an hour later, Sebastian collected Zee and her things, and whisked her off to his place. Now she stood before the massive wall of windows, looking out over the city. The sun wouldn't set for hours, but the hazy day cast a shadow over the sky and silhouetted her before him. He felt as though she were untouchable and yet so down-to-earth. A princess of quaint and chickens but also a goddess of beauty and frolic. Yet he couldn't forget when she'd told him she wasn't sure where life would next lead her. He had a few ideas. But he cautioned himself from overstepping with her. She was skittish. And rightfully so.

Since returning to Paris from Ambleside he'd had opportunities to date and had refused them all. No woman interested him like Zee did. The idea of proposing to anyone but Zee didn't even fit into his brain. And now there was another reason for him to invest in their relationship.

He agreed with Zee on one point: he did not want his child to be a tool to lever his position in the family drama. That was unfair. And reeked of his own childhood. Not an unpleasant upbringing, but even he could understand it wasn't normal, and most certainly was not in Zee's range of comfort.

"How are you feeling?" he asked as he pulled a bottle of sparkling water from the fridge, then poured them both a glass. "Am I allowed to ask?"

"Of course, you are. We are still…friends." She swallowed.

Unsure about that title? It wasn't what he would label them, and it poked at his heart to hear her declare such. On the other hand, who was he to claim something more? How to navigate this delicate balance between them?

"I'm feeling good. I assume you're asking baby-wise? I had a little morning sickness for the first few months but it's gone. It's just odors that bug me now. Although you smell great. Very subtle. I like it."

"Thank you. I finally got the last remnants of Câlin out by hiring a cleaning crew. Remind me never to attend another perfume party."

He handed her the glass and kissed her cheek. He wanted to hug her and never let her go, but she'd flinched when he'd met her at the hotel. Keeping a bit of distance between them? That killed him. He daren't offer a pinkie hug either. She'd not responded the last time he'd tried that. He'd react to her cues.

"I still can't get over how beautiful Paris is," she commented. "It's a cloudy day and still the sky looks like a painting. Is that Notre Dame over there, with the scaffolding climbing the structure?"

"It is. Under repair following the fire a few years ago. Though soon it will be complete."

If she intended to pussyfoot around the subject that he'd not been able to stop thinking about the past few weeks, he would pull out his hair. But he reminded himself to give her some measure, and to allow her the lead.

"I'm sorry it took so long," she said. "I mean, to come here. Dad got back a few weeks ago and I told him about the baby. He's over the moon to become a grandpa. Pops is what he's decided the baby will call him. Diane, his girlfriend, is excited as well. She's been doting on me."

"Doting is good, yes?" Some things got lost in translation.

"It involves lots of stories about when she was a mother, shopping for baby things, and stories about how to breastfeed properly and select the best pram. So, yes, very good." She set down the water and splayed her hands before her. "So. We need to talk."

"I don't intend to make talking to me a hardship, Zee. Are you so against the idea that we now have a connection? You called us merely friends. I thought we got along so well."

"We did. We do. It's just…everything has changed." She sat on the sofa that faced the windows and patted the cushion beside her. "First tell me how things are going for you at work. You had a meeting you had to get home to? How did that go?"

"It was for next year's spring line. All signed, sealed and sent to the tailor. And work is always a pleasure for me."

"I know that about you. That's why I also know how important it is that you win the CEO position."

He sat next to her and took her hand, kissing the back of it. The softness of her skin brought him instantly back to her farm, sitting on the porch, watching the sun beam across the pond. With chickens. An odd moment to remember, since it should be the very last thing that he cared to repeat, the country retreat part. And yet, if Zee were beside him, would he be comfortable spending the rest of his days living such a scenario?

"I don't want to talk about work, Zee. I've done a lot of thinking these few weeks. About us."

"I don't think there can be an us."

He turned abruptly to search her gaze. She looked down, avoiding his nudging desire to find the truth in her eyes. "Zee?"

"It all comes down to that stupid competition. I won't be a part of it. It's unfair to me."

"First, I haven't asked you to marry me. And second, I'm not so insensitive. You mustn't believe I would use you in such a manner, Zee. You mean too much to me."

"That's lovely to hear, but I will never know if you're saying it because it's what I want to hear or if it comes from your heart."

"It comes from my heart. I know we haven't known one another long, but you should know that I am a man of my word. I do not tolerate lies."

"I think I know that." She sighed and leaned against the cushions, closing her eyes. The hazy light emphasized her freckles. "I can do this on my own. I just need to find a job. Get a little place in London—"

"But you told me London is too big and noisy."

"It is, but it may be the only option. And Dahlia has already started scoping out potential flats for me."

"A London flat is expensive. And you have no income. Zee, I don't want you to sacrifice your comfort for the necessity of earning an income. And who will take care of the baby?"

"I'll hire a sitter. Day care is also an option. Both are… well…" She winced.

"What you can't say is that they are expensive. So you'll

work to pay someone to watch our child while you work… to pay for childcare? Sounds like running in circles to me. You don't want to do that, Zee. I know you. Your best friend is a cow. You thrive when you are wandering the grass barefoot and dancing with the flowers. I can't imagine you'd want to raise a child in London."

She shook her head. "Not really. But it's a place to start. I can find a job at a florist, or maybe a supermarket."

He cringed. "You, a supermarket clerk? Absolutely not. Such a menial job would extinguish your bright light."

"A person can find joy in any task if they look for it. Even shelving canned tomatoes. Sebastian, I'd do anything for my baby. I want to give it the best life."

"The best for our baby is to have its mother there for it. As well as its father. I want to be a part of my child's life," he insisted. "I need to be a part of his life."

"His?"

"I'm sure of it." He smiled. "I have a feeling. But I won't force you to allow me into his life. I don't want to be that man who controls people with his money. I want to be in his life because you want me there. And Zee, I will take care of you. No matter what you decide. I'll find a place for you to live. Or you find the perfect place and then I'll finance it. You'll never want for anything. You simply need to enjoy being a mother."

"No matter what I decide? Like I have options? Sebastian, this is one choice I know isn't a mistake. I'm having this baby."

"Of course, you are. I'm sorry, I didn't mean to imply there were any other options."

"I didn't plan for it, but now that it's here…" she patted her stomach "…inside me, I'm actually excited about this little bean. Boy or girl, I'll be happy either way."

Sebastian wished she could be as excited about inviting him to share in the baby's life. But then, he hadn't given her any reason to do so. Proposing felt wrong. She'd flee, insisting he wanted to marry her to become CEO. It wouldn't be like that. Maybe a little like that? If he wasn't even certain himself, then he could hardly be certain with her. But he could understand how she would think. So taking care of her was his only option.

For now.

To win her over and change the course of his future was the question. Because winning Azalea and his baby meant forfeiting the CEO position.

He kissed her cheek and nuzzled his head aside hers. Raising a hand to place over her stomach, he stopped before touching her. "May I?"

"Uh…yes." She took his hand and laid it over her stomach. She didn't appear pregnant, though perhaps she'd filled out a bit? "The baby doesn't start noticeably moving around for a few more weeks. I read about it online. I'm about four months according to my doctor."

"I'm pleased you've seen a doctor. I'll cover all your medical bills. Will you allow that?"

"The prenatal visit was free, and most of the rest is, including the midwife, but there will be expenses…"

"I'll make sure you get a card to use for any and all expenses. Medical, baby supplies, food, anything, Zee. You've only to ask."

"You know you can't buy my baby with the slash of a credit card."

Sebastian gaped at her. "How can you say such a thing? I would never."

A curious anger forced him to stand and stride into the kitchen where he grabbed the bottle of sparkling water. He was not buying her baby because—it was *his* baby, too! How dare she use such an accusation to repel him? He had as much right to watch their child grow up as she did. Why was it the woman always got the key role and more say in what would happen with the baby? It wasn't right.

He was still embracing this news about being a father, but more and more he was excited about it. And he wanted to share those feelings with her. He wanted to hear the stories about the best prams and how to survive the sleepless nights that would come with fatherhood. He wanted to be there for his child's first smile, his first words, his first toddle across the yard.

"I'm sorry," she said quietly. "This is an unusual situation to navigate. If not a little weird. Don't you think so?"

He took a swig directly from the bottle. "I do think it's out of the usual. Though not by my family's standards. It would be easier if we were..." At the very least, in one another's lives. In the same country. On the same page. "Am I to believe you don't want to be my girlfriend, then?"

"I...wasn't aware that title was on the table. I've only ever considered us lovers. Friends. Sebastian, I don't even live in Paris!"

"But do you live in Ambleside? Not for much longer."

She shrugged and gestured dismissively. "I will probably have to move before the leaves drop from the trees."

"Which is fast upon us. What about a cozy little town on the outskirts of Paris? Something wooded and with cobblestones and cows and chickens?"

She laughed, then looked up at him, as if realizing he was not joking. She had her dreams of being a princess; he could dream, too. Yet he wasn't quite sure what the dream of his future looked like. He was winging it. Trying to please her and not make a wrong step.

"So that's a possibility," he boldly decided. "Good to know. As I've once said about you, you teeter between village life and big-city life."

She agreed with a nod. "A happy medium would be perfect."

"At the very least, will you stay in Paris for a while? Grant me some time with you? Let me romance you as I've wanted to do every day we've been apart."

"I do like how you romance me."

"I think you're talking about the sex part."

"All your sex parts are quite lovely."

Was that a blush he felt heating his neck? "I'll work half days so I can spend all my time with you. We'll have a grand time."

"Until?"

He wasn't sure what she wanted him to say. He didn't know where this relationship was headed, or how it would get there. But if he could win another day, week, or more with her, then he'd snatch it and honor it as something precious.

"Until you need to seriously start wife hunting," she said.

Sebastian clutched the neck of the bottle. That was a sticking point she wasn't able to get beyond. Something that he should not overlook. Life had delivered him an interesting curve. He could follow it and see where it led him or try to straighten it back on course.

He wasn't at all sure which was the better choice. And really, what *was* his course?

"Should we make a deal not to talk about wife hunting or baby heirs?" she asked. "Just have some fun for a few days?"

He nodded. But it wouldn't be simple fun. It could mean the start to something grand.

Or the beginning of unbearable heartbreak.

CHAPTER TWELVE

Days later

THE LIMO PULLED to the curb and Sebastian leaned over to kiss Azalea. “Ready?”

She inhaled and said, “Give me a minute.”

“We can sit here as long as you like. Are you nervous to meet my friends?”

Yes, she was. She had spent the afternoon shopping for the perfect dress to wear tonight. Not too fancy, not so country bumpkin as her favorite floral dresses were. She’d landed on a simple white linen dress that did not have a tucked waistline. Red sandals were a necessity since lately her feet were swollen. So much for doing this pregnancy gracefully. Everything was growing larger. Puffy. Although she’d take the swollen breasts since they did now make her look like a B-cup.

She was confident she looked passable, but the key now was to not come off as uneducated or a farm girl. Lloyd’s words had embedded themselves into her soul. She wanted to ignore what he’d said, but right now it was hard not to feel those words wrap around her like a bold red flag. Surely Sebastian’s friends were rich and elite and maybe even snobbish?

“A little nervous?” she offered.

"You mustn't worry. They will love you. And they are not pretentious. If anything, they laugh at me when I have a model on my arm. They are always telling me to find a woman of substance and elan."

"And look what you've come up with. The chicken lady from England."

He laughed heartily. "That's a good one. I will have to tell them that one."

"No, don't! Sebastian, please, I just want to make a good impression."

He kissed her. Each time they connected, no matter how briefly, it fortified her courage a little more. "The only one you have to impress is me, and you've already succeeded on that front. Come on. You'll be surprised at how down-to-earth they are."

She nodded. Just the fact he'd arranged for her to meet his friends had to mean something. Had he told them about the baby? She hoped not. It was too big a topic to get into with people she didn't know. Right now, she just wanted to get through the evening. And perhaps learn a little more about Sebastian in the process.

They got out and entered a cozy restaurant walled with black steel and blue furnishings. A circular fireplace at the center was viewable by all the tables. Sebastian held her hand firmly, and when they arrived at a half-circle booth, three men and two women greeted her warmly.

"Azalea is not fluent in French, so tonight we will speak English for her, please?" he asked.

"Of course!" they all chimed.

An hour into drinks—nonalcoholic for Azalea and Sebastian—and a round of appetizers and desserts, Azalea had relaxed and was laughing along with everyone else as they went round the table telling tales about their adventures with Sebastian. From boating excursions in Marseilles that resulted in a broken-down engine that left them stranded for hours, to college lacrosse days when he'd led the team to a championship. They genuinely cared about him, and he was right when he'd told her they were not pretentious. She did not feel as though they were judging her. And she relaxed even more, her thigh hugging his, her head tilting onto his shoulder occasionally.

The past few days had been adventurous, visiting the Paris sights, afternoons wandering lush city parks, and evenings spent making love and staring out the window at the city lights. As well, carrying the weight of the situation between her and Sebastian, which had begun to sink in deeply. There was no easy resolution to what they'd created between them. She was thankful no one had brought up "the rebound baby." It was still her and Sebastian's secret.

When she yawned, she tried to disguise it behind her hand, but Clemente, the gorgeous redhead with silver dangle earrings, noticed and suggested that they end the night. "I'm as tired as Azalea looks," she said sweetly. "How about we split the tab?"

"No, I've got it." Sebastian gestured to the waiter to bring the check. "It's been a marvelous evening. *Merci, mon amies!*"

"And thank you for going out of your way and speaking English for me," Azalea added. "That was very kind."

"Not a problem." Charles, who worked for Sebastian's competition as a marketing exec, said with a pat to the back of her hand. "You're adorable, Zee. We hope to see you again, and soon."

"*Oui*, very soon," echoed out as everyone rose and began to leave with kisses to cheeks.

Consumed by a whirlwind of cheek busses, she finally

stood in Sebastian's arms out front of the restaurant. "I like your friends." She sighed and sank against his chest.

"I'm glad. They very much liked you."

"Thank you for not telling them I'm pregnant. I'm not sure how to deal with that announcement yet."

"No worries." He held up his hand, pinkie out.

She met his hug with her pinkie, glad for the secret code that meant to her that they did care for one another and no matter what happened, she trusted he would treat her well.

"Shall I also keep it a secret this weekend when we do supper with my family?"

"Your family?" Suddenly Azalea's throat went dry. Her heart pounded. "Oh, I don't know about meeting the family, Sebastian."

"Why not? We get together once a month, all of us, including all of the moms and girlfriends and kids. They'll love you as much as my friends do."

"But I thought you said your family wouldn't approve of me?"

He winced. "That was a crass thing to say. I regret it. I realize it doesn't matter to me what my family thinks of anyone in my life. All that matters is how I feel when with you. We're not trying to impress anyone, are we? Let's go and have a good time and you can meet Philippe and my dad. Roman has been working with a speech therapist. He still has trouble enunciating words but he has a manner of getting his point across."

"I'm glad to hear he's recovering. But seriously, you may not think it a big deal, but this is going to be my first impression on them. I might need something different to wear."

"You have the card I gave you. Buy what you need."

"It's generous of you to give me whatever I want but I could take advantage and buy a car or something."

"If it makes you happy, it makes me happy. Besides, what good is it to have money if you do not use it to buy things you enjoy?"

"Oh, mercy, you will corrupt me."

"And I intend to enjoy every minute of it."

Making love to Sebastian was the best feeling in the world. Besides taking off her bra after a long day. Nothing could compete with that feeling. But she'd never tell him he had competition. And that her mind wandered to silly things like undergarments after she'd just climaxed—for the second time—bothered Azalea.

Because after the bra she started thinking about his family. She didn't want to meet the family! Did she really have to? But of course, if she was to have Sebastian's baby, she should probably assess the relative situation. On her side the issue was easy enough. One grandpa and grandma and their respective partners. On Sebastian's side it was the one grandpa and…how many grandmothers? She'd lost count. And would they be called step-grandmothers?

Kisses to her spine stirred her from her mad-making thoughts and she rolled over to snuggle against Sebastian's chest. Heated vanilla, cedar and saltiness scented his skin. She nuzzled closer and licked him. "You are a talented man."

"And you are a vocal woman. I love when you climax."

She smiled against his skin. "You're not so quiet yourself."

"Fortunately, I own the whole top floor of this building, so we can be as loud as we care to be."

With that permission, she let out a long and bellowing call that ended in a giggle.

"Is that so?" He tickled her ribs in punishment.

Her laughter turned to shrieks and kicks and then she collapsed in a huffing sigh of relief as his tickles turned to kisses from neck to breasts, to stomach. Gentle and reverent, he took his time covering her entire growing belly. Then he pressed his ear against her stomach.

"Can I help you name him?" he asked.

She'd not yet given thought to names. Hadn't any favorites. And how he guessed it was a boy was cute, but she'd not gotten confirmation during the ultrasound on the sex.

"Of course, you can. As long as it's not Clifford or Harry."

"What's wrong with Harry?"

"That would remind me of my lost love," she said with a dramatic tone.

"Do tell?"

"When I was in primary school I intended to marry Harry Marks. He once gave a report on how he wanted to be a prince when he grew up. At the time I didn't realize you had to be born into the title. Anyway, you know about my aspirations to princess-hood. Alas, the last I heard, Harry works as a bartender in the West End."

"Alas," he mocked gently.

"Oh, come on! I could have been a princess."

"You already are a rural princess, Zee. And I'll fight Harry any day to win your regard."

She assessed him in the pale beam of moonlight that shone across the head of the bed. "You did offer to punch the photographer that night you rescued me. You must be quite the brawler."

"I did punch him."

She gaped at him. "What?"

"I brought back the dress and made sure he understood he'd done wrong."

"Seriously?"

He shrugged.

"Wow. You're my knight in shining menswear. Your suit is your armor."

"I suppose it is." He kissed her belly and tugged her against him, her back to his chest, and nuzzled his face into her hair. "I'm falling in love with you, Zee. And I'm not using the word *think* this time around. This time I can feel it right here, in my entire being."

His words sounded so real. Just what she wanted to hear from him.

"Don't be mad?" he added.

"Of course not." And yet, she wasn't happy.

And why she wasn't happy astounded her. Because the man of her dreams had just confessed his love to her. Or almost love. And he wanted her to have everything that would make her life, and the life of her child, perfect. She should be dancing with joy. Over the moon. Wearing that princess crown with pride.

Yet how to get over the self-imposed caution that would not allow her to believe Sebastian was only in this for the CEO position?

CHAPTER THIRTEEN

TEN DAYS HAD passed since Azalea had come to Paris. Puttering around the neighborhood, slipping in and out of the trendy shops, and browsing Sebastian's home while he was away at work felt like the most normal thing in the world. There was plenty to keep her busy, from exploring the parks and cafés, to exploring the elegant suits in his closet and laughing over his meticulously ordered fridge. Yes, there were hues of wine and each bottle was arranged in order from pale to dark. As well, the cheeses were in alphabetical order!

She'd not even considered when she would return to Ambleside. Though she had thought about finding a job. She could look into teaching English as a second language, or even apply at one of the florists on the main strip hugging the river, using her English as an attribute considering all the tourist business that must demand a command of the language.

"Possible," she muttered as she scrolled through a website that sold baby furniture and clothing.

She preferred the plain pinewood furniture and simple clothing that wasn't frilly or the declarative pink or blue. Her toddler would amble through the grass barefoot and chase butterflies in whatever color inspired her that day.

"He has to," she said with the dream swelling in her

heart. "That's how I want to raise a child. Free and wild. Respectful and prone to common sense."

She would definitely homeschool. But that was a lofty dream for a penniless, pregnant woman who had no home or job.

Sebastian's offer to pay for everything was not to be disregarded. Which was why she'd accepted the credit card he'd handed her. She wasn't going to refuse it on some arrogant moral ground that she was too good for charity. Heck, he was the father. He could chip in to raise their child. However, she did want to make her own way as well. A happy medium must be achieved. Because while she was living it up, enjoying the luxurious life in a swanky Parisian penthouse, eating at exclusive restaurants and buying fabulous clothes, she didn't want to take advantage of Sebastian. Nor did her aesthetics require such swank. Not all the time, anyway.

Simple things. A simple life. With a side of Weekend Parisian Princess added to the mix?

The thought made her smile.

"How to incorporate Sebastian Mercier into my simple plan?" she murmured. "And at the same time give an inch and occasionally slide into his world?"

Could she incorporate him into her life in a meaningful way that would allow her to accept his need to keep a wife? No. If he married, or even if he dated someone else while keeping her on the side as his family, the way all the Mercier men seemed to keep women, Azalea was absolutely sure she did not want a part of that.

But convincing him *not* to go for the CEO position would be unfair to him. He wanted that job. He had plans, dreams for the company. She couldn't deny him that win by insisting he not marry another.

It could be as simple as telling him they should get married. It would give him the win. Could it ever be a real marriage?

Maybe?

"I only want it if it's real."

"Hey, Dad, how's it going on the farm?"

"Casual, as usual, with a side of packing and tossing all the junk we don't need. How's it with you and Sebastian? Are you working things out?"

Azalea bit her lip. She never lied to her dad. And really, even she wasn't sure they had worked things out, so a straight yes or no couldn't apply.

"Lea, sweetie, you've got to get things straight with him."

"I'm not sure what is straight for me, Dad. I'm still working this out in my heart, if you can understand that."

"I do. You don't want to be treated any lesser than what you deserve. Nor do I wish that for you. You know Diane and I will support whatever decision you make."

"I know you will. So, what's up?"

"I just called to let you know we've had some offers for the property."

"Dad, that's wonderful."

Was it? Azalea's heart sank. Such good news would allow her dad to take the next step. But she felt some panic in that it felt as if her life, her very roots, had just been torn up and were dangling like dirt clumps above a hole in the earth. Her escape to the farm would soon be gone. Then where would she go?

"What about Stella and Daisy?"

"They sold two days ago."

"What?" He'd just up and sold her best friend?

"You knew I was selling them, Lea. The neighbor is going to pick them up in a few days. He's promised not to eat them, I swear."

That sounded so not reassuring.

"The hens are..." He exhaled heavily and she knew that meant he and Diane would be feasting on chicken for the next few weeks. "It's going well, sweetie."

"I'm glad for you, Dad. Though I wish I could be there to send off Stella." She slid a hand over her not too round belly. Still, she was proud of it. "I have a feeling no matter where life takes me and this little one, it may involve a cow."

Her dad laughed. "Sure you don't want to buy the farm from me? There's still time."

Not that she could afford such a thing. Would it be possible? No, it wouldn't be fair to her dad to work up an arrangement to keep something that she loved, yet also felt would keep her from moving on. She needed to forge her own life.

"If you're selling at fire sale prices, sure."

Another laugh. "Let me know when you've plans to return. I'll drive to London to pick you up."

"Thanks, Dad. I'm not sure how much longer I'll stay. I'll ring you when I do. Love you!"

She hung up and tossed the phone to the comfy sofa and walked up to the window to look out over Paris. The sun was bright and tendrils of some vine twisting about a nearby tree snaked toward the window. The city of lights was so pretty. And here in Sebastian's home, it felt not quite so busy and hustling as London had to her. Still, it wasn't exactly her style. Even if it was home to a man she couldn't imagine pushing out of her life.

Sebastian's trajectory and hers were not aimed toward

one another. His life was here in Paris. Hers was…not here. And there was nothing left for her in Ambleside after the farm was sold.

The door opened and Sebastian breezed in, as was his habit. Even after a full day at the office he always seemed light on his feet, his smile seeking hers. If a person's eyes could speak his screamed happiness. It was difficult to sulk when in his presence.

Azalea sailed toward him and he swept her into an embrace that suddenly turned into a full-on, dance-floor dip. She let out a hoot, and he pulled her upright to kiss her. Her Frenchman's five-o'clock shadow tickled her skin, perking her nipples and zinging desire through her system. As their kiss deepened, they swayed to an unsung melody backed up by the timpani of their heartbeats.

When she came up for air, she asked, "What was that for?"

He shrugged. "The best part of my day is coming home to find you here, smiling at me."

"I was thinking much the same."

"Another dip!" He spun her before the window and when she swirled back to him, he bowed her low. "Do you think we could qualify for that dancing show on the TV?"

"Why not?" He spun her upright and she landed in his secure embrace and they kissed again.

Everything was perfect. And everything was wrong. His kisses only managed to distract her from the more serious stakes.

"Can we make this work?" he asked.

"I'm not sure."

"Do you want to make it work?"

"Honestly? I want to, but I'm also cautious because I don't want my heart to get broken."

"I would never do anything to hurt you, Zee. Or our baby." He spread a palm across her stomach. "I think you've got a little belly?"

"Don't remind me. It's not so much a belly as a full spread. I feel like a lump."

"A beautiful lump." He bent to kiss her stomach. Feeling him there, paying respect to their child, made her question if she were being too protective of her heart. Should she give him a chance?

"Are you ready for tomorrow night? The dinner with my family?"

"Oh." Her consternation switched to panic. "I haven't found a dress yet."

"We'll go shopping in the morning. Don't worry, Zee, I'll hold your hand." He clasped hers and kissed it. "It won't be so terrible. Dad is more quiet than usual. The girlfriends are all a bit materialistic and focused on fashion and jewels. Like those housewife shows on the television."

Azalea laughed. "And your brother. Will he have a date?"

"Not sure. I haven't spoken to Philippe for a few weeks. But we do try to show up at these family soirees with a date."

"To show the other you're committed to the competition?"

"This—us—is not competition," he said. "I've found the perfect woman. And she's already told me she won't marry me, so I must suffice with merely adoring her for the rest of my life."

"Don't be foolish, Sebastian. You wouldn't give up the CEO position to stare at me as I grow fatter and my fingers and toes swell to sausages."

"Honestly? It's something I wrestle with daily."

"I hope the CEO position wins."

"Really?" He studied her with that perceptively delving gaze that always brought her to her knees. "You don't want me to choose you?"

"I want you to be happy. And the CEO position would make you happy."

"It would. But *you* also make me happy."

"You can't have both."

He sighed. "No, apparently not."

"Besides, don't you know happiness is an inside job? Only you can make yourself happy. And if you're not happy on your own, then it doesn't matter if another person comes into your life and makes an attempt to create that happiness."

"Profound," he said. "Are you happy?"

"I am. Mostly. I would be much happier if I had definite future plans, but I feel as though things will work themselves out."

"So you don't require me in your life to be happy?"

Answer truthfully, her conscience nudged.

Azalea shrugged and shook her head. "But you are a nice bonus."

"The bonus guy. How utterly romantic."

"Don't take it the wrong way. I adore you, Sebastian. And… I really do hope things can work for us. But I'm not going to make plans for something that I feel isn't a sure thing."

"What about life *is* a sure thing?"

"Not much." Her father had said much the same to her. *Life is meant to be lived. Go off and live it!*

"Well, we'll see how things go, eh?"

Yes, they did like to dance around making a final decision on this situation. And she was fine with that. Because

Azalea sensed any decision would result in heartbreak for one, if not both of them.

"No matter what happens between us?" he said. "I am going to create a stipend for you and my child. You'll never want for anything, Zee. I promise you that."

"Oh. Well." That was very generous beyond the credit card he'd already given her. But not so surprising, knowing Sebastian for the kind and generous man he was.

"Tell me you'll accept?"

It would help her in the interim until she could really figure things out, decide what the future looked like for her with a child, and maybe or maybe not the child's father.

She nodded. "Thank you. But I only need a little help until I get my life on track—"

The kiss he often employed to stop her from rambling senselessly never failed to be successful. And to shift Azalea from brain mode to soft and accepting heart mode. Could she seriously imagine life without Sebastian's kisses?

"You'll have an account forever, Zee. That's how it's going to go. Like it or not. Now, I ordered food on the way home. I'm going to wash up. If the bell rings, answer it!"

He strolled down the hallway, leaving her feeling floaty from his kiss, but at the same time she could feel the chain tighten about her ankle that bound her to the floor. His floor. His chain. His money. She'd become one of those women his father collected, mothers of his children the patriarch wasn't willing to commit to.

Would Sebastian feel he could direct her future, and that of her child's, because he was financing it? She didn't want that.

Had accepting his offer been a mistake?

She shimmied off a creeping tightness in her shoulders and shook out her hands. "No, it'll work. It has to."

While Zee was in the shower, Sebastian washed the dinner dishes. Night hugged the windows with a glint of moonshine across the glass and an ambient pink glow from the city's neon. The neighborhood was old and quiet, but the heart of Paris was always present no matter where one lived or stood within the city. Lights, river, history. This was his home. He loved it. Couldn't imagine living anywhere else.

Now that he was to become a father, he had some hard choices to face. He wanted to see his son raised in Paris, or at the very least, France. His child must speak French, and of course English. He would know his family and their history—with some careful edits and alterations regarding what a family really was. And that meant he should consider going traditional and marrying his child's mother. Bring him up in a nuclear family surrounded by those who loved him.

Yet how to convince Zee of that? Surely she must want the best for their child? And she couldn't believe denying her son his father would be for the better. He knew she didn't believe that.

Was he ready to make the commitment and propose to her? He'd twice already made a proposal. Hell, he even had the ring. But those times had meant nothing more than winning a competition. They hadn't been based on love, respect or even like.

It was different with Zee. As much as she teased that he couldn't possibly love her—and perhaps he was mistaken, for the only kind of love he knew was that which he'd experienced from his family—he did feel a deep respect and attachment to her. And what better basis for starting a family, something formed from friendship, laughter and passion? All of which had nothing to do with the competition. He didn't want it to be associated with the infernal contest. Because that detail was the one thing that kept Azalea from seeing him.

Could she ever see him for his own man? Someone who had not followed in the footsteps of a pleasure-seeking rogue who could not commit to his children's mothers?

Dinner with his family would either cement Zee's opinion or change it. And he wasn't feeling very positive about which way that pendulum would swing.

CHAPTER FOURTEEN

WATCHING THE SUNRISE from the balcony that wrapped around Sebastian's penthouse, a soft blanket wrapped about her naked body, Azalea felt as if she existed inside of a dream. She had crept out of bed, leaving Sebastian sprawled on his back, arms out and legs wide, still asleep. The guy was a master at the unconcerned sleep. She loved it.

Now she leaned against the ornate wrought iron railing. The city was quiet, and a foggy heaviness sweatered her with the heat of August. It felt like a hug from Paris. Seeming to rise from the dash of rose light that hugged the horizon, the Sacré-Coeur Basilica, far on the Right Bank, pierced the gold sky with its bleach-white spires. Closer, wearing scaffolds like intricate lace, Notre Dame announced to all that she would not be taken down, no matter the strife she endured. Below on the sidewalk, a woman in sleek jogging wear ran by, earbuds depriving her of the peaceful morning.

It wasn't like rising to Big Bruce's call and then wandering through a meadow barefoot, each step stirring wild and earthy scents, but Azalea wouldn't neglect this moment. This was the Paris she could manage in her life. Quiet, beautiful, something out of a postcard. But give it a few more hours and the rush and hubbub would change her mind.

Dinner with the family tonight. A dreadful clutch at her heart forced a swallow. But really, she was a grown woman. She could do this. A few hours seated before the eyes of a klatch of snooty girlfriends, a virtually speechless and likely judging father, and the brother who viewed Sebastian as his greatest competition?

What could possibly go wrong?

Smirking at the disaster scenarios that deluged her brain, she shook them all away. This night would go well. And she did want to meet the family that had influenced Sebastian's life. They were going to be her child's relatives. Whether or not they were included in that child's life was a matter for another day. First, she had to gather basic intel and check out the gene pool.

"Zee," Sebastian called from the bed. She'd left the balcony door open. "Come back to bed."

"It's perfect out here." She remained by the railing, despite his wanting moan that seemed to vibrate through her erogenous zones.

A glance over her shoulder saw he'd rolled to his side, back away from the morning light, derriere exposed. Now, that was a sight she couldn't resist. And it gave fun definition to the word *manhandling.*

Enough city-gazing. Time to put her hands on that.

Sebastian tugged at the violet silk tie that added some color to his simple black velvet smoking jacket and trousers. From last year's summer line, the violet silk was tied in a trinity knot. The single button on the jacket was a Louis d'Or minted in the sixteenth century. The gold coin added a touch of flair to the look. He felt comfortable. On trend. Fashionably right on the mark.

Roman Mercier appreciated his sons' attention to even the smallest fashion details. Rather, he expected such diligence. Sebastian could recall, as a child, watching his dad dress and being tutored in the correct arm length for the various dinner, smoking or tuxedo jackets. Proper shirt styles for all suits, jackets and occasions. How to pair shoes with trousers, and what colors went with what seasons. Styling the perfect suit was like breath to Sebastian. It was his second language, even before English, which he got to use so much lately with Zee.

Another tug wasn't necessary to loosen the tie, but rather readjust it slightly. It was being stubborn. Hmm… Ties never gave him bother, so why…

With a wince, he realized he was nervous about tonight.

He'd wanted to accompany Zee on her afternoon shopping adventure to select a suitable dress, but a call from the office concerning an emergency fitting for a visiting celebrity hadn't allowed such. And when she'd asked him if he didn't trust her fashion sense, those big blue eyes had lured him to tell her of course he did.

He hadn't lied. Maybe a little. But he'd also the sense to encourage her to be herself. And she had found the perfect dress. This evening his rural princess teased big-city casual chic.

Flicking off the lights and spinning out to retrieve his date by the front door, he took the elevator with her to street level.

Now, sitting next to him in the back of the limo, Zee smoothed at the white fabric splashed with florals. It was cut just above her knees and hugged her figure with a sweetheart neckline. Her soft blond hair was done in loose waves that framed her face and the red lip matched the flowers on the dress. Sweet yet elegant.

Now, if he could just get his head straight on how to handle the situation of her pregnancy. It could mean the win to him. If they married. That was the calculating way to look at things.

Yet a softer, more heartfelt, side of him simply wanted to do right by her and make her happy. And to be a father to the baby that he had helped create. He couldn't imagine not being involved in the upbringing of his child, unplanned or not. But that way also looked exactly like the path of Roman Mercier. And that did not suit him either.

Realizing she'd given his hand a squeeze, Sebastian then noticed the limo had stopped. "Right. We're here. You ready for this?"

Her nervous nod told him so much. Honestly, he shared her butterflies. His mother could be judgmental at times. *Merde*... All the time.

"I've got you," he promised. "We can do this together."

She exhaled heavily. "Yep. Together."

The Mercier family met monthly in a private top-floor room at an elite four-star restaurant in the 8th arrondissement. The owner was a former lover of Roman Mercier's, though she'd not produced a child and therefore didn't qualify for the family dinners. Sebastian had lost count of all the women who had passed through his father's life over the years. It would be madness to try and keep a tally.

Once out of the elevator, they were greeted by a friendly hostess, and he accepted a drink from the waiter who offered wine and champagne. He suggested sparkling water for Azalea, and the waiter dashed off to get that.

"Ah! There are my baby brothers." He walked up to greet them.

"Sebastian, so good to see you!" A woman in an elegant black silk gown walked alongside the nanny dressed in plain black linen, who toted a baby on her hip. In a stroller sat another rambunctious baby.

She bussed Sebastian on both cheeks, then eyed Azalea. "And who have we here?"

"Elaine, this is Azalea Grace. My…girlfriend." He smiled at her and she affirmed the label by returning the smile. "Zee, this is Elaine Desmauliers. And this here—" He bent to the baby in the stroller. "Is Henri?"

He got a nod from the nanny that his guess had been right. The twins were only nine months old and were always dressed identically. Tonight, they sported black onesies with a designer logo in leather applique across the bellies. Who could tell the dark-haired sprites apart?

"Hey, Henri." He waggled the baby's toe, clad in matching designer socks. "How's my little brother?"

"So nice to meet you," Azalea said to Elaine and offered her hand to shake.

Elaine leaned in and bussed her cheeks. "Lovely, *cherie*. What a pretty dress."

Sebastian picked up on the snide tone and returned his attention to Zee. He slid an arm around her waist and tugged her close. "There's never a moment Zee is not the most beautiful woman in the room."

Elaine's elegantly tweezed eyebrow lifted. He had seen the bills come through the L'Homme Mercier accounts that authorized twenty thousand euros monthly for the woman's coiffure and wellness spa expenses. "Well, well. Have you found the one?"

Sebastian smirked. "I'll leave Zee to decide whether

she has successfully captured me. But we must get on to the dining room. How is Father tonight?"

He hooked his arm in Zee's and led her as Elaine took up his other arm. Behind them, the nanny followed, pushing the stroller.

"He is doing well," Elaine said. "His inability to get some words out frustrates him, but he is easier to understand every day. He's changed, Sebastian. You will remark it, I'm sure."

"Changed? How so?"

"He's softening. More so even than he did following the first stroke." She patted his hand and looked up at him.

He read the success in her eyes. She would love to be the one woman who finally procured a ring on her finger from Roman Mercier. Sebastian doubted that would happen, but he wished her luck, if only for Henri's and Charles's sakes.

They entered the dining room through elegant Art Deco stained glass doors. Zee's grip on his arm tightened as they stopped before the long dining table. The rest of the family was already seated. All looked up to take them in.

Sebastian leaned in to whisper at Zee's ear, "Ready?"

"As I'll ever be."

After introductions, and some initial questions from each of the family members regarding Sebastian and Azalea's relationship, everyone seemed to settle and sniff at their wine and poke at the hors d'oeuvres.

The room was amazing, featuring more of the Art Deco stained glass, lots of dark woods, gold flatware—was it *real* gold?—and a bottle of champagne so large Azalea wasn't sure anyone would even be able to lift it to pour.

Her nerves did not settle. Maybe her upset stomach

was more baby-related than nerves. She hoped not. Now would not be a good time to start delivering on the vomiting she'd avoided during morning sickness. So she sipped water constantly, then realized that must look suspicious. Pushing the goblet forward on the table she clasped her hands on her lap.

Roman Mercier's girlfriends were all glamorous, and there wasn't a single one of the three of them—Elaine, Angelique and Cecile—who did not look artificially enhanced with breasts that defied gravity or cheekbones and lips that plumped just a bit too unnaturally. But on the surface, they were kind and, beyond catching their assessing gazes of her perfectly plain dress—spangles and rhinestones seemed *de rigueur*—Azalea didn't feel like a piece of overcooked meat that none of the elites wanted to touch.

Yet.

Philippe, the brother—son of Cecile—who shared Sebastian's dark hair and gray-blue eyes, but was stockier and more built with thick biceps, eyed her suspiciously. He also had a girlfriend sitting alongside him, not as uber-plumped but certainly working the sequins and glamorous hairstyle, and with eyebrows that defined perfection. He kept a keen eye on Azalea. Was Philippe sizing up his chances at being first to the marriage stipulation of the competition? What might it do to him if he learned his brother had successfully completed the "produce an heir" portion of the race to the win?

And the fact Sebastian introduced her as his girlfriend both annoyed and excited her. They hadn't agreed on such a designation. Sure, they'd spent the last days with one another as if they were in a relationship. Had chatted with his friends as if they were a couple. *Did* that make her his girlfriend? She loved the *idea* of being Sebastian's girlfriend.

Though certainly carrying the man's baby did give the girlfriend label some credence.

Oh, Azalea, stop analyzing! Just try to enjoy this night. The sooner it will be done.

And then later at his place they could discuss the way they would label their relationship. Because it did need a label. For her sanity.

The woman seated on the other side of the table from her, next to Sebastian's father, was Angelique, Sebastian's mom. Dazzling in pale pink beaded chiffon, the woman eyed Azalea covertly through long false lashes. Wicked red nails caressed a champagne goblet. Sebastian had to have told her a little about his date. Was the woman musing that Azalea was just a country bumpkin and how dare she insinuate herself into her son's life? Most likely.

When the main course was served, Azalea took some solace in being able to eat and not make eye contact with anyone. Sebastian reached under the table and gave her thigh a squeeze. He leaned in and whispered, "Still good?"

She nodded. Yes, as long as he was by her side, she was good. So far, none of the women had scratched out her eyes. Not that they had reason to. It was the competitive brother who worried her. And at that moment, Philippe stood, gesturing for everyone to silence.

Azalea met Sebastian's gaze and he shrugged, indicating he had no idea what was to come.

"Family," Philippe began, "I have exciting news I must share before the desserts arrive. I want to announce that Colette and I are engaged to be married!" He bent to kiss the exuberant Colette as everyone gasped. Then the girlfriends all clapped and cheered. Roman, who used his words sparingly, tapped his spoon on the side of a goblet in applause.

Azalea did not miss the wink Philippe directed at his brother. Yet beside her, Sebastian raised a goblet and said, "*À la nôtre!* To a good life!"

All echoed the toast and drank.

Colette extended her hand to reveal an acorn-sized diamond ring. "I didn't slip it on until just now," she said. "We wanted to surprise everyone."

"It's lovely," Cecile cooed. Philippe's mother walked around to hug the couple and congratulate them.

And Azalea noticed Roman's expression as he quietly observed. There was not so much a proud smile on the father's face as a curious moue. He cast his glance between both of the sons he'd pitted against one another. Was he reveling in the competition? One had already achieved half success. Or was he plotting something else? It bothered her in a way she couldn't quite label.

And then she realized how this must make Sebastian feel. She slid her hand under the table and clasped his hand. A good squeeze brought his attention to her and she kissed him. "He hasn't won yet," she said.

"Doesn't matter," he murmured. "It…really doesn't. What matters is the way you look at me."

With that, Sebastian stood and made another toast to the couple's future and the entire family.

Once desserts were served it was Roman's turn for a speech. He stood and thanked them all for their support. According to Sebastian's whispers in her ear as he translated for his father. The family had been speaking both French and English through the night, but Azalea would not expect the patriarch to employ English when he already had difficulty with speech.

"Family means more now than ever," Sebastian translated. "He is happy."

Dear old Dad having a change of heart about family? Interesting? And she hoped, for Sebastian's sake, it would develop into gentler, less aggressive expectations of his sons. But still she felt uncomfortable about the whole thing. Something was brewing inside Roman Mercier's brain.

After desserts were cleared and the champagne was poured with elan by the sommelier, everyone chatted quietly. Philippe was showing off his fiancée's ring to his dad and Cecile, explaining how it cost two million but he'd got it for half that thanks to his connections in the jewelry industry.

"Sebastian," Angelique said over a sip of champagne, "you look so well. I don't think I've seen you since Roman was in the hospital. What is it that's got your eyes so bright, my love?"

"Well, isn't it obvious? Zee here is the one who makes me happy."

Eyeing Azalea over her goblet, Angelique made a dismissive noise. Red nails rapped the crystal. "Interesting. Not your usual type."

"Mother," Sebastian admonished.

She shrugged and Azalea felt that the woman would not be dissuaded from what felt like a venture into villainy. Likely she'd been waiting for just the moment to toss out a few comments.

"She's rather unkempt," Angelique said. "And so thick around the middle."

"Mother!" Sebastian remanded with a pound of his fist on the table that alerted everyone to hesitate in their conversations. "That thick middle is a baby."

Everyone at the table turned their full attention to Azalea.

Sebastian, not seeming to notice he'd silenced the room, continued, "*My* baby, Mother."

Now gasps swept up like a violent wave that crashed against Azalea's skin and flooded into her heart. Philippe swore. Roman tilted his head, and then nodded in what looked like approval. Elaine cooed, saying "*Ooh, la, la!* Another Mercier baby!"

The heat that rose in Azalea's throat to circle her neck felt suffocating. Why had he announced that? They'd agreed not to tell anyone tonight. When she felt him reach for her hand she tugged away and stood. "Excuse me. I need some air."

She fled the table, leaving surprised gasps, remarks that she was rather touchy, and someone congratulating Sebastian on having secured one half of his success.

CHAPTER FIFTEEN

AZALEA MADE A beeline for the ladies' room. Thankful no one was inside, she aimed for the last of the three sinks and leaned over it. She wanted to splash water on her face but thought better against ruining her makeup. The oval mirror showed no black mascara smears from the few teardrops that had escaped as she'd rushed away from the dining room.

What Sebastian's mother had said about her had been cruel.

But Sebastian announcing to all, in a boasting manner, that she carried his child, had gone beyond. How dare he? It hadn't been his place. They had agreed not to tell anyone tonight. This was her body, her baby. And if Sebastian thought to use it as a means to gain control of L'Homme Mercier, he had another think coming.

It had to have been a slip of the tongue. He wouldn't throw her under the bus like that. Or maybe he'd simply needed to feel some pride at that moment? Some small win after Philippe's engagement announcement.

Wrapping her arms across her chest she paced. She studied her stomach in the mirrors as she passed before them. Thick in the middle? Why couldn't she have a baby bump instead of this full-middle swelling? It did look like she'd gone a little too hard on the sweets and carbs. Maybe she had been enjoying Diane's homemade crumpets a little too much lately. With blueberry jam. And lots of butter.

Azalea Grace was definitely not one of those glamorous women sitting out at the table. As nipped, tucked and contoured as they were. Not…sophisticated. So how had she even caught Sebastian's eye in the first place?

Right. She'd taken him by surprise by commandeering the back of his limo. And then they'd spent the best night together. And since, whenever they were together, she really thought they enjoyed one another's company. Had amazing chemistry. She was happy that if she were to have a child, half its genes would be from the smart, sexy, adorable and terribly funny Sebastian Mercier.

But if she had to raise that child within the family sitting out in the dining room?

She shook her head.

The door opened. Azalea turned to the vanity and made it look as though she were checking her hair. Angelique sidled up alongside her, sequins hissing with her movements, and studied her reflection in the adjacent mirror before speaking.

"Sebastian says I must apologize for calling you thick. Apparently, truth is not always welcome. I am sorry."

What an apology. So genuine. Not.

"You are unlike any of my son's previous girlfriends," she said to Azalea's reflection. "They were all very stylish and…"

"I'm sorry, Angelique. I don't meet the standards you have set for your son. I know the Mercier family is rich and has style and a certain social standing. It's not my world, and it never will be. But his abrupt announcement about the baby—"

"Ah, that is the bright side to this startling evening, *oui*?"

Azalea turned to face the woman who granted her a bright smile quite opposite of the treatment she'd just served her.

"You are going to have my son's baby! He is already halfway to the CEO position. You've only to marry him and he wins."

Azalea's mouth dropped open. Tears again threatened, but she held them back with an act of willpower. The woman was truly lacking in empathy.

"I would have chosen a different mate for him," Angelique continued, unaware of her stinging words, "but it gets him what he deserves, so I will go along with it."

Go along with it? As if the woman had any say over any of this!

"You will marry him?"

"He hasn't asked." Why had she said that? It didn't matter! She wasn't going to insert herself further in this messy family drama. "Besides, I wouldn't marry your son. And he knows that."

Angelique's expression remained the same. Because everything on her face was unnaturally tightened. But Azalea suspected she would frown, if she could.

"Just because I'm carrying Sebastian's baby doesn't mean he gets to jump in and assume control. I have choices. And I'm not going to marry a man just to help him win some stupid family competition. It's so cruel that his father subjects him to such a thing!"

"You mustn't speak of Roman like that. He simply demands the best from his sons. His expectations are exactly the reason why Sebastian and Philippe have done so well. They are highly respected by their peers in the industry.

Both are millionaires. And how dare you suggest you will keep my son from his child's life!"

No, she could never do that, but— Walking into this crazy argument had not been on the books for tonight. The past few months Azalea had felt emotionally fragile, and as if she were walking uncharted grounds. And speaking with Sebastian's mom only lifted that fragility to the surface. She couldn't hold it together much longer.

"I don't want to argue with you about something that should be between me and Sebastian."

Angelique grabbed her by the arm. "Sebastian is my son. And…" Was that an attempt at a frown? "I don't want him to be like his father."

Her desperate confession startled Azalea. Had the woman empathy after all? Of course, who would want their child to be a man who collected women and sons as if prizes? And now that she thought about it, she realized Sebastian was doing just that! He had emulated his father's example. He'd offered to pay her expenses for a lifetime. Just as Roman had done for his sons' mothers. And she had accepted!

What a fool she had been to allow herself to get sucked into the Mercier family drama.

"I know that as his mother, you think very highly of your son," Azalea started, "as you should. He's amazing. Talented, smart, kind and so funny. We seem to get one another despite our differences. But I could never marry him, even if he did ask. If it was simply to win a competition, then it could never be real. I don't want to live like that."

"Has Sebastian told you he loves you?"

"Well…he has." At least, he'd said he was falling for her. "But…"

"But what? If you know my son as you think you do, you know he does not lie."

No, he did not. Azalea couldn't imagine a lie coming from Sebastian's mouth.

"So, if he has told you he loves you, why do you believe that is a lie?" Angelique challenged.

Because there were too many other conditions distorting that truth. And maybe she just needed to step back from this crazy family to see it all clearly.

"I know he wouldn't lie to me," Azalea replied. "And I do believe I love him. But it feels wrong. This. Your family. It's…crushing in on me. I'm sorry."

With that, Azalea fled the bathroom, but waiting outside across the hall from the door stood Sebastian, hands in his pockets. He straightened, pleading with his soft yet devastating gaze.

Azalea put up her hand. "I don't want to do this. Not here. I'm going home." Dash it, she couldn't flee. Home to her right now was Sebastian's place. "I just need to get away from this drama."

"I'll text the driver to pick you up and take you back to my place," he offered.

"Thank you." When he made to take her hand, she shook her head. "I need some space, Sebastian."

Angelique strolled out of the ladies' room and took her son's arm. "I tried," she said to him. "She's not got the Mercier dedication to family."

"Mother, enough. You were only to apologize to Zee."

"She did," Azalea said. "And there are some things your mother and I agree on."

Angelique lifted her chin proudly.

But there had been no agreement on the definition of family.

"You are a good man," Azalea said to him. "I have never believed otherwise." She wandered toward the elevator. "I'll talk to you later. Please, just give me an hour or so to myself."

"I can do that. I'm sorry, Zee!" he called as she stepped onto the elevator.

Before the doors closed, she saw Sebastian with his mother standing beside him, clutching his arm like the protective yet unknowingly wicked mother who could never unfurl her tentacles from around her child. Azalea felt terrible leaving in such a manner. It didn't reflect well on Sebastian. And she didn't want to hurt him.

But this was all too much to process.

The man had once offered to defend her honor. What had happened to his valiant promise? Did his family stifle that individuality, his genuine impulse to do right? It seemed like it. They loved him but they wanted certain things from him, and he had unknowingly fallen right in line.

CHAPTER SIXTEEN

BEFORE SEBASTIAN ENTERED his home, he leaned against the wall and took the ring box out from inside his suit coat. It had been nestled there all night. He opened the velvet box. Inside sat a 10 carat diamond ring surrounded by sapphires as pale as Zee's eyes. It wasn't the same ring he'd utilized two times previously. He'd returned that and purchased one that was fitting of Zee's beauty, her soft innocence and her bubbly nature. He'd intended to propose to her after a successful family dinner.

Now? He'd blown it. Everything felt wrong.

His mother could be cruel in her forthright manner. Angelique was a judgmental person but also honest. Yet he hadn't expected her to treat Zee with such open disdain. He should have never allowed her to go into the ladies' room to apologize. After they'd watched Zee's exit, she'd told him Zee had threatened to take the baby and never allow him to see it.

He couldn't know if that was true or an exaggeration. He suspected the latter. It was Angelique's habit. What was it that she and Zee could have possibly agreed on? He should have asked his mother, but he'd wanted to get away from her as much as Zee had. They had returned to the dining room. He'd hugged Colette and Philippe, congratulating them both. To Sebastian's surprise, their engagement didn't bother him at all. He didn't feel as though he'd slipped in the race to the prize. And yet…

Tucking away the ring box, he blew out a breath. He should have never blurted to all that Zee was pregnant. In that moment he had felt pride and exhilaration to make such an announcement. But at the sight of Zee's sad expression, he'd immediately known he'd done wrong. He should have asked her permission to make the announcement. And…when he was really honest with himself, the first set of eyes he'd met after breaking the news had been Philippe's. His brother's gape had pleased him. He'd successfully created an heir! Halfway to the prize. He and Philippe were still on equal ground.

He swore and caught the heel of his palm against the doorframe. Was he so callous as to use Azalea in such a manner? To gain the CEO position? The baby hadn't been planned. It wasn't as though he had plotted his way to the win. But any proposal of marriage now could only be seen by Azalea as his final step to securing that position.

And maybe it was.

That his father had patted him on the back and told him, "Good job," had again bolstered his pride. For a few moments. And then he'd surfaced from that false emotion and realized that Azalea didn't see any of this in the way his family did.

Or maybe she saw it for exactly what it was.

He was following in Roman Mercier's footsteps. Because if he did propose, Zee would surely run away from him. And that left him only with the option of providing for her, financially taking care of his family. Just as his father did for his sons and girlfriends. Sebastian hadn't even seen it coming. It had obviously been ingrained in him all his life. But that was no excuse. It couldn't be.

Damn this stupid competition!

There was no way to erase the damage it had inflicted on his and Azalea's relationship. And they did have a relationship. He cared deeply about her. He loved her.

Or was he telling himself he loved her because it felt like what was expected? He couldn't know if it was because his heart hadn't taken the full jump or rather if it was all this family stuff that was deflecting any real emotion from fully forming.

Again, damn it all!

He knew this was difficult for Zee. And that she was pregnant on top of all this had to compound her stress. But it was hard for him, too. He didn't want to mess this up. But he wasn't sure how to make it right. And…what was right?

Inside his home it was dark save for ambient city lights beaming through the wall of windows. Was she already asleep? She needed to rest for the baby.

He tiptoed through the house, leaving his suit coat on the back of the sofa and taking his shoes off before slinking into the bedroom. The lamp by the bed was on and Zee stood beside it in the red silk negligee he'd bought for her.

"Hey," she said.

"Did I wake you?"

"Nope. Can't sleep."

"I'm sorry. I wanted to give you some time."

"Thank you for that." She sat on the bed and patted it beside her thigh. "Let's talk."

He noticed her pallor. "Are you feeling okay?"

"My tummy was a little unsettled after dinner. Might have been that taste of octopus."

"Or the judgmental mother?"

She smiled and clasped his hand, tilting her head onto his shoulder. "Angelique is an interesting one. But she's your mother. And I can see that you both love one another. I don't want to do anything to change that between the two of you."

"You wouldn't and you haven't. Angelique can be abrupt and has a tendency to speak her mind. She wants the best for me."

"I know that. And I realize that, no matter what happens between the two of us, those people I met tonight are forever going to be my baby's aunts, uncles and grandparents."

"Henri and Charles will have a niece or nephew close to their age with whom they can play."

"It was nice to see you interacting with Henri. You really like the little guy, don't you?"

"He's my brother. And he's silly. Loves when you blow on his toes. You should hear his giggles. Charles, on the other hand, is a sober bit of pudge and baby goo."

"The fact that you notice such defining traits in them makes me believe you would make the best dad, Sebastian."

"You think so? Better than Roman?"

"Well, I don't know your dad at all. And I shouldn't judge him on the one quality alone. But he does seem to want to pit his sons against one another for reasons that are—" She sighed. "I just can't see you doing something like that to your children."

"I would never." And yet…here he was. Committing much the same crime against the family structure as his father had.

"And your mother…well, Sebastian, she's quite dependent on your father, isn't she?"

"He does finance her entire existence." As he had offered to do for Zee? *Mon Dieu*, why had he not seen that one for what it was?

"And is that how you wish me to be? You offered to pay for things, and—I shouldn't have accepted. I'll give back all of it."

"Don't do that, Zee. I don't want you to be dependent on me. You won't be. You'll get established with the baby and then find a job that suits you so you can feel as though you are making your own way."

She frowned.

"Or not?" he added with a shrug. He didn't know how to read her mood. Whatever he said would be wrong, no matter if it sounded right to him.

"I won't become another kept woman like those girlfriends who sat around the table tonight."

And he didn't want that for her, but his offer would do just that. How to allow her the freedom she obviously desired but also provide her the help he knew she required to survive?

"Despite it all," she said, "your mother loves you and she only wants the best for you and your family."

"Is that so terrible?"

"It isn't."

"As for my dad, I sometimes think the competition and race for the top is all he knows. His father was the same. Roman was one of four boys who eventually won ownership of L'Homme Mercier after much the same sort of competition. Except my dad had to produce an heir *without* marrying. My grandfather didn't want the woman involved in the family wealth. Which is why he's never married."

"That explains some things. Yet I wonder why he's insisted now his sons marry?"

"Might have something to do with his brush with mortality. The first stroke is what served as catalyst to this competition. On the other hand, Dad is always energized to watch Philippe and me compete."

"So odd. But again, I shouldn't judge. Sounds like the only lifestyle he's ever known. I find it interesting that he still keeps all his sons' mothers in his life."

"Kind of crazy, eh? Roman does love family. In his manner. And if he had refused my mother to be a part of my life, I may have hated him for that."

"I suppose. You are not a playboy like your father."

"A man can't work in the fashion industry, surrounded by beautiful women, and not have his roguish moments." He clasped her hand and kissed the back of it. "Not anymore. I honestly have no desire to date any other woman, Zee. And it's not even about the fact you're carrying my child. I care about you. I want you in my life."

"I want the same."

"You do?" He searched her gaze, smiling a little. "Then why are we at this crossroads that feels as though one of us is going to turn in the opposite direction and leave the other standing alone?"

"You know how I feel about us marrying."

"Fake. Which it wouldn't be, Zee. Not to me."

"That's where your mother and I agree. We both know you are true to your word. When you tell me you feel as though you are falling in love with me, I know you are speaking from the heart."

"I am. And I promise you nothing about a marriage between us would be fake."

A kiss was necessary to his wanting heart. Their connection did not cease to make his world feel right. Even if in reality it was not right. He caressed her hair and she sank into their kiss. He didn't want to lose her. He didn't know how to keep her. He'd never been more at odds in his life.

"My father has made this difficult," he said when he pulled away. "I don't want to blame him. It's all on me. Where I'm standing right now. The situation life has presented to me." He stroked her cheek and she leaned against his hand. Her quiet acceptance both filled his heart and broke it at the same time. "I don't know how I could have made a different choice, Zee. You did hijack me."

She smirked. "Guilty. But you did invite me to the party, and your bed."

"You could have refused."

"I couldn't have possibly refused the sexy Frenchman who danced into my heart."

"Would you stay with me if I asked?"

"Here in Paris?"

He nodded.

"That's just it. I don't know. I can use the excuse that Paris is another big city that makes me feel uncomfortable, but the thing is, I feel comfortable wherever I am as long as you're holding my hand."

He pressed her hand to his lips. Losing her felt inevitable. Because at the moment, this—whatever it was they had—felt more forced than right. As if they were both avoiding speaking the truth. But he didn't know his truth. *Did* he love her? He'd been speaking the word, but had he a grasp on its true meaning? How to know what love really was when all his life it had been expressed through expectations, challenges, boasts and achievements?

"I love you, Sebastian."

His heart thudded and then dropped. It felt too tremendous and too small at the same time. Because if he replied in kind he wasn't sure if it would be accepted in kind.

"But I don't think we can make this work," she said. "Not the way your family wants it to look."

Now his heart dropped to his gut. A swallow tasted of acrid heartache.

"Can you tell me it can work?" she challenged.

"I don't know what you want to hear, Zee. Rather, I do. I know what your heart craves from me. But…right now? I feel like I'll break your heart no matter what move I make. And I don't want to be like Roman. I can't be. Someone has to break the cycle."

"I'm proud of you for recognizing that."

He closed his eyes. Yes, and he'd only just made such a realization this evening.

He hadn't swept Zee off her feet and given her good reason to surrender to a future with him in it. Because that ring box in his pocket out in the living room was not the thing to make it all better. He needed to win her heart, soul and trust.

If he'd ever had her in the first place.

"I'm returning to Grace Farm tomorrow," she said. "I think it's best. I need to spend time on the farm before it's sold and gone forever. It holds a lot of memories for me."

"I don't want you to leave me, but I understand. Of course, you'll need to send off Stella and Daisy."

They sat in silence for what seemed a lifetime, though he suspected it was only a few minutes. Zee laid her head on his shoulder and snuggled against his arm. How was it possible she could smell like summer when the moment felt like winter? Was this the end? Were they breaking it off forever? He didn't want that. But he didn't know how to ask for forever from her.

"We've come to a certain agreement about the baby," she said. "I will accept the financial help you've offered. If it's still on the table."

"Of course, it is. I would never rescind that offer."

"Thank you. Sebastian. But I won't take your money forever. I promise I'll figure my life out and get a good job sooner rather than later. I'll be able to support myself. And eventually I won't need your assistance. Because it feels like we'd be perpetuating your dad's…"

Yes, his father's ways. And his father before him. What a legacy the Mercier family flaunted.

"There are some aspects of what we have that feel different than Roman and his girlfriends. It does to me. I mean, the emotional part of it all. With hope, you'll realize that as well. I will never stop supporting you, Zee."

"I…" She sniffled and tears rolled down her cheeks.

That she hurt so deeply tore apart his bewildered heart. He felt that sadness as much as she did, but he didn't know how to express it. So he settled for ignoring the shards of his heart that seemed to crackle and fall.

He pulled Zee into a hug and kissed the top of her soft, sweet-smelling hair. "Things will go as they should," he said.

It was more of an encouragement to his own heart. It was all he could manage without crying himself.

She would leave him. Take his baby with her. And he might never see her again.

No. He wouldn't allow that. And not because he was some rich bastard who could have anything he wanted with the wave of his wallet. No, he wanted Azalea in his life—baby or not. And there may yet be a way to win her.

"Will you go with me somewhere tomorrow morning?" he asked. "It's someplace I want you to see before you leave. I'll put you on a private jet back to England after."

"What is it?"

"Just something I want you to see. I promise there will be no Mercier family members there."

She nuzzled her head onto his shoulder. "Sure. One last trip together, then."

Such a final announcement. Now Sebastian had to tilt back his head to staunch the tears from falling. He was so close to losing her.

CHAPTER SEVENTEEN

AZALEA HAD NO idea what to expect when Sebastian pulled around the front of the building in a blue sports car. He'd told her he kept it for summer driving and hadn't yet had it out this year. Now they cruised out of Paris to a destination he said was an hour's drive away.

Anything to spend a little more time with him before she left for home. Because while she knew going back to the farm was best for her, she hated that decision in equal measure. Leaving the one man she loved couldn't be right. Was it pregnancy hormones screwing with her mental reasoning? Possibly.

Her life had suddenly become so big. She was swimming in new experiences and yet grasping for something solid and familiar. It was hard to process the entirety of it all. So she decided to take it one day at a time. And do it with pastries. Sebastian had kindly pulled over in front of a patisserie and she'd bought croissants and chocolate-stuffed rolls. But when he'd given her the side-eye as she started to pull one out of the bag, she'd said she'd wait until they stopped. Didn't want crumbs on the leather upholstery.

Now he drove down a quiet country road lined with thick emerald grass that wavered in the breeze. Tall birch and lush maple blocked the sunlight for a second, then a dash of warmth hit her nose again. Rolling down the window filled the car with fresh air.

"You know that Pierre Hermé in Paris delivers pastries on subscription?" he said as he pulled into a driveway before a medium-sized, stone-faced château.

"Really? I wonder if they'd deliver to England?"

"I can look into it."

The offer was too rich to accept, but on the other hand, when pregnancy cravings nudged… "Go for it."

With a kiss to her cheek, he leaned over and opened her door for her. "I appreciate that you don't argue the simple things, Zee."

"When life offers me a party, I party. And when it offers pastries, I am no fool. Where are we?" she asked as he swung around the back of the car and met her as she stepped from the car.

Before them rose a château that could almost claim quaint cottage-ness for its size, were it not for the tall windows on the two floors and so much slate tile on the roof. The yard hugging the gravel drive was overgrown, the grass as high as their knees. Oak trees dipped their boughs over the front doorway where pink flowers bloomed and designed an elaborate trellis.

"Oh my gosh!" Azalea rushed toward the frothy pink blooms. "Do you know what these are?"

Sebastian shrugged. "Flowers?"

She plucked a bloom and tucked it in her hair, spinning to declare, "These are azaleas!"

"Really? Then this adventure was meant to be."

"Whose place is this?"

He shuffled in his pocket for a ring of keys. "It used to belong to my grandparents on my mother's side. When they passed away, the property went to me. I haven't been out here since I was a kid who got dumped with Grand-père and Grand-mère every summer while Mom and Roman took a vacation overseas. Or Mom and whom-ever she was dating at the time. Though I did stop in a few years ago when it came to me. A grounds crew and clean-ing service stop in twice a year. Let's go inside."

The house was cool and bright enough to navigate with-out switching on the lights. The electricity was kept shut off, he explained, as well as the water. Sturdy white canvas dust covers hugged the furniture in the front sitting room. In the kitchen, counters were also covered and glass-faced cupboards were bare. The place had been cleared of the smaller things and decorations, leaving behind only large furniture and appliances. He led her toward the back of the main sitting area, which opened to a stone patio over-grown with weeds.

"It needs some love," he said as he walked out onto the grass and weed-frothed stones. "Maybe a cow or some chickens?"

"Are you asking me or telling me?"

The air smelled so good that Azalea felt compelled to spin, eyes closed and head tilted back. This felt like her dad's farm. Safe and cozy. And the sun beaming on her cheeks made her forget about last night's debacle.

"I'm asking."

Suddenly he twirled her and they did a little dance. It was always easy to find their silent rhythm. Kicking off her shoes, she shimmied her hips and plugged her nose, performing the dance move that he mirrored. Then with a grand flair, he spun her under his arm and performed their patented dip that activated her libido every single time. When she rose in his embrace, he kissed her deeply.

Kissing Sebastian always felt right. Like something she

deserved. They knew one another in an intimate, silent way that said more than words could ever begin to define. Safety in his embrace. And excitement. An exhilaration of discovery and a confidence of ease. There was no one else in this world she'd rather be kissing. And she could kiss him for the rest of their lives.

That thought made her pull back.

"Why did we come here?" she asked. "Did you want me to see where you were most happy as a child?"

"That and… I want you to have it, Zee."

"Have what?"

"This place." He dangled the keys before her. "The property. It would be perfect to raise a little boy, yes?"

"Well, yes, but…"

"You like a farm, but you still prefer to be close to a city," he pointed out. "I know it would mean you'd have to move to France, but…will you accept? I promise it's not like I'm tucking you away out here to keep you for myself."

Now that he brought it up… "That's exactly what it sounds like, Sebastian."

"I…" He exhaled heavily. "I wrestled on the drive here with the whole 'tucking away the girlfriend and her child' scenario. It might look like it, but it doesn't feel that way in my heart. I'm not Roman Mercier. At least, I hope that I will not follow in that most egregious of his traits. I so desperately want to be different, Zee."

She could see that in him. She wanted it to be that way if that was what he truly desired. But could he rise from his conditioned ways to forge a new path?

"I want you to have this place to do with as you will," he said. "A place that will make you feel safe. But also, I want to be close so I can visit my son. You will allow me to do that?"

"Of course, I wouldn't forbid you from being a part of our child's life. But. This is a very generous offer, Sebastian. This home holds memories for you. How can you give it away?"

"Maybe I want to put new memories here to share with the old ones? And as I've said, I haven't used it since it came to me. It would be a shame for it to sit empty when there's a bright soul who could bring happiness to its walls and grounds."

"It's a lot to take in. I mean, it's beautiful. And it would require a lot of work…"

Which would keep her busy. And she'd start with this patio, plucking out the weeds and maybe planting some rosemary along the borders for fragrance. And wouldn't a birdbath painted in bright colors be a lovely addition?

"The grounds and cleaning crews can come in this week and polish it up for you," he said. "You can select a decorator to do up the inside. Or do what you like by yourself. It's completely up to you."

Oh, baby, what fun she could have making the place her own. Could it ever be her own coming from a man who struggled with doing the right thing and who may eventually revert to his father's ways? Then, the place may become like a cage to her and her child. Oh!

"I have to think about this."

"Of course, you do. You only jump into things when the door is open and you're being chased."

She smirked at his reference to their first night together. That was the night her heart knew Sebastian was the man for her. Yes, even when her brain continued to insist he was not.

"Here." He took her hand and placed the key ring on her palm. "Take these with you. I'll text you the GPS coordinates for the property. You can come here whenever you like. Move in. Do what you wish. But please accept this from me, Zee?"

"I…" She dangled the key ring from her fingers, thinking how much fun it would be to decorate the place and make it her own.

To make a life for her new family.

It was too generous. But that was simply Sebastian doing what made him happy. And what a perfect place to raise her child. "…will take these keys and give it a good think. How does that sound?"

"I can't ask for anything more. Well, I could, but I don't want to push you into anything. Now, let's get you to England."

"You want to be rid of me so quickly?"

"No, I want you to stay with me." He slid his hands down her arms. His touch always served her a good shiver. Was it her heart responding to his heart? Nah, it was base and wanting, completely lustful. "But I also want you to do things your way, in your time. And I did arrange for the pilot to meet us at the airport in about an hour and half."

"Then let's get going."

Azalea locked the door and clutched the keys to her breast the entire ride to the airport. It felt like she held her future in her hands. And within her body. Yet beside her sat a piece to that puzzle that didn't seem to orient itself to fall neatly into place.

CHAPTER EIGHTEEN

Weeks later

STELLA AND DAISY, carefully loaded on a livestock trailer, rolled down the driveway and away from Grace Farm. Azalea waved, and—dash it—sniffed back a few tears. It was silly to get so attached to a farm animal.

"Hormones," she muttered. That was her story, and she was sticking to it.

Oliver Grace returned from the front gate, having pounded the Sold sign into the ground earlier this morning. They had two weeks to vacate the premises. Both her dad and Diane were ready to go, with most of their possessions packed. They weren't taking any large furniture. Only clothing and necessities. Because they intended to travel the world for a few years before—if even—settling somewhere.

"Where do you think you'll ultimately land?" Azalea asked as her dad wrapped an arm across her shoulders and they stood before the cottage watching the trailer disappear down the road.

"England will always be my home. I'm not sure I could ever leave it completely. Diane thinks Greece."

"Beautiful water and the sun." She tilted her head against her dad's. "Sounds like a dreamy place to stay for a while."

"How you feeling, Lea?"

"Great, actually." She smoothed a palm over her belly. "Finally this extra weight is turning into some semblance of a baby bump so I don't just look fat."

He laughed. "Your mother was the same way with both you and Dahlia. When are you due?"

"February."

"Then we'll plan to be in France after the New Year."

Yes, France. Because she'd spent the last few weeks muddling, creating scenarios, mentally arguing, and then finally deciding that, yes, she would move to the château south of Paris. She would be a fool not to accept such a generous offer, especially since her desire to go job hunting never seemed to match her need to take it easy. To honor her changing body and heart.

Besides, this farm was no longer her home. And she couldn't be a rural princess in a low-rent London flat.

She looked forward to the adventure of it all. And while she could never know if Sebastian would be a common fixture or an infrequent visitor, she had talked herself into accepting whatever he decided would work best for him.

Did she want him to live with her? To help her raise their child? Yes. And…she knew she could do this on her own, if need be, but…yes.

"You going to be all right, sweetie?"

"I am. Off to adventure! And with Dahlia helping me move in, I think I'll have a great start."

Her sister had vacation time and planned to stay with Azalea for a couple of weeks. Painting, weeding, decorating and lots of gossip, was how she'd put it. And shopping for baby things.

Her dad kissed her cheek and then mentioned Diane would have supper ready soon.

* * *

It had been days since Zee had texted him. Sebastian stood in the office before the window. The sun had set, and the coffee his secretary had brought in earlier was cold. The instant his phone buzzed he spun and picked it up. His heart fluttered to see a text from Zee.

I'm at the château. Here to stay. My sister is helping me move in and make it a home. Wanted you to know I think of you every day. Want to see you. But give me some time?

She'd accepted his offer to stay at the château. That was immense. He would give her all the time she needed. It wouldn't change the way he felt about her. Now more than ever he had to win her heart. Because being CEO of the company wouldn't matter if he didn't have Azalea Grace in his life.

"That turned out much better than I thought it would," Dahlia said of the bedroom wall that they had dry-brushed with shades of maroon, violet and pink. "Gives it some warmth in a rustic kind of way. Not my style, but I think it's you, Lea."

"I love it." Azalea tilted her bottled water against Dahlia's wineglass. "Thanks for helping me with everything these past few weeks. The baby's room is adorable."

They'd found simple pine furnishings for the small room next to the main bedroom. It was a sunny room with a balcony, so Azalea could sit in the rocker on warm summer nights.

"I'm excited about this," she said with a smooth over her belly. "I feel like this little guy is eagerly waiting to come into my life."

The doctor had accidentally revealed the baby's sex after a sonogram and Sebastian had been right. A boy. Azalea hadn't cared whether it was a boy or girl. She was simply ready to hold the little tyke and mom the heck out of it.

"You do have that proverbial glow, sis. You know I'm not the motherly sort, but you almost make me want to have one, too."

"Do you think Clyve would make a good dad?"

Dahlia's boyfriend had proposed last year but they hadn't set a date. They were in no rush, both working in the legal sector and having eighty-hour workweeks. Who had time to say vows?

"Maybe. I don't know. It wouldn't be fair to a kid with our work schedules. That's what I love about your situation. Your man is taking care of everything so all you have to do is be a mom. How perfect is that?"

It could be more perfect. Like having that man in her life to actually be a father to her son. Not being relegated to the cottage where she had her own life and he had his in the city. She tried not to overthink it. Sebastian had gifted her the world with his generosity. And if that meant she'd be just another girlfriend sitting around the monthly family dinner, she had to accept that.

But did she really?

"You're thinking about it again," Dahlia warned. "I shouldn't have brought him up. You always go all melancholy on me when I do."

"I love him, Dahlia. This château is a dream, but it's not the perfect dream."

"You need the father in the picture rather than floating around the edges."

"Exactly."

"Do you think Sebastian would make a good father?"

"I actually do. The little I've seen him interact with his baby brothers makes me believe he would be a kind and gentle dad. But then, what do we ever know about how well we can parent before we've even given it a go? I just hope I can be the best mother and raise a boy who is respectful and kind."

"You will. And if his dad does more than float around the edges that would be ideal. Maybe you should ask him to marry you."

"Can I do that?"

"Heck, yeah. But I get the struggle you have over that stupid family competition debacle. You'd never know if he married you for love or money."

"His brother is engaged right now. There's always a chance Philippe could win. But I really want Sebastian to win. Oh, why am I being like this? I can help him to win something he wants more than anything."

"At what price? Your heart? Your trust for him? Standing in line next to the other girlfriends? I can't see you getting a boob job."

Azalea sighed and settled onto the floor before the bed. The fake fur rug was soft and dark pink to match one of the colors on the wall. "Tell me what to do, Dahlia."

"I think you're doing it." Her sister sat next to her. They each slanted a foot toward one another, touching toes as they'd always done when they were kids. "You're capable of doing the single mom thing. It'll be much easier with financial help than not. And you've got a dream home. What more is there?"

"A dream man."

Dahlia sighed dramatically. "Give me the bloke's address. I'll stop in to Paris to have a word with him."

"You will not. Sebastian will…*we* will make this work. One way or another."

"Fine. But I'm not going to promise to babysit once the little man arrives."

"I wouldn't expect you to, especially living as far away as you do. But you will have aunt duties."

"What will that involve? I don't think I can bring myself to change a nappy."

"How about throwing a baby shower?"

"Oh, I can do that! Let's go online and shop for baby stuff!"

When, within five minutes of introducing himself to Oliver Grace, the man asked Sebastian to help him out back, he agreed eagerly. A means to ingratiate himself to Zee's dad? And to get to know him better. He'd flown over specifically to talk to the man. What better way than to do it within Oliver's comfort zone?

Apparently, comfort meant mud and hay. Donning the rubber boots once again, Sebastian helped Oliver heft a dozen bales of hay that had been dropped off by a neighboring farmer to store in the overhead loft of the barn. They were heavy but not overly taxing. After a few bales he got into the swing of it, and it felt good to work up a sweat. Even wearing a dress shirt and trousers.

When they had finished and Oliver invited him to stand at the back of the barn where it opened to the fenced field, which was absent any cows, Sebastian had to ask. "Where are Stella and her baby?"

"Sold them."

Right. Zee had mentioned something about her dad selling them. She had been heartbroken. He'd seen it in her expression. A woman and her cow were not so easily separated by the heartstrings.

"Then why the hay?"

Oliver shrugged. "I bought those bales this spring. Forgot about them. They'll be good starter stock for the new owners."

"When do you move?"

"Few days. We're headed to the States for six months. Diane wants to tour all fifty states. Not sure we can do it all in that time, but we'll give it a go."

"Why the time limit? If your intent is to travel, then why set a schedule?"

"Exactly." He smirked. "But she's the one with the schedule in her head. You must know how schedules work. Big-city businessman like you."

"I do, but I've learned to be more lenient thanks to your daughter."

Oliver nodded, but Sebastian noticed his tight jaw. He could guess what the man must think of him. So he'd end the torture.

"I had to talk to you face-to-face," Sebastian said, "because your daughter is important to me. I love her." He waited for Oliver's reaction, but the man merely inclined his head. Listening.

Yes, he did love Zee. He'd created his definition of the word, and it felt right in his heart. It was that immense feeling he got every time he saw her blue eyes crinkle and her freckles dance. The feeling that all things were right.

"I know she'll be the best mother."

"Yes, she will. But what about the father? What does he intend to do?"

"That's why I'm here. Monsieur Grace, I want to ask you for your daughter's hand in marriage. I love her. But

I don't want to ask her to marry me without your permission."

Oliver stood from his lean against the barn wall, crossing his arms over his chest. Defensive? Not a good sign.

"I'm sure she's told you about the competition with my brother."

Oliver nodded. Swatted at a fly.

"It's why I haven't felt right about asking her to marry me. But I intend to tell my dad I'm out. I love Zee too much to risk losing her. And if that means I have to step out of the competition, then I will."

"Won't marrying my daughter make you the winner?"

Sebastian exhaled heavily. "It would. But it wouldn't be right. Not to Zee. I know she would always wonder if I asked her to marry her out of love, or if it was to win a competition. I can't do that to her. It must be real with her. The one thing we value most between us is truth."

"Noble. But…"

Sebastian met the man's gaze. Same pale blue as Zee's eyes. But not so fun-loving and perhaps even cynical right now.

"Lea's told me that winning that CEO position would make you a happy man."

Sebastian nodded. "It would. I believe L'Homme Mercier should remain true to its legacy by continuing its attention to menswear, but my brother has different plans. Much as I hate to see the company add a women's department under Philippe's control, stepping out of the competition is a sacrifice I am willing to make."

"Not for my daughter you won't."

"I…don't understand."

"I don't give you permission to marry my daughter."

"But—"

Oliver held up a hand. “I understand that you love Lea. It fills my heart to know my grandchild has a father who will love him and his mother. Even if he isn’t in their life.”

“But I want to be—”

“You asked for my permission? Well, you’ve got your answer. I won’t have you marrying my daughter if it means sacrificing something that would make you happy. It wouldn’t be fair to Lea. Happiness is an inside job. That saying about making another person happy is nonsense. Only you can make you happy.”

Zee had once said much the same to him. The apple hadn’t fallen far from the tree.

“And then?” Oliver continued. “Once you’re happy? Then you can find another person who complements that happiness in their special way. But if you think you’re doing something noble by walking away from a job you desire to prove your love to Lea? Nope.” Oliver shook his head. “Not going to happen.”

“I intend to tell my father I’m out of the competition,” Sebastian reiterated. “No matter what.”

“That’s your choice. But if you’re serious about my opinion on the future you may have with my daughter? You’ve heard my say.”

Sebastian nodded and bowed his head. The man had a point about making himself happy. But he hated to hear that. That meant he’d have to continue the competition.

He wasn’t about to lose Zee, though. There had to be a way to make this right. Which meant, his happiness first, and then he could begin to imagine embracing his family.

Family? Yes, that was the key to all of it. He had to talk to his dad. And he knew what had to go down. Truths must be honored.

"Can I get you a bite to eat before you go?" Oliver offered casually. As if he'd not just torn out Sebastian's heart.

"No, I'm… I just came to ask that one question. I should be on my way."

He started to walk through the barn. What had just gone down? He didn't need Oliver Grace's approval for a single thing. Because that man's approval did not make him feel like a smile from Zee did. Her smile gave him such pride and he felt respected by her, seen. That was all he needed.

And yet, Oliver had a point. Could he truly stand as head of a family if his heart were not made happy by his work? What sort of example would that set for his son? He'd grown up watching his father flit from woman to woman, never committing, and—

It had to stop! It would stop. With him.

"You seem like a good man, Sebastian," Oliver called after him. "I know my daughter loves you."

That small comment landed right in his heart. The Grace family had a way of gifting him respect in a manner he'd never experienced.

Sebastian paused in the open end of the barn and turned back to Oliver. "I'll make it right. I promise."

CHAPTER NINETEEN

DURING THE SHORT flight from London to Paris, Sebastian pulled out his phone. The screensaver was the photo of him clasping Zee around the waist so she wouldn't be carried off by a bouquet of bright balloons. That had been a hell of a night. One that had changed his life.

He opened the video that had been taken moments after that photo. He and Zee had marveled over the display crafted entirely from paper. It had looked like a Japanese cherry tree, spilling blossoms from its slender branches to the ground. They'd stood in the middle of it all, posing for a few photos, and then…their first kiss.

At the time, Sebastian hadn't been aware the photographer had switched his phone to video to record. Afterward, when she'd handed him back the phone she'd apologized, but had said it was a moment she'd thought worthy of capture.

Indeed.

Now he watched as he kissed Zee. They'd both been exhilarated from dancing and getting to know one another. Like two magnets, they'd instantly clicked. Her freckles had dazzled him. Her bright smile had seeped through his skin and flooded his system with joy. And he realized now he was watching himself as he lost his heart to a woman he had only known for hours. At the time it had felt as if they'd been searching for one another all their lives. Their souls had finally found one another.

A silly thought? No. It had been real. And that beautiful soul now carried his baby. They'd made a new soul together. They belonged together. And not in some weird arrangement where he kept Zee on a farm and visited her on weekends because they weren't married. Or even married because he wanted to gain the CEO position. Their souls wouldn't survive with anything less than true, real connection. No conditions attached.

His heart ached. He'd thought it a noble gesture to fly in and request Oliver Grace for his daughter's hand. He'd never expected a no. But if Sebastian were in Oliver's position, he would have delivered the same answer. And while it wasn't binding, and wouldn't keep Sebastian from doing as he pleased…he would honor that *no.*

Until he could make it right.

Roman Mercier was recovering slowly but surely following the second stroke. With the use of a cane, his gait touched stability. He'd initially refused the cane, but when Elaine had presented him with a stylish walking stick, he'd ceased argument. It was his voice and his ability to speak fluidly that still troubled him. He could speak but his words were jumbled together and sometimes he chose the wrong word. Aphasia, a condition of the stroke. A speech pathologist worked with him three times a week. Elaine made sure he did not miss the private, in-home sessions. She'd told Sebastian she wanted her twins' father to be able to communicate with them. As well, she'd mentioned her plan to win his father's softening heart by convincing him he should marry the mother of his latest sons.

Sebastian had wished her luck. And he truly hoped she would be successful, if not for his youngest brothers, but for the Mercier family overall. The toxic sins of the father had to be redeemed.

And today Sebastian was taking a step to do just that. There was no time to dally or hope for change. Action must be taken. His future would look different than his father's past.

Sebastian found his dad in the conservatory, which overlooked the narrow garden against the ancient limestone wall that separated their property from the neighbor. Roman was going over some paperwork for L'Homme Mercier. Sebastian realized that even though their patriarch had been felled by the stroke he was still an able and important part of the business. He had connections, a certain trust built up with their oldest and some of their largest clients.

But the man also had two capable sons. It was time he retired or took a smaller role.

Still, Sebastian did not see Philippe as the best choice for CEO. Even if he had no designs on a women's line, the man could be easily distracted by recreational pursuits, which also included women.

"Business on a Saturday?" he asked his dad. He strolled to the window and stood beside his father's lounge chair.

Dressed impeccably, as was his mien, and nursing what looked like whiskey on the rocks in a cut-crystal tumbler—but which smelled more like coffee to Sebastian—his father gestured he sit. He used gestures more frequently as opposed to talking, though Elaine insisted it was important to be patient and allow Roman to speak. That was the only way he was going to improve his speech.

"What are you drinking? Doesn't smell like whiskey."

"Coffee," Roman said with a wince. "Elaine insists… less alcohol."

"Coffee has been touted to have some excellent health benefits. Though cold coffee sounds horrid, if you ask me."

Leaning over to inspect the papers on his father's lap, Sebastian watched as he pulled out a red file folder and handed it to him.

"What is this?"

Roman held up a finger to pause him from opening the file. "Important changes. Life."

"Life?" Curious, but also fearing that Roman had made those changes to the company, Sebastian didn't open the file. "Before we get into this, there's something I came here to tell you. Ask you. Well, both." He sat on the window seat before his father. "I'm in love, *mon père*. With Azalea Grace."

His father nodded. "Your…baby."

"Yes, she's the mother of my child, but that's not why I love her. I fell in love with her months ago. On the first night we met, actually. It just took my brain a while to realize what my heart has known. I know you probably can't understand…"

His father clasped his hand and squeezed. He opened his mouth to speak, so Sebastian waited to allow him to form words. "I…have loved. Do. Love."

"I know. You love your children. You love the mothers of your children. I wasn't implying… Well." To even begin to understand the intricate heart of his father could be a mad-making venture.

"I want to marry Zee," he said. "But not because of some family competition. And yet, if I ask her to marry me, she'll only believe it is because of the competition. And I thought I would come here to tell you I was out. To allow Philippe the win. But I can't do that, either. I genuinely feel I would be the best choice for heading L'Homme Mercier. And certainly, I understand how much you enjoy the work you do with the company, but you must realize it has come time for you to retire, *mon père*. You and Elaine should be spending your hours enjoying the twins."

Now his father leaned forward and slid a palm over the back of Sebastian's hand. They had never been demonstrative in their affection. Winning approval and a congratulatory nod of the old man's head had been the morsels of emotion and fondness Sebastian had learned to accept over the years. So the feel of his father's warm hand on his loosened something inside him. He clasped Roman's hand and bowed his head over it. At a loss for words. He simply wanted to experience this moment. He had almost lost him to a stroke. Twice.

Family did mean something to him. It was everything. And he could have something wondrous if only he'd step up and do it the right way. For perhaps the first time in his life, his heart was telling him which was the right way.

"I don't want to compete with my brother anymore," he said softly. "And I need to change the family dynamic that has existed for generations. It's not what I want. Can you understand?"

His father nodded. He tapped the red folder. "Wrote it. Too much to say. Mean it." He slapped a hand against his heart. "For my sons. Family."

With a heavy sigh, Sebastian opened the folder. He'd not clearly explained what he needed to his father—Zee, and nothing else.

Inside the folder were a few pages of printed text. It began with *To my sons...*

As Sebastian read his father's words tears formed. He clasped Roman's hand. The old man had had a change of heart. Elaine, and the strokes, had been the catalyst to opening his eyes. To seeing his family in a new way. He didn't want to someday pit his youngest sons against one another. He regretted doing as much with Sebastian and Philippe. It had been what he'd known. There was no way to take back the years. But he wanted to move forward in a new way. To learn a new way. He intended to ask Elaine to marry him. He would surprise her in a few days.

Sebastian nodded with joy. This really was a change for his father!

"Read the back," Roman said.

Sebastian turned over the page.

I watched you at the family dinner. The way you looked at Mademoiselle Grace. You admire her. You respect her. I've never seen you look at a woman that way.

Sebastian swallowed back a tear as he nodded, "I do admire her. Everything about her is everything to my heart. I love her."

He read the remainder.

I want to earn that same look of respect and admiration from you, my son. Someday.

Another nod. It was all he could do not to blurt, "Yes, someday, I want to look at you in that manner." It would happen. This family could change. And it would begin with this letter.

It made Sebastian's heart swell to read the next lines that detailed how Roman intended to dissolve the competition. And he wanted both his sons to agree to what he'd decided.

Sebastian stood and leaned over to hug his father. It didn't feel unnatural. Because he'd had some practice with Zee. "I love you, *mon père*. We can do this. As a family."

A week after Dahlia left, Azalea sat on the stone patio out back of the house, finishing a braided daisy crown. A pile of uprooted weeds sat to her left. The plants with the little yellow flowers remained untouched. Though she suspected they might also be weeds, they were too pretty to pull up. And she liked how they spread across the stones forming a soft carpet for her bare feet. Later, she'd surf online to find out what they were and if there were uses for them such as a natural elixir or even tea. Since settling into the château, she'd become all about using what the land gave her and DIY-ing the heck out of things. It was fun and gave her a sense of satisfaction.

She set the circlet crown on her head. "Rural princess!" she declared to the symphony of crickets. "Well, you don't have to bow, but I would appreciate a little less chirping come late night."

And thinking about noisy animals… Now, to get some chickens for the little coop that sat beside the barn. Fresh eggs every morning? She was living the life.

Sebastian had texted her this morning. He intended to stop in tomorrow and wanted to know if she needed anything. She'd given him a list of foods that she hadn't a chance to get to the grocery store for, despite the little car that had been stored in the garage for over a decade and which ran like a dream. Milk, eggs and lots of chocolate pastries. She was labeling it a pregnancy craving, but really? She just loved pastries.

She'd added "live chickens" to the list but did not expect that one to actually be fulfilled.

With a satisfied sigh, she tilted her head to take the sunshine into her pores. She could do this. She was doing this. It felt right, like the thing that had been waiting for her to finally turn around and declare, "Oh, yes, that's for me!" Her aspirations to find a job had slipped away. Supporting herself completely wasn't doable at the present moment.

In a few years, she'd revisit her goals and desires and if a job felt right then, she'd explore her options.

Yet she knew the country life was not something that Sebastian could get behind. Visits on the weekend might be all he could manage, or even want. The man had an important job that kept him at the office and in the city where he needed to meet with contacts face-to-face. He thrived on the busyness of Paris.

He might feel obligated to treat her as a girlfriend since she was having his child. But he couldn't sustain that forever. Could he? Perhaps she should tell him he should start dating so he could find a wife and win that CEO position? The competition did not stipulate the wife and baby had to be from the same person. And really, Roman Mercier should be proud his son was spreading his DNA around.

She could be okay with that.

Sighing, she shook her head. "You love him. Don't deny it. You got pregnant by the rebound guy and now he's taken over your heart."

Time to start listening to her heart.

If she was to be true to her heart, she needed to make it clear to Sebastian that she did love him. To, well, to fight for him. If they did marry it could be good. It could be real and based on love and caring for one another. It wouldn't have to be simply because of the competition. And if part of it was? Then she was going into the marriage eyes wide-open.

"I'm denying him an easy win if I insist we never marry," she said. "I want him to win. The CEO position will make him happy."

With a sense of renewed purpose, she nodded. Tomorrow she was going to ask Sebastian to marry her. Hopefully, it would be the best choice she had ever made.

CHAPTER TWENTY

SEBASTIAN WAS ARRIVING this morning. And Azalea had a plan. She'd picked wildflowers from the overgrown field behind the barn. Armloads of them. Now she stepped back from the front stoop, looking over her work. The azaleas had shed their blossoms weeks ago. She'd managed to create a bough of wildflowers cascading over the entryway. It looked lush and romantic and smelled like heaven. Here was where she'd ask him to marry her.

"It could work," she whispered with hope.

No woman was going to share her baby daddy's surname but her. Azalea Mercier had a certain ring to it.

"A ring?" A proposal wasn't a proposal without one. "Dash it. I need to find something..."

She wandered barefoot around the side of the château. The grass was soft and freshly mown thanks to the grounds crew that stopped by once every two weeks. She plucked up the daisy crown she'd made yesterday and placed it on her head.

If he said yes. Would he? She couldn't know what his answer would be. Their lives had been altered with this pregnancy. Their needs and desires had been brought to the fore, amplified. Perhaps he wouldn't be willing to commit if she demanded real love from him?

Mostly, she wished he'd just walk back into her life, kiss

her silly, make love to her until they were sated, and stake his claim to her. That was how it happened in the movies.

"Life is not a movie," she muttered. Plucking a daisy, she decapitated the white-petaled head. "This rural princess has to work a miracle if she intends to win her prince."

She busied herself with creating a ring from the stem.

When the sound of a large vehicle rolling down the drive turned her head, she dropped the daisy stem and wandered around from the backyard to see a truck backing up to the gravel side lot before the barn.

A livestock trailer? She hadn't ordered any animals. Though the barn was clean and ready to receive any stock she might wish to own. She'd already looked into finding a rescue animal, or two, in the area.

The driver got out of the truck and—

"Dad?" She rushed up to meet Oliver Grace, who sported a big smile and wrapped her in an even bigger hug. "I don't understand?"

"Hey, sweetie." He gave her tummy a pat. "You look beautiful. Wow, it's nice out here, isn't it? Diane and I will have to spend a weekend with you sometime."

"You are always welcome."

He tapped her crown, then gave her a kiss on the nose where once he'd teased that each kiss added another freckle.

"I'm glad you decided to stop in for a visit, but I don't understand why you're here? What's in the truck?"

He held up a finger. "I've brought you a few things that I know are important to you. Hang on." With that, he opened the back of the trailer and pulled down a ramp, walked up it and opened an inner gate. He then guided down a cow. And it wasn't just any cow.

"Stella?" Azalea took the reins from him as he again disappeared inside the truck, where she saw another smaller cow. "Daisy! But how? I thought you sold them, Dad?"

"I did." He shrugged. "But someone bought them back because he knew how much they meant to you. That's the other important thing I brought today." He leaned back and slapped the metal side of the truck. "Hup!"

A door slammed and from around the front of the truck walked another man, wearing sunglasses and an expensive suit perfectly fitted to accentuate his physique. On his feet were wellies. A rather stylish pair with a designer logo splashed around the tops. And he carried something she would have never thought to see a man in a suit carry. A chicken with lustrous brown feathers that gleamed blue in the sunlight.

Azalea handed the reins to her dad as she gaped at the sight of the new arrival. "Sebastian?"

"You were expecting me, yes?"

"Of course, but.... What is this?" She looked to her dad, who smiled widely but offered no explanation. But of course! She'd written *live chickens* on her grocery list. And he'd actually come through? What a guy!

"I talked to your dad days ago," Sebastian explained. "Asked him something important and...he told me *no*. It made me do a lot of thinking."

"I have no clue what you're talking about. You two are in cahoots?"

"That's a good way to put it." Sebastian pushed his sunglasses to the top of his head and winked at her dad. "That conversation with Oliver sent me to my father's doorstep and we had a long and good conversation. My dad has had a change of heart. The strokes have him viewing his life and his family with new eyes. He proposed to Elaine last night."

"Really? That's amazing. That's good, right?"

"It's incredible. She's taught an old dog a new trick. Elaine insists the twins do not grow up like Philippe and I have. Always competing. Dad agreed."

"He did? But that's…"

"That's what led him to dissolve the competition for the CEO position."

"But—Sebastian, you wanted that position. Now what happens?"

"Now Philippe is going step into the role of CEO of the new company Dad wants to form. A women's atelier. It will be completely separate from L'Homme Mercier. As it should be. And I will take the reins of L'Homme Mercier."

"You got the position!" She plunged forward for a hug but stopped abruptly as the chicken in his arms clucked. "It's what you deserve. I'm so glad your dad had a change of heart. And to celebrate you brought me the chicken I asked for."

"Actually, it's more than that."

Sebastian stroked the calm chicken. Its feathers were sheened blue and green and his strokes revealed a bright orange undertone as the soft feathers moved. The fowl was perfectly content on his arm.

It was almost too much to take in. And now she noticed his wellies had a splotch of chicken doo-doo on them. The man was out of his element. And yet, he fit in like a shiny new garden implement just waiting to be dirtied a little.

She looked to her dad, who still wasn't offering any explanation, not even a helpful gesture. The two of them had been talking? This was crazy!

"Of course, Stella and Daisy will love the field," she offered, unsure what else to say. "And there's the old chicken coop beside the barn, but…"

"But there's something more." Sebastian approached her. He held the chicken as any experienced farmer would cradle a cherished farm animal. Now he bent a knee and kneeled before her. "It's a proposal."

A pro—? But she had planned to— She'd dropped her makeshift ring upon hearing the trailer drive up. Azalea's breath gasped out as she slapped her chest. Her dad nodded, smiling widely. She wasn't sure how he was involved, but did it matter?

Sebastian, on one knee, held up the chicken in offering between them and said, "Azalea Grace, you've changed my world and my heart. I don't want to spend a day without you. I want you in my life because I love you. Because we have fun together. Because I want to dance with you until our knees creak and we can no longer move. I asked your dad permission to ask you to marry me and he said no."

With a gape, she looked to her dad.

Oliver shrugged. "He was going to refuse the CEO position and concede to his brother. I knew he loved you, and you loved him, but I also knew he wouldn't be happy. I couldn't let him ask you if it meant he wouldn't be happy."

"That's why I talked to my dad," Sebastian said. "I had to make him understand that you had won my heart, but I also knew your dad was right, that I wouldn't be completely happy if L'Homme Mercier went to Philippe. I told him all that, and then he showed me the letter he'd written stating all the plans he had for dividing the company. As well, we…shared a hug."

His smile now seemed to surprise him. Azalea understood exactly what that hug must have meant to him.

"Anyway…" He held up the chicken before her, a grand gesture if there was one. "Would you accept this chicken from me and say yes to becoming my wife?"

Azalea clasped her hands over her heart. The proposal was absolutely perfect. And everything she wanted from him. And…she glanced to the flowers hanging over the entry. Like nothing she could have imagined or planned. And that her father was here to witness made it even more special.

Still holding out the chicken, Sebastian waited for her reply.

The proposal was genuine and real. It was the most enduring gesture he could have made. And she'd already decided how her best future could look.

The chicken cooed. Sebastian tilted it to look at its little face and cooed back at it. "She'll say yes. She has to." He held the bird higher for her to inspect. "Is the chicken not enough?"

"The chicken is perfect." She took it from him and it settled in the crook of her arm and on her belly as if the bird knew there was a baby inside and it needed to nest and protect it. "You know the way to my heart, Sebastian."

He embraced her gently, including the chicken. "Do you love me?" he asked.

"I do."

"And I love you. I wouldn't have worn rubber boots and traveled for an hour with a chicken in my arms for anyone but you. Will you be my wife? Will you live with me here in the château, but also in Paris? I've already figured I can work four days a week. We can make our schedules work. Maybe you'll live in Paris a few days and then back on the weekends to the country, where you can wear your rural princess crown as I see you've already begun?"

She blushed and tilted down her head. Yes, she had created the crown and wore it with pride.

"I'll do anything to be with you, Zee. Can you be okay

with me working but being home every night in your arms? Will you share our boy's life with me?"

Our boy.

Those words landed in her heart and swelled to her extremities with the most wondrous joy.

"I will." She held up her hand, pinkie crooked. He entwined his pinkie with hers. "I love you, Sebastian. And I want to make a family with you."

Their kiss was sweet, indulgent, welcoming, and laced with a thrill of desire. It was the perfect representation of the future that waited them.

The chicken crowed and leaped to the ground. Stella nudged Azalea's arm. And her dad said casually, "Well, that's a bit of all right."

Azalea's heart fluttered. "I'm going to marry you."

"That's the plan."

"Can we get married here? Next summer after the baby is born?"

Sebastian took her in his arms and spun her. "Anything for you, Zee. Oh." He patted his suit pocket. "Almost forgot." Reaching inside his coat, he pulled out and revealed a big, sparkling diamond ring. "You didn't think I'd expect you to wear a chicken on your finger, did you?"

EPILOGUE

The following summer

THE WEDDING WAS a simple affair catered by a posh restaurant for the few dozen people who had come to celebrate Sebastian and Azalea. Now four months old, Zachary Mercier had won the day by attracting the attention of everyone by simply existing. Cute baby wearing a polka-dotted onesie sleeping on a blanket under the willow tree? Haul out the cameras!

The twins were not to be outdone. They attracted as many photo opportunities and were currently tearing apart pansies and nibbling on the petals. Roman and Elaine, who had married over Christmas, were contemplating house hunting in the south of France now that Roman was completely retired. Oliver and Diane were headed almost the same direction, to Spain, for a few weeks before then trekking to Hawaii.

After most of the guests had left, and only their closest family lingered in the château—some staying the night in the guest rooms—Sebastian and Azalea danced slowly on the patio to the music of their hearts. Zachary slept quietly in his nearby cradle, rocked gently by the breeze. Sunday, the chicken—because Sebastian had proposed on a Sunday—was perched on the bow of the cradle, her favorite place to rest when the baby slept.

The moon was full and bright. The summer air just right. Sebastian had shed his suit coat and unbuttoned his collar. Azalea's pink spaghetti-strap dress dusted the grass because she'd not worn shoes all day. Her hair spilled in thick curls—thanks to Dahlia's styling—and was circled with a frothy pink crown of her namesake flower.

"You are the most beautiful woman in the world," Sebastian said as they swayed under the moonlight. "You have my heart. And so does Zachary."

"We're doing rather well at this family thing," she said as she rested her head against his shoulder.

Since taking over as CEO, Sebastian had been able to reduce his in-office hours to three days a week, then home to the country for two days day of online work, with the weekend free. Azalea and Zac commuted to Paris for two or three days midweek. She enjoyed the change of pace, which allowed her to stroll Zac around the parks and discover all the endless tourist attractions and hidden wonders of the city.

On the days she was in Paris, the neighbor girl, a sixteen-year-old with dreams of becoming a veterinarian, looked after their livestock and chickens. It was a perfect situation.

"I sometimes wonder," he said softly. "If you hadn't been such a strong and fearless woman, I might have never experienced you charging into the limo. I'm so glad you kicked the photographer and ran to me."

"I'm glad you were there to catch me."

"Always and forever, Zee."

* * * * *

IT STARTED WITH A PROPOSAL

Susan Meier

'So, where's the bride?'

He frowned. 'Bride?'

'Sorry. Where's your fiancée?'

He continued to look at her as if he didn't understand.

'The woman you're going to ask to marry you.'

His mouth fell open a little bit. 'I thought you were bringing her.'

'I don't even know who she is.'

'That's the point. There is no one. So just like the flowers and the mandolin players I thought you'd provide someone to fake propose to.'

This time her mouth fell open. 'I assumed you'd bring the woman from the restaurant.'

He squeezed his eyes shut. 'No.'

'Okay,' she said, thinking on her feet. There were three cute young women arranging the flowers, but they were dressed in dark trousers and golf shirts with a florist logo on the breast pocket.

'I…' She looked around.

He tapped her shoulder to bring her attention back to him. 'You're here.' He looked down at her dress. 'And you're dressed for it.'

Damned if she wasn't.

Antonio's voice brought her back to reality. 'Please. We've gone to all this trouble already.'

She took a breath. 'You're right. It's no big deal and technically I am dressed for it.'

'And you look beautiful.'

Her heart fluttered before she could remind herself that he'd only told her that because he wanted a favour.

She forced a smile, then turned to Jake, the videographer. 'I'm going to be playing the part of the fiancée,' she said, holding her smile in place as if it was completely normal that she was standing in for the role. Because it wasn't. This was a job. Period. Nothing more.

'Once I get to the centre of the gazebo, you start filming.' She faced the mandolin players. 'Same instruction to you.'

The three guys nodded. Jake scrambled to get into position for the best angle for the simple video.

Riley took a long breath and put her forced smile on her face again. She walked to the centre and turned.

Jake said, 'Action.'

The mandolins sent romantic music wafting through the gazebo.

Antonio started up the steps. He walked to her, got down on one knee and took her hand.

When his warm fingers wrapped around hers, she had to work to stop her heart from pounding. The man was simply too darned good looking and sexy.

'I love you, Riley Morgan. Will you marry me?'

Continue reading

IT STARTED WITH A PROPOSAL

Susan Meier

Available next month

millsandboon.co.uk

NAIMA
SIMONE
JULES
BENNETT
DANI
COLLINS
Sinfully
Yours
3
BOOKS
IN ONE
THE ENEMY